A Portable Egypt

A Portable Egypt

a novel by

Catherine Madsen

Copyright © 2002 by Catherine Madsen.

Library of Congress Number: 2001119910
ISBN #:   Hardcover   1-4010-4183-3
             Softcover   1-4010-4182-5

"The Getting of Wisdom" was first published in *Pandora* v. 1, no. 1, Winter 1998

Cover: Karla Gudeon, "Baby Boys and Their Balls." Courtesy of R. Michelson Galleries, Northampton, MA, www.rmichelson.com

All rights reserved. No part of this book may be reproduced or transmitted in any form or by any means, electronic or mechanical, including photocopying, recording, or by any information storage and retrieval system, without permission in writing from the copyright owner.

This is a work of fiction. Names, characters, places and incidents either are the product of the author's imagination or are used fictitiously, and any resemblance to any actual persons, living or dead, events, or locales is entirely coincidental.

This book was printed in the United States of America.

To order additional copies of this book, contact:
Xlibris Corporation
1-888-7-XLIBRIS
www.Xlibris.com
Orders@Xlibris.com
13994

for Herman Koss and Dorothea Hunter

PRELUDE:

THE GETTING OF WISDOM

Ibbur, or spiritual pregnancy, refers to a mystery. As a woman becomes pregnant and gives birth, without losing anything from her nature, so also the souls of the pious and righteous become pregnant and give birth. From them sparks radiate out into this world, in order to assist the age, or for some other reason, and it is as if one light kindles that of another.

—Gershom Scholem

And the sons of God saw the daughters of men, that they were fair.

—Genesis 6:2

Sarita Bunge was a dressmaker in the port town of Easy Landing. She had a little shop over a bookstore, with windows that caught the sunlight off the bay and a narrow glimpse of the water. In the anteroom she kept bolts of fabric and portfolios of her designs, and in the back was the cutting room with a big table and sewing machines, and a corner curtained off for fittings. Businesswomen from town ordered from her, and officers' wives from the base, and the summer people; for these last, and for the occasional arty professor from the college town, she could invent the unexpected. For the rest, she rearranged the expected.

She did it well: the garments were finely finished, and her designs were both striking and comfortable. A growing number of people recognized her work; she had been written up in the local weekly, and over the last year and a half had had to hire two assistants, and could pay them. But she was haunted by a sense of indirection. Tailored suits and evening gowns were interesting puzzles, but she did not want only puzzles: she wanted to invent, or discover or encourage, some new spiritual grammar of clothing.

The paper had spoken of her "simplicity of line" and wondered whether to compare her silhouettes with the twenties or the twelfth century; this was a deliberate confusion, and represented her effort to combine the erotic with the stately, which she thought the clothing of both periods sometimes achieved. Her customers understood the erotic, but they could not manage the stately: they were likely to mar the subtlety of a sage-green silk with a smear of red lipstick, or the sweep of a V-necked jacket with a perky bow. Some of them understood the art of spareness, which was better; they understood her aesthetic principles, but they did not grasp the moral effort behind them. And how is one to speak of morals in the same breath with clothing?

There was a look in women's eyes she could detect sometimes, a profound disillusionment with all clothing that could be bought. When she saw that look she would drop her impersonal courtesy and ask them what they really wanted to wear, but they didn't know; it was as hopeless as trying to ask for a new haircut by telling your hairdresser the books you read. The roles were reversed, but the principle was the same: two languages that should have translated each other did not connect.

She was disturbed to find that she was becoming personally offended by this state of affairs. She restrained herself, several times a year, from seizing a woman by the shoulders and hissing into those anxious, smiling eyes, "Look: you are going to die: will you never dress as though you had a soul?" She was ashamed of this, and never told anyone; and when she raised the subject of her discontent to friends, she got back answers that astonished her. "Maybe you should go to New York and try for the big time." "Maybe you should go back to school and try a career change." "You spend all your time in the shop; you hardly have a private life at all. Why don't you look for a lover?"

In theory Sarita would sleep with anyone she liked, but she liked very few people. She did not think it probable that someone she liked would appear in answer to the present need. She had had two lovers by the age of thirty-two, a man and a woman. The former was a divorced art history professor who made love sweetly but treated all conversation as an argument to be won, and who was beginning to drink too much. For the latter, a penniless graduate student fond of flannel shirts, she had commissioned a piece of calligraphy: *Let Ithamar minister with a Chamois, and bless the name of Him which cloatheth the naked.* But her lover was studying psychology, and so of course had never heard of Christopher Smart, and would not hang anything on her wall that referred to God as He. So the calligraphy hung in the cutting room, where occasionally a customer would read it and look puzzled.

So she thought she would not look for a lover. Instead she went to lectures and readings: the visiting poet, the flamboyant new Blake scholar, the translator of the lost books of the Bible. She joined the ranks of the invisible: the exiled nation of people who love ideas, which exists (outside the university) only for a few days a year, when, gathering around some speaker or occasion, it constellates itself and then disperses: the floating world. She read poetry and history—"nurture and torture" as she called them to the woman at the public library—and tried to meet there the minds that would not meet her in life.

At last she turned to anatomies of the soul, diagrams and lists of qualities, hidden names of the angels and of God. She could not have told why, except that this seemed to be a center, a focus of light around which something turned.

The angels of service are the fowl of heaven, Sarita reads. An exegesis of the hundred and fourth psalm by Rabbi Akiba, who ought to know. Then why should it not be possible to attract one by the same means one uses with other fowl? She begins to make a dress out of translucent white wool, severe as lightning, soft as cloud: with big wings made out of net and wire, each separate quill cut out of horsehair interfacing and drawn on with blue chalk. She will give it to the Episcopal Church for their Christmas pageant when the experiment is over. She pads the front with batting into a maternal, pouter-pigeon shape. There are three plaster mannequins in the shop, spray-painted with metallic auto paint; she puts the dress on the silver one, posing it as solemnly as the flexed wrists will permit, and gives it a white and silver headdress. She does this on a Friday when the customers and the assistants have gone home. She sets the decoy in a lighted window. Is it necessary to open the window? She does. She lights candles and pours wine for herself and another; then settles herself with a book, not facing directly the open window, and waits.

The sound stunned her: a noise like the battering of swan-wings against the walls of a box. Nothing else had changed: the mannequin stood without swaying, the scraps of fabric pinned to the walls did not flutter. The candle-flames held steady. But the sound shook the room, pattering against her eardrums, beating at her mind, until she leapt up and cried, "Wait—Welcome—Shalom."

The noise diminished. Beside the cutting table a light began to collect, as though sound were changing into visible form. A shape roughly human, but not solid: the size and aspect of a person, but translucent and hollow. She could see the contour of its back through its front. Blurred lights around its head and feet and shoulders subsided into wings. Under its feet the floor rose slightly to meet it, as though matter were yearning upward toward spirit; the boards were covered with new grass.

An androgynous face, impossible to call male or female: long and severe and intent. She glanced over its body for other evidence of sex, instantly abashed at the thought that it might spot her, but there was only a gathering of light at the root of the body, too bright to reveal a shape. Another light within the head, where humans have their brains. All unreal and remote and strange, until she looked into the eyes—and then she caught her breath, because there was no longing in them. Whatever she desired, those eyes had seen.

"שבת שלום" it said.

It spoke within her mind, not audibly. But she understood that she must reply in language. She was certain that the angel could read her thoughts, but as a mortal she was bound to the sayable: language was the boundary between them, and if she could not articulate she would be consumed. But trying to speak was horrible: automatic, unpremeditated, as if the angel touched with its beam of thought the center of language in her, and language came up, as bile would have come up if it had put a finger down her throat. Ugly, superfluous, external to her body when it should have stayed within: it exposed her.

What are you? it said, and she babbled, "Functionary, feminary, just another of too many; tailor to the lawyer ladies, dresser to the wives."

How do you know? "Apple-knowledge, no college would offer it. They can't test what you ingest on your own."

How do you love? That made her pause, and she began to answer more slowly. "By flesh and warmth, a wave of the first water, breaking. Hands remember and follow the skin trade. *Coito ergo sum*," she added, tears springing to her eyes.

How often does it happen? Did even angels want to know that? Lines from old songs skipped through her head. "When I can . . . going to the fair with my young man." But what was the true answer? "Not often enough . . . and too much grief . . . too long a sacrifice. For she that may not when she would, she dare not when she can."

How long does it last? The tears spilled over; she could think of nothing at all. "Till the stars fall from the sky, and she cry."

What are those tears? "Helplessness, automatic . . . like automatic writing." She began to struggle against the invasion. "I can't. I have a standard transmission, *I* shift the gears. This nakedness of not thinking, too tender, no one should have to see that."

Are you ashamed? "Yes, damn you! Have you never seen it before?"

The voice in her mind grew gentler, the eyes were averted. *I am sorry. We in the World of Formation understand all things through feeling; emotion is our substance. I cannot recognize you except by what you feel.*

"I had read that," she said. "I had not imagined how it would be."

She turned from it and sat down on the edge of a chair. The decoy caught her eye, suddenly ridiculous, and she shook her head: the difference between what you wanted and what you got.

You called me. Why?

"I was longing to talk to someone about spirit." She did not meet its eyes. "I don't suppose you can know what it's like not to be able to. The customers aren't really interested—it's all their kids and their jobs and their vacations; and people in the clothing business just laugh that kind of thing off the runway. It's a sort of assault on reality to say anything about God or one's inner life. They'd think I was trying to evangelize them or correct them, and it has nothing to do with that."

God is an assault on reality.

"Well, then, reality proceeds from one assault to another; and what is one to do about it? We try not to talk about these things, so as not to be assaults on each other. But we seem to do it by pretending that assaults don't happen at all, or happen to someone else. Only to people who ask for it, I suppose."

What would you prefer instead?

"Oh, to be able—I don't know how it can be said. To have spirit mean something besides ethereal vapors, or whether you've been saved. Poets and scholars know, sometimes, but it's in their work, you can't go up to them after the lecture and have a real conversation. What would you say? *Look, I made this dress, it says just the same thing you were saying.* Right."

Clothing is an arcane language.

"It's a corrupt language. People think of it as a sort of Stepin Fetchit routine, or advertising—something that's innately not serious. Comic dialect or salesman's jingles. Self-mockery, servility, sentimentality, despair, all rolled up together. They think it means you enjoy being a girl."

And it could mean—?

"It could mean you love God with your whole body, and you know your body is going to die. It could mean you see the pain of the world and are grieved for it. I don't mean that all lightness is wrong, but it shouldn't be a frantic lightness." She stopped herself. "I'm not saying it well; let me try again. Ask me the other way."

It smiled; a coruscation of light flashed over its whole body, starting from and returning to the eyes. *What is the dress of the spirit?*

"Eirenical, ironical, not caught in the duress of success. God's image is no old cheese, to be bound in a cloth; it's a star, to shine between clouds, and not be unseemly." The beam of thought was not imperious now; it was searching, generous, throwing light on synapses she had not known she possessed. It tickled her mind and made her laugh.

Courage! Now you have asked for a witness.

"What else are wits for?" She smiled back at it, full of an energy and daring she had never felt in her life. Her gestures became wider; her step and her grasp were firm as she got up and reached for the two cups of wine. "I'm a fool, but I won't be a coward. Will you drink with me, for a blessing?"

It sang something over the cups, and added, *Blessed are You who separate work from rest.* Then, as she held one cup out to it, it drew back from her a little. *Set the cup down,* it said.

She set it on the cutting table near where the angel stood, and moved back. She had not considered that touch might be impossible, that even the transfer of an object might cross some explosive boundary. But if she must speak aloud to maintain her separate existence, could touch be a less dangerous frontier?

It raised the cup, and drank. The wine altered its color: from bright gold it turned a sort of rose gold, mellow and subdued. She was astonished that anything material could affect it. As she drank in turn, feeling the wine blush through her tissues, she wondered if the angel felt a similar physical change.

But the immaterial affects you. Why should not the material affect me?

"Well... one is told that matter is grosser. That you are too ethereal for such interminglings."

A laugh like a wind blowing. *Oh, these self-pitying humans! Matter is slower than spirit, not less clean. If I come in answer to a decoy, who can suppose I need fear matter?*

"Maybe you ought to fear decoys; ducks are shot because they don't. Aren't you afraid I'm going to send you here and there, and make you do my bidding?"

No.

"No?"

Could anyone who calls an angel by decoy be content to send me on errands?* It was looking at her with frank delectation. *How rare, how lovely, to be asked to witness, not to serve!*

She laughed and looked away. It understood; she was not sure she understood in herself all that it understood. She had a sudden vision of it wrapping its wings around her before a crowd of admiring onlookers, praising her work: saying things that would prove her finally, incontrovertibly, as good as her ambition. Oh, God, this was just like having a crush on a teacher: the same shy vanity, the same rancid self-regard. She recoiled.

"Oh, but I am a fool: why should I ask you to witness *me*? As though you had nothing to do but improve my life. Imagine meeting you across such a gulf and doing nothing but wanting help."

That is the usual condition of such meetings.

"No doubt; but it isn't much different from sending you on errands. I don't want to be usual; my whole effort in life is not to settle for the mediocre and the mindless and the stunted. But I think what I really want from you is some assertion that I'm special and good, and what could be more usual than that?"

How troubled you are by what you seem to be.

"Exactly. If I weren't, I wouldn't want help; I would just do the work."

What prevents you?

The thought was searching and gentle, and yet the place in her mind that it searched was so scarred over, so enclosed in some thick membrane without nerve-endings, that the ready flow of sounds did not come forth. Emotion sought for emotion and encountered nothing.

"I—I don't know. I suppose if I did, it wouldn't."

You have buried it deeply. Then tell me instead what drives you.

That was something she understood. "Fury. Fury at the women I dress, that they really prefer clothing to be apologetic and whimsical, that they *want* in some way to be stunted. And fury at the whole structure that keeps clothes on that trivial level. And fury at everything I can't have, at the certain knowledge that if I told any other designer all this he would laugh himself silly, and if I told it to my customers I'd probably never sell them another rag. It's shameful; I should be moved by something better, because this is as dangerous as it is powerful. If I really let it out it would blind me. It would offend other people and make them feel wretched, and I have no right to do that. But it's an ugly feeling to try to sublimate into beauty."

Something underlies that fury, something disappointed or unsatisfied. What is it?

"Longing," she said less steadily. "Wanting to tell people what I'm doing. Wanting to turn them from despair. Wanting to bring into the world—God knows how much time we have left in it—some recognition, some meeting of soul and soul. Wanting to tell them what I love, to bring out this extraordinary tenderness that's in me all the time. But how can I do that if they don't? Who's to begin it? How am I to know that they want it, just because I do? I don't know whether longing drives me or prevents me. I only know it never stops."

What would appease your longing?

She searched its face, its golden and unclouded eyes. "What appeased yours?"

A scent flowed out of it like sandalwood; the whole room sighed. She had not asked it anything until now, and she saw that it depended on words even less in answering than it did in asking. She did not grasp whether it was giving her an answer or saying it had never longed; the whole change of tone overpowered her with such longing of her own that she could barely breathe. It was like the hush of a May twilight when the world has just become green, the grass thick and soft, the leaves full out and the trees seeming denser and closer because they have become opaque; the window as you look out of it full of green shadows, weighty, erotic, still. She put her hands to her breasts.

"Oh," she said, the involuntary motion recalling her, "I'm sorry. I hadn't—I'm not used to being spoken to that way. You make me wonder—"

Yes?

"Whether I want my longing to be appeased or just want it to be the right longing."

The stillness deepened. She saw that in the grass at the angel's feet blue flowers had sprung up: scilla and chionodoxa little and bright. With infinite gentleness the voice in her mind went on.

How do you judge the right longing?

"It recurs, it returns, it draws the mind like a tide. Sunken thoughts rise like drowned rocks. Pumice and porousness, floating on waterwastes, O even stones might rejoice in levity. It's no longer my longing but simply something that longs; I could live in it like a house."

Will you not live in it?

She was startled back into reason. "But, after all, can I? Isn't that some sort of sainted craziness, remote from everything, stranger to people than fury? What would I be? Could I do the simplest things, handle the most ordinary objects, without falling at their feet?"

You might approach the most ordinary people without dreading to offend them. Whoever lives in the house of that longing learns not to despise.

She gave a sad laugh. "That would be a change."

She was silent, thinking. Could longing be anything but a private failure, a sign of impotence and isolation? Could it be lived in, openly made a condition of her work, a part of her public truth? If it were the right longing, could it?

Think. No one lives in a house at every moment: they go in and out, they have their work and their errands, they visit in other houses. But their own house is the one they return to: it shelters them.

"And something that feels so much like exposure could shelter me?"

If you will.

She drew breath. "I will."

It stirred. Its wings opened, hugely; the tips of them pierced the ceiling and were visible through it. Every feather glimmered, luminous and trembling, gold reflecting gold till she seemed to stand within a shimmering dome. *B'rucha ha-ba'a,* it said. *May He who understands the speech of the rose among thorns—*

She felt it in her body, because that is where human creatures feel it; as with Bernini's Saint Teresa, it was a sexual ravishment that flowed over from the spiritual. But unlike Saint Teresa, she felt not one inconsiderable arrow-shaft, but a whole surroundment of angelic substance. It was like making love to water, but water that resisted and kept its shape, and went everywhere at once, meeting the rise of shoulder and breast and pelvis along every surface, glowing; gripping under the arch of the thighs and beneath the buttocks, sliding up to push at the neck of her womb and loosen her inner muscles, and slipping along the wet exterior parts, insinuating the merest tendril into the hinder orifice. Her ears hummed with a sound like audible gold. Her body was at once helpless and purposeful, not simply unresisting but rejecting resistance, refusing any response but transfixed involuntary motion. There was no distracting move, no absence or sudden slacking; no moment when the sensations became too fierce, for every movement or convulsion brought her against some surface that held her; no muscular contraction that turned to a cramp or griped upon empty air. But what undid her most was how her mind was held: how its desires were grasped, its half-formed impulses taken up and played on, even its failures caressed into some lovelier shape. No thought too shocking, no speculation too complex, no weakness too contemptible to be met—and met not with consolation or instruction but with an eager recognition and protection more enflaming than any bodily embrace. She did not hear her breathing or her cries; she did not know whether she lay upon some surface or hung in air. For a moment or a day she rested in it, and did not know whether longing was intensified or satisfied, and did not care.

She knew it ceased. Not like the cessation of any other lovemaking: no unceremonious popping out of her body, no pulling apart of itching sweat-drenched skin. Only the desolation of distinctness, angel and woman, the miraculous occupation withdrawn and gone.

She was chanting names: cup, table, candle, matches, pins. She lay in the stuffed armchair she kept for customers to sit in; she was clothed, though she was sure she had been naked. Her eyes wandered slowly over the room, registering its contents: sewing machines and sergers, heaps of cloth and half-assembled garments, the steam iron with its little tank of water, a half-tailored jacket on a dummy. The candles had gone out. The angel waited at a little distance, its wings folded again.

"So," she said, and tried to smile. "Even with an angel, it has to end."

Its brightness seemed a little dimmed. *Even for an angel, the embrace is arduous*, it said. *We have light, but you have warmth.*

She stared at it and blushed. "You also desire it, then?"

We are given the task of blessing; we desire above all things to bless.
Only a little ironically, she asked, "How often does it happen?"
We do not live time as you do. All who desire the blessing are given it.

Its distance annoyed her suddenly: to go from that mighty joy back to questions and answers! "A kind of celestial whoredom, is that it?"

It smiled sadly. *Celestial promiscuity, you might say if you wished; but not whoredom, surely. No one I bless renders payment.*

"They don't have to," she said. "You're on salary. Heaven's payroll, to which we all pay a tithe. It's a service profession, right? And you've serviced me." She turned her face away.

Ah, will you regret it? the angel said. *You who desired a witness, who wanted to be searched and changed? Will you refuse it after all, and continue to despise?*

She stared fixedly at a wastebasket in the far corner. "No," she said at last. "I called you and I wanted you; I will never be sorry that you came. But how will I bear your leaving? Jacob at least had his brother to meet in the morning. And the angel gave him a new name, which became the name of a great nation. But I have no people at all."

It did not answer. The wind changed; the feathers of the decoy rustled together. The real angel stirred its wings. *Dawn is coming,* it said.

"Oh, God," she said. "Then tell me one thing. What are the consequences? If you were human—if you were a human man—I would be worrying whether you had made me pregnant and whether you had made me ill. Surely this encounter has its own dangers. What are they? What have I risked by having knowledge of you?"

Knowledge.

It was drawing into itself again, its gentleness receding; it was becoming the implacable noise of wings that had entered the room at first. She jumped up; holding off that beating sound with both hands, she cried, "No! You won't go without telling me. What pregnancy have you left me with?"

Your work, it answered remotely. *Before tonight it was only fertile; now it will bear fruit.*

"Thank you," she said, and bowed her head. But the wings beat louder, and the bright shape began to dissolve, and over the sound she cried again, "And what illness? What contagion do you spread from one mortal to another, every last one of us craving to be blessed?"

It gave an indescribable flicker of dark gold, a spasm of grief that left behind it a scent of wet earth. *Limit*, it said. *Your work will never be enough*. The wings drummed louder and were gone.

Down the stairs she stumbled in the darkness, the dawn just beginning outside, the decoy trailing its skirts from under her arm. Down to the restaurant next to the bus station, coffee and an omelette, home fries and toast. The waitress staring at the decoy, propped opposite her in the booth. "A costume," Sarita explains. She reads the paper: ground broken for the new city hall, red tide subsides along the coast, our young people need more discipline; the Anima Clinic, an alternative healing center and bookshop, opens its doors next week. She sketches on the placemat. Pregnant with work: already morning sickness is setting in, making the sketch ungainly and distorted.

Too much cheese in the omelette. She leaves a lump of it at the edge of the plate, pays at the register, and maneuvers the decoy backwards out the door. Saint Michael's is two blocks down and one over. She leaves the decoy on the back steps, where Andrew, her assistant Todd's lover and the church organist, will find it when he comes to practice. He can return the mannequin later. On an impulse she writes on the back of a business card *Please bring my baby up a Christian*, and tucks it in the neck of the decoy's gown.

She takes the long way back, past the piers where the fishing boats are going out and birdwatchers are gathering for the early harbor cruise. She watches everyone. As once after a firework display, when she found her eyes suddenly opened to traffic lights, headlights, streetlights, illuminated doorbells, all of them appearing no longer as common signals but as the brilliant jewels of modernity, so now she sees in everyone she passes a bright reflection of the angel's lineaments. The human form divine. All their clothes perfect on them as if they had grown there:

uniforms, T-shirts, nylon windbreakers, the sublime serenity of blue denim. Nothing without dignity, nothing needing alteration.

Not that they dress as if they had no souls; that's how a soul dresses. But is her work necessary to do, if she is not correcting some lack in the world by means of it? Is her ambition a mere redundancy, an insistence on finding something wrong with other people's designs so that her own might be right? Is her moral vision only a brazen little shout of her own name endlessly repeated, a cry of *Notice me, notice me, let me not perish unnoticed*?

Only not to have to open the shop. Only to be able to sleep.

When she arrives back at the shop the light is streaming in the windows; the little strip of water sparkles. She packs the candlesticks and the cups and wine into a paper bag to take home. No one would suspect that anything had happened. But walking across the room to turn on the steam iron she almost falls: there is a place where the floor is not level. Disoriented, she stares at it blankly; then flings herself down next to it, shutting her eyes, pressing with both hands the damp uneven spot where grass grew. *Not in order to be right*, she whispers. *Rightness is half a blessing. Witness is all.*

•

CHAPTER 1

> What is it that men call an issue? It is to make a tragic problem (for all problems are tragic) so small and so empty that everybody can understand it.
>
> —Edwin Muir, "Against Optimism and Pessimism"

Sarita went to a rally; two of the lawyer ladies were speaking, and she thought she ought to appear. She was bad at politics: her very compulsion to read political writers gave her an aversion to crowd scenes, and she was always uneasy with friends who knew exactly what was the matter in Nicaragua or whether economic sanctions against South Africa were imperative or unconscionable. She was not sure why she made an exception now, except that it was an anxious moment for legal abortion and somehow abortion politics were not quite the same; when she read about women crossing lines of shouting protestors at the local clinic she always felt obscurely that those women were taking punishments meant for her. If witness were all—if witness were anything—surely she owed them something. Surely she owed some action on their behalf. But what action? She bought a pin and took a blue-and-white placard and stood feeling foolish. The plaza in front of the post office was crammed with people; they squinted in the bright July heat.

The lieutenant-governor—wearing her new summer suit—opened the speeches: firm and resolute, passionate in the stylized manner of politicians, well in control. Sarita tried to summon an answering passion, but the speech seemed to have no rough edges; her passions slid off. Our choices must be protected, the law must be safeguarded, we shall not be moved. She was not. She struggled with disappointment.

She ought not to hope; politicians were like this, one couldn't imagine them being *relaxed* enough to get pregnant by accident. She scanned the faces of the women waiting to speak, hoping for something more. *Will you never talk as though you had a soul?*

But something was going wrong. Several women at the foot of the steps had laid their placards down and were shouting, no, singing, in a treble whine that rose in counterpoint to the lieutenant-governor's voice and floated over the crowd. The tune was "The Old Rugged Cross," though they seemed to have done something to the words. The lieutenant-governor stammered on one syllable and then recovered; she raised her voice. The crowd coalesced into one nervous entity. Unease rose out of its pores like a sweat; the very smells changed in the air. Young women with curious haircuts began to shout slogans; the police, parked across the street, muttered into their radios.

Sarita hoped it would not come to a fight. As a child she had seen the Chicago convention on television, heads running with blood for the sake of a principle, and had wondered if any principle in the world were enough to endanger her head for. She supposed this one was, but she devoutly hoped not to have to make good on the supposition. She looked cautiously around for an escape route. When she looked back, the line of speakers was in disarray; the announcer was beckoning frantically to someone at the foot of the steps. A small dark-haired woman was coming up, looking hesitant. Several others from the line rushed forward and formed a little knot of chaos around her; they moved her toward the podium in a slow dance of gestures and expostulations (the lieutenant-governor, meanwhile, shouting the text of the First Amendment over the noise). At last the speech ended, and the others stepped back, leaving the dark-haired woman alone. She looked tiny and petrified. The crowd clapped distractedly, and the hymn-singers booed.

The announcer gave the woman's name as Miranda Como: no title, no Attorney or Reverend or Professor. The hymn-singers seemed to know no more about her than Sarita did; they began singing again, but not at full volume. The woman looked down at them. Something seemed to shift in her face; calm came over her all at once, and she said:

"I'm here to talk to you about God."

There was a confused silence. Both sides clearly wondered if something had slipped: had a heckler infiltrated the line of speakers, and was the rally about to be hijacked? She gave no sign, but went on.

"God is a god of justice," she said; "all of us would say we are here today in search of justice. But there are women here today who've passed themselves off as supporters of abortion rights and turned out to be opponents, and that's unjust; they've prevented another woman from being heard, and that's unjust; and they want to make it appear that all the religious conscience is on their side, and that's most unjust of all."

A ripple of appreciation passed through the crowd, and the silence turned friendly. She acknowledged it with a flicker of the eyes, and went on.

"To be unwillingly pregnant is many young women's moral awakening. It's the first time they realize that being moral doesn't mean never doing anything wrong: it means trying to repair the wrong you've done before it's too late. Where abortion is still illegal, women risk their lives to repair that wrong; that's a moral act."

She paused and looked at the hecklers, but they seemed to be unprepared. Apparently they had been expecting some other argument. She went on.

"Our opponents don't think the birth of a child can be wrong. It can; it can be the death of the mother's spirit. Having a child changes your life absolutely, and if you have no veto against that change, when conception is so easy and by its nature isn't a thoughtful moment, you become a slave. Men kill and die for freedom, because they're afraid of how slavery will stunt their humanity. Women are afraid of that too."

The hymn-singers were beginning to recover; one of them shouted a long accusation, unintelligible to Sarita in the back except for the final word, which was "Holocaust". Miranda gave her a long look.

"If you want a historical comparison," she said, " it's Masada: women are killing the fruit of their own bodies, as early and humanely as they can, because they can't prevent the world, and their own families, and their own selves from brutalizing those children once they're born."

More cries rose from the hecklers, but Miranda looked at them sharply and held up her hand.

"Now you may think," she went on, "that a brutal childhood is nothing new, and a mother who's been reduced to a slave is nothing new, and what's one more broken spirit? But someone who thinks that way has no religion. And someone who takes this choice from a woman, who forces motherhood on her as if there were no escape, also takes *her* religion from her, because they take the nexus of her responsibility. They take her chief means of reducing the cruelty in the world." Her eyes took in the whole square.

"There's a longstanding tradition in the Church that says choice—any choice, the act of choice—is subversive. The word *heresy* comes from a Greek word meaning choice. But that's an institutional convenience which directly opposes a far more ancient idea, an idea at the core of the Hebrew scriptures: that choice is the central act of religion—the choice to do what is most humane and responsible in the circumstances given, and not to leave everything to fate or the will of authority.

"Because the spiritual is not the pious and obedient thing. The spiritual is not what knuckles under to the inevitable. The spiritual is not what says *Be it unto me according to thy word*. The spiritual is what is concrete and practical and sane, and resists the inevitable to the limit of its imagination, and deals not in condemnation and punishment but in *remedy*—and until you can offer a remedy to unwillingly pregnant women that's as humane and responsible as legal abortion, don't dare to tell us you speak for God."

A cheer went up from the crowd, and a sea of placards waved above people's heads; but Miranda Como had already turned away and was walking down the steps. A few of the hecklers shouted inaudible accusations at her as she went, but most seemed to be arguing among themselves about what she had said.

Sarita met her at the foot of the steps. From her position on the edge of the crowd she had been impelled right through it, pushing between people in a way she had never done in all her life, cutting between the hecklers— "Praise the Lord!" she said to one of them, pressing a VOTE FOR CHOICE button into her hand and smiling warmly—and arriving at the front with her heart pounding and her ankles trembling as though she would fall. A tangle of cameras and microphones had closed around Miranda as the rally went on, but even into this she insinuated herself, and after a few impatient moments found herself looking down into those alert dark eyes.

"Who are you? Do you live around here? I didn't know there was anyone in this town who could talk like that," she stammered.

"There isn't," said Miranda shortly. "I'm a figment of the imagination." She gave a wry smile that might have been defensiveness, or resignation, or anything.

"Can you come for coffee somewhere?" said Sarita, still trembling, trying not to sound foolish. "Caffeine can provide the illusion of existence."

"I'd like that," Miranda answered. "But I'm due back at work; I can't. Maybe we can run into each other somewhere."

"Come to my shop," Sarita said anxiously. "It's right in town here: 59 Water Street, above Harbor Books. SB Designs. I'm always there." She fumbled in her wallet for a card.

"Always?" said Miranda. "Well, I'm always somewhere; sometime I'll be there." She took the card; although it was a hot summer day, her hand was icy.

Sarita was sure nothing would come of it; anyone with a mind like that must be wholly preoccupied with using it, and Miranda must have a circle of friends far worthier of her company. She still suspected that the intellectual center of the world existed, by definition, somewhere that she was not; when it saw her coming it moved itself, rapidly and silently, to somewhere she could not disturb it. She cautioned herself to expect nothing, and waited.

She was working that summer on a series of shrouds. Really they were not shrouds—or no one could have walked in them—but hooded robes adapted from a combination of Eastern and Western monastic garments; but through perversity she thought of them as shrouds. The present series were in rayon gauze and light silk, which she dyed streakily in shades of yellow, orange and crimson; occasionally she used black linen, which she bleached to a patchy gray, and then scattered a pattern of blurred stars across it with a spray-bottle of chlorine. In winter she would do a similar line in wool and cotton velvet. Somewhat to her surprise, they were selling well; women put them on and saw some unexpected power in their reflections, as though the clothes revealed a part of their character they had despaired of. "Oh," they would say, as if something were made clear, and take out their credit cards. One of them told her she was like Fortuny, cutting her own eccentric path through the jungle of the fashion world, and that she would be remembered when more famous designers were dead. She knew that some of them were dying, and did not think it a fair contest.

She was experimenting one evening with the drape of the front, swearing pensively through a mouthful of pins, when Miranda appeared at the door. "You are always here," she said. "Are you always doing something so magnificent?"

"Miranda! Come in," she said, standing up hastily, flustered. "Yes, when I can."

"Call me Mim; everyone does," Miranda said absently. "Let me look at this stuff. I've seen clothes like this in dreams." She wandered about the room, fingering the half-finished garments.

"Would you like to try one on? Try one on!" Sarita held three different shades under Mim's face in quick succession. "This one," she said. "I knew I hadn't seen the person this red was for."

Mim disappeared behind the curtain and emerged, regal. The robe was too long, and she held it before her to walk, like a lady from an illuminated manuscript. "Let's try a head wrap with that," said Sarita. "I've still got some of the scraps." She worked on Mim's head for a moment and stood back. "Now look."

"Good heavens," said Mim at the mirror. "You've made me into a Rembrandt. I don't know if I deserve this."

"Everybody capable of being a Rembrandt deserves to be one," said Sarita. "Some are only capable of being Fragonards."

Mim broke into a wicked smile. "Who were not born to keep in trim with old Ezekiel's cherubim, but those of Beauvarlet," she murmured. "Well, I'm not convinced, but I'm willing to pretend for a while. Here, I've brought you some wine."

"Oh, good! Only we'll have to drink it out of these teacups. And you can tell me all about yourself. Where did you learn to talk like that? What have you published? I've got to know more about you."

"Oh," said Mim shamefacedly, watching her pull the cork. "There's not very much to know. Certainly I've never published anything. I'm a secretary."

Sarita leaned heavily against the cutting table. "Jesus Christ," she said, stunned. "Why? I'm sorry, I know that's rude, but I would have thought you'd be teaching philosophy somewhere, or writing speeches or something. Damn it, you can think; not everybody can think."

"Do you call it thinking?" said Mim uncertainly. "I'm not sure. It frightens me. I mean, I reason it out, up to a point; it's not that it springs full-blown out of my head without any work. But the rhetoric, the way it ties itself to the situation, that's a kind of seizure; it just presents itself and I do it, and it's terrifying."

"It's extraordinary. How could anyone have said anything more appropriate, and more intelligent? You saved the day."

"Oh, yes, that's the problem. People listen. They're generally eating out of my hand by the time I finish. Do you have any idea what that's like?"

"Mightily satisfying, I would think. It's not as if it was just the latest polemic."

Mim looked away, her face troubled. "But if they hear it, *is* it anything more than polemic? If I get the ideas across, have I raised people's sights or diminished the ideas? The fact is, I'm a born demagogue. What does one do with a gift like that?"

"What a scruple!" said Sarita. "Use it, if the cause is good enough."

"Is any cause good enough, in the long run? I believe in this one—God knows I owe it enough—but who's worth risking for it? Who do I put in jeopardy?"

Sarita was puzzled. "What?"

"This business of choice in the Bible," Mim said reluctantly. "You don't talk about the Hebrew Bible to right-to-lifers. Right under the surface, for some of them—"

"Well, right under the surface it's their Bible too."

"Under a set of conditions that changes it utterly. It's not safe to point that out. It's too easy, where Jews are concerned, to—my God, it was only fifty years ago. You don't go adding more fuel."

There was a silence. "Sit down, Mim," Sarita said gently. "Yes, I see what you mean. But—surely even that doesn't give you license to submerge yourself in some dreadful job, just bury yourself out of fear. Christ, whose secretary are you? Whoever he is, you're worth ten of him."

She sat down. "Well, there are six of them. The book selection staff at the university library. Two of them are women. It's not as bad as it sounds." She took the wine from Sarita, and for a few minutes they sat in silence.

"But you're really asking about my life, aren't you?" she finally said. "Since that's how I learned to talk this way."

"I suppose I am, really, yes," said Sarita nodding. "But of course it's prying and I have no right."

"No, I think you do," said Mim. "Anybody who can make one into a Rembrandt can bypass the usual conventions. I don't mind telling you. But it's a shameful story: just one more woman who started out as a thinker and threw it all over to be normal." She sipped her wine. "Everybody knows what happens when young men feel disenfranchised: they act it out violently on the body politic, where everybody can see it. Young women look more civilized because they don't do that. But they're not: they act it out quietly on themselves, and their lovers, and their children—born or unborn. Young wives are the real female delinquents. Their crime against the body politic is their disappearance from it."

"Nine people out of ten will tell you that's our duty to the body politic."

"And nine women out of ten will agree. But I knew better, and in the end my mistake was worse than most young women's. After all, once you've learned to think you can't really be normal: you forfeit common sense, and then if you give up thinking too you have nothing at all."

Sarita laughed, and was not sure she should have. "At least you have words."

Mim shook her head. "My father's a poet. Do you know what Blake said about poets? *The poet is independent and wicked, the philosopher is dependent and good.* What's odd is that poets can produce philosophers: I admired my father and didn't want to disappoint him, and the minute you think like that you're dependent and trying to be good. I suspect that being a poet takes so much energy that there's not enough left for the next generation: a kind of congenital entropy, like congenital syphilis. And as you can see, I'm not even much of a philosopher—only this peculiar dormant kind who can't do any real work, but just emerges at odd times and saves a day. When I die they'll have to publish my collected crank letters; there won't be anything else."

She was looking away, and seemed to be settling in for a long narrative; Sarita decided to say nothing. She could barely decide not to break into an idiot grin: another human being in this town who could quote Blake!

"Being dependent and good, I was naturally drawn to religion. I was brought up without any: my father's a lapsed Catholic, and my mother was raised Presbyterian but she's a musician really. My father used to say I could get all the religion I wanted from the B minor Mass. He was right in a way, but I needed people to talk to about it, and the easiest place to find them was in church. So I did disappoint my father—if there was anything he hated worse than the Church of his youth it was the Church trying to modernize. But that's how these things go: you have to work out your life, and your timetable meshes very oddly with the rest of the world's, and you disgust the very people you mean to honor, and you just have to keep on.

"Besides, I'd met a man: a lawyer nine years older than me—I was twenty-two when we married, just out of college—who had wanted to be a priest and found that he couldn't, and who was looking for a serious woman.

"I was relieved and grateful to have found a serious man. And I was overwhelmed by his age and position—the possibility of an ordered life, when my friends were scrounging along from job to job and lover to lover. I'd never really expected to get married; it seemed to be something that was on the way out, like the Latin Mass, and the only men I was interested in were ones like my teachers that I couldn't have. But here was Alan, who found me miraculous, and who seemed to know everything I wanted to know, and wanted to live it out with me.

"He was devoted to the authority of the Church in a way that at first I found beautiful: it's astonishing to see a man in his thirties empty himself of pride, defer in the deepest decisions of his life to some outer rule, let himself be commanded. He'd come under the influence of some writers who said that the drive toward mastery was at the root of our social problems—that the world isn't perfectible by our own powers, that to do God's will we have to embrace defeat. I found the whole idea very attractive; so far I'd failed to master anything much, and it was an unexpected pleasure to hear that my failures put me ahead spiritually, gave me a head start on all those busy, competent people who had such a head start on me in all the other ways. And of course, being much younger and very grateful, I admired Alan rather uncritically. I—it's a seductive combination, you know: someone intelligent who thinks you're intelligent, and who talks theory to you, and thinks you're beautiful too.

"What it meant, though, was that I failed to master the rhythm method."

Sarita spoke without meaning to. "Oh, my God. Mim."

"Well, I—Alan was very serious. Some people do manage to make it work, I think, but it takes a good deal of body knowledge, and I barely had enough body knowledge to make love. I liked to think I was rather worldly and bold, but I was very backward about actually touching the body I lived in. I didn't feel at all prepared to have children, and Alan was nice about it, but he wouldn't do anything against the Church's directives. Almost no one obeys them; even most of the people we read thought that was one place the Church had gone wrong. I didn't want to distress him; I said I would try. But I was horribly confused and embarrassed at trying to keep track of my cycle, and stunned by the power of sex, and for the first few months I was like any haphazard sixteen-year-old, waiting in terror for the blood to show.

"Once or twice I asked him whether we couldn't possibly consider the Pill for a year or two, so I could prepare myself for the sheer permanence of motherhood and get through graduate school, and his answer showed me a new side of him: he was willing for me to be defeated *there*. I don't think it was . . . indifference, you know, or hardheartedness; it was—"

"Obliviousness," said Sarita. "Did he really care about children?"

Mim looked at her: beseechingly, as if she had been puzzling over it ever since. "You know, I don't know. He didn't spend much time with his nieces and nephews, but then he'd never been close to his sisters, who were all much older and hadn't had a real education. I think he really felt we weren't supposed to have control in that realm. We were supposed to be taken by surprise. How you felt about it wasn't quite admissible as evidence; if I was afraid of pregnancy, it was the fear that had to go. Fear was almost a form of willfulness or pride, a self-preoccupation verging on sin.

"All of which I could assent to in theory by that time, and even find rather moving, but I couldn't live it in practice. And when it became clear that I couldn't talk to him about it, I did something that really was a sin: I went and got a prescription for the Pill and didn't tell him. I'd grown up like we all did, more or less knowing that birth control was there, taking for granted that any sane, responsible person would use it; I couldn't adjust my mind to living by the lottery. I felt furtive and sad every night when I took the little pill, and I knew I wasn't worthy of my husband—but oh, God, the assurance!

"And so things went on for a year or so, till Alan went to the doctor for a routine checkup and decided to have his sperm count taken."

Sarita winced.

"When he told me about it—the results were fine, of course—I saw what the year had looked like through his eyes, and I was ashamed. It's merciless to lie to someone who trusts you: it creates a false world, where they move with ease and serenity, and which all the time you could destroy with a word or two. He thought that because I no longer seemed afraid of pregnancy, I'd accepted the possibility. He'd assumed I would naturally turn up pregnant in the course of things, and had been kindly refraining from comment in case I was anxious about it. He'd gotten anxious about it himself."

"In other words, he expected rhythm to fail. So much for sympathy."

"But, Sarita, he thought it ought to fail, really. I keep telling you, he believed in defeat."

"Then why have his sperm count tested? Sterility is a defeat too, if you're looking for one."

"The official line is that pregnancy is the natural state, so it's permitted to assist it. It's just not permitted to avoid it—or not to avoid it effectively. There are subtleties to this defeat business, as I was beginning to find out.

"But just then I had to deal with the consequences of having lied to him, and they were dreadful. I'd never seen him so angry—thin-lipped and stone-faced and untouchable. It wasn't only the bitterness of having been lied to, it was the certainty that I held the Church in contempt. I hadn't even stopped receiving the sacrament. Obviously, he said, I was younger and more shallow than he'd realized; he hadn't imagined me capable of this kind of moral collapse. If I didn't want children yet that was fine, he was quite willing to do anything within the limits of the teaching, but he couldn't make love with me in a state of sin; it was just too painful to contemplate." Mim hesitated. "And he stopped. Wouldn't go near me. Slept on the edge of the bed. Not hateful, you know, not impatient; he just wasn't there. He said it was my choice." She drew a shaky breath. "So I chose."

Sarita whistled. "And this is the man who didn't believe in mastery."

"When it came to his loyalty to the Church he could be quite ruthless. I couldn't understand it. It was a good-natured, durable ruthlessness at its best—Catholics are in it for the long haul—but sometimes that broke down and there was an awful woundedness beneath it. I suppose that was how he lived with not being a priest: if he was going to be married, he was going to be married by the rules. That's all I can make of it. He was a generous man, and on the whole very kind, but when that nerve was touched he was irrational. He wanted to put himself under obedience, whatever the cost. That was different from what I wanted. I wanted to obey a just authority."

Sarita, who had never wanted to obey anyone, did not know what to say. "Nine years' difference between you," she finally ventured. "That's a bad position to be in. Was there no one else you could talk to?"

Mim looked down at her hands. "Not really. I mean, one doesn't tell one's parents this kind of thing. And I was in such a different position from all my friends. I did once go to confession—the modern kind, where you sit in an office and talk to the priest face to face—but what could the poor man say? Talk it over; work it out. *He* didn't care what we did. And I was shy, and didn't want to seem to need help, and didn't want to push him to say anything he wasn't supposed to.

"We did talk it over—and over and over, but we always seemed to go in circles. Alan thought I was incapable of restraint, and unused to obedience, and blamed it all on my age and the excesses of my generation. I couldn't seem to convince him that birth control *was* restraint, and that my allegiance to my generation—which was his generation too, after all, though we came from opposite ends of it—was just about nil. But I kept thinking of a fear I'd had before: that I and all of us born after the war are just half missing morally, that there's some necessary piece of a human being we just didn't get. There were so many of us that I wondered if most of the later ones, like me, were born with only parts of souls; I've imagined the souls standing in line for their bodies, and there being too many bodies—a glut, a congestion of bodies, so that the angel in charge began to split and patch the souls any old way, like a bored assembly-line worker during a speed-up. I was sure I was the result of a patching like that, and half my fear of pregnancy was the fear of passing on my insufficiency to the next generation. But of course if I was so insufficient, maybe Alan did know better; maybe my only hope was not to oppose him.

"So I gave in," she said; "he thought it was acceptance, but it was really a kind of despair. He thought I'd taken the Pill in order to be unrestrained, but I became unrestrained without it; God knows after weeks of forced abstinence I wanted to. I did try haphazardly to locate my fertile period again, but I had no idea what my cycle was doing as I went off the Pill. It was, which may or may not surprise you, the most passionate time in our marriage: despair is like that, it charges everything with emotion. This terrible moral hothouse, where there's nothing but the terms you've set for yourselves, forcing you to flower out of season.

"I never got the next period. Soon it was obvious why. I had several days of extreme clarity—the clarity you have when you see a truck barreling toward you on the road, and time slows down, and your every movement seems to take an age as you do precisely and only what's needed to get out of its way. Another woman might have felt at that point that her body's wisdom was stronger than her mind's, and had been driving her toward what she really wanted; I saw that neither my body nor my mind had any wisdom. Maybe I do have only half a soul, that I couldn't be glad at that point—after all, I was married, we could afford a child, we lived in conditions most people in the world would have envied. But I felt a shame that made me double up on the floor: I was bearing down, over and over, as if to expel the fetus through sheer force of will. I couldn't stop till I was exhausted; it was all I could do not to scream. It makes me wonder whether abortion is as instinctive as labor in some cases, except that you need help to accomplish it. People talk about the miracle of birth, and how it changes you; this was a miracle in reverse, with all the power and none of the deliverance.

"Alan was at work; I was curled up in the bathroom as if I were locked in a cell. There was no alternative ahead of me that wasn't fearful. The drive toward mastery—how can you raise a child without a drive toward mastery? It wouldn't live if you were willing to accept defeat. Malnutrition, earaches, falls and burning and drowning and the common cold. You can't let all those things win. And *the child* has to be mastered: its own drive toward mastery is so relentless and so inexhaustible, and wears everyone out. Submission to God's will doesn't get you very far when you're dealing with a two-year-old. There's nothing but mastery in motherhood; not that it always succeeds, but there's never a moment when you don't need it.

"A competent person would have laughed in Alan's face, and in

God's face, and accepted that nine-tenths of everything men say to women is wishful ignorance, and come into her strength there and then. It would have been her and the child then, the one stable unit in the world—Mary and Jesus, who don't really need Joseph to get by. But I couldn't do that. I loved Alan, I loved the men we'd been reading, I didn't want all that to stop. Pregnancy was a sentence to solitary confinement with someone who couldn't talk theory. I'd be locked away in some other understanding of the world that Alan could never share. I walked the house as if I'd been told I had cancer, seeing everything with the light of mortality on it. I stared at the bookshelves and said, *I will have to learn mastery, and Alan will despise me, and God will forsake me.*"

Sarita shook her head slowly. "Either way; either way. Whether you have the baby or not, it changes you; you learn mastery in a way men can never understand."

"I think some can, but Alan wasn't one of them. Certainly I couldn't imagine telling him. I tried to force myself to be happy: thought of nursing, thought of Alan watching the baby with his tenderest look, thought of telling my mother. None of it helped. I couldn't feel anything for the child. Or no, that's not true: I couldn't let it long for me when I hadn't longed for it. There are enough times in the life of a child when you have to be efficient and perfunctory, and disappoint its love for you. If you didn't want it at all—

"So I went to the doctor. When we got married I'd stayed with my usual doctor at the university clinic, but now I went to another one: Morgenzahl, who was quietly known among the students as the best man for these jobs. Of course everyone knows him now, because of all he's gone through to keep his clinic open; back then he was still in a private office on Green Street. I found him a little frightening—he's a formidable intellect, they say he reads Kant and Wittgenstein for fun— but where I would have expected him to treat me condescendingly, he was wholly gentle and tough-minded. He knew what to listen for. He dealt mostly with unmarried women, of course, and occasionally with a married woman who didn't want more children, so I was an odd case; he wanted to be sure I wasn't being coerced. Once he was satisfied of that, he said, 'You're a purist: you have the husband and the income and insist on the willingness too.'

"'I'm a religious woman,' I said. 'I don't believe inadvertent acts are moral ones.'

"He gave me a strange look—and it was really one of the strangest things I'd ever said—but all he said was, 'What have you been using for birth control?'

"I could barely answer him: my eyes filled up and my throat constricted, and I could only shake my head. 'My husband,' I said finally, 'is a religious man'; and then I was sobbing as if my heart had broken on the spot, covering my face for shame, trying to wipe my eyes on my paper gown.

"Morgenzahl got me a kleenex and let me cry, and when I'd pulled myself together I saw him looking at me. 'What a world,' he said. 'He gets a thinking woman and all he can think of to do with her is try to stop her thinking. What do you really want? If your religion is going to come back to haunt you, are you better off having the baby? What's it going to cost you to go through with this?'

"My voice wouldn't work. 'What's it going to cost me not to?' I said. 'You don't bring someone into the world, a whole new life with a history, on orders from your religion. The baby doesn't deserve to have parents like Alan and me. Oh, God, the baby probably doesn't care; it just wants to live. Am I justified in not having it because I've been living under false assumptions? Who kills a child to shore up her integrity?'

"'You'd be surprised,' he said. 'Though if we're going to work together I would caution you that there is a distinction between a six-week fetus and a child. That's the whole point of abortion: it's not the slippery slope to infanticide, it's a complete repudiation of infanticide. Do you ever hear people saying, "If *Roe* is overturned, women will start killing their newborns?" Of course not. You do it now *because* you wouldn't do it later. If, that is, you want to do it at all, and I don't make that decision for you.'

"He was quite beautiful, I saw just then: my eyes were still struck with that preternatural awareness, and I saw the way his hair was thinning on top, and every wire of his beard, and the way his eyes held compassion and distance at once, as if seeing beyond you. A face like an eagle's, sharp and aloof, but not predatory: there was quickness of judgment there, but no cruelty.

"'Then you're not going to tell me I deserve what I get for using rhythm, and I should go home and bear my punishment?'

"'I'm not in the business of handing out penances,' he said, a little acidly. 'I'm a Jew; so far as we believe in anything, we believe in damage control. Can you make an appointment for Tuesday?'

"I said I would; I knew I wouldn't change my mind. I wanted it sooner—I didn't want to spend another week lying to Alan—but he said it was safer at seven weeks than at six: there would be less chance of a problem. Then he gave me another of those piercing looks, and said, 'Are you going to tell your husband?'

"I didn't want to face that question at all. 'Oh, God,' I said, 'I don't know. Don't ask me to tell him beforehand.'

"'I don't ask you to do anything. But unless you're afraid that he'll hurt you, I think you should tell him. Soon. It's disastrous for people of principle to keep secrets from one another.'"

Sarita stared. "What an extraordinary man."

"Yes. And it was extraordinary how that one conversation returned me to a world in which 'people of principle' could include abortionists and their clients. I wish they had more certainly included husbands and wives. In college I'd had friends who got pregnant without meaning to, and their boyfriends had gone with them to the abortions, stricken and gentle; they would never have thought of being angry. I thought far more of Alan than I did of those vague boys, but it was unimaginable he should come with me."

Mim sighed, looking down and away. "But I told him, or rather I helped him figure it out for himself. He noticed Tuesday night that I was looking depleted, and he was worried; he didn't know what to do about illness. When he asked if I was all right, I just said, 'I was pregnant for a few weeks,' and the rest happened without words. It hit him in reverse order, first 'pregnant' and then 'was': the shock of that enormous possibility at last becoming actual, and then the question, *What happened?* I saw him arrange his face in a look of sympathy, and I just shook my head a little, rejecting it, and met his eyes. And so he knew. He tilted his head as if he were trying to clear it, deep distaste and the effort to understand both dawning at once in his face. 'Oh, no,' he said. 'Mira. Why?'

"That was what he called me, you know; he didn't like my other nickname. Of course he was a Latinist, and he loved the way *miranda* meant *to be marveled at*, and we'd found a medieval hymn to the Virgin that went

> O mira novitas
> et novum gaudium
> matris integritas
> post puerperium.

I've never been able to listen to it since without a certain irony: O wondrous news and new joy, that a mother should keep her integrity after childbirth!

"'Either way, Alan,' I said, 'I would have had to commit the sin of mastery. Either through raising the child or through—killing it. We've been wrong, and our teachers are wrong. You can't get by on submission alone. You have to have confidence in your powers.'

"'Mira,' he said, 'that's crazy. We're talking about a human life, not a theory. Which of our teachers has ever said you don't have to be able to rise to an occasion? Which of them has ever said you don't need self-discipline? When they say *mastery*, they mean usurping God's place; they don't mean the ability to take care of yourself. What does all that have to do with having a baby?'

"He didn't see it, and I was in no state to explain. I just waited. Finally, since he said nothing, I said, 'You know we can't stay together now.' He sagged in his chair; I thought he gave a sigh of pain, but it was actually a weak little laugh. 'Oh, not that too,' he said. 'Every easy out in the book, every possible escape route. No, love, we'll stay together. Marriage doesn't end because of a—a lapse of faith. We'll put it back together.'"

"Oh my God," said Sarita. "Where is this man? Let me get my hands on his silly neck."

"Don't," said Mim in real distress. "He meant it; he meant *well*, even if he didn't understand. Once he saw I was beyond cajoling he was terribly upset. He even said that if it was the only way to keep me he would disobey the Church. I said it was too late for that; I wasn't going to be the occasion of sin for him and never be allowed to forget it. I wouldn't ask him to go against his conscience, but I'd found I couldn't sacrifice my own. He started shouting that individual conscience was never the point, didn't I know that, and why was it so hard to understand that we were part of a *community* of faith? That was the trouble with all that existentialist trash I was brought up on, it threw people back on their own resources, as if anybody was ever really alone. Hadn't it taken both of us to conceive the child? Wouldn't it take both of us to sustain the marriage? Did it mean nothing to me that man and wife were one flesh?

"'I notice one thing, Mira,' he said finally. 'You haven't cried. I take that as a sign that you were acting for your own happiness—that you still think you're entitled to what you want, and that you got it and are satisfied. Did you know that people very advanced in Eastern meditation, whose goal is perpetual happiness, eventually lose the ability to cry? I find that horrible. To become incapable of suffering, either for yourself or for others. Don't go that way.'

"Of course he hadn't seen me on the bathroom floor or in the doctor's office. I let him say it: let him think what he wanted of me, if it would comfort him. But I did wonder . . . 'Alan,' I said, 'Did you *want* children?'

"I don't know what I expected. It wasn't what happened. He just looked patient and reasonable and said, 'Mira, you keep trying to cast this in terms of personal feeling. Personal feeling is fine, but it isn't the point: children are also the purpose of Catholic marriage. We're supposed to live by a certain pattern. It doesn't matter whether the pattern makes us happy or not. It does make us good.'

"I started to tremble. I had thought I believed that; I couldn't believe it now. 'I can't be good, then,' I said, and I got up and groped for my coat—it's not easy to make a clean exit in November—and left. Disastrous for people of principle to lie to each other. Disastrous to tell the truth, too."

She sat still for a moment not speaking, sipping her wine. "Why can't we be good?" she said finally. "Why does even being good make us so bad? When Alan and I were married my parents gave us some money, and my father wrote that Hopkins poem out on the card:

> *God with honour hang your head,*
> *Groom, and grace you, bride, your bed*
> *With lissome scions, sweet scions,*
> *Out of hallowed bodies bred.*
>
> *Each be other's comfort kind,*
> *Déep, déeper than divined,*
> *Divine charity, dear charity,*
> *Fast you ever, fast bind.*

How can a poem like that have no effect on a marriage? But it didn't. And I still don't know, really, whether it was Alan's doctrines or my youth or narcissistic modern life that did the damage."

"Doubtless all three, plus the nature of the menstrual cycle," said Sarita. "And Hopkins, being celibate, wouldn't have known about that."

Mim smiled wryly and forgivingly. She rose; it was dark, and the bay was lit with white lights and reflections from the dockside restaurants and the navy yard. She went behind the curtains and changed out of the shroud. "It's lovely," she said as she handed it back to Sarita, a limp twist of red and maroon. "If I ever fall in love, I hope you're still making them."

CHAPTER 2

> A strong belief in the inevitability of a catastrophe attracts the catastrophe.
>
> —Eric Gutkind

The idea for the shrouds had come to Sarita when she read in a craft magazine of some Hmong women who, prevented by the exigencies of war from clothing their parents properly for the grave, still carried a weight of guilt for the omission. Only the graveclothes could mark the dead as members of their clan; unmarked they might wander forever, lost in the afterworld, and their ancestors would not know them. Sarita had felt the familiar unease of reading outside her culture: the stricken sympathy with the women's burden of guilt, helpless and irremediable, and the simultaneous busybody wish to dissuade, to enlighten, to absolve by despiritualizing. "Oh, we in the West don't *believe* . . ."—and all their grief wasted, inoperative, consigned to the realm of quaint pathetic myth. How much anthropologists have to answer for, she thought; and how the rub between cultures itself erodes the certainties of each culture. Not to accept another's myths and rites is a tacit denial that the rites are effectual and the myths are true; in spite of one's best intentions it is an insult. And one must either refuse to insult, and call into question the worth of one's own past, or anxiously reassert one's own certainties against the other's. And then—suspicion, pogrom, gang warfare, government surveillance, the banning of religions and languages. It was a few years before the term *ethnic cleansing* etched its way into the maps, but its potential always waited, a corrosive seed in some politician's mind or gonads, to spill and spread. Meanwhile Sarita, untrained in combat or diplomacy and wanting to respond through her own work, translated the graveclothes into evening dresses and made more money from them than the Hmong from their intricate cutwork. No use: in the rub between cultures, America efficiently band-sands everything down to the commercial—death, kinship, exile, war's agony, filial duty betrayed. On such terms even homage is damage.

Mim and Alan, it occurred to her, had been caught in the same trap: two warring cultures seeking a truce, but only one willing to give ground, and only until the price became painfully clear. Sarita felt for them both, but underneath feeling a small anthropological voice kept whispering, *How could intelligent people live this way? We in the West don't* believe, not like that and not any more, and if Sarita had had the power she would have gone back in time, stopped Mim at her first church door, and told her to listen to her father. She bought a recording of the B minor Mass to play in the shop.

Between Easy Landing and the college town, where Mim lived, lay a network of inlets and tidal flats. The roads went over causeways and bridges, crossing nearly as much water as land, with the water reflecting the color of the sky so that one seemed to be suspended in a bath of pure color—blue or grey or at sunset a luminous pink, and just after sunset the water turned a pearl color paler than the sky. Sarita tried periodically to mix those colors, puzzling over which surface best gave them back: silk satin, silk broadcloth, China silk. At one end of the longest bridge a derelict hotel perched like a rookery; a disused nuclear plant loomed on the far horizon. Sarita did not make the trip often, but sometimes she went halfway: there was an expensive grocery with organic vegetables and tempting imported condiments placed strategically between the two towns, and in an extravagant mood she sometimes went there.

She walked through the grocery now, musing, checking out the customers' clothes with a practiced eye, picking up greens and yogurt and Thai deli food. Someone was demonstrating a new brand of whole-grain pasta. "Cook it till it's just done," he was saying, "*el Dante*." She turned and took a package so that she could. Back to the underworld: no avoiding it anywhere. Imagine wanting to join your ancestors after death. She was not sure she would find eternity with her ancestors tolerable. Surely not everyone wanted their ancestors: not everyone wanted their children. If you were not buried according to the right forms and your ancestors did not know you, would there be some wide cosmopolitan society of the unfamilied, more congenial than kin? Could you be buried by the right forms to be known to your friends?

She thought of a line from the Gospel of Matthew: Whatever you bind on earth shall be bound in heaven, and whatever you loose on earth shall be loosed in heaven. If she bound the body in cloth on earth, what did she bind in heaven? A shroud for Mim's unwelcomed baby, at seven weeks a curled, translucent bud with a skeleton of cartilage like a shark's, infinitesimal gonads, a heart that pumped and a stomach that secreted acid and ears almost ready to hear? For Mim, still burdened by what she had not borne, and by the memory of misplaced trust and mistrust and failure?

She thought and wondered, and tracked down some conservative Catholic writing, and let it all work on her sewing. Once she had lunch with Mim, and they talked about poetry and politics. ("But these writers were talking against *Marxism*, Mim, not against basic human competence; how could you mistake them?" "What did I know about Marxism? I knew about private life; I knew that submission to God was submission to chance, refusal to take charge of your future.") But after that they did not speak again till late September, when a news bulletin sent her scrambling through her litter of telephone numbers and grabbing for the phone.

"Mim, have you been near a radio? Morgenzahl's been shot."

"Oh, my God, no. Is he—? Who—?"

"As he was going into the clinic this morning. One of the protestors. I don't know. They said he's been taken to the hospital. I don't suppose they know yet."

"Damn it, is he alive?" Mim cried.

"Mim, I don't know! They're probably still finding out how he is. They know more about the gunman, because he turned himself in."

"Oh, Jesus. Oh, Christ. It's because of what I said at the rally. Somebody's decided to hunt Jews. Oh, Christ, even to call attention—"

"Oh, Mim, I doubt it. Surely doing abortions is enough. Anybody who's going to shoot him for that wouldn't scruple about his religion. Calm down. Find a radio. Are you going to be all right?"

Gradually, through the day, the story emerged. The gunman (as the news reports invariably called him, as if he were the villain of a Western) was a fundamentalist unknown to any local church, who had sporadically attended protests but had never worked steadily with the local group. He had recently lost his job and was determined to make a difference of some kind in the world. He had been clumsy and rather slow in pulling the gun, so that a couple of the other protestors, horrified, had time to seize him and deflect his aim somewhat. He had surrendered calmly to the police, only sneering over his shoulder at the protestors, "You poor saps. Think you care about babies, but are unwilling to take up arms in their defense. Sometimes you have to take a life to save a life; remember I told you that." His one phone call at the police station was to the newspaper.

Morgenzahl had been struck in the left shoulder; the bullet had broken his collarbone and lodged in the neck muscle. The subclavian artery was torn, and he had lost a lot of blood, but he was alive and not badly damaged. He issued an elegant statement thanking the protestors for their timely intervention: "Good people to have on one's side, if only for a moment." Within ten days he was out of the hospital and convalescing.

What Sarita did not hear about till later was the note he had been sent there, as soon as he was well enough to get mail. It came in with hundreds of cards—solidarity from the national women's organizations, outrage and fear from his colleagues, gratitude from former patients, incoherent scrawls of disappointment from his enemies—and thirty-two floral arrangements. His brother and sister-in-law opened the mail and read it to him, extracting the hate letters for a study the sister-in-law was doing on comparative bigotry. "Here's a strange one," she said. "She's trying to take the blame. Is this somebody you know? Miranda Como?" He squinted, puzzled, but as she read it he started up, winced, and relaxed again on the pillows. "Give it to me, Lisa," he said. "I know who she is. She was years ago, before I had the clinic." He reached carefully for the plain handwritten note.

Dear Dr. Morgenzahl,

    I was greatly relieved to hear you were not badly hurt. I cannot help feeling I am somewhat responsible. When you are well enough to have visitors, may I see you and explain? Perhaps I'm only having an attack of nerves, but you may be able to judge better than I can. Even inadvertent acts may have far-reaching consequences.

    I have always been grateful for your help ten years ago, which has changed my life in wholly unexpected ways.

Yours sincerely,
Miranda Como

"No phone number, just an address. Is she in the book? Oh, good. Dial it for me, Jay, would you?" A short wait. "It's an answering machine. Beeep! Yes, this is Bob Morgenzahl and I just got your note. I'd be delighted to see you. I saw you on the news this summer, giving this extraordinary speech, and couldn't remember your name. It's so good to hear from you again. I can't think what you mean by feeling responsible for this nut with the gun. Come in any time. Don't tell anybody else I'm seeing visitors."

Mim arrived the next evening, moving nervously and dressed rather formally in a dark suit. "My God, what it is to be appreciated," she said, looking around at the flowers.

"Oh, this is only half what there was. You should have seen it yesterday. I've been giving them away to the other patients, and I sent some over to the clinic. The place was starting to look like a state funeral."

"You seem thoroughly alive."

"Transfusions and morphine," he said. "That and the powerful elation of not having had my head blown off. Sit down and tell me how you're to blame."

"I begin to think I'm not, really," she said, sitting in a straight chair at the foot of the bed. "The man's statements don't seem to bear out my fears. There are always so many more variables than you think, and I suppose very few people remember speeches at rallies. But all I could think was that I'd let the cat out of the bag. If you make odious comparisons between the Catholic and Jewish ideas of choice, with pro-lifers standing right there—well, once you know anything about history you're deathly afraid you'll make it repeat itself. I couldn't stop thinking that somebody would revive the blood libel."

"Blaming the Jews for the death of babies," he said. "Oh, yes; I get mail like that now and then. They don't need you to help them think of it. But you might have made them think of a few other things. Talking about God to the antis!"

"I talk about God to anyone who will let me," said Mim. "It's one of my character flaws. I don't know why; I haven't had any religion since I left my husband. I just can't seem to forget it."

"Ah, so you did leave him," said Morgenzahl sadly. "That's too bad."

"My God, do you remember all your patients' dilemmas?"

"Yours was memorable. It's the philosophical ones that stick in my mind—those and the really desperately awful families. Though most families are pretty awful in those conditions. But there was something so curious about your situation—this scrupulous mind, and this medieval religion based on absolute self-distrust."

"Self-distrust was what I made of it, anyway. I'm not sure my husband did. He talked that way, but he was in a position to take more for granted. Perhaps he needed to be reminded to distrust himself; I didn't."

"Where is he now?"

"Teaching law at some little school in Maryland. Remarried. Writing for some religious magazines; I've seen a few of his articles. And I'm floundering in an office job, wishing I had the courage to go back to grad school. And coming out of the woodwork to give the occasional uninvited speech."

"Still operating on the self-distrust theory?"

"I suppose so," she said slowly. "I wouldn't defend it any more, but it's still how I live. That was really the reason I wrote you, wasn't it? I don't trust what I say. People say I should publish, and I couldn't publish: so much that I think is dangerous, and even if the arguments are sound they could do awful damage. But it's so evasive, isn't it? That's the story of my life. I get married to evade the problem of finding my real work; I have the abortion to evade the consequences of marriage; I leave the marriage to evade the problem of turning a dishonest relationship honest, and now I'm back to evading my real work. I'm sorry; you're the one who's in the hospital. I'd better shut up."

"No, no," he said easily. "I asked you. It's my fault. Go on."

For the moment she could not. "Damn it," she finally gasped, "every time I see you I cry." With his good arm he proffered the bedside box of kleenex; she waved it away. "No, don't. You need a break from handing women the kleenex." She fished in her pocket. "I don't know what more there is to say. I'm just stuck with a self I can't bear. I can't seem to rise reliably to an occasion. I can do pretty well in the short run, but as soon as I have to make a sustained effort I cave in and disappear." She stopped and blew her nose. "Do people just get their character given to them, along with their DNA? And however they try to escape themselves, do they just keep getting that same character given back to them again? As if the universe were saying, 'No, I told you, *this* is you. Do it until you get it right.'"

"Maybe the universe wants you this way."

"What possible use can it see in my being this way?"

Morgenzahl shrugged, with one shoulder and one eyebrow. "You seem to have read a good deal about Judaism since we last met."

"Yes. Because of something you said, originally. Damage control."

"Good Lord, really. Well, have you run into the little story about Reb Zusya? He was worried about his prospects in the world to come, and he said, 'The Recording Angel won't ask me *Why weren't you Abraham?* or *Why weren't you Moses?* He will ask me *Why weren't you Zusya?*'"

"Yes, I've run into it," said Mim drily, "and it strikes me that the answer is *What if I didn't trust Zusya?* What if I thought being Zusya was liable to create more problems than it solved? What if the essence of being Zusya is so puny and vulgar that it's a shame to Abraham and Moses? Isn't he justified, then, in refusing to become?"

"Puny and vulgar? Where does that come from? Something your husband called you? It looks nothing like the reality."

"Perhaps it doesn't. I can't judge that sort of thing for myself. I suppose that's where the Recording Angel has the advantage over Zusya—

he can see the true self, whereas Zusya can't tell the difference between the true self and the false." She stared off into space, and he did not answer. "Oh, hell," she said finally, "this is appalling. What a thing to do to someone who's risked his true self in every way so that women can have theirs. Such ingratitude—to have lived this way, and then to come here and drivel on about it. I'll go. Thank you for everything, still." She got up and clasped his hand briefly, and turned toward the door.

"Something occurs to me," he said.

His voice was quiet; he was growing tired. "You could do me a favor. They're going to be letting me out of here in a couple of days, and my brother and his wife are going home. I don't need anything practical; the clinic staff and the rehab people have worked it all out. But Monday is Yom Kippur. I haven't been to shul in years, but being shot by a goy has made me sentimental; I think I'd like to go. Would you take me there?"

Mim could feel expressions crossing her face three at a time: surprise, confusion, awe, trepidation, embarrassment, the ghost of a smirk ("sentimental"!), rapid calculation of how to get the day off. She nodded and said, "Of course."

"Thank you. I think you might find it useful."

"So strange," she said to Sarita. "I walk in and all the fear evaporates. Not that history is any different, or the consequences of what I say any less dangerous, but I'm only one of a zillion people talking and in a sense it's my business to talk. Shutting up doesn't solve it. And there he is in this ridiculous blue-and-white sprigged hospital gown, bandaged and full of tubes, and totally in control. And the conversation goes on, ten years later."

"Given the way it started, I suppose it might."

"I suppose so. But it's rather overwhelming to be taken seriously by someone that sure of himself. And it's not over yet. I've got to take him to this all-day service, which is bound to dredge up God knows what emotional muck. It's the Day of Atonement; you think about your sins all day."

"But you think about your sins all the time," said Sarita. Mim wadded up her napkin and threw it at her (they were in the restaurant next to the bus station, having Sunday breakfast). "Not with anyone who knows what to do with them," she said. "I look forward to seeing what happens with someone who does."

"We wait until after Yizkor." They were parked in the town parking ramp, overlooking the old synagogue, whose façade was a sort of New England-Byzantine amalgam. "That's the memorial service. People crowd in for it, and there's no space. Being a bad Jew, I don't belong to the shul and don't have tickets, so we're missing about half the show. But there won't be any problem about getting in once this part is over."

His arm was in a sling under his tweed coat, and his energy seemed a little dimmed since the day in the hospital. He looked extraordinarily out of place in Mim's little Japanese car, as if she were transporting the president or somebody from the movies. This was the first time she had seen him conventionally dressed, and it disturbed her a little for reasons she was not sure of. But as the crowd streamed out and they began to make their way against it, she forgot to think of how she felt. There were a few people there that she knew from the library, who looked surprised to see her. Several others waved to Morgenzahl, or stopped to ask how he was, and at the door the usher said, "Bob. Good to *see* you. In fact I'm amazed to see you. Are you okay to be out so soon?"

"I thought I'd try it, for part of the day anyway," he said. "Join the die-hards."

"Thank God, you deserve to join the die-hards," said the usher, waving them in.

"A stiff-necked people," grinned Morgenzahl, gesturing toward his bandages. And they made their way up the aisle.

They let him in, she thought. *They know what he does and they let him in.* "You know him?" she said.

"He's a pediatrician," he said. "We run into each other sometimes."

The cantor was singing a long elaborate solo. Mim found that she could follow a few of the words in the prayer book. She and Alan had studied a little Hebrew together, and recently she had begun to read it again by herself. But it was difficult to keep up: she found herself jumping ahead several lines and waiting to catch the words as they went by. Whenever she looked up, her sight was blurred from too close focusing. The service alternated between standing and sitting, cantorial flourishes and congregational folk tunes, and a sort of random, free-for-all chanting that made the big room hum like a holy beehive. Morgenzahl had acquired a yarmulke and prayer shawl from somewhere and stood beside her wholly unfamiliar. He sang the words of the prayers in a rapid mutter.

The room's attention focused: it was as if the air stilled. Mim had encountered the prayers for the Day of Judgment before, but she had not taken in that it happened once a year. It was not Paul's or Michelangelo's Last Judgment, doomsday and the dead being raised incorruptible; it was the reading of the year's deeds in the book of remembrance and the sealing of one's fate in the book of life. A harsh verdict could be softened by repentance, prayer and kind deeds, but even the angels trembled at the coming of the judgment. On the New Year it is written and on the Day of Atonement it is sealed: who shall live and who shall die, who in the fullness of years and who before. (She had encountered the prayers, but she had not heard them standing next to someone who might have been killed a mere two weeks ago.) Who by fire and who by water, who by the sword and who by a wild beast; who by famine and who by thirst, who by earthquake and who by plague, who by strangling and who by stoning. Mim's eyes filled up again, uncontrollably: *My God, he will think I do nothing but cry.* But then she became aware that people all around her were quietly sniffling; no one could get through this prayer unmoved.

She remembered with a sense of unreality the last service of repentance she had gone to. It was at the Newman Center on campus, a few years after her divorce; it had been listed in the student paper as a Lenten service for women. For the most part she had stayed away from the Church—a few times she had gone to mass on Christmas or Easter, losing herself in the crowd and not going up for communion—but she had hoped for something transforming in a service for women. But it had been strangely unsatisfying, the artificial folksiness of the new Catholic liturgy and the presumed intimacy of the female world combining to nullify every serious feeling. One notion behind the service Mim found arresting: women's sins were different from men's, the deadliest being not pride but abdication. Women's humility lay not in self-denial but in self-reclamation, the full possession of the self's unique powers and duties. But the service itself was unendurably saccharine: a tape of soft rock was played, with flaccid words that a few of the women followed in muffled voices, and the prayers nudged them softly to a fuller realization of their potential. God was a mother, caring and supportive. They were Her daughters. They could depend on Her for every need. These gentle encouragements to rise one rung higher on the ladder of self-esteem could not hold the ferocity of Mim's terror at being pregnant, or begin to answer the quiet violence she had done. Perhaps she was liable to the sins of both sexes: she could identify the abdication quickly enough, but as she sat listening to the dreadful words she felt a contempt that was surely pride, and when the leaders passed a chalice of salt water, telling each woman to mark a tear on the cheek of the woman next to her, she had shot out of the circle and stood cursing and shivering in the hall. Alan's voice still accused her tearlessness; she was unwilling to surrender her tears to anyone who could not heal as strongly as he could wound. *Libera me de sanguinibus Deus*, she whispered, *et exsultabit lingua mea justitiam tuam*—Deliver me from bloodguiltiness, God, and my tongue shall extol your justice—not because, in her ineradicably secular upbringing, she had ever really believed bloodguiltiness would send her to hell, but because it was strong enough language. One of the leaders had followed her out at once, but she had refused sympathy: "Damn it, I've killed someone. *That's* abdication: it's not just too bad, it's lethal." But away from the ritual the woman was earthy and competent, and Mim had spilled her whole story—the first time she had told it to anyone but close friends—and felt relieved, if not absolved, in spite of herself, though she had refused to go back to the circle. The woman—her name was Teresa Treviso—was, it turned out, a pro-choice activist in perennial trouble with the bishop; it was she who later encouraged Mim to speak at rallies, and who had beckoned her up the steps at the rally this summer. She handled Mim carefully, a bit overawed—she could not really see how anyone dared judge feminist language—but she knew good words when she heard them, and for that Mim was grateful. But that was the last service she had attended. Repentance was stricter than—

She was hauled back into the present with a jolt. She thought she heard her name called. She was lost on the page, the liturgy rapt in some vision of angels, the congregation responding with the *Shema*, everything moving too fast. She was glad to sit down. She tried again halfcompetently to read; she gave up and let the beauty of the music wash over her; she rose and sat on cue, and tried to understand the confessions from the translation across the page. She was beginning to feel fatigued. But there was satisfaction in the fatigue, a sense of simultaneously laboring with a community and being alone with God. Was there a God? She was not sure it mattered.

More standing and sitting, more confessions, more prayers, more pleas. At last dismissal for a two-hour break, with Morgenzahl looking rather grey.

"Do you want to go home?"

"No. There's something I want you to hear in the next part. But I'd better have some food. One's supposed to fast, but there are exemptions for the infirm."

They went to a café in the next block, where Morgenzahl had herb tea and a sandwich, and Mim decided to have nothing; she was under the spell of the liturgy. "Awful the way the chanting seizes on an apostate," she said. "You don't realize, all those years, how you've been starving for it."

"You're probably starving for the Latin Mass, *requiescat in pace*. At least we still have our holy tongue."

"I never knew the Latin Mass, except on records; I was raised an apostate. It was only later I became fanatical, and by then it was all gone."

"Ah. I was raised fanatical. Orthodox, at any rate, which looks fanatical once you no longer are. It sticks, though. I could still get up and read from the Prophets, cold, if I had to—or from the Torah scroll with a week or so of prep."

"How amazing. And you seem right at home—not like I am when I walk into a church, wondering if I deserve to be there. And you know all the people."

"Well, the people are other doctors, and psychiatrists and social workers and lawyers and professors; I bump into them all the time. There aren't a lot of us around, and we're all overachievers."

"It makes me wildly envious."

"Envy's one of your sins, not one of ours."

"That's not true; I noticed it on the list. You just have a longer list."

"It's said that Jews have as many words for sin as Eskimos have for snow. What are we to make of this? A heightened sensitivity to nuance? An oversupply of sins?"

Mim laughed. "Whatever it is, it's liberating compared to what I'm used to. You know that confession, the short one that piles up all the abominations so fast? It looks so crushing on the page: we've trespassed, we've lied, we've blasphemed, we've committed perversions, we've counseled evil, we've led others astray. And people are literally beating their breasts—which must be the origin of *mea culpa*. Yet the tune changes it utterly: it's just simple and sorry, like a kid's apology."

"It's an acrostic, did you notice? All the sins in the book, from aleph to tav."

"No, I didn't. So it's even a kind of game. Not that it isn't serious, but it's conscious of itself as artifice. It's saying *This is how we delineate things, this is our* method *for comprehending and containing what we've done*. There's a kind of ego-strength in it. The point of the ritual is not to make you grovel till you're abject enough to receive what the religion has to offer."

Morgenzahl shot her a look. "A little angry, are we?"

"We are." Mim smiled thinly. "But that's what confession means where I come from. In modern times they try to dress it up differently, but it's not different enough. Thank God it's easy to lose one's faith. I couldn't have confessed the abortion—put it into their framework and been forgiven, and forfeited my own deserved consequences. The reward wasn't great enough, even if I could have: a little white wafer, not even as alive as a fetus, the dead body of Christ. And all that misery with Alan to be gone through again. No no no no. I don't believe in sacraments."

He nodded in sour sympathy. "You still seem to think the abortion was a sin, though."

"Of course I do. Who doesn't feel wretched, stopping a life that's started? It was a hideous experience for poor Alan, too; what kind of person puts her husband through such a thing? But it was a sin to get pregnant, knowing I felt that way; it was a sin to get married to someone who lived like that. It was a sin to fall in love with religion on the terms I did, *because* it encouraged abjection. I still think the abortion was the most responsible thing I could have done, but that's because everything leading up to it was irresponsible. When you've been living dishonestly, how can your first effort at change *not* be a sin?"

"That's probably specious logic," he said, "or at least I can think of cases where it wouldn't apply. Do you really mean it's the kind of sin your priest would have thought it was, or—"

"What could he have known about it?" she said shortly. "No, it's not that kind of snow. He'd have thought marriage and pregnancy were good in themselves, *a priori*. I don't. I think all those people think they mean well, and are trying to handle terribly painful moral questions in a conscientious way, but they have no idea what they're asking of people."

He hesitated. "Then you don't think I've given you evil counsel."

Startled, she looked at him. "Bob. You. No. My God, don't let them get to you. Is that what you've been lying there thinking all these days?"

"No, no; not about them," he said. "They're not going to convince me of anything. They may be trying hard, but they're moral idiots; they're operating at the lowest level. No, I mean you: do *you* think, now, that you did the wrong thing and that I encouraged you?"

"Do you remember what you said? You were about as encouraging as the Sphinx."

"I don't remember what I said, but I know the *sort* of thing I said; I never make a patient's decision for her. But I'm not so much talking about what I did as about what you think I did. It's a postmodern distinction," he added, "but it's crucial."

"I see the distinction," she said. "But you only did what I asked. If you hadn't been there, or if somebody hadn't been there . . . you know, I tried to resist calling you for several days, but when I found myself looking at benign household objects and noticing which ones had sharp points I said this is crazy, there's a perfectly safe clean way—"

"Jesus," he said. "And this was in nineteen seventy what?"

"Nine," she said. "Yes. So no, I don't reproach you with anything. I don't see how anyone could. I mean, all too obviously they do, but . . . but they're moral idiots."

"Never mind them," he said. "Their reproaches I can handle. Yours—I'd have thought you were all wrong, but I'd have had a hard time with it."

The break was over. A Torah scroll was taken out and carried around the room, which was now considerably emptied. People reached out to touch it as it went by. Morgenzahl reached out the fringes of his prayer shawl to it, and kissed them with a practiced gesture. A succession of people were called up from the congregation to sing blessings over the scroll, and they too touched their fringes to it and kissed them. Morgenzahl himself went up and spoke a short phrase, to which scattered men in the congregation responded loudly. He pointed it out to her in the prayerbook in a whisper: the blessing for having escaped death. The Torah reading itself was appalling—a levitical catalogue of forbidden sexual unions—but the intimacies between people and scroll almost made up for it. And the chanting took on a new form, a sunny confident monotony in major key, like water over stones.

Then the scroll was taken away and the chanting changed to minor, and Morgenzahl touched Mim's hand. "Here we go." The book of Jonah: Mim had never paid it much attention except for the episode of the whale, but it was about to be read in full. Indeed, after a brief chanted introduction, it was read in English, and simultaneously acted out in mime by the Hebrew School children. It was comic relief, but the moral of the tale was blushingly clear: Jonah is called to prophesy and evades his calling. After his prayer from the whale's belly earns him a second chance and he fulfills his duty, he's disgruntled: wouldn't God have spared Nineveh anyway, with or without his preaching, wasn't He just waiting to forgive? Jonah sulks outside the city walls, morose as if constipated with undelivered brimstone. God makes a gourd grow, to shade him from the sun, but the next day sends a worm to eat the gourd, which makes Jonah want to die of rage. God, in a marvelous piece of illogic, asks whether, just as Jonah pitied the plant (no, Mim thought, it was the plant that had pity on Jonah) He Himself was not bound to pity Nineveh—"that great city, wherein are more than sixscore thousand persons that cannot discern between their right hand and their left, and also much cattle?" Mim had never been so charmed at being accused. *He laughs as he judges*, she thought. *The pity is real, the judgment is severe, but he laughs.*

More prayers. More confessions. More singing, which became intense and fervent as the evening fell. People had drifted back in: the room was near full again. A long blast of the shofar, and the day was done. Mim smiled into the eyes of strangers, euphoric from hunger and thirst and strained attention. She felt she knew everyone there. "Good yontif," she replied to their greetings. "*Shanah tovah.*"

"Shall we stop for more food?"

"I have a surfeit of food at home. People have heaped me with offerings. Just drop me off."

He was visibly tired, but Mim was disappointed; she supposed there was no reason she should ever see him again, and she wished she could prolong the time. As they spiraled down the parking ramp in the dark, she asked shyly, "How soon do you expect to go back to work?"

"It should be another month to six weeks, depending on how fast the rehab goes," he said. "It's just a question of building up power and mobility again. There doesn't seem to be much in the way of nerve damage."

Mim gasped. "Thank God." The thought had not occurred to her.

"It's appalling, all that can happen to you in a split second."

"It is," he said. "And I hope they give the man a good long sentence. But considering what he could have done to me, it's very minor damage, and he's not going to scare me off. It's my kids that are pressuring me to quit."

Mim paid the attendant and pulled out into the street. "They're worried about you, of course. How old are they?"

"My daughter is twenty-one, deep into computers at Berkeley. And my son's nineteen, in media at UCLA. We don't know each other all that well these days; I missed a good deal of their adolescence. I think they blame my work, or the whole situation surrounding it, for the divorce, because it was around the time I started the clinic that things got openly wretched between me and their mother. But of course it's never that simple."

"No," said Mim sympathetically. "But naturally they want things to be fixable. No one wants to face their parents' failure in love; it's so ominous."

Morgenzahl's condominium was about a mile away, in a renovated mill on the waterfront. When Mim stopped the car, he made no move to get out. "Listen," he said slowly. "I'm wondering what you'd think of this. There's this group, Clergy and Laity Concerned for Choice, that's putting on a conference in Boston in the spring. They want me to speak—now that I've been in the news I'm a hot property—but it occurs to me that they really ought to hear you speak, and I'm wondering if you could be persuaded."

It was the last thing she expected to hear. "Oh my God," she said, "no. I can't imagine anything worse than talking to clergy."

"Why? You talked to fanatics at that rally. This should be a good deal more congenial."

"I'm not a congenial person," she said. "Not in a group like that. You have to be reasoned and moderate, and assume that everybody you're talking to is reasonable, and meanwhile they're picking your arguments apart and getting ready to call you a gnostic or a neoconservative or an enemy of the family or a running dog of the patriarchy. I'd rather talk to fanatics: you know where you stand right away."

"But this isn't a random bunch of clergy," he said. "These are thinking people who are on your side; probably most of them are women."

"Women who've finished grad school and have *real* jobs."

"Oh, Mim, that's not even honest self-doubt talking, just cringing underdoggery. You know you're good enough for them. Can I tell them about you, and tell them you're thinking about it?"

She stared at the dimly lit brickwork of the mill. "Well, I—perhaps. I don't promise you anything, but . . . but when I stop to consider, I'm probably a better thinker than some of them."

He laughed aloud, a great resonant "Hah!" that made the little car vibrate. "That's the attitude! Think of all the clergy you've ever known that you could run rings around. Half of them will be like that, and they'll be grateful to you, or at worst just mystified; the other half will be as good or better than you, and they'll want you to sit down and think with them. You'll be exhilarated. When's the last time you were exhilarated?"

Mim laughed in spite of herself. "I don't know; probably before I was married. No, actually, it happens every once in a while, when I find just the right book in the stacks. In fact I've been exhilarated today, for about the last two hours. I suppose it's the fasting. How long do I have to think about this? What do I do if I decide to say yes? Write them an abstract?"

"I'll find out," he said. "Or no, if you decide to do it I'll just have them call you. I imagine you can stall for about a month; they'll need to put their program together at some point, so you can't make them wait too long. Just call me when you make up your mind."

She helped him out of the car and went with him to the door, trying to arrange all the layers of her gratitude into some articulate statement. Finally all she could say was, "Why are you taking all this trouble with me?"

"Apparently because nobody else knew how," he said. "But it's not trouble; it's such a delight, to find out what happened to you and just to make contact again." He took her hand and gave her a serious look. "Don't frighten yourself about this conference. It's nothing. Compare it to what's really at stake. Have you read *Pirke Avot* yet? *You are not required to complete the work, but neither are you free to desist from it.*"

Something fell into place; for the moment she could not tell gratitude from fury. "Damn you," she said, "you're trying to trick me. You're trying to make me be Zusya."

"What I don't understand, Del, is what you hope to accomplish by this kind of tactic. Won't the women just go upstate for their abortions, or down to Boston? Do you think you've interfered with even one procedure by doing this?"

Del Marlin dragged on his cigarette and fixed the questioner with a pale-blue eye. "You got to look at the long term," he said. "No, maybe this time I haven't saved any babies; I saw in the paper where they got a man from the hospital to come in and take over the killing operation the very same day. But how many doctors are willing to live with the fear? Even if this one, what's his name, Mergenzell, is still alive and ready to go back, how many others are doubting the wisdom of what they do, thanks to what I did? What happens when there's nowhere to go upstate, and nowhere in Boston, just the one little clinic here, and I come round again?"

Jerry Kaplansky, whose father was a district attorney in Newark, brightened visibly: if the man was fool enough to make such threats in the presence of a journalist, what would he do in the courtroom? "Well, women will go back to where they were before *Roe*, won't they—having to do it themselves, or go to back-alley butchers, and a lot of them will die. Do they have a right to life?"

Del rolled his eyes, looking around for someone to share the joke; there was only the prison guard, who gave him a bored stare. "Aw, man," he said, "a woman who will even go near a back alley, is that a nice woman? Or a woman who will stick a knitting needle up herself, is she treating her body like the temple of God? I ask you, why should I value their lives so highly if they value them at a straw? Besides," he added, "in terms of sheer numbers, not all those women will die; whereas *all* the babies will die with the laws we have now. And they're innocent."

"So innocence is the key," said Jerry, making a note of it. "The guilty can fend for themselves. And all those women are guilty, right, 'cause they're pregnant?"

Del gave a wheezing laugh, coughed a little and wiped his eyes. "Oh, my," he said. "I only ever heard of one innocent girl getting pregnant, and she certainly wanted that baby. I can tell you're no Christian, but I bet even you can tell me her name. Yes, sir."

Jerry decided to rise to the bait. "I've always understood that forgiveness is a big part of the Christian faith, Del," he said blandly. "Any forgiveness up there for a woman who's had an abortion?"

"Well, of *course*," said Del, shocked. "There's forgiveness for any sinner who truly comes to repentance. But mind you, she has to repent. Nobody's going to tell you she can go ahead and do it with a clear conscience just because God forgives. Shall we do evil that grace may abound?" he said, his voice rising in pitch and volume. "God forbid! That's what the repented sinner Paul said, *God forbid*, and I say it with him."

What a mixed bag the man was, Jerry thought: a religious sensibility tender as a raw wound, combined with a worldly cynicism the equal of any pimp's. A notion of language, though; half of what he said seemed to be for the music of the words, whether they helped his logic or not. The lyricism of an oral culture? "Where are you from, Del? Originally, I mean; where'd you grow up."

"Michigan. Up in the Thumb area. Right—" he raised his left hand and pointed carefully to a spot at the base of his thumbnail— "here. Raised in the Nazarene Church. Oh, I've slidden back sometimes—the world is full of temptations—but if they start you right, you always know where to return."

"You're not disappointed with religious people?"

Del dropped his eyelids haughtily. "Whatever would you mean by that?"

Jerry shuffled his papers. "Well, when you found out that the charge was attempted murder, here's what you said: 'You mean he ain't dead? Shoot. Those wimps, they don't know what's good for them. I was on their *side*, and they pulled me down. How can you expect to win a war if you don't counter bloodshed with bloodshed?' It just makes me wonder if you feel betrayed."

Del looked composedly back at him. "The Son of Man was betrayed unto his death," he said. "I'm in real good company."

CHAPTER 3

> Between every woman and God there is always the moment when their mutual attraction threatens to dissolve the distance between them. It is up to each of us to prevent God from going too far.
>
> —Ann Diamond

It was an obsession, a moral weakness, and Mim knew it. For weeks now she had been haunting the synagogue, singing whatever fragments of chants she could pick up, reading with eyes too slow, syllable by syllable, the Hebrew words that rushed by in others' voices. The hours on Yom Kippur had broken something in her: they had turned her outward, so that she could no longer read and think by herself but must make the fourteen-mile drive from the college town, Friday night and Saturday morning, to be with others who read and thought the same. In a lifetime of passion for religious poetry and liturgical music, she had never understood that spiritual ardor is like drink: that it eats your life, that it demands more and more of your time, till you wander from service to service like a shell of your former self, and your work suffers and your friends lament the change in you.

It was the sanity of it she was drunk on (irony of ironies, that sanity should be the headiest drop of all!): that she could sit through hours of services in that amazing language (she was never sure whether the words were more like rocks or more like waves) that made angels sound palpable and moral qualities angelic, *and never hear a word about Jesus.* Everything she loved and trusted in religion, without that sickening center around which all church services revolved. An undreamt-of freedom, just as standing rather than kneeling was an undreamt-of gift of bodily integrity.

There was a time, in her late teens and early twenties, when she had loved kneeling in church: the sheer gesture of it, flinging oneself down before the cross in the posture of supplication. She could not have imagined, then, that a religion in which one did not pray on one's knees could feel quite holy. *A religion for adolescents*, she thought now. *Nothing so easy as surrender.* She appreciated the tension between respect and challenge implied in standing, the insistence on a certain reserve. Not abjection but partnership; not salvation passively received but readiness for the uncertainties of action; not even law—the one thing Christians were sure of in Judaism—but the vastly more complicated dance of the *mitzvot*, which (though some of them seemed to her very strange) were not stern and joyless but almost breathing, almost beating, with the effort to integrate will and compassion. *You don't take No for an answer from the universe*, that seemed to be the thrust of the Torah: you strengthen yourself to live in a world where danger and cruelty have been endemic from the beginning, and to provide something other than danger and cruelty to the people you meet. In a good cause you argue even with God. And you are never free of God either: a still small voice follows you around, whispering uncomfortable commandments in your ear, reminding you to resist, to stand out against the expected, never to become resigned to the world as it is. She liked a God who did not lay traps for the innocent; she admired a people who would not let him get away with it.

One morning she watched a bar mitzvah boy race competently through his chanting. The rabbi had known the boy since his birth, and spoke to him with respect for what he was and concern for what he would become; it was clear that there was a whole community of adults besides his parents that the boy could talk to if he wanted. Envy shot through her like adrenalin. If she, as a child, had had adults to trust—! If she had had a way like this, gradual and expected, of turning into an adult—! If, when she was pregnant, there had been this prospect . . . but she could not think that thought through to the end, not without grief and fury, for her own half-competent self and for the baby whom, years too late and without any possibility of recovery, she could finally imagine herself raising.

Of course she was only a visitor, and doubted that she could be more; you could walk away from your origins, but you could not very well get new ones retroactively. At the social hours after the services—the *oneg*, the *kiddush*—she met a few converts and asked them questions, but did not think herself worthy to take that step. Yet something like it seemed to be demanded as she woke up morning after morning with all that music in her head. Her mother was a choir director and voice coach, and she learned music easily; she began to sing harmonies to the service music. That more than anything else made the language real to her, put it right into her breath: she metabolized Torah, she took it into her body. In an anguish of indecision she talked to the rabbi, and the conversation was almost comic in its marking of the bounds between the two religions—he saying, "What about Christianity?" as if to hint *But Christians are your own people,* and she talking endlessly about her love for Jewish thought as if belief were the real question. And sometimes Alan's voice whispered disdainfully in her ears (carefully mimicking the inflections of the still small voice), "Still trying to escape your obligations? Liberation is only evasion, Mira; all Western culture is Christian finally, and you can't be free of that."

She did not hear from Morgenzahl, and did not call him; whenever she thought of speaking to clergy at a conference she grew bewildered at what she could say to them, and kept putting off the decision. She was not entirely sorry to postpone another conversation with him: they talked so easily together that it was uncanny, and she felt out of her depth. She had nearly said she would speak at the conference just because he thought her competent to do it; she could not understand what had come over her. Conversation with him seemed always to create possibilities, to clear a way. Was it his trained habit of not taking No for an answer from the universe? Was it just what happened to people by the time they reached their mid-forties? Was it because he was a man? Mim darkly suspected that it was the last, both because maleness allowed him to move more freely in the world and because she herself more readily believed that what a man called possible was possible. She found herself rather demoralized at the thought.

On the fourth Friday night after Yom Kippur she did not go to services. A friend at the university had published her first book and was giving a reading from it. Laura was the first "out" lesbian on the English faculty, and the reading was being hailed as a political triumph by some of the gay students, though Laura was too good a writer to be unequivocally glad of their endorsement. The department chairman was hosting a party for her, and late that night there would be a dance at the women's center with the band "Bartholin's Revenge," and Mim had been invited to the whole apotheosis. She was glad of an excuse to get back to her real life.

But she found that a Friday night had become something like a minefield. She could not do anything without seeing it through the lens of Jewish observance; she found herself thinking that it was better in one sense to walk two blocks to a reading than to drive fourteen miles to the synagogue. She lived across from the campus, in a large three-room apartment over a restaurant, and could walk to everything in town (though of course Hal Benning, the department chair, did not live right in town, and she would have to drive to the party). She was not sure she knew anyone who walked to services, or who observed much of the obsessive point system that governed what one did or did not do on Shabbes, but she wanted to honor the way of life behind the way of thinking; what else could one do about it? She thought of what she had done to honor the last way of life she admired, and scorn almost knocked the breath out of her: surely Judaism deserved better than that. But she did not know what else to give it that it would want.

The reading was in the small auditorium off the English Department offices. There was a good crowd; there were even a couple of writers she had met at the synagogue, who smiled and nodded without a trace of guilt for being somewhere else on Friday night. She sat down, feeling dreamlike, and then thought *When the Lord turned again the captivity of Zion we were like them that dream*, and then wondered whether she were in or out of captivity. But the lights were dimming and Hal Benning was getting up to introduce Laura; at last she would get a chance to think of something else.

Laura was a Jungian feminist; her work was full of myths and blood mysteries. She had spread a cloth with mauve blots on the wall behind her, and placed candles and heaps of pine cones on the stage. She wrote a rhythmic, incantatory prose, and quoted old songs, which she sang when she came to them in the reading. Time slowed down when she sang:

> O see you not yon narrow road
>   So thick beset with thorns and briers?
> That is the path of righteousness,
>   Though after it but few enquires.
>
> And see you not yon braid braid road
>   That lies across the lily leven?
> That is the path of wickedness,
>   Though some call it the road to heaven.
>
> And see you not yon bonny road
>   That winds about the fernie brae?
> That is the road to fair Elfland,
>   Where you and I this night maun gae.

Music hath charms; Mim felt quietness return to her. It was the first time in weeks she had heard anyone sing in English, except for restaurant muzak. Laura went on:

> A third destination, neither hell nor heaven, a destination one does not have to die to reach. A third path, leading neither to the clouds nor to the flames, but winding into the midst of ambiguity. In the wood of Broceliande, trees grow straight out of the water in full leaf. There the land has sunk or the sea risen; there the creatures of earth and water meet. This is the wood with its feet in the flood, the borderland between solidity and flowing.

It was lulling, almost liturgical; not with the insistent rhythm of the Kaddish, which seemed to her almost sexual or maternal, as if one were being rocked, but enough to touch the same place in her mind. It was, after all, human, the instinct to incant; the content in a sense did not matter, as long as you had the right rhythms. She listened:

> How have I found this path? Is it only the lost, the exiled and the outcast who ever stumble on it? Those who seek heaven expect a strait and narrow path; they bind its brambles ever more straitly against mere tag-alongs and tourists such as me. Those who seek hell (though no doubt they call it by some happier name) are advertisers: they praise the scenic views and luxury accommodations, and the smoothness of the highway, so well paved. But those who take the third way, are they always astonished that there is one? Are they surprised that anyone before them went the way they go?

Mim began to listen; there was more to this than the sound of the words. "The path of righteousness": a few weeks ago she would have dismissed that phrase as readily as her friend did. But Laura assumed a Christian cosmology, or at least the ballad assumed it and Laura did not contest it, and Mim had encountered a kind of righteousness that was nothing like that thorny creed. The Hebrew word for righteousness, *tzedakah*, had nothing to do with deportment; by a kind of traditional shorthand it meant almsgiving, justice to the poor. In the midst of her reverie another phrase went by, "Good, evil and green"; from the distraction of her thoughts she produced an inelegant equivalent, "Heaven, hell and hasidut," but she gave it up in despair. What did she know, what had she seen, but some liturgy with amazing life in it and some exact and admirable thinking? She had fallen romantically in love with a religion she had never lived with; how could she suppose she knew it well enough to start using its language? And was romantic feeling not the sheer antithesis of sanity? Damn it: drunkenness, shameful, unconscionable.

> ... *strange and utterly familiar, known in the bones. On the roads to hell and heaven the voice of God resounds, I AM, I AM, and no other voice is heard. But here that voice is a great silence, and*

within that silence sound the voices of all things that run or trample on the earth, and all the green things growing, and all the winged things flying, crying the ineluctable blasphemy that life wrings out of them: SO AM I!

Suddenly the air seemed very close. Mim had to get out or start asking questions; she could hear the high, strangled voice in which she would ask them, and she had better get out right now. She rose cautiously, catching the seat as it sprang up to keep it from thumping, thankful that the door didn't stick or rattle; she went out through the lobby, where a great coffee urn was sighing on a laden table and a stack of Laura's books was waiting to be sold, and out into the crisp darkness.

The reflecting pool in the quad was drained for winter, its corners full of dry leaves; she stood on the ledge and breathed, and listened to silence. The night of the Yom Kippur service, arriving home, she had heard wild geese fly over: starved and shaking, she had looked up at them with wonder, their cries, which had always sounded to her like dogs barking, taking on a new shape and substance. She heard them singing in bird-language the blessings before the Torah, that swift succession of notes in minor key, thanking God for the great gifts: *Baruch atah Adonai Elohenu melech ha-olam, asher bachar-banu mi-kol ha-amim, v'natan lanu et* . . . wings? instinct? migration? For what has God chosen the geese? And Laura, soaring on the wings of her own rhetoric, would have their multiplicity be a mere challenge to God's unity, as though God *wanted* the only voice in the world to be his own! Mim shook her head. She began to sing softly: all the bits of the evening service she could remember, fragmented and out of sequence, some of them over and over, till the reading broke up and people came bumping through the lobby doors exclaiming. Then she was stricken with embarrassment: she had missed nearly everything Laura had read, standing out in a November night in some foolish trance, and she was cold. At least she had better go back and buy the book.

Dendrogyny, it was called, *Woman into Tree*; on the cover was a trick photograph of an aspen trunk blending into a woman's face, the scar of a fallen branch serving as one eye. It was a loosely knit collection of prose pieces, personal and critical; its wordplay was less arcane than the prevailing academic jargon, and its ideas were substantial, and it would have been worth listening to aloud. What kind of person stands outside singing to God when she might be inside listening to a friend? She waved to Laura from a distance through the crush of people, hoping her face was not too evidently red with cold. She would talk to her later, at the party.

The Bennings lived a few miles out, in a split-level house on the edge of a big pond. Ghostly willow-branches trailed into the water, their leaves mostly shed. The stars were thicker and brighter than in town. Mim, comforted by the sight of water, would have liked to stand by the pond a while, but she did not trust herself not to pray. There was a long string of cars parked on one shoulder of the country road; she left her own car at the end of it and went in.

In the house it was dim and warm and she hardly knew any of the people. Hal Benning was taking coats and shouting genially into the din about food and drink. His wife Linnea, an assistant professor of art history, was bringing trays of food to a long table. The guests were an odd mix of tweedy male professors and their wives (some of whom were professors too, but whose whole presentation shouted "wife" in its respectability and unobjectionable attractiveness) and women of all academic ranks in political T-shirts and confrontatory haircuts. They mingled uneasily, without rancor but without small talk, seeming to know what to do only with Laura.

Mim drifted toward the table as toward a refuge. She picked cubes of cheese and little sausages on toothpicks off a tray, saw them with new eyes and wished she could put the sausages back, and moved on to the raw vegetables and dip. A jazz record was playing in the background. Someone behind her was saying, "—inherent in the symbolism of the pentagram, as Shuttle and Redgrove point out. The extremities of the female body are head, hands and feet, there are five of them; so what better symbol for women's religion? But when you add the extra male extremity, changing the five to six, you get the star in patriarchal form. So it's clear that—"

A spear of broccoli in her hand, Mim turned and launched herself at the speaker. "Good God," she said, "doesn't anybody know how to behave any more? Is intellectual anti-Semitism back so soon?"

"What anti-Semitism?" said the woman, affronted. She was wearing a T-shirt that said WITCHES HEAL, and she was talking to Laura. "I'm talking about patriarchy. I suppose you're here to defend it?"

"Ceridwen, this is Mim," said Laura. "She's an old friend of mine; of course she's not going to defend patriarchy. And Mim, I don't think Ceridwen meant any harm."

"Well, pick your metaphors better," Mim said irritably. "We've had enough trouble with the Star of David."

"Jesus, Mim, what's got into you?" said Laura. "I don't think I've ever seen you mad. Are things okay at the library?"

"At the library? Of course they're okay. Do you think I'm talking in code about the library? Why shouldn't I be talking about what I'm talking about?" She felt exposed, suddenly, and her hands began to tremble; a little sausage rolled to the edge of her plate. She ate it.

"Well, I'm talking about the old religion," said Ceridwen. "It does have a valid symbol system, and I don't see why we shouldn't discuss it as something useful to women today. Unless," she added unpleasantly, "you're afraid of having your stars castrated."

The old religion. What wasn't the old religion? "All I'm afraid of is history," Mim said. "What makes a symbol system valid? Do women have a special set of exemptions? Are you going to revive the swastika as a benign old symbol of the seasons?"

"Look, woman," said Ceridwen, "I don't know who you are, but if you're accusing me—"

"No, no," Mim said, waving her free hand before her face, "not you more than anybody. Not you more than myself. Laura's right; it doesn't come out of nowhere. Do stop it. It's obvious you didn't mean a thing; not that anybody ever means a thing, and people die just the same."

Ceridwen regarded her with exasperation. "All right," she said. "Obviously you're on some planet of your own. Later, Laura." She patted Laura's shoulder and disappeared rapidly into the crowd.

Mim laughed miserably. "Poof," she said. "How to vanquish your enemies: fall apart before their very eyes."

"I should really thank you for it," said Laura in her ear. "She's in divinity school, and her thesis is the most self-indulgent thing I've ever. . . . Pictures of herself doing rituals among the rocks, robed in white samite. Are you okay now? How did you like the reading?"

"It's very fine stuff," said Mim, making an effort. "That business about the third path is extraordinary. I want a chance to read the whole book before I say much, but I did have one minor quibble—"

A pinch-faced man in a corduroy jacket with elbow patches appeared beside her. "But you know, Laura," he cried merrily, in tones he probably meant as collegial raillery, "Daphne didn't escape Apollo by turning into a tree. He appropriated her leaves."

"Well, he won't get mine," she shot back. "My leaves belong to Danu. The Irish goddess," she muttered to Mim as the man went affably by. "Not really apt, but all right for the spur of the moment. Now, your quibble?"

Mim took a deep breath. "The creatures crying SO AM I, it isn't a blasphemy. I don't mean you should change it, of course it's a wonderful line, but—" How on earth did one say it? "Holiness and creaturehood are not incompatible. Holiness and blasphemy are not incompatible. Holiness isn't what we thought it was at all: it's practical, it's solid, you just do it. God doesn't despise us for not being him, and we don't have to despise him for not being us."

Laura regarded her, puzzled. "Well, of course, if you get me in the mood where I can put up with the word *God*, I can look as ambiguously at him as I can at anything else. I'm not sure he wouldn't rather have us blaspheme. But where can you possibly do it? Religion won't have you; religion just wants you to shore up its pieties. They may offer you a more interesting God on paper, but they don't want you to talk to him the way Job did. And in art he's right up in your marrowbones, too close for talking. That's really all I meant: the only place you can use your own voice is where God is silent."

"I've been going to Jewish services," Mim said. Her heart was pounding, her hands were damp, she felt as if she'd been caught stealing. "He's silent because he's listening."

"Oh," said Laura slowly, enlightened. "So that's what it's all about. You've got religion."

"Oh, Laura, don't," said Mim. "It's so awful. I'm so impossibly in love with it—as I have been for years with the thinking, but now there's this music connected with it, and suddenly the prayers all make sense, and everything seems to say I should practice it as religion. And I don't want to practice religion. I've told you what it did to me before. I'm back to square one, after fifteen years, and I'm so frightened."

Laura was sympathetic at once. "It's not square one; you have too much sense for that," she said. "It isn't the *same* religion. You must be looking for something the first one couldn't supply. After all, at midlife people try to go deeper than they could in their youth; they may follow the same pattern, but it's at another level."

"Midway in our life's journey," said Mim. It had not struck her before. "But why is my pattern religion at all? Some people have affairs; some people drink; some people write books. Why do I go on these spiritual benders, leaving all this wreckage behind me for something no more reliable than an atmosphere?"

Laura thought it over. Another well-wisher approached; she smiled noncommittally and signaled her to wait. "What's in the atmosphere that you want?"

"Oh, God, what isn't? Intellect, this endless poring over texts and stories, those inexhaustible books. This extraordinary combination of awe and irony, neither at the expense of the other. And this relentless drive toward self-discipline, with no taint of fear: it's not obedience to God, it's a kind of magnetic attraction." She was about to start babbling; she knew it was wrong to monopolize Laura's attention, and to rave on about a subject that Laura knew nothing about, but she could not seem to control herself. "In the Mishnah it says you should serve God with both the good impulse and the evil impulse—not repress evil, not split heaven apart from hell and project all the hell onto the Shadow, but integrate it and give it a use." Laura nodded; Mim was deliberately using Jungian language, and she followed it well enough. "It's as if the good needs some small admixture of evil, maybe only a millionth part, to leaven it and make it rise. There are endless ways to get it wrong, to let the evil impulse get out of hand and rule you, but what Judaism is for is to show you how to do it right—how to work in the midst of that danger all the time and not be destroyed. And knowing all the time that you're in that danger, it liberates you, Laura, it heals you, it makes you incredibly comfortable to be with—" She broke off. "No, you might not survive it. But while you're alive you're twice as alive as the rest of us."

Laura looked at her, disturbed. "You know," she said, "it may be everything you say, but you're also doing a tremendous amount of animus projection, and you're in terrible shape. I mean, damn it all, it's *your* intellect, *your* sense of awe, *your* self-discipline that's been captured by all this; these aren't attributes that the Jewish religion has and you don't."

"Well, that's sort of the point, Laura; people don't fall into these things by accident. Of course I know I have those qualities, but they have them developed to a point *more* intelligent, *more* beautiful, *more* disciplined than I'm capable of alone. People don't pick just any old place to project their animus."

"But you know enough Jung, don't you, to know what happens? The projection isn't the reality. The disappointment when the object turns out to be itself, with its own direction and its own flaws and its own imperatives, is as bad as when a lover turns out to have quite a different personality than you thought. I'm sorry, I don't mean to upset you—I was trying to help, but I see I haven't. You just seem to be in such awful pain."

Mim's eyes swam instantly. "Do I? Do I? Yes, I am," she said, and staggered away. Laura followed, putting a hand on her arm, but she said, "No, really; people are waiting to talk to you. I'm sorry. What a place to have an identity crisis." She found the bathroom and ducked into it, and sobbed silently and furtively into her hands.

When she emerged—having put cold water on her face and composed herself—Laura was deep in conversation with three other women, and facing away from her. She got her coat and left quietly, thanking Linnea Benning on her way out. She would call Laura tomorrow and thank her too. She went out and stood by the pond, unable to think or reason, empty as if her self had been bled away. The waning moon floated above her in the trees. As the moon sidles up must she sidle up. His light had struck me blind dared I stop. My language beaten into one Name. I am I, am I; all creation shivers with that sweet cry.

She would have to speak at the conference. There was no getting out of it; it was mere cowardice to refuse. Her life was leading her, against her will, out of solitude and into demagoguery. She would have to convert, whatever that might mean and whatever self-annihilating future it might involve her in; perhaps it would provide a check on the demagoguery, but more likely it would upset her balance in ways she could not yet imagine. She wanted to be another kind of person, one who was immune to religion, one who did not need help. She leaned against a willow tree, pressing her forehead into the furrowed bark. To be inanimate—a tree, a stone, something without the power of choice, never to be accountable for her actions, never to act. Somehow she had been chosen, in some minor and not quite comprehensible way, to act and to speak, and she could no longer evade it. Morgenzahl knew; he was driving her there, as a sheepdog herded a sheep. *You don't take No for an answer from the universe, and it won't take No for an answer from you.*

She drove home. She could not face the Women's Center and noise and dancing; she felt fraudulent there even at her most confident. She went up the back stairs to her apartment, with its shabby-genteel 1930s fixtures and ten-foot ceilings, the secondhand Persian rug she had paid too much money for, and the books overflowing the bookshelves into piles on the floor. Drunken students were yodeling in the alley. She found her brass candlesticks and two stub-ends of yellow beeswax candles, and set them out on the counter. Next week, before sunset, she would kindle the Sabbath lights.

CHAPTER 4

Life, as we find it, is too hard for us; it brings us too many pains, disappointments and impossible tasks. In order to bear it we cannot dispense with palliative measures.... There are perhaps three such measures: powerful deflections, which cause us to make light of our misery; substitutive satisfactions, which diminish it; and intoxicating substances, which make us insensitive to it.... It is no simple matter to see where religion has its place in this series.

—Sigmund Freud

The word moves a bit of air, and this the next, until it reaches the man who receives the word of his friend and receives his soul therein and is therein awakened.

—Rebbe Nachman of Bratslav

Monday. The return to work was numbing, if not calming. There was mail to be opened and a stack of publishers' catalogs to be filed, and at nine-thirty Cedric Post, the chief bibliographer, stormed in and said accusingly, "Do *you* believe in the nationalization of culture?" "Certainly not," Mim said without hesitation, though she had not heard the term before; Post was a bully and she was damned if she would ask him to explain it. "Oh! Good!" he said, taken aback, and strode into his office. Outside the door the Acquisitions clerks were talking interminably about their cats.

She stared unthinking at an annotated weekly listing of new books.

There were some children's books this time; someone had done new illustrations for *Pinocchio*. "A wooden puppet," the description read, "who wants more than anything else to become a real boy." *Don't flatter yourself,* she said inwardly, to herself or to God. *A real boy who wants more than anything else to become a wooden puppet.* Woman into tree: if she had been born a tree, there would be no sin in it.

The phone rang. "Mim?" said an uncertain voice. "This is Gina in Circulation. There's a package for you. From the florist. It's not flowers, though, it's . . . it's really kind of strange."

Mystified, Mim told the nearest bibliographer (Irina Kalganova, German and Slavic Languages) that she was leaving her desk, and went out to the lobby. The package—done up in lavender plastic tissue—was a trailing philodendron vine, a crooknecked gourd attached to it with florist's wire. The card read (in round and guileless shop clerk's handwriting) "Nu? R. M."

She whooped with laughter; she laughed all the way back to her office, loudly and helplessly, the ridiculousness of the missive balm to her soul. She put the plant on her desk ("Never apologize, never explain," she said to the perplexed all day) and was about to call Morgenzahl's private number when she hesitated. He might be back at work by now; and even if he were not, the message deserved a different sort of answer, a reply in kind. She went out to Reference, with laughter still threatening to erupt, and found the interlinear Hebrew-English Bible. Isaiah's calling: what were the words? *Hineni sh'lacheini,* she copied clumsily in Hebrew letters on the back of a catalog card. On her coffee break she wrote it several more times till it looked less shaky, then wrote it again on a piece of library letterhead. She signed her name in Hebrew letters—this she had been practicing for weeks—and wrote underneath, "Nobody's dared me to do anything in years. You're on." She sealed the letter, and mailed it in care of the clinic on her lunch break. *Here am I: send me.*

"Who named you that, anyway? It was either a Jew with a sense of humor or a non-Jew with unusual luck."

"It was a friend of my parents', Herb Raskin, when I was eight.

Before that, God help me, I was Randi. He used to call me by it in full whenever he saw me. 'How are you today, Mimcomo?' 'What are you learning in school these days, Mimcomo?' He got a great kick out of it, but I never knew what it was all about until last month."

They were in a little seafood shack on the coastal highway. It was Tuesday, and the phone had rung as soon as she got home. ("Mim? I got your note. I'm so pleased you've decided. I've just left a message on the program coordinator's machine; she'll be calling you. Mary Christine O'Connell, a name that should tell you everything necessary. Meanwhile, they tell me I can go back to work next week. Let's go celebrate. When are you free? Any time? Now? Oh, good. Shall we meet at Brock's Landing?")

"Randi. Good Lord. It doesn't suit you at all. But you weren't walking around with this name ten years ago; I'd have noticed."

"No. I took Alan's name, like a good wife. And he gave me another nickname. But I've been Mim all the rest of the time."

"And on Yom Kippur you were alarmed to see your name in the prayer book?"

"More or less," she said. "I heard it called in the middle of the service." On going back the next Saturday she had seen it: the seraphim crying *Holy, holy, holy* and the ophanim answering *Blessed be the glory of the Lord* mim'komo, *from his place*. "Rather a shock to find that my name's been part of an angelic utterance for hundreds of years."

"Thousands," he said. "The rabbis swiped it from Ezekiel. 'The spirit took me up, and I heard a great rushing voice: *Baruch k'vod Adonai mim'komo*." He chanted the words in liturgical style. "*Makom*, the root word, is interesting too."

"I know it's one of the mystical names of God, and that there's something marginally pagan about calling God after a visible and tangible thing like *place*. Though I don't see why the same isn't true of *rock*, which you hear more often—or *father*, which you hear all the time."

"Inconsistency," he said. "Reaction against the Canaanites, maybe. Some anthropomorphisms are more pagan than others. So is some food," he said happily, as their plates arrived. "Oh, isn't this good stuff."

"Very," she said, taking a bite. "It's so easy to cook scallops just a minute too long." This would be harder to give up than little sausages. "But my name isn't worth talking about. How are you? What have you been doing, besides being rehabilitated? I hope you've had a good rest."

"It's been nice," he said. "Enforced leisure is very soothing. I read *Crowds and Power*, which I'd never gotten around to, and wrote a paper for *Family Planning Perspectives*, and last week I skipped town and went to New York. The mail has tapered off again, and most of it isn't too nasty, and that's a relief."

"How much nasty mail do you get?"

"It varies quite a bit. In a slow month there might be none at all; when the faithful get riled, there might be a spate of twenty or thirty. It's not the worst they do, but some of the letters are pretty crazy. I send them to my brother's wife. She's a sociologist. She knows what to do with them; write 'em up."

"I got a couple of letters after I spoke at that rally. They weren't crazy or threatening, but they were very contemptuous; they scared me. I had my address taken out of the book. Do they get any easier to read?"

"I don't read them carefully. You can't; you'd be mad all the time. I just open them up to distinguish them from the thank-you letters—there are some of those too, and often they're pretty emotional—and file them away for Lisa. I'd rather have letters any day than pickets—or being followed around by bright-eyed stalkers with Bibles."

"My God, do they do that?"

"They do all sorts of things. They've chased people out of the business that way. Not only doctors but staff and lobbyists. I hear stories at meetings—Jesus, just evil stuff. They can do anything they want, you know—publish your kids' pictures all over town, or leaflet your neighbors, or call you names on the street—because any indecency they can dream up is nothing beside abortion. I've been lucky till now. Pickets, a little arson, preachers in the waiting room, some telephone games—"

"Some what?"

"Oh, you know, filling up the message tape with propaganda, or booking phony appointments. They don't have the energy to do it often, but they're relentless little bastards when they do."

Mim shook her head, amazed. "And they say *we're* doing evil that good may come."

"No, they just say we're doing evil. Actually they say YOU DIRTY BABY KILLER, I HOPE THEY GET YOU NEXT TIME; that's one of the recent ones."

Mim winced. "I hope they don't. Eat your nice treyf, and don't think about it."

They were silent. Conversation drifted towards them from the other tables: "—told him it was cheap paint, and now we see the results of it." "—a storm like that one last December—" "—and her mother up in Castine with a house full of cats." And in the next booth, a young woman: "It's a respect thing, too. I mean, they don't have to *know* I'm going away with him after they told me not to. I don't have to *say*, 'I'm going to do this and you can't stop me.' I respect them enough I don't have to rub their noses in it."

"Who pays your rent?" said her friend.

Sheepishly the girl answered, "They help me." Mim bit her lip to keep from grinning, and saw that Morgenzahl was doing the same.

"Poor kid," he said in a low voice. "Her logic is very involved. Lie to your parents if you have to, sweetie, but don't say it's out of respect. And for God's sake take your pills." He shook his head sharply. "Let's talk about something else. How have you been? Is there life after politics? Bring me news of the world."

"The world *is* politics, isn't it? And anyway, that's not quite where I've been."

"Where have you been?"

"In the heights," she heard herself saying. "*Bimromav*. Oh, hell, I wasn't going to talk about it, but I might as well tell you. I've been going to shul ever since I last saw you, and getting into an awful state."

"Good Lord," he said. "Is this something I precipitated? I had no intention—"

"No, of course you didn't. I'd surely have done it on my own sooner or later. You just supplied the excuse, and once I saw what it was like I had no resistance. To find out that all these magnificent words I've been reading for years are *sung*—this incredible moral language that seems to me absolutely incorruptible because it's not Latinate, and intimate as—damn it, I'll shut up, I'll shut up, I could go on about it for hours, and I'd bore you and bother you. I'm completely dislocated; I think I may have to convert." She had said it: she was astonished that she had said it without shame.

"Good Lord," he said again, disconcerted. "I hope you know what you're doing. For God's sake don't get yourself mixed up with some born-again Hasid. They don't believe in birth control either."

"Where would I find a born-again Hasid at Beth Jacob? I don't think you should worry. He wouldn't have me anyway—not unless I were terribly strict about practice, and I don't plan to be." The words danced out of her mouth, decided, decisive; how did they know what to do?

"Well, nobody at Beth Jacob will bother you about your practice—not unless you do something egregiously wrong right there in the synagogue. But of course to the tidy mind that's mere hypocrisy."

"My mind is very untidy since Alan. I'm not going to follow anything strictly no matter how much I respect it. You're not telling me *you* have a tidy mind?"

"How can you ask?" he said, peeling a shrimp. "My family did, though, and one never really gets over that. It leaves me in the equally untidy position of despising all halfway measures while taking no measures at all myself."

"I suppose orthodoxy seems very confining if you grow up in it."

"Confining and trivial—or at least an insufficient response to what we have to respond to. I mean, how we ever got from Moses at the burning bush to a kid sneaking out for a cheeseburger—and then if the kid is sneaking out in 1954, as if at that moment in history there's nothing more critical in the life of the Jewish people than what you put in your mouth—"

"Maybe that was the kid's misunderstanding?"

"Oh, probably; but the kid had plenty of help. It was a messy time: all these displaced persons trying to cope, and you couldn't talk about what had happened—you couldn't talk about a tenth of what you needed to; and all these competing groups of Hasidim who hated each other like poison but hated us even worse. Actually I liked shul, and took it pretty seriously at one point, but it didn't seem to cohere with the real world. Anyway, you can be a perfectly good, obsessive Jew without being observant; I saw that by the time I was sixteen, watching people who'd become artists or academics or Beat poets and were teaching a perfectly recognizable Torah all the time—one that didn't need a fence around it."

"That's it! There's a sort of continuum: people who grow up with it must notice only the distinctions, but people who grow up without it notice the pattern, and observance or nonobservance is the least of it. There's a way of thinking that's almost independent of the practice—and just about indestructible. You, for instance, can go anywhere at all, you can sit here with a shiksa in a seafood restaurant, and you're still a Jew; nothing could make you adopt some other mode of thinking, you'd despise it. It's written on your heart, as legibly as Jeremiah could have wished—energy, compassion, the obligation to fix what's fixable, and some sort of absolute refusal of other people's compromises. It's a covenant you couldn't escape if you wanted to, and you don't want to."

"Jewishness is overdetermined," he said. "There *is* a way of thinking, but there's also what the world thinks of you—since if you don't insist on the difference, it always will. It's written on my face too, after all; no one would mistake me for a Yankee. Do I have this way of thinking because I grew up religious in Brooklyn, or because my parents couldn't be mistaken for Germans in Berlin in the thirties, and decided to get out while the getting was good? Either one will make you suspicious and hypercritical, and force you to use your wits to the limit. It's a difficult question for a people that believes in distinctions. But you're right, practice is no indicator. There are left-wing radicals who wouldn't set foot in a shul who are still driven to do mitzvahs; there are pious old men who show up every day for the minyan—my father was one—who sound a lot like atheists when you get them talking. It's not a religion, it's a people with an attitude."

"Yes, yes, exactly! And nothing in life can take that attitude from you. The Torah insists on it, whether you live by the Torah or not; the world insists on it, which is nothing to be grateful for but which has the effect of a gift in spite of itself. I suppose I insist on it too, and you probably think I'm a fool; philo-Semitism must seem fawning and silly to people who just live with being Jewish. But—it's like Santayana's little joke about Mary: There is no God and the Jews are his people. Permanently, irreversibly, no matter what you do. As if you're a compass, always pointing one way, from anywhere on the globe showing the direction of God, whatever God is. *Ani l'dodi v'dodi li.*" The great cry of the Song of Songs, the bride calling out to the bridegroom or the soul to God: *I to my love and my love to me.*

Morgenzahl looked bemused, as much by this outburst of lyricism in a shabby beachfront restaurant as by his own part in the picture. "You've got it bad," he said. "A terrible case of allegory. I wish you luck with it. But I can't help wondering how they'll deal with you: a woman of—whatever age you are; I suppose I'd better not guess—coming in by herself, in this complicated wound-up state of metaphysical love, sounding like a cross between John Donne and some unlikely female Kabbalist. I'm not sure Beth Jacob is ready for this."

"I'm sure they're not. But I don't seem able to stop." She sipped her water and wondered if she could even stop talking. "I'm not coy about my age, by the way; I'm thirty-four. A friend of mine tells me that's just the age one has to expect these disasters. She's a Jungian; she says it's all animus projection."

"Good Jungian orthodoxy," he said. "What do you suppose a Freudian would say?"

Mim looked at him sharply. "Something insinuating, no doubt. Sublimation; displacement of sex onto religion; failure to accept my feminine role; should have had the baby. All praise to Vater Sigmund, who by his own admission didn't know what women want." She speared her last scallop vengefully.

"Freud was as indelibly Jewish as the rest of us," he said. "And that's a streak in Jewish thought, or at least in Jewish life. Women belong in families, having babies, involving their sons in Oedipal relationships, the whole nine yards. Things have loosened up considerably in the last couple of decades—both in psychology and in Jewish life—but there's still a lot of that thinking around."

"So I'm told. It's maddeningly stupid, of course, but at the level that really matters I can scarcely bring myself to care. I want this way of thinking; by one means or another I'm going to have it, whether anybody wants to give it to me or not. I can't be put off by what men think of women."

"No, of course not. Of course not. Mim, I'm no champion of the status quo; relax. I just don't want you to be unpleasantly surprised. If you've come to this passion mostly through reading, in one sense what you want is to be a Jewish man; that's where all the intellect has been. But nobody's going to let you do that."

"No, and I don't qualify in any case," she said. "Let's find one of the local shrinks to write me up: *A Case of Shabbes-Envy*, full of words like *cathexis* and *countertransference*. Though it's more involved than a simple gender reversal: what I want isn't simply to be a Jewish man, it's to be a heretical Jewish man who knows all about the tradition but doesn't obey it, or not in the usual terms. Preferably one who writes magnificent, intelligent verse."

"Damn," he said. "Till you got to that last part I was going to offer to trade. I'd be curious to try being a heretical ex-Catholic woman with a quiet job and unlimited access to books. Too bad. What do you want for dessert?"

"Lemon pie," she said to the waiter. "And some sort of nice tea; Earl Grey, if you have it. Bob, I'm sorry; I had no intention of talking about all this, and I've gone on about it insufferably. I need a twelve-step program for people addicted to religion."

"*We admitted we were powerless against the opiate of the people*," he chanted. "*We took a searching and fearless inventory* . . . how does it go?"

"I don't remember. There's a hitch, though: the dependence on a higher power. How do you ask God to help you hold out against God?"

"Oh, that's no trick," he said almost scornfully. "There's nothing God's better at with the Jews. You want to surrender to God, go be Catholic again; he'll sweep you away on a flood of emotion, and you'll never have to think or resist. He doesn't want *us* on those terms—not even at tame, assimilated Beth Jacob. Not to worry."

"But the Song of Songs? The terrible case of allegory?"

He impaled her on one of his looks. "Pay attention to Reb Sigmund," he said. "Find out what it's an allegory for."

Mary Christine O'Connell called the next evening, and Mim liked her at once: she had a high, clipped, unpretentious voice and a decisive manner. Mim wondered if she were a nun, or more likely an ex-nun. "Call me M.C.," she said. "We'll be very glad to have you. Dr. Morgenzahl has been praising you to the skies, and we've also heard great things from Terry Treviso—she says she pulled you out of the audience at a rally where things were getting iffy and you really gave 'em what for. What are you thinking of saying?"

"It may change a good deal by May," said Mim, again sounding oddly competent to her own ears, "but I was thinking over the whole question of playing God. That's thrown at us as if there were simply nothing worse to be said, but I've never seen why: it doesn't seem self-evident that playing God is wrong. Or rather, I can see that it's wrong, even for God, but I can't see how it's avoidable. If it's playing God to end a pregnancy, isn't it playing God to start one? Isn't it playing God to give birth and teach your child morals and bring it up in the way that it should go? Isn't it playing God to take any initiative whatever, and then isn't playing God our business? We may not know how to go about it very competently, but there's some evidence that God doesn't either; he and we just have to muddle on with it anyway, doing what we think we have to and then cleaning up after it."

"Oh, I like this," said M.C. firmly. "No apologies here. This is something the whole group needs to listen to. I may have to put you in some horrible time slot, but I'm going to see if I can't get you a real hearing. No need to use male pronouns for God, by the way; this is an enlightened bunch. Okay, write me all this in a letter so I'll have something to show the committee, and give me a title—never mind if it changes by May, you just get up and say, 'Well, back in November I thought I was going to talk about that, but now I'm going to talk about this.' And I'll need a short bio from you too; I don't need it this instant, but if you can do it now that's one less thing to keep track of later. If you can get it all to me by the end of the month that'd be great. We'll forget to be in touch with you—it happens all the time, the organizers get up to their necks in organization and you think they've disappeared from the face of the earth—but we *will* send you the registration flier, and we *will* send you the schedule, and if you want anything else at all you should just call me. Oh, mercy. I don't have your address. Of course, Dr. Morgenzahl only gave me your phone number. Where should I send things?"

What on earth did one say in a bio? She could, she supposed, call herself an activist without stretching the truth too far. Her only real connection to the subject of abortion was having once had one, and she was not going to say that in anyone's program notes. In a sense it didn't matter who knew, but it repelled her to think of using her own private misery as a credential. She wondered if she ought to audit a course in philosophy or medical ethics, just to say she was studying something. She stalled over sending the letter.

In the next Tuesday's paper there was a small news item on the third page:

ABORTION DOCTOR RETURNS; PROTESTS RESUME
by Jerry B. Kaplansky, *Monitor* Staff

> Dr. Robert Morgenzahl, shot and wounded by an anti-abortion protestor September 28, returned yesterday to the Women's Health Center to find the protestors there ahead of him.
>
> Led by Rev. Calvin Hardy of Universal Gospel Church, the group held a peaceful prayer service in front of the Market Street clinic, which they called "the abortuary." Hardy stated that while he deplored the assault on Morgenzahl, the protests would continue "for as long as the killing goes on."
>
> Morgenzahl, appearing well rested and unafraid, spoke briefly with the protestors before entering the clinic. He repeated his thanks for their assistance during and after the assault, and urged Hardy to have "the same compassion" for the clinic's patients.

Police say that without the intervention of two of Hardy's group, Morgenzahl would almost certainly have been fatally wounded. Delbert Marlin of Bethel has been charged in the assault.

Mim stood at the kitchen table, furious, reading. In the background her messages were playing themselves: call your mother, pick up *Crowds and Power* at the bookshop, try our new credit card. Then, "Mim! There's a string quartet at the public library Sunday afternoon. Want to go?" She spun around, punched in Morgenzahl's number, listened to his taped ironic voice—"If you've reached this number, I assume you know what you're doing. Please leave a message"—and said, "This is Mim. Thanks, yes, I'd love to go to the concert, but—I've just been reading about these damned protestors. What can I do to help?"

CHAPTER 5

Only when Christianity is politically dead, that is to say as unorganized as Greek mythology, will its great imaginative resources be available to the poets.

—*The Sweeniad*

Through being profane, the profane assists . . . the coming of the Messianic kingdom.

—Walter Benjamin

On Christmas Eve Sarita held open house in the shop. There was always the chance of selling a scarf to someone doing last-minute shopping, and anyway it was pleasant to have regular customers in without selling them anything; festivity supplied its own excuse. She plugged in a big electric crock and mulled cider in it, and brought in pfeffernüsse and Russian tea balls, and played early music tapes above the hum of the sewing machines. People wandered in and out, and talked and ate, and the calligrapher down the hall emerged from her cubicle for a half-hour's foolery, and no one worked very earnestly. A few New Year's orders remained to be finished, but not today.

Sarita celebrated Christmas more by default than by conviction. Vestiges of quiet and mystery still hung about the day, if one could manage to ignore the frantic cult of gift-buying; besides, she did not feel entitled to any other holiday. She had tried for a few years to do without one, but that felt wrong too. She was interested to see how her two assistants handled the question. Todd Erway, though he lived with a church organist, was a thoroughgoing pagan: he celebrated the Winter

Solstice and insisted that that was all anybody *really* did who lit any lights in December. Edith Tyrell was a convinced Christian, of some austere Calvinist stripe, and while she abhorred the business of Christmas shopping could talk an eloquent line about the Word made Flesh; it was the day's theology that appealed to her, not its mood. They managed to work together without open hostility, but interesting fights broke out now and then between them; Sarita felt that (quite apart from the matter of their skill with cloth) she could hardly have been luckier in her hiring.

Toward the end of the afternoon Todd's lover came in. Occasionally through the year he stopped by on the way to or from the church, with snacks and stories; today he appeared in the doorway with a mighty fruitcake, which he elevated on the spread fingertips of both hands, proclaiming in a stentorian baritone:

> "The boar's head in hand bear I,
> Bedecked with bays and rosema*rye*!"

There was no point in working after that; they switched off their machines and sat eating fruitcake with fingers too sticky for sewing.

"Everything ready for the big night, Andrew?" said Sarita. "Did you convince them not to use the light bulb?"

"I did," Andrew said. "I told them it would light Mary's face from below and make it look ghastly. I couldn't, of course, approach it from the standpoint of mere good taste."

"A light bulb?" said Edith.

"In the manger; to represent *le divin enfant*," he explained. "The aesthetic management at St. Michael's is uneven—distinctly uneven. Your angel costume is the best thing in the show, Sarita." Sarita inclined her head with a private smile.

"Only an Anglican could coin a term like 'aesthetic management,'" Edith said with a snort.

"I'll admit that the word *management* is not of the highest order," said Andrew, cutting another slice, "but I suppose you mean to imply that aesthetics aren't either."

"Well, aesthetics is surely below ethics in the scheme of things."

"I categorically deny it! What's wrong with having aesthetics for your ethics?" said Andrew expansively. "Let me tell you my new theory. All that raving against idols you get in the O.T.—that constant grousing about asherahs and graven images—it's not a prohibition against art as we know it, not at all. Think of the Canaanite household gods as Hummel figures, garden gnomes, teddy bears, pink flamingoes—all those kitschy interchangeables that people insist on cluttering up their lives with. Wasn't Abraham's own father supposed to have been an idol-maker? So what could God say to him except *Get thee out of thy father's house and get thee some standards*? Vote of thanks to Abraham for trashing the garden gnomes!" He raised his mug of cider.

Not everyone could make Edith laugh, but by the end of this she was squeaking behind her hand, holding her mouth shut to prevent the crumbs escaping. "I like it," she said. "You're a heretic, but I like it."

"It's very fitting," said Todd. "What's more suitable than for God to appear to the interior decorators as an interior decorator? And to their clients, too, of course," he added graciously.

"Well, it goes for all the arts, including yours and mine," Andrew went on. "Think of the implications! The prophets were divinely inspired; what can that mean but that *God wants us to have good taste?* Thanks to their efforts, we're now in a position where the individual talent—you, Sarita!—can partake of that same divine inspiration, bringing down a little of heaven to earth."

"If you think a woman's business suit isn't the sartorial equivalent of the garden gnome, you haven't thought about it much," Sarita said gloomily. "Still, that's proof that aesthetics has something to do with ethics, or ought to."

"Ah! But *ought* is an ethical word, and prevails," said Edith, triumphant. "Can you say that ethics *ought* to be aesthetic and make any sense at all?"

"Um, I think so," said Sarita, considering. "What about that old phrase *the beauty of holiness?* Should ethics have to be ugly?"

"Or look at the Book of Common Prayer," put in Todd in high excitement. "The Anglicans are throwing it out on its ear because it's old-fashioned; they're getting rid of all those wonderful quotable phrases like *the quick and the dead* and *meet, right and our bounden duty—*

·

anything you wouldn't understand if you got all your words from TV. Isn't there something unethical in that? They're ripping out of the language something that gave shape to it; they're discarding their history. English lit. is going to be unintelligible without it. Grad students will have to read it as a reference book, and they'll miss things; it's not the same as having it drummed into you week after week."

"Todd, what are you so upset about?" said Edith, amazed. "You don't believe a word of it."

"No, but if the people who *do* don't care enough to do it right—! It's the tackiness that gets me, the deliberate indifference to sound. It's not even casting your pearls before swine. It's—it's sending them to the landfill."

"You don't understand." Andrew's voice soared. "The churches are profoundly self-abnegating institutions. They know they have to renounce their worldly goods. Mother Rome began it, of course, in the sixties; we, as usual, are just following along. Gregorian chant? Too beautiful; sell it to Telefunken and bring in those guitars. The Book of Common Prayer? Too complicated, too hypnotic, all those compound sentences; chop 'em up and feed 'em to the worms. Renaissance iconography? Too obscure, we don't want to have to *teach* people anything; what do you think religion is, a degree program? It's only people like you, Todd—you and Sarita (and me too, of course, in private life, but as the only Anglican here I have to take the official line)—who think ethics and aesthetics owe each other anything. Damned elitist worldly intellectuals! Take your *Dies Irae* and your triptychs and your Thomas Cranmer! We strip ourselves of all these gauds, these trappings of the Whore of Babylon. We bring it down to the primal simplicity of—well, there was this billboard I saw once, a rent-a-sign in front of a gas station:

        GOD SAID IT
        JESUS DID IT
        I BELIEVE IT
        THAT SETTLES IT

Thither the Anglican Church."

"Trappings for me, every time," said Sarita. "You can have Jesus if I can have Gothic painting."

Todd got up and refilled his mug. "What I find politically interesting," he said, "is that they're getting rid of the beauty right at the time when women and blacks are finally getting their due in the mainstream churches. I know the official line is that they're being sensitive to women and blacks, but I think that's just blaming the victim. *I think the people in charge are really saying, All right, the rabble can come in and take the place over, but we're going to turn it into a slum on our way out.* If they can't have beauty on their own terms, no one else can have it at all."

"It amazes me, how much difference all this makes to you," said Edith, shaking her head. "Surely the point is Christ, and the demands his life makes on us, and not the beauty of the words you say it in?"

"Ah, but it isn't," said Andrew sadly. "It isn't the same truth if you say it differently. Besides, when you take away beauty, isn't the failure of the whole thing that much clearer? How can you say *Your sins are forgiven* when people still suffer from them, or *Christ redeemed us* when clearly nothing has changed, or *Where will you spend eternity* when you can't face up to this life? So you have to stress the aesthetic, to cover it up."

"It's these sacramental churches," Edith muttered. "No idea of faith *or* works. I wonder you keep going at all if you feel like that."

"Well, I tried other things, you know—Goddess worship, and sweat lodges, and shamanic initiation for white boys—all this stuff Todd goes in for—but the thing was, I found I couldn't swear any other way. Anything else I tried sounded euphemistic, as if I were simply too prudish to use the real stuff. Finally I said to myself—'Jesus H. Christ on a raft,' I said—'if these new religions can't generate any convincing blasphemies, I'm not convinced that they're valid.' And I came back."

"To the church of Henry VIII, the *only* one that would—"

"Honey, the Christian hegemony guarantees—" Todd began simultaneously.

"Oh, stop it, you idiots," Sarita called over the noise. "Look, here's

Mim. Let's make ourselves civilized: she's the one who's doing really ethical work. How are you, Miranda?"

"Ethics and aesthetics have met together; righteousness and peace have kissed each other," Mim said. "I'm afraid I've been eavesdropping. It's all too wonderful; you people ought to go on stage."

"I've tried," said Todd, "but nobody cares. You get outside the context and it's too esoteric; nobody wants to hear what an ex-religionist has to say about his ex-religion. And of course anyone who's still in it would be highly offended, so you can't say it there."

"All theause who with haughty repentance and treu faith tuhn unto Him," intoned Andrew, somewhat irrelevantly. "But you're the one who's going to do it, aren't you?—by giving this paper to the pro-choice clergy?"

"If I can manage to get it written; it proceeds by fits and starts. But that's not much like talking to a random audience of churchgoers. It's a very self-selecting group."

"Preaching to the converted, in fact," said Edith.

"Well, I've preached to the other kind too," Mim said mildly. "But they *were* offended. I agree, it's a problem; people don't cross the lines often enough."

"You've been crossing lines, though, I hear," said Sarita.

"Oh, the—? Oh, that! Well, it was just too infuriating: as soon as he's back on the job they start sending pickets again."

Edith and the two men looked blank. "I've been escorting patients into the Women's Health Center," Mim said; "the protestors harangue them and make them feel awful. You remember, the doctor there was shot in September; you'd think they'd have the decency to let him alone."

"It's not, of course, indecent to *do* abortions," Edith said. "And the one thing you mustn't do to women about to kill their unborn children is make them feel bad."

"Oh, Lord, Edith, are you another one? All right, let's get it over with."

"Don't leap to conclusions," said Edith. "I think abortion ought to be legal; people are going to do it anyway, so they might as well do it in sterile conditions. But it's not like blowing your nose, you know: it really is a human life. They ought to feel something more than if they were having a tooth out."

"How do you know what they feel?" said Mim, and they glared at each other, trembling on the edge of accusation and confession.

Sarita, fearing an explosion, leapt in. "They say you've been doing unheard-of things—shaking hands with the protestors and learning their names, and keeping your temper when all about you are losing theirs, and generally behaving like a saint."

"Some of them saved Bob's life," Mim said simply. "That much is decency; I suppose I'm pragmatic enough to think they might do it again, if they're treated like—human lives."

"Turn the other cheek," said Todd. "And you call yourself an *ex*-Catholic."

"It's not turning the other cheek: it's ghetto strategy," she said. "*Where there are no people, you be a person.* Maybe it'll rub off."

"This Dr. Morgenthal," Edith persisted. "Fred, my husband, is a lab tech. at the hospital, and runs into him now and then on ob/gyn business. From what Fred says, he seems to be quite a connoisseur of women."

"Morgen*zahl*," said Mim. "I wouldn't know."

"Well, he has a reputation at the clinic, or did at one point, for practically exercising *droit du seigneur* with the staff. And it makes me wonder: does he find it so easy to do abortions *because* he's a connoisseur of women? Does he think women's ideal state is to be young and unburdened and frivolous, so that the best thing he can do for them is relieve them of responsibility? Is he trying to keep them from getting hard and practical and resentful of men, whereupon they're no longer accessible?"

"Good God, what a train of thought," said Mim. "Damn it, Edith, we're told to help the widow and the orphan. Is there nothing to be said for helping people not *become* the widow and the orphan? Can't we ever prevent poverty and misery, instead of haphazardly trying to relieve them once they're there? If the choice is between abjection and frivolity, maybe it's better to be frivolous."

"I'd go for abjection every time; it teaches you something."

"If," said Mim fiercely, "you're prepared to learn it; if you're not, it teaches you nothing, and it infects all the people around you. You'd *go for* abjection because you have a chance to choose it in a principled way. But thrusting it on others without their consent is—" She stopped, with effort. "I'm sorry. Excuse me, everyone. I shouldn't do this. Edith, you asked a question, to which I don't know the answer. I suppose I don't think it's a relevant question. If he does acts of kindness because he's a connoisseur of women, what does it matter, as long as he does them?"

"I'm sorry too," Edith said. "That's a more civil answer than I probably deserve." She turned awkwardly to her machine and fiddled with bobbins.

"This isn't good Christmas Eve conversation," Todd complained. "Can I open my presents now?"

The others turned to him, glad of the relief. "It *is* six o'clock," said Mim. "Are you going to close up, Sarita, or just stay through the holiday?"

"Six!" said Edith, with palpable relief. "I meant to leave at five. Fred will be stuffing the turkey, and he'll do something exotic and horrible with it; last year it was pineapple chunks and water chestnuts. Goodbye, all. Mim, I'm sorry; let's have a real talk sometime. Merry Christmas."

"And to all a good night," said Andrew conclusively as she shut the door. "Mim, you are a woman of valor."

"Edith's all right," said Mim. "She just doesn't have any tact. I could use less myself."

"Not tonight," said Todd. "I think you stood up to her pretty well. Why don't we all go to our place for some food and spiked eggnog? I take it none of us are going home to our families."

Todd and Andrew lived on the top floor of an old house a few blocks away, with a collection of Art Nouveau posters (reprinted) and a large dog that they called Raoul, not because that was its name but because that was the noise it made. ("No, her name's Shasta, but the first time she howled like that we said my God, it's a woman wailing for her demon lover. And what else would a demon lover be called?") They fed Sarita and Mim on Swedish meatballs and a big salad and a mocha soufflé, and then being too full for eggnog they made hot buttered rum instead. Then they all went out for a walk, ostensibly to look at the Christmas lights but also under Andrew's tutelage to sing carols, till Todd and Sarita dissolved at "A Virgin Unspotted" and said it made them think of leopards and Kipling, and Mim said she felt spotted herself, singing these things after three months of going to synagogue, and they started lampooning the words. It went on and got worse until, silly drunk, they wandered the downtown streets four abreast, passing Town Hall with its crèche and a hastily added menorah, shouting out loud an improvised carol of Andrew's:

> Take no scorn to wear the horn,
> *Morally, merrily,*
> So our savior Christ was born
> *Of our pretty lady.*

And then Mim left to drive carefully back to the college town, and Todd and Andrew wended toward midnight mass, and Sarita was left alone to climb the stairs to her apartment.

She sat without music, turning the pages of a book on Gothic painting, her eye—she could not help it—turning the fantastic gowns into pattern pieces. She could not relax. The quarrel between Mim and Edith and the evening's subsequent hysteria had destroyed the uneasy truce she usually kept with the holiday; she vacillated between envy and distress. She could not keep her memories selective: from childhood up, the mysterious beauty of the tree was tarnished by the disappointment of the presents, and the promise of deliverance by the reality of dogma. Twenty centuries of stony sleep. What she had once loved about Christianity had been the glory of it, the assertion that the world's true nature was magnificent; Jesus and morals had had very little to do with it. They could have been talking about Osiris or Persephone or Balder for all she cared. But magnificence was not in the repertoire of Christianity's current defenders, and Sarita had ceased fairly early to hope for anything from them. Only in little impromptu communities of unbelievers, like the one this evening, could she approach anything resembling her real religion, the mockery serving partly to cover and partly to reveal it.

She was not so much hostile to Christianity as immune to it: its profound doctrines and art, given to her before she could believe, had acted on her as a kind of inoculation against belief. C. S. Lewis, she had once read, had come to Christianity through myth; she had come to myth through Christianity, and found it hard to tell the difference. (Except that myth did not produce militants: nobody would block an abortion clinic in the name of Osiris or Persephone or Balder.) But if she had built up a resistance to the system it was through the potency of the system itself, and she was in debt to it—and there was nowhere to pay the debt. It was unimaginable that anything said in the shop that afternoon or in the streets that evening should be said (for example) at St. Michael's; the priests would say, kindly enough, that such jibes were out of place, that they would cause the little ones to stumble. A hushed and reverential atmosphere must be maintained: loud laughs might shatter faith. Concessions were always made for the fig-leaf hangers, the painters of nighties in the Sistine Chapel, never for the outright mockers. The faithful could never believe that faith had resilience. The mockers, who tested it constantly, knew it was indestructible.

She had once read a tale of a Lithuanian kabbalist who had called up Ivan the Terrible from the dead, three centuries after, to accuse him. She had wondered then, who would she call up? Who would she accuse or question out of the past, to understand the workings of history and the losses of her own life? She shut the book and went into the kitchen; she took a rope and a bucket from the broom closet and dressed to go out. She took the shortest way to the docks, down past the great pile of salt that three or four huge cranes were always adding to or depleting; it stood ghostly in the streetlights, swaddled in black plastic and old tires. Finding a bit of sea wall that had not been fenced off as private property, she lowered the bucket and brought up a little water. She took it back to her apartment building and carried it up to the roof, bringing also a blue bowl from her kitchen and a length of white watered silk.

She poured the sea water into the bowl, and walked carefully around the roof for several minutes, looking into the water as she went. Finally she put the bowl down and smiled: the crescent moon overhead was mirrored thinly in the water. She draped the white silk around it, trailing the ends along the snowless tar.

"Miriam bat Joachim v'Channah," she said softly. Mim had told her that this was the formula for being called to the Torah—at least at the egalitarian Beth Jacob; traditionally only the father's name was appended to one's own. She was not sure whether *Joachim* was proper Hebrew or an English approximation, and she stumbled over the unaccustomed guttural *ch*, but she thought this was how it ought to be done. She stared into the bowl of sea water, drawing her eyes back to it again and again when they wandered, and after some time spoke again.

"Why did you do it?"

> *And Mary said to the angel, Get thee gone. If the Lord intend to take flesh of me, shall he not speak to me himself? And the angel departed from her.*
>
> *And the Lord spoke to Mary, and said, Mary, and she said, Here am I. And he said to her, See, it is my purpose to be born among men, to ransom them from their sins and deliver them. Thou art my chosen vessel. Why hast thou dismissed my messenger?*
>
> *And Mary laughed; and she said, Behold the handmaid of the Lord. I make to myself no graven images, neither do I bow down and worship them. Shall I bear a son and call my own flesh my God? How then should I do thy commandments?*
>
> *And he said unto her, Man and woman I made in my image; the son of man is no idol but very God. I come that all men may see and believe.*
>
> *And she said, Hast thou not told us aforetime that we are made in thine image? And shall we trust the seeing of the eye above the hearing of the ear? Hear, O Israel, the LORD thy God, the LORD is one; what needs more to believe? I am of Israel, father: I am thy lover, but I contend with thee. Be it not unto me according to thy word.*
>
> *And the Lord laughed aloud and said, My daughter has won*

against me, my daughter has won.

And Mary sang, but Sarita was becoming fatigued, and it was not the Magnificat that ran through her head as she came muzzily back to night and rooftop, but an old medieval lyric Yeats had borrowed, with the words oddly skewed:

> *"I am of Israel,*
> *and the holy land of Israel,*
> *and time runs on,"* said she.

Disoriented, she gathered up her things and went back down, feeling the experiment had failed. The last impression she had as she fell asleep was of a scene from an illuminated manuscript, Gabriel standing before Mary with the message unfolding from his mouth on a little scroll, and Mary not meeting his eyes but staring away at the floor at middle distance. *History must be carried out,* he was saying. *There is Constantine to be converted, the Holy Roman Empire to be raised, Jews to be persecuted, heretics to be burned, music to be written and churches built. The peasants of Europe wait to call you Queen of Heaven.* Mary listened and stared. Her expression was uncannily not modesty: she was like Rembrandt's Bathsheba, chagrined and gentle, her eyes under lifted brows focused on something unseen, her mouth bemused in what might have been a smile had there not been such trouble in it. *This, then, is what it means to be desired.* And then God overbore her: Gabriel's *Ave,* pricked out in Gothic letters, pierced her ear, and her womb began to magnify the Lord.

Bathsheba, in the painting, holds a letter: the king's summons, or the news of her husband's death. Mary, whose ear had swallowed the little scroll, held all the words within, foreseeing all: becoming in that moment the sort of woman who ponders things in her heart, who does not forget complexity, who will always take the side of the compromised daughter or the pregnant nun, not because she condescends from her great purity but because she is defeated as they have been: resigned, maculate, worldly, no longer virgin.

CHAPTER 6

It is up to us to accomplish the negative. The positive is given.

—Kafka

The clinic was in a large yellow frame house down the street from the hospital; it had been built in the 1830s for a sea captain with daughters, and had a ballroom on the third floor. Easy Landing's old-timers still called it the Bennett House, all the more pointedly when deploring the protests. To think of the dignity of that house being marred by political controversy! And those lovely spacious rooms simply gone, divided up into little cubicles, when the doctor could have put up a one-story brick office anywhere and nobody would have cared. But in fact old Mrs. Dore, descendent of the first Miss Bennett, had offered the house, and paid part of the cost of the remodeling (which had actually been done with restraint, and under her direction): she had been an early disciple of Margaret Sanger's, and thought a family planning clinic was a noble scheme. Margaret Sanger had had racist eugenic notions, and that was disgraceful, but of course there should be a safe place in town for abortions now they were legal, and if there were no woman doctor available to do them, Dr. Morgenzahl was certainly the next best choice. She had him to tea once a year at her apartment in the Buckingham Hotel around the corner.

There were a thousand abortions a year, more or less; they were first-trimester abortions, the later ones being referred to a hospital in Boston or performed by Morgenzahl at the local hospital. The clinic also provided birth control, referrals to adoption agencies, testing for venereal diseases, and (through a separate waiting room) prenatal care. On the second floor there were other medical offices, a chiropractor and a dentist. In the third-floor ballroom there were classes some nights of the week: yoga, Lamaze birthing, and "Women's Health Awareness" (breast and cervical self-examination and instruction on birth control and avoiding sexual infections). The folklore society rented the ballroom monthly for a contradance.

Saturdays were the hardest days, though some Wednesdays were "procedure days" too; women who lived upstate, or who could not leave their jobs during the week, came in on Saturdays, and the protestors showed up early to prevent them. Mim, who drove into town to go to services anyway, simply came earlier to bring the women through the picket lines. As time went on she did not always leave when nine-thirty came, and when she did she came back afterwards; she had already become one of the steadiest volunteers. The two paid counselors were often overworked, and when it became clear that she was willing they trained her to do their job. Morgenzahl had been worried at first about this ("No, you're fully qualified, but you're complex; they may need somebody simpler and less troubled"), but after he heard her first few pre-operative briefings he was reassured. Counseling did not mean simply listening to the woman as she justified or reconsidered her choice; it meant, for each one who chose to go through with it, being present at the operation, holding her hand and helping her breathe slowly, answering her questions and comforting her when she cried. Attending, in fact, to her soul, while Morgenzahl and the nurse attended to her body. The nurse, Anne Shattuck, was a tough maternal woman in her fifties who had done illegal abortions in the old days and had been with the clinic since it began; her reading of the women's physical reactions to the process seemed nearly infallible.

Mim found the procedures extraordinarily moving. Having already a peculiar consciousness of simultaneously keeping and breaking the Sabbath, and of restoring the balance of one life at the expense of another, she had a heightened sense of everything that went on; she tended to find herself breathing along with the women. Her own past did not trouble her at these times, but was subsumed in their present.

Sometimes in the calmer intervals she got a glimpse of Morgenzahl's face as he worked between the woman's knees: it was abstracted and intent, as if he somehow listened with his instruments. "It's a kinetic process," he explained when she asked him. "You're in a very vulnerable part of the body which you can't see, and the range of motion is rather narrow. You have to be sure you're getting all the tissue, but you can't move too far or too forcefully. The two big risks are infection and perforation." He was utterly kind to the women, in a voice she remembered instantly from ten years back, not the ironic voice of his intellect but an inward and compassionate voice: "Hold still now. Thanks, that's fine. Do tell me if you feel another *kind* of discomfort; that's very important for me to know. Okay, I'm going to use the suction again just briefly . . ." The cannula gave a discreet little slurp as he withdrew it. "There, we're done. You're not pregnant any more."

The worst of the procedures so far—the fourth one she had attended—was on a fifteen-year-old girl, at the upper limit of the first trimester, who had not understood that she was pregnant. "My mom caught me throwing up and started screaming at me. When was my last period, and how could I do this to her, and on and on. How was I supposed to know? Sometimes I have periods, sometimes I don't. I thought you couldn't get pregnant if you weren't regular.

"Have the baby? Oh, please. I'm not going to be one of those cute little sadder-but-wiser teenage moms. I'm a dancer: I'm just starting to do choreography. What am I going to do, go lumbering around the gym in a leotard at nine months? Give me a break. These creeps out there with the blood-covered baby dolls, that's the sort of thing they'd want. Why do they even care? Just because Kevin squirts some stuff up me, I'm supposed to drop everything and become a mommy for the rest of my life? I don't even have a *driver's license*, for God's sake. 'Abortion stops a beating heart'—all I can say is, it better damn well." And to Morgenzahl, nastily, as he put on his gloves, "You'd really like to see me cry, wouldn't you?"

"Shh," he said. "You do what you need to. Just keep very still in the lower body, because otherwise you could get badly hurt. Mim says you're a dancer: that means you have very good control over motion and stillness. Right now we need stillness."

It was a longer procedure than the others because of the age of the fetus and because the girl fainted midway: it happened occasionally, Morgenzahl said, when the cervix was dilated. The vasovagal reflex. He held a stethoscope to her chest. When she recovered he resumed the abortion. Mim held her hand for what seemed a long time, listening to the growl of the machine, trying not to watch what passed through the clear tubing but seeing that Morgenzahl watched it intently, smelling the smells of blood and antiseptic. At the end the girl did cry, squeezing Mim's hand and talking unsteadily: "I'm sorry. You've all been so nice, and I've been so ratty. I just feel so fucking stupid. Nobody ever told me it was like this, that it takes three people and a lot of expensive machinery to get the baby out. Too bad sex isn't this hard. I don't know, in a way I don't even like Kevin that much, but while it's going on it's like you can't stop. Can't anybody just tell me, how do you stop?"

They all three winced. "Oh, Cassie," said Mim. "We don't know either. That's why you use birth control."

"If a man ever tells you he *can't* stop, he's lying," said Morgenzahl. "That's the oldest line in the book. They can. But of course they don't want to."

"Don't even tell her they can," said Anne, collecting the instruments for the autoclave. "How likely is she to find one who will? Don't listen to him, honey; he's better than most of them, but none of them get it. Come on, let's get you into recovery. You must be wicked hungry; you want a snack? You want your mom to come in?"

For the next hour the girl would sit in a reclining chair resting and massaging her lower belly, and Mim would come by and make sure she got contraception, and Anne would watch her for excessive bleeding and signs of trouble. If all was well they would give her cookies and tea. Mim lingered at the door as Morgenzahl prepared to take the jar of blood and tissue to the lab. "What a waste," she said. "Why do we handle things in this haphazard way? We train boys of eighteen to use judgment about life and death; why don't we train girls? Why didn't she know by the time of her first period exactly what was at stake?"

"Because we believe in accidents," said Morgenzahl sourly. "It's cozy and reassuring to pick up the pieces after a disaster; it brings out the neighborly instinct. Think how nice it would be to say Oh sweetie, poor little lost lamb, let me knit you some booties for the baby, and I'll look after him every third Tuesday, and isn't it comforting now that your life's been wrecked to know that at least you've got *his*. Here we're not nice. We recognize perfectly well that she's not a lost lamb, that in fact she's kind of a weasel, and she'd make a pretty weaselly mom at this point. We're picking up the pieces too, but . . . well, they're smaller pieces." He swirled the jar apologetically. "It's cold, it's mean-spirited, to prevent the disaster from happening. You take all the despair out of things, and all the consolation goes with it."

Sometimes at the end of the day they would stay and talk, or go out for a drink or for dinner and twice to a concert. They talked expansively, and yet by tacit agreement never about what they were doing together; their physical contact was limited to affectionate handshakes and later to such hugs as they might decently have exchanged in the synagogue. He showed no sign of the reputation Edith had given him, and she wondered where that had come from; perhaps it was something from the aftermath of his divorce. Perhaps, even, the shooting had shocked him out of it: a brush with death might make even a connoisseur think of other things than collecting.

One evening she stopped at his apartment after a concert, to borrow a book; she had not been inside before, and was struck by the magnificence of the design. The old mill had been built with lofty ceilings and enormous many-paneled windows, and the architect had preserved them; the living room looked like something from Versailles. She wondered if the other rooms were the same, or if something dreadful had been done to them with lowered ceilings and acoustical tile. Perhaps there were lofts: there was a round window high up in one living room wall, which suggested a place on the other side to stand and look through it. Gaping at the bones of the design, she saw nothing of the contents until Morgenzahl's voice came floating back to her in midsentence: " . . . not in the Thoreauvian grain, with that fatuous 'simplify, simplify.' Complicate! Complicate! It's the only way to keep one step ahead of the world." Then she saw that the place was cluttered with books and art; one section of wall was filled with a large collection of records and CDs and the equipment for playing them, a computer sat on a desk in one corner playing a complicated geometric game with itself, and a week's worth of *New York Times* littered the couch. A young ginger cat woke up and jumped from a chair, and a book slid to the floor behind it. "It's nicely complicated," Mim said. "One step ahead of the world in civilization."

"Sit down; take off your coat," he said, patting the newspapers into a stack. "I thought I knew right where this was, but it seems to have moved. It can't have gone far."

"I'll just read your shelves, I think," she said, craning her neck at the nearest one. Kafka and Dante; Nietzsche and Gershom Scholem; the Proceedings of the National Abortion Federation back to 1977; a book on the Nuremberg trials; art books (Kollwitz, Holbein, Baskin, Barlach, Jeanclos); medical books and random volumes of the Talmud; Whitman and Dickinson; D. H. Lawrence; Sander Gilman on Freud; Freud on Moses; it went on and on, according to no system that she could discover. At eye level on one shelf, a little bronze of a pregnant man, a snarling face incised upon his belly. On the walls, two abstract paintings of somber delicacy, and an etched landscape of an autumn field. And on the desk with the computer, some old family photos.

"Here it is," he said from across the room. "Janet Chance—how's that for a name—*The Romance of Reality*, 1934. It's a curious little salvo: that maddeningly complacent English anti-Semitism, too decent to persecute but perpetually on the edge of tittering, and this perfect faith in the ability of human reason to sweep away Christian fear and prudery in a generation or two, which seems to the *fin-de-siècle* American baby killer a bit too touchingly misplaced. Here's the passage I was thinking of: 'For the final outcome of these experiences is serenity, and this serenity owes its being to the constant presence of disillusionment, and disillusionment's resultant ecstasy.' See? You don't have to be Jewish to know that. Not that serenity is quite—I mean, if you're going to keep one step ahead of the world you don't have the time for it. But she's onto something, I think. And take a look at what she says about sex education. The same mix of the idiotically utopian and the marvelously sane."

"These are your children?" she said, still at the photos.

"Yes; Marcie and David. And my parents when young," he said, pointing out two faces in an old black-and-white group portrait. "With my mother's family in Prague. All gone now, except for one cousin who wasn't in the picture."

He did not elaborate, and she did not ask; there was nothing that could be said. Then she observed, gently, "That David's a gorgeous young man. Did you look like that at his age?"

"Oh, no; I was a terrible nerd. I don't know where he gets it." He rummaged in a drawer. "I don't have one at that age, but here's one at twenty-five. Not much to look at." A thinner version of himself, with more hair, in a studio portrait with a young woman in an angular empire-waisted dress and a pouffed hairdo. Both of them wore 1960s-shaped glasses with heavy black rims.

"How style dates us, especially women," Mim said. "I'm trying to imagine what she must look like without all that, and I can't."

"Here's a recent one." Now the woman was thinner, greying and handsome—it was obvious where David got his looks—and caught in mid-laugh between the two adolescents and a tall athletic-looking man. "That's her new husband. Ben Carlin—math professor at Cal Tech. A much better match."

"I don't think you've told me her name."

"Ilene." He looked at both pictures and shut them back in the drawer. "Nobody's fault really, is it? Just one of life's little ironies. You get desperate to marry *somebody* in your twenties; you want to grow up. God knows, just to be having children, when—" He gestured at the old group portrait. "But there's more to it than that, and nobody tells you. You don't marry *somebody*; you don't have children in the abstract. You're creating a world, and Ilene and I didn't create a good world together. I'm not even sure why. Some mismatching of personalities. Perpetual misfirings in conversation, having to guard yourself all the time; you stand it as long as you can, but you both resent it. Finally you can't look at each other without seeing resentment, and then in some fundamental sense you don't have a home." He drifted toward the middle of the room and sat in an armchair.

Mim sat on the couch. His mood was quieter and more exposed

than she had seen it before; she should not try to leave. "It's always some gap between souls, isn't it?" she said. "Something you take for granted and can't explain in yourself, or something you never learn to anticipate in the other. You keep trying to work it out by the means you know, but since they're already your means they only compound it."

He nodded. "And keep on compounding it—both of you signaling for all you're worth, and both of you totally misreading each other's signals. Or *missing* them. And finally it occurs to one or both of you, this is worse than being alone."

She looked at him curiously. "There's a lot worse than being alone," she said. "I've been alone for ten years, and it's not for a total dearth of opportunity. There are prices I won't pay."

"You must have terrifying standards."

"I don't think so. I only have one standard really—some sort of essential serious-mindedness—but it's not easy to find a man who has that, or who if he has it doesn't have to keep making sure of it at my expense."

"That jerk," he said, meaning Alan. "Hell of a thing to do to a young woman. Serious-minded men are all monomaniacs. Stay away from them." He laughed darkly. "But who am I to talk? I keep on going to work every day, in spite of all the vicious mayhem the antis inflict, and the official story is that *that's* what cost me my family. This weird humanitarian obsession that I can't walk away from."

"Surely that's rather different," she said. "You prove your seriousness every day in the public realm; you don't have to insist on it at home." She stroked the cat, who had decided that she was all right and curled himself delicately in her lap, purring heavily. "Bob, you know, I've never asked you and you've never said—how did this all begin? For as long as I've known about you you've been a byword: your name comes up in late-night conversations or in ladies' rooms, kind of soberly, you know, *She went to Morgenzahl*. But at some point you decided you were going to do this work. How did it happen?"

"Through an irony," he said. "I liked delivering babies. That was the part of the hospital rotations I couldn't get enough of as a student. That euphoric moment—the kid pops out, and the crisis is over, and the mother's so happy, and how can anything in medicine be nicer? It's not one of those uncertain questions of cure or palliation that make med students so cynical and crazy, it's just *more life*. The hours are godawful, but the satisfaction is immense; there's just nothing like it. But of course when you start seeing pregnant women you meet a certain number who don't want to be pregnant.

"Growing up where I did, it hadn't occurred to me until late adolescence that a woman might not want to be pregnant; I suppose it did happen among my mother's friends, but they didn't tell *me* about it. As a rule, women were trying frantically to get pregnant; some of them had lost other children in the camps, or been worked on by Mengele and didn't know what was left. When I overheard anything about pregnancy as a kid, it was usually that kind of thing. By the end of high school I did of course know that girls got in trouble, and that abortion was one of the things they did about it; in college I knew a few couples who got into that situation. It was all pretty matter-of-fact. I mean it was miserable, but it was no big moral issue. Medically I knew there were certain risks, and by the time I was doing rotations I had a fair sense of what they were, but that didn't prepare me for this little room full of women with perforations or sepsis—"

He broke off. "God, they were sick. You don't see it any more, these massive pelvic infections, enough to leave a woman sterile if she even lived, just desperate illness. This was the mid-sixties; there were pretty safe illegal abortions if you had the money, and even some legal ones if you could convince the hospital you were crazy enough. But if you were sane and didn't have money, or you didn't know where to go ... there was a congressman's daughter who died because she didn't talk to her father, she got some name from a friend and the guy was incompetent. And with poor women that happened a lot more. And it was all so unnecessary. Of course if you look up the congressman's daughter it won't say *abortion* on the death certificate; that's another thing money can buy."

He was looking away, at one of the abstract paintings. "It's sad, of course—pulling a fetus out of its mother and checking to make sure you got it all; sad to be the cause of its death, when a minute ago it was safe and swimming in place in its little sac. One doesn't think of it every time, but it's always true. Nobody likes it: the mother doesn't like it, the doctor doesn't like it, the fetus doesn't like it. The Hippocratic Oath doesn't like it either. So it's unanimous, right? But it's not: women do it even though they don't like it, and they do it a lot. Because what's worse is to give birth when you don't want the child—to have all the resources of your body go to protecting and building up that child when somewhere you profoundly don't consent to it. It's like rape, only it's as far beyond rape as torture is beyond, I don't know, mugging. The despair you saw in these women—good God, in Brooklyn we knew the look of despair. You don't force another human being to go through that. It doesn't matter whether you like her reasons. You don't put her through it.

"Ever read Jean Améry?—né Hans Mayer, actually, but after going through Auschwitz he abandoned his German name and wrote some remarkable essays under his new one. He said the intellect didn't matter a damn in the camps—you became your body, and you were lucky if your body got out alive. Often it only did if you gave up your principles. He says, 'There are situations in which our body is our entire self and our entire fate.' Pregnancy is another of those situations, isn't it? Happily it's a situation you can want, which the other wasn't, but if in fact you don't want it—I'm sorry, are you okay?"

Mim blotted her eyes. "I've read him. I never made that connection. I—the intellect—of course there *is* no connection, pregnancy is the most normal thing in the world, whereas. . . . But there is this sense of just being stolen. Taken out of your place. Thinking was all I knew how to do, and thinking was worthless." The cat was asleep in her lap. "Of course most women lose their intellect long before that; if I'd had any self-preservation I would have too."

"No, you wouldn't," said Morgenzahl. "You've seen some of those kids; you know perfectly well that losing their intellect didn't preserve them."

"I suppose one does tend to envy the wrong people," she said. "But please go on. You saw these women, you saw what was happening to them; and within a few years it was legal?"

"It was in New York; we were the first state, in '70. It all happened very fast. No one was ready: there was no setup, there was no time, nobody knew what they were doing. There was this little underground that knew about the Karman cannula, and a few people willing to do training, but the demand was just overwhelming. A group of us went off to Japan to find out what *they* did—they don't really do contraception in Japan, so they're very good at abortion—and by the time we got back women were converging on the state. It was a crazy time; we were trying to put together a clinic, and trying to train people from upstate, and in the midst of it all Ilene was giving birth to David—she was in her eighth month when I left for Japan, she was furious. When I look back I'm amazed I got through it at all. In fact it was a pretty busy three years, until *Roe* came along and some of the pressure was off.

"We moved up here soon after that. Ilene wanted to get out of the city, and I wanted to get out of the clinic—it was one of those assembly-line places, very depressing—and I wanted a private practice. I thought it would be nice to deliver some babies again. But I was certainly going to keep doing abortions, and gradually it turned out that people were just as happy to send those cases to me. I was better at it than they were, having had all that practice, and also I wasn't an old-timer in these latitudes. It's hard for some of these people to face women they went to high school with, or those women's daughters; they can say very tactless things. As a rootless cosmopolitan I feel no compulsion to do that. So after a few years I thought it made sense to open the clinic, *not* as an assembly line but as a place where you could get whatever you needed relating to sex and pregnancy and be treated like a civilized person. It's a lot to keep in the air at one time—if I had any sense I'd probably give up the obstetrical piece—but that's the part I like best, and it does help remind some of my colleagues that I really am a physician and not a sleazebag. And if not for these wholly uncivilized fanatics, who won't leave me alone—who'd rather shoot me or set fires in my waiting room than lift a finger to really help one of these women—"

Mim sighed. "And here we are back in the present. How sad that it's gone this way. You can have either safety or privacy, I guess: either you risk life and health in complete isolation, or you go to a real doctor with half the world looking on and telling you not to. If the courts would just find a way—"

"Yes; if. And if the federal government would stop playing games with funding for poor women. And if hell would freeze over." He stared morosely at the stack of newspapers. "Well, there's no point in talking about that, is there? I shouldn't be sitting here desponding. I should be offering you a drink, or at least some tea. Would you like—"

"I should be getting home," she said. "Look how late it is. It's all right; you don't have to be a good host. I thought you were just going to hand me the book. I was the one who got you to tell your life story."

They both rose, Mim still holding the cat, who was sleepy and trusting. "Well, I must say it's a nice change," said Morgenzahl quietly. "Most people just want to know how I could do such a thing, or why I would want to look up women's—um, anatomy—all day, and they don't really want any answers. Or how I put up with the controversy, which I don't really know. Here, want me to take him?" he said, reaching for the cat.

"It's a shame just to put him down. He's so happy. What's his name?"

"This? This is Yitz," he said, touching a finger to the cat's pale nose. "He's what, about ten months old. A good kid, on the whole; only he wakes up half an hour before the alarm goes off, and starts playing tag. Here, don't forget this."

She finished zipping her parka and took the book from him. He glanced at their various encumbrances, smiled and shrugged, and pulled her in for a half-hug, kissing the side of her mouth. "Good night. Nice person. Good night."

CHAPTER 7

Mine, O thou lord of life, send my roots rain.

—Gerard Manley Hopkins

Mim stared mutely at several pages of notes. She had been right to dread talking to clergy: the very thought made all her prose soporific. She did not have one line she would be willing to use in a crisis. "The charge of playing God, often leveled at pro-choice advocates . . ." Who, hearing even that much, would want to hear more? "The anti-abortion movement clings to religious language; the pro-choice movement disdains it. The true humility, I think, is on the side of those who will not use God as a slogan, but a principled secularity need not prevent us from . . ." Who, hearing those cadences, would suppose Mim knew a thing about secularity, principled or unprincipled? "If an unintended pregnancy is always God's will, where is the distinction between God and chance?" That was better: at least it was a complete thought, and her language was not so swathed in cotton wool, but why was it so impossible to get from that question to a coherent twenty-minute speech? Was it simply impossible to talk about God if one wasn't singing in Hebrew? Was it impossible to talk about abortion except by telling a story? Was there anything theological or theoretical in this question at all?

She needed real language. The shock troops: Hopkins or Dylan Thomas or James Joyce, someone who would blast her out of the priggish, decorous mind and back into the body. Hopkins, even in prose (she got up and found the little blue paperback) was never anywhere else: even when dissecting the mind he was never anywhere but the body. "When I consider my selfbeing, my consciousness and feeling of myself, that taste of myself, of *I* and *me* above and in all things, which is more distinctive than the taste of ale or alum, more distinctive than the smell of walnutleaf or camphor, and is incommunicable by any means to another man . . . searching nature I taste *self* but at one tankard, that of my own being." And in verse—she turned to the poems, but did not get any farther than the first stanza of the first one before she was stricken with shame.

> *Thou mastering me*
> *God! Giver of breath and bread;*
> *World's strand, sway of the sea;*
> *Lord of living and dead;*
> *Thou hast bound bones and veins in me, fastened me flesh,*
> *And after it almost unmade, what with dread,*
> *Thy doing: and dost thou touch me afresh?*
> *Over again I feel thy finger and find thee.*

It was like a physical pain to read the words; she shook her head slowly, her eyes staring away, her mouth agape and tensed as if on a cry. The man meant it: there was no guile in him, no resistance, only the absolute tension, the instress (his own word) by which God held him in being. Not even the first stirrings of self-protection: that last line, which no modern reader could look at without ribaldry, was written straight and meant to be read so. Not a ribald bone in his body, nor inch of recalcitrant flesh. She was staring at stripped innocence, robust and tempered, the chaste heart naked to the spirit's eye. She could not equal it. Worse: the words turned her back to her past, and she found herself thinking *If this was what Alan wanted, he had no business to love me.*

She had been reading Hopkins long before she knew Alan—since she was nine or ten; one way and another he had been there most of her life. When she was fourteen or so her father had pointed out the homoerotic charge of "lissome scions" and of the boys bathing "with dare and with downdolphinry and bellbright bodies" in water that was the analogue of "spousal love"; before that she had scarcely looked for meaning in the tumble of sounds. Her father enjoyed dismantling the innocence of Christian poets (and, perhaps, of his daughter): even younger, she remembered him smirking at the prospect of teaching Herbert's "Love Bade Me Welcome" to freshman. *"You must sit down, sayes Love, and taste my meat: So I did sit and eat.* If you were one of the Love Generation—or even a boneheaded jock—what would *you* think of?" At twelve, Mim hadn't known, and her father had been a little abashed and had not explained; but the lesson was clear, that a double entendre (whatever it might mean) displaced all other meanings. Whatever seemed innocent and merciful concealed some Freudian slip, or else some outright ignorance of the ways of the world, for which one had to look with keen suspicion. After that the dark suspicions of feminism, that femininity and family were themselves modes of ignorance—that even innocence and mercy were the daylight terms of some sordid double entendre—had come easily to her. (Perhaps the most recent and most necessary pattern of suspicion, indeed, would not have been possible to her without the first two: the double entendre of Christian mercy was Jewish history.) What had Alan seen in her—or she in Alan—after that training?

No, that was not fair: she knew what she had seen in him. Relief, a respite from compulsive lewdness, a chance at intellectual virginity even if it coincided with her bodily initiation. She had wanted the simple sensation of uninterrupted trust. And in a sense—at a price—she had had it, with a man whose principled innocence had increased the force of his sexuality. One didn't talk about Hopkins' homoerotic charge to Alan—or only once, and hesitantly, and he replied, "Yes, but the main thing is that he restrained it." A terrible, perdurable male chastity, next to which her own repose in her body seemed an accident of youth, finite and perishable. But as soon as she understood the workings of sex she had known it was not corruption: it was candescence, levitation, eroticism and purity at once.

But Alan was not at ease with that combination. He was delighted with her forthrightness and joy—the early loss of innocence had at least left her with no inhibitions—but he could not sustain his delight: he seemed to mistrust it or to resist its power. He loved to give her pleasure, but when her pleasure (or his own) rose to a certain height he was frightened by it and drew back. When her mood was calm he was reverent and wondering, and marvelously tender; when her mood was voracious he would try to make her calm, and when (a few times) she managed to change his mood to hers he was troubled afterwards, as if he had done violence to her. "You don't regret, Mira—?" he said once. "This incursion of the body on the soul?" "Oh, no," she had answered, glowing with bone-deep satiety, "Alan, it *is* the soul. Carnality *is* incarnation." Of course he had not liked that way of putting it, and had said nothing; she could see him trying to work out in his mind whether she was wanton. She had no brassy pornographic habits of movement, but since those habits are merely exaggerated and codified versions of the spontaneous motions of desire, he seemed to see in her a sort of innocent brazenness, like Eve just reaching for the apple. Just the other side of innocence from him, but it was too far: the little distance between them was the fence between the garden and the wilderness.

    She closed the book. She would have to come back to it later, when Hopkins could be hers again and not Alan's. There were other books on the table—Aquinas, Noonan on the Catholic doctrine of contraception, Feldman on the Jewish laws of sex and marriage, Harrison on the feminist ethic of abortion—but the one she picked up was the one Bob had just lent her, the political tract on disillusion. Idly she turned its pages. The paper had a comforting smell of old book: it smelled like the library stacks. Its prose was dreadful. "The real cleavage," she read (oh Lord, the pitfalls of language!), "lies not between those who approve of birth control but not of abortion, or those who want divorce but not too much divorce; it lies always and in every sex question between those who have known and loved sexual experience and those who have not." She wondered sadly which category she fell into. Could you love sexual experience with someone who found it disturbing? Perhaps in the end there was no other choice—there was so much to be disturbed about in sex that one or the other of you was always bound to be making some difficulty—but it was years since she had been willing to make the experiment. The disaster with Alan had confirmed in her what she now began to see as a pattern of sexual hesitancy—a fear not of the experience itself but of everything it took to have the experience, the absolute risk of one's future and one's equanimity to someone who might not use them well. The ecstatic part of sex was easy enough to supply for oneself; the more complicated ecstasy of seeing oneself discovered in another's eyes, and discovering another, was more difficult to come by. (Her practiced ear caught the possible double entendre of the last phrase, and she angrily let it stand: who could keep track of them all?) And without that tentative and compulsive mutual discovery, sex was simply not worth the hazard.

In another sense she was always discovering and being discovered; she was doing it with Morgenzahl right now, helpless to stop herself. Nothing was easier, as soon as the intellect came into play, than to light up, to respond eagerly to the other's slightest move, to make one's own moves confident of the other's quick response. The intellectual attraction between them could ignite the physical any time they let it. But why let it? Conversation at that pitch was always partly erotic: she had understood that early in life, from her father and later from a succession of college professors who were equally extravagant talkers, and nothing was clearer than that one could not always act on the attraction. She had accustomed herself to not acting on it; with men her own age her recurrent mistake had been to think one could talk at that pitch, even about the nature of the erotic, without going to bed with the person one was talking to. A man in her circle of friends in college had told her she was lucky not to be raped; another old friend she had gone out with after her divorce had called her an intellectual cockteaser and refused to see her again. Bob Morgenzahl was made of sterner stuff—perhaps his work had taught him the hazards of insistence—but clearly the time was coming when he would want both kinds of conversation. And would she? Did one have to act on the attraction, sooner or later? Was every man, however improbable, at one level merely a sort of pheromonal signal, calling forth the matching signal in her whether she wanted to send it or not? Was every conversation between a man and a woman essentially a sort of predatory search?

Once she had overheard the clerks in Acquisitions, just outside her office, talking about men; Faye, the newest unmarried member of the section, had said she was "waiting to meet . . . *him*," and two or three of the others, married and unmarried alike (she could picture them putting their heads together and rolling their eyes), had immediately chorused, "*Himmm*." Carolyn, Mim's own age and also divorced, had slid in the door an instant later, shuddering histrionically and brushing imaginary cooties off her sleeve. But if you had heterosexual leanings at all, there it was: every man you met was not simply a personality but perforce a Yes or a No.

Morgenzahl looked unnervingly like a Yes; when she was with him she found herself inflecting every word and gesture with special force, as if his own force of character deserved to be met with nothing less. She had moved and talked with that much force before, but mostly on the speaker's platform—as if it took a whole crowd to muster the energy that he could produce with one look, to call forth the corresponding energy in her. What would it be like to live at such intensity all the time? Perhaps exhausting, like being perpetually on stage. But perhaps profoundly satisfying, the actor before her right audience, alert and uncompromising, making the strict and subtle choices of one who is intelligently seen. Who was it that had said, at the death of his friend, "The theater of all my actions is dead"? Imagine, Mim thought, one's actions having a theater.

Alan had been an attentive audience, but he had been anxious about what kind of play it was: he had wanted a morality play, or at least a comedy in which all ended well without unsettling too many of the audience's morals, and instead had suspected that he was getting some inconclusive modern script in which one could not tell the gender of the characters and the symbolism was obscure and the plot turned on events that did not seem to be events. What would be possible with an audience that did not fear the play?

At the end of that week the weather warmed. There had not been much snow that winter, but there was enough to cover the grass and pack tight on the sidewalks; its melting caused great steaming fogs and a pungent smell of pine. Mim's office did not have a window, but she opened

Cedric's window surreptitiously while he was out, and took great gulps of moist air and listened to the river.

There was a choral concert that weekend at the music department: the students in the January intensive term presenting their work. As it happened, there were only five abortions scheduled for that Saturday, so Mim was not needed at the clinic; she went to services with the little university minyan she had recently discovered (which met in the basement of a Congregational church) and stayed for lunch and study. In the course of the discussion it turned out that at least half the group called themselves atheists—the Torah reader and the woman with the good voice who had led the service and the man leading the study session who had brought all the interesting books. Nobody turned a hair. Mim was exalted: these were people insistently drawn to prayer, people in love with the old texts, who yet refused to capitulate to the usual terms of belief. She resolved to begin the formal conversion process, and spent the afternoon reading a book on the Sabbath. In the evening she met Morgenzahl at her favorite restaurant, downstairs from her apartment, and they went on from there to the concert.

She had not seen him on her home ground before: it was like a collision of worlds. Her senses were sharpened, as if she could not quite believe them. She felt exposed before the staff of the restaurant, uncloseted even to the campus trees. Simply to hear his voice in these surroundings was disorienting, as if the sounds of one geography had been imposed on another. He, of course, did not feel it, and strode on talking happily about a new Mozart record he had found. But she had seen their waitress blush, as if she had met him before under painful circumstances, and she wondered how many other women heard that voice with a sense of disorientation. The angel of death, civilized and humane in a tweed coat. *Who by strangling and who by stoning, who by suction and who by sepsis, who by a bullet and who of a broken heart.* For the women who had gone to him, his unexpected appearance must bring back the whole air of the disaster, just as for the protestors he must move surrounded by a cloud of little ghosts. She shivered; she took his arm.

Cedric and his wife Elise were at the concert. Cedric, who had no diplomacy, started visibly at seeing Mim in male company (or perhaps in that particular company; there was no telling what Cedric knew). Doubtless he would have some flaying remark for her on Monday. She smoothly made the introductions, with an inward sense of unholy glee as if she were mixing some explosive compound. *You thought all I was good for was to process your words. Now you know.* She identified the odd feeling she had had when she first saw Morgenzahl in street clothes, on Yom Kippur: it was *prestige*, the heady vanity of being seen with a nicely dressed man. She wished she had a new coat instead of her three-year-old parka. Then she was furious: Good God! Were twenty years of feminism as nothing beside the powerful lure of appearances? Did she give a damn how he dressed, as long as he talked like a thinker? Was anything more contemptible than feeling like one half of a handsome couple? Her anger distracted her, and he noticed and looked at her curiously. "What's making you monosyllabic?" he said. "It's not like you." But the concert was about to begin, so she did not have to answer; perhaps by intermission they would both have forgotten.

It was a good choir: Mim's mother had worked with both kinds, and Mim knew what to look for. Fifty people worked as one eye, that stayed trained on the director even as it read the difficult passages in the music; as one lung, filling for the attack, emptying slowly and with control, separating during the long lines back into fifty pairs of lungs that staggered their breathing so seamlessly she could barely detect it. Like a colony of Volvox, those microscopic animals that live in spheres, functioning as a unit though they were all separate beings. Mim wondered for the thousandth time why she had not followed her mother's profession: why music, though she knew her way around it, had always seemed to her a freemasonry from which she was excluded.

They sang a short Bach cantata—B.W.V. 50, about the casting out of Lucifer from heaven; a psalm (the 24th) by Lili Boulanger; John Tavener's settings of Blake's "The Lamb" and "The Tyger", and some interesting and disturbing settings by Carl Orff of some Franz Werfel poems. They did a jazz piece which must in its early stages have been improvised; during this one a manic beeping broke out in the seat beside her, and Morgenzahl hastily silenced it and during the applause stole out in search of a phone. They did a Te Deum by Britten and an Ars Antiqua motet by Perotin. It was all strong, demanding stuff, and that made it the more surprising when the encore turned out to be a simple setting of the old Scots ballad "Ca' the Yowes tae the Knowes." (Yowes, the director explained, were ewes, and knowes were hillocks.) One of those achingly pure modal choruses, with big open chords and just enough modulation in the last line to remind the audience that this was a modern setting. The movement of the choir's voices was limpid and tender. The verses were sung by soloists—in the personae of shepherd and shepherdess—in a free rhythm that the choir followed expertly with soft humming. But what verses! Robert Burns had had a hand in them, the director said, and Mim could believe it; there were very few flies on Robert Burns. The shepherd began with a gentle invitation:

> *Will ye gae doon the waterside*
> *An' see the streams sae sweetly glide*
> *Beneath the hazel spreadin' wide?*
> *The moon it shines fu' clearly.*

The young woman met these fond overtures—in the same melting tune—with a slap of practicality:

> *I was bred up in nae sic school,*
> *My shepherd lad, tae play the fool,*
> *A' the day tae sit in dule*
> *Wi' naebody tae hear me.*

Thus rebuffed, he answered unprotesting in the same kind, with practicality:

> *Ye sall get rings and ribands meet,*
> *Calf leather shoon upon yer feet,*
> *An' in my airms ye'll lie an' sleep,*
> *An' ye sall be my dearie.*

And she, with sturdy tenderness, replied,

> *If ye'll but staund tae what ye've said,*
> *I'll gang wi' you, my shepherd lad,*
> *An' ye sall roll me in yer plaid,*
> *An' I sall be yer dearie.*

Instead of courtship, a bargaining session; instead of requited love, a warranty. Or rather, no distinction in their minds between the love and the bargain: the shepherd's willingness to provide for his lover (and for the eventual child, so obliquely referred to as the cause of "dule") *was* his love, and the shepherdess's flintily conditional consent was her earnest of being his "dearie." Mim nearly laughed aloud. *This* was romance, this was pastoral, when all was said and done: the heterosexual contract. I will love you, genuinely love you, if you will put your money where your mouth is; that is the measure of your care. If not, nothing doing. The same bitter terms as in the church and the right-to-life movement and for that matter all Western literature back to *Medea*. Love is not the streams and the moon, or heat and sweetness and nerve-endings: it's the long-term willingness to shoulder the consequences, and don't you forget it. "He's buying her!" she said to Morgenzahl afterward. "My God, no wonder people made such a rigid distinction between marriage and prostitution in the old days: you can barely tell the difference."

"I *think* this was marriage," he said. "At least, that business of rolling her in his cloak comes up in the Bible as a pledge. Ruth asks Boaz to do it after she uncovers his—well, feet—on the threshing floor in the middle of the night. And in Ezekiel God finds Jerusalem as an abandoned infant, all over blood with the navel-cord still uncut, and makes sure she lives to grow up, and when he comes back and finds her grown to nubility he spreads his robe over her nakedness and betroths himself to her. Of course it ends badly; as soon as she has nice clothes she goes a-whoring with the Egyptians, and God becomes jealous and abusive, and the rest, as it were, is history. But it bears thinking about: God rolling Israel in his plaid and promising everything."

"Why didn't he just turn himself into a swan? He could have had her for free."

"Mim! Rape is for goyim. He really wanted a marriage. Did she come looking for him? Did Abraham think up the covenant? No: it was all God's notion, and he knew how risky it was. Have you run into that bit on Sinai, after he puts Moses in the cleft of the rock and tells him his thirteen attributes? He says, 'It's a terrible thing I'm about to do to you.' It had to be marriage; otherwise she might have got away."

"You missed your calling," she said. "You ought to be teaching the Bible to adolescents."

Without thinking about it they had started walking; the sidewalks were clear, with little runnels of water trickling across them, and the night air was cool and damp. "Do you have time for this?" she said. "What was the beeper about? Is it a labor or a complication?"

"It's all right," he said. "It was one of the women from this morning, worried about bleeding, but I think she's okay. There's no fever, and everything looked complete in the lab. Mostly she's scared, I think. Banerji is at the ER tonight if she needs help, but I doubt that she will. Don't worry."

They walked on toward the sound of the river. "I'm surprised how uneasy covenants make me," Mim said. "The one between God and Israel is scarier than the one between the shepherd and the shepherdess—I *think*—but with both it's simply a deal. You come across with this and I'll reward you. And the shepherdess saying, I don't come across *unless* you reward me. (Israel is easier, come to think of it: she doesn't set any conditions, the people just stand there at the foot of the mountain saying *We will do and we will hear*. Maybe that accounts for her constant unfaithfulness—she doesn't know how to hold out.) It just seems cagey and calculating at a moment when mutual consent is all you need."

"But consent to what? You've got to know that. You're both going to be disastrously hurt if you don't. It's the question of children, of course, partly—in real life, I mean, not in the Torah—do you want them, and when, and who's going to pay for their upkeep, and what do you do if you get one without intending to, and is it a disgrace to have them at all. And the other question of permanence, and how you can promise it, and whether you can trust the promises if you've seen them go wrong before. I don't know, I guess I believe in covenants. They don't always work—you can't second-guess everything—but they're better than nothing."

"Maybe," she said. "But I hate the way someone always seems to have the upper hand. God says, You belong to me but only on these terms; the shepherdess says, I belong to *you* but only on these terms. What happened to simple belonging? Can't there ever be a mutual covenant? Like that line in the Yom Kippur liturgy, 'We are your chosen and you are our chosen'? Can't both parties ever mean well at once?"

"Not in the long term," he said. "Not in my experience so far. How about yours?"

"No, not in mine either," she said. They had come to a little bridge, where the river came out of the woodlot; she leaned dejectedly on the rail. "No, Alan set all the terms really—until suddenly I found that I had to, covertly and desperately. Nothing mutual there. But what could I have done? Refused his terms altogether? Told him, I belong to you but only at the price of your faith? I couldn't. I couldn't. The most contemptible form of playing hard-to-get."

The water was high with snowmelt, heavily moving; puffs of foam drifted along the surface, spinning against the banks. "So you belonged to him at the price of your better judgment," he said. "No wonder you're hard to get now."

She looked at him in utter confusion. "Am I?"

"Sure," he said easily. "You said it yourself, the other night—I heard you—'There are prices I won't pay.' What could be clearer? You paid too high a price to begin with; you're not going to do that again. You talk a wonderful line about mutual consent and free agency, but if you see anything short of that you're not going to be tempted for an instant. The most powerful terms in the world: absolute trust or nothing."

"But they're not terms at all," she protested. "I'm not ungettable: anybody could get me who wanted to, if—I'm not saying nobody's good enough for me; I want to be good enough for *them*, and I can't if there's no—Damn it, you try to be what somebody needs, and all the time you're being backed into playing this hideous game of advantage; surely it's better just to stay out of the running, unless—"

She heard herself and stopped. He laughed one grain of sardonic laugh. "See?" He leaned next to her on the railing, looking down into the dark. Under their feet, the water slid away from them.

After a while he spoke. "The game plays you, I think," he said. "I don't know a way around it; it's anatomy, and destiny, and all that familiar stuff. We try to break the pattern, over and over, and just when we think we've circumvented it we find that we're trapped again. Birth control, abortion, open marriage, feminism, they're all attempts to solve this agony between men and women, and it won't solve. No wonder the antis, who believe in being trapped, are so angry. Walking into the trap doesn't solve it either."

"No," she said. "I suppose you're right; I suppose everything is part of the bargaining, whether we like it or not. But I wish to God it weren't so; it means that friendship between men and women is never possible, or is possible only when love isn't, and that you constantly have to defend yourself from the person you're closest to. That's no way to live."

"No, it isn't," he said. "Don't I know it; several times over by now." He stared away at the river bank. "Of course," he added, "sleeping with the enemy isn't the only way to handle these problems."

"I know it," she said. "But I've never found the right woman either."

There was a difficult silence. The conversation had turned a corner while Mim was not watching; she saw that she had just told him, in the space of five minutes, everything one should not tell a man. Again she had the sense of sending him signals whether she wanted to or not, and she moved uneasily and wondered if that too were a signal. He gave another faint snort of laughter beside her, and something under her ribs received it, powerfully as a blow and summarily as the shutting of a box: she wanted to send him signals. There was a tone in that laugh that drew her, a total disillusionment without any loss of intelligence or kindness: as if even in the face of repeated failure he did not despair, as if some equanimity underlay all disappointments and meant more to him, finally, than even the defense of his own interests. A contract with him, of whatever duration and at whatever level, would be something more interesting than a trap. She looked up questioningly, to find out the reason for the laugh. "Mm?"

A PORTABLE EGYPT

He jerked his head toward the sky; his eyes signaled complicity against some trick of the universe. "Look at the moon." It rode half-high and a little lopsided, hazy and lucent as an out-of-focus pearl. "Oh, my," she said. "Don't they ever get tired of coincidence up there?"

But a little tremor started in her body, as if all her bones shook. She felt him look at her, and she looked back; he was familiar, not frightening, the penetrating eyes, the wry mouth, and her eyes softened as she looked at him. She saw his do the same. She smiled, in a warmer and more trusting complicity, and turned her face up; his at once bent down. He kissed her, briefly at first—affection, soft dry lips, a zone of warm air around him—and then again, long enough for her to learn the smell of his face and the texture of his beard, and for each of them to feel tentatively muscle against muscle as their mouths turned minutely on each other. She felt the inrush of blood to the root of her body, subtly and faintly like the buzz of an electric field, and drew back: too much sensation all at once, too sudden a remembrance of forgotten joy. She turned back to the railing, her eyes withdrawn, stunned at how quickly daring turned to reticence.

Again she felt him look at her, and gradually understood that he was anxious. She had drawn back too quickly: was she afraid, offended, repelled? She had not lost daring altogether; she looked at him again, and rose to language.

"I won't ask you what you meant by it."

"Yes, you will."

CHAPTER 8

> Words are the salve with which we heal the wounds inflicted on us by our actions.
>
> —Quentin Crisp

"Mim, can we talk?"

His voice was tired and peculiarly contrite; he sounded as if he had barely slept. It had been a difficult parting. Daring had deserted her at the end of the evening: standing by his car in the lit parking lot behind her building, the air perfused with pizza and ripe dumpster, she clinging with both hands to one of his, shaking her head and refusing another kiss. She had not slept well herself. She had dreamed of praying in the synagogue on Sabbath morning, her hand stroking the pages of the prayerbook, smoothing the letters as her body swayed back and forth, while over the hum of prayer a voice cried out an old denunciation of Hasidic worship. "They move their bodies back and forth as in the act of union. They say one must be potent at the time of prayer, to unite with the Shekhinah. So aroused are they by this union that they squander their seed." She woke and slept again, and dreamed of her father laughing at a poem she wrote. "A philosopher, not a poet, kiddo, no question. Stick to dependence." Again she woke and slept, and dreamed of Alan in a priest's robe, putting wafers into the mouths of the kneeling faithful, and when she stood apart and refused to kneel he came to her and put a tiny curled fetus in her hand. Dawn came, and she got up and tried to read: a page and a half of the morning service laboriously in Hebrew, the first act of *The Tempest*, and an old nurse novel for little girls, until the phone rang.

"Whenever you want," she said. "Now? Of course now. Come over for breakfast."

The last collision: his presence at her door and at her table. His eyes, she had never noticed, were a mid-grey, lighter than hers. She gave him French toast and coffee and half a grapefruit. "Mim, I'm sorry," he said. "I said a stupid thing, and I don't want you to feel pushed into some obligation towards me out of pride or a sense of fairness. You don't owe me anything."

"You're very kind," she said. "But what did you say that was stupid? I don't think I caught it; I must be stupid too."

"No, you're not; you're a forgiving person, blotting out my transgressions. I said you were hard to get. I was just stealing your words, but it came out all wrong; I knew it as soon as I said it. I'm not trying to get you. Or rather," he said, with a glimmer of his usual self, "I'd like very much to, but not in that grabby way. I'm not going to bother you."

"You don't bother me," she said, feeling unequal to the occasion. "It was mostly that terrible song. All the mechanisms of the trap right out in the open, and nowhere to go but straight into it."

"Yes; no more approach-avoidance, no more pretending these questions don't have to be faced. It's such a hard moment. You either go on . . . or you stop."

He looked at her sadly. She thought of not going to concerts, not going to the clinic, not hearing his voice. "I don't want to stop."

"You're sure?"

"Well—I'd really miss talking. Do you dare—with someone you can talk to—"

His posture subtly relaxed. "No. *I* don't. I'm glad you don't. But there's so much that can get in the way-—if you go on."

"You mean anatomy and destiny."

"Well, yes. All those questions of children, and permanence, and dominance—things that as friends we don't have to ask each other, but as lovers we'd have to answer, and might answer differently." He tilted his coffee mug, staring into its depths. "It's all so uncertain. You pay a heavy price for someone to talk to. You pay a heavy price for sex. Sometimes you pay one for the other, and can't talk to the person you make love to or can't make love to the person you talk to. And you never know which it's going to be until it happens."

She searched his face for a sign. "Are you sure you want to go on, then? Hadn't we better try to get out of the trap?"

"Sure," he said dryly. "You gnaw on my leg and I'll gnaw on yours, and we'll limp off together into the sunset. Is that an escape or not? It's hard to be sure."

Mim had not been expecting to laugh; it came out in a squeak. "You're good company in a trap," she said. "That must count for something. I don't know; it's a risk, but I'm tired of not taking risks. But you may be tired of taking them."

"I'm—" His look became abstracted, and he sighed. "It's just been a long time. Of trying and failing, I mean. So much is just luck. Who's ready for what at what point, and what kind of attraction is enough for the long term, and—well, I don't want to bore you with all my sad stories."

"Why not?" she said. "You know my whole sexual history, such as it is; I don't mind hearing yours. As much of it as you want to tell me, I mean; I don't insist on hearing it, either. I just—if you're trying to get me, I'd like to know how ambivalently."

He focused again, surprised. "Oh!" he said. "My God, I'm not ambivalent about *you;* I'm ambivalent about the whole setup. Who isn't? No, if you're gettable I'm trying to get you with absolute singlemindedness. Only . . . I don't know how to speak for the long term any more."

"Well, I'm not sure I do either. Perhaps we don't have to decide that all at once." She waited encouragingly. "Tell me about luck."

He thought and sighed, and made a couple of false starts. "Ilene and I—there's no reason go into all the details, which will no doubt unfold unpleasantly enough as the need arises, but . . . well, essentially we got together to play grownup. This was the very end of the old days, when you married somebody you kind of liked in order to have a family, and of course to legitimize going to bed with them, which you'd started a little bit early while pretending not to, and . . . and you had no idea of how much you needed to like each other to keep going over the long term. We had different notions of what being a grownup was, and no sense of how to talk about it; we couldn't learn on each other. We didn't have the vocabulary, we didn't have anything but hormones when I look back on it. And it took us fifteen years of sniping to figure it out, this George and Martha routine . . . God, I really think we were casualties of the old dispensation. It was better—even for the kids, though of course they don't think so—for us to stop living that way."

Mim nodded and waited.

"I was so tired after we split up—just glad to be alone, though I missed the kids terribly and my whole private life had disappeared. I just read and listened to music and worked and slept. It was a couple of years before I even wanted to look for somebody else. I mean, I indulged in this sort of compulsive flirtation with the whole clinic staff, but it was shallow and silly and nobody ever took me up on it. I'm amazed they didn't take me to court. I suppose I looked so pathetic they could see there was nothing in it.

"And then when I did start looking . . . I mean, I can do the dating routine and find it enjoyable, but it's such a weird mixture of total self- . . . self-*offering*, and almost total withholding. You sit there speculating on how this person would be to live with for the next thirty years, and at the same time you might not call her next week; and she's doing the same to you, only forming some definite opinion on whether she's desperate to see you again or really dreading it. And there's such desperation—there are a lot of Jewish women around looking for Jewish men, or maybe more accurately for the means to have a Jewish family, and there's this whole mission in life that they need you for; there they are waiting to start it, and here you are being choosy about personalities. It puts you in the position . . . I mean, all this is supposed to have changed, but there you are acting like some sultan, saying this one's not pretty and that one doesn't read the right books, and this one's voice is too grating, and this one seems so depressed, and how can you live with yourself after too much of that? And then, did I want to have another family?—just make more kids to replace the first ones, as if that would compensate? I really didn't know. On the other hand, did I have the right *not* to when one woman after another was clearly hoping for that, and couldn't live the life she wanted without it? Bad enough that I do what I do, here I am aborting *wanted* babies by not being willing—"

Mim shuddered. "You can't take it that far. It's like those people who say the womb cries every month if it isn't pregnant."

"I know, I know. Rationally, I do know that. But, you know, there you are—you see women all day who are desperate not to have children, and then in the evening you go out with women who are desperate to have them, and everybody's getting exactly what they don't want, and it's so hard to bear. Finally I just took my name off the list. I developed this Portnovian reflex against the whole Jewish dating scene. I . . . it's kind of embarrassing to say this to *you*, all things considered, but it was such a relief to go out with non-Jewish women—to go out with them because I met them and liked them, and not necessarily to think about living with them for the next thirty years. Or if I did, not to have Abraham, Isaac and Jacob breathing down my neck while I thought about it. To get away from that burden. Of course there was a level at which we could never connect, but that didn't bother me; at the time I almost preferred it."

Mim nodded, interested; she had heard of this phenomenon before, but always from Jewish women and in the bitterest terms. "Did they see it that way?" she said. "Or were they looking to get married too? They may have been desperate for their own reasons."

"Well, the pattern was rather different. Non-Jewish women in their thirties and forties—those who were willing to be seen with me—tended not to want marriage or kids. That's liberation: all they had to worry about was their own choices, the conduct of their own lives, not what their ancestors wanted of them. I imagine the ones who wanted marriage would have wanted a kind of normalcy I couldn't supply. After all, if all you can get is an abortion doctor who's tearing apart the fabric of society . . . there was just more of a chill with some non-Jewish women when they found out what I did. They couldn't show me off to the folks."

"But that wasn't all of them, obviously."

"No, not at all. And there were two that I—got seriously involved with; not for very good reasons, but when you're lonely enough you don't really need good reasons. Or maybe *you* do, being a strongminded woman, but I didn't, and they didn't. One of them you may even know; she teaches some rarefied form of lit. crit. at the university, and is having some success with her curiously named new book—"

"My God, not Cleo Seldane?" This was one of Laura's colleagues, a cadaverous and flamboyantly dressed woman (she must, Mim realized belatedly, be one of Sarita's customers) who had recently published a book of postmodern criticism called *Penile Dementia*, to some public outcry. "I had no idea. I see her sometimes in the library; of course she doesn't see me. Are you in the book? What's she like?—no, that isn't fair. Don't answer."

"She's all right," he said. "Not very companionable—too busy working on her persona—but a brilliant thinker in that convoluted, punning sort of way. No, I'm not in the book, but that section on the semiotics of the fetus was stuff she tried out on me. As you can imagine, it wasn't the sort of relationship that could last long; someone who thinks of herself as mercurial isn't going to stick to one person. She's getting to be well regarded, and even in my time that meant taking up with sundry opportunists at the MLA conference. It was a problem. I tried not to be jealous, but one doesn't know where they've been. I worry about her."

"I worry about *you*," said Mim, blanching. "Have you—did you—"

"I am thoroughly clean," he said gently. "I am not one to trifle with viruses. You don't think I would offer—"

"No," she said, "no, of course not. And I know how careful you are at work. But the thought of—and my God, you've had transfusions . . . the world's such a dangerous place."

"The transfusions were clean too," he said. "The blood supply is all right. Mim, sweetie, I wouldn't—"

"No," she said again, "no, you wouldn't. I'm sorry; I know; it's just panic."

"Of course. That's all right."

"So you were saying. There was Cleo and someone else."

"Yes. And I won't tell you the other one's name yet, if you don't mind, because I don't think she'd want me to. It was complicated. She's a lesbian, and she'd gotten nostalgic for men; politically speaking that's not supposed to happen, but it does, and she'd been sort of quietly looking. Enormously flattering to be chosen out from the mass of men for such a purpose. Though of course rather utilitarian too. But she was very troubled about it all—afraid it would interfere with her art, afraid she'd get servile, finally I think ashamed—well, of wanting . . . *like a fish needs a bicycle,* you know. And I—it didn't bring out the best in me: there was this awful sense of dependency, my own desperation. Trying to convince her I was worth wanting. I'm pretty good at civilized manners, as I hope you've discerned, but I had some bad lapses. She decided it was better to stop."

"Ah, I'm sorry. It sounds very painful." She reached for his hand across the table and held it.

"Well, I—it made me serious at a new level," he said. "That a woman would risk so much for a physical act that she missed and a man that she liked, and then just decide no, the risk isn't worth it: it's terrifying to be in the presence of that much purpose. I mean, even apart from my own feelings. One of the last things she said to me was that just to live, we have to give up necessities: we don't choose between wholeness and mutilation, we choose between mutilation and death. Self-actualization isn't even in the picture."

There was a silence. "And then," she said, trying to be diverting but feeling merely clumsy and obvious, "this little secretary shows up and puts scholars and artists to shame."

He sighed and came back to the present. "Mim, you're no secretary: you're a prophet evading her calling, incognita among the denizens of Tarshish. Come out from behind your smokescreen. Your job isn't you."

"Maybe not. But how did you see what *was* me? I walked into your hospital room and dissolved in a puddle; I was a mess."

"Oh, that; I see that all the time. That's not so important. In a sense you were asking for help, and that's simply practical; one can get it out of the way. And there was this undercurrent—as if you were saying *I'll make it so interesting for you to help me, you won't even think it's work.* This irresistible mind."

Mim took this in, with a sense of exposure. "In the dark all minds are grey," she said. "Is that good enough for the long term? People don't stay helped; they revert to being themselves. What if you have to keep helping and helping me, and we settle into some treadmill of love as therapy, where you always know best and I'm always two steps behind? That's how I lived with Alan. I won't do that again."

He was distressed. "Oh, Mim. God forbid. No, of course not. I don't think it's ever one-sided. It's one of those things, it's sort of like sex, you know, where if you stop to analyze who's on top and who's sticking what into whom what percentage of the time it can make you crazy, but while it goes on it's just—*daat,* as it's called in Genesis. Knowledge. You know what each other wants—at best, anyway—and you give it, and what each of you really wants is the other to want you. You think you don't help me? My God, everything that went wrong between Ilene and me in conversation goes right with you; there's this sort of mutual agreement on the deep structure."

She had never attached an erotic meaning to a linguistic term; she did now. "I wasn't sure," she said. "You seem so self-sufficient."

"All an act," he said. "All the thinnest integument on a raw mass of quivering need. I'd do—well, *almost* anything for you. Tell me what you want in your covenant, and I will deliver. Calf-leather shoon, marriage, children—or no marriage and no children, if that's what you want—an account with my favorite Judaica book dealer, any enticement and any security I can possibly offer. I'd better add that I hope you never want to keep kosher, but if you do I promise not to be rude about it; I'll just sneak out quietly for the occasional orgy of shrimp. I believe this is what's called midlife crisis."

Mim laughed: he couldn't even make an avowal without giving it a codicil of wicked irony. "Bob, you won't have to—" She reached for his hand again; then she found that tears had sprung to her eyes, and sniffled, trying to contain them. By reflex he looked around for the kleenex, and they both collapsed into laughter: sorrow and hysteria and love and dread all at once. She could not say anything rational. "Damn it, I can't call you Bob. Bob and Mim, Mim and Bob, these two monosyllabic palindromes, there's something so silly about it. What's your Hebrew name?"

"What?" he said, disoriented, still laughing. "Aryeh. Aryeh ben Mordecai. You can't call me that either. What is this all about?"

"Palindromes are treacherous," she quavered. "You're liable to start thinking ABLE WAS I ERE I SAW ELBA, or A MAN, A PLAN, A CA-

NAL—PANAMA, or—or STEP ON NO PETS, at the most inopportune moments. I'm trying to look ahead." She lost her voice entirely and lay whimpering among the plates; he got up and crouched beside her and stroked her back.

"You all right now?" he said presently. "Here, let's go sit somewhere soft. You don't have to give me an answer."

They sat, half-facing each other, on her small couch in the living room. He rested one hand between her shoulderblades, and with the other took the ends of her hair and dried her eyes. He kissed her a few times, comfortingly; at first she responded, but again responding so stirred her that she traveled too quickly beyond comfort. "I'm sorry," she said, "I can't take very much of this at once. It's a while since anyone's kissed me."

He smiled; it was a new smile, supremely confident as always but stripped of defenses, unguarded. "If you'd like to get used to it," he said, "it can be arranged. But never before you're ready; there's no need to hurry—until you say so. We can wait as long as you want."

Mim looked away: "until" struck her with all the force of an awakened imagination, and she hoped he did not see her blush. If these were the wiles of an expert seducer, there was something to be said for expertise. She spoke in a cracked voice, unwillingly. "I don't want to wait."

His look became simply defenseless. "My God, you're right," he said. "You're not hard to get. Do you want—how soon are we talking? I thought you just said—"

Her voice would not clear. "I did. I don't mean right this instant. But as soon as—as soon as . . . I want to have something reliable—"

"Of course," he said. "Always. I'll never do to you what he did. Do you want me to bring you—"

"I'll go to my doctor at work. For heaven's sake, Bob, you're not going to examine me."

The thought was sobering enough—or surreal enough—that it broke the mood; they relaxed and sat back. "There's that palindrome again," he said.

"Don't you like Aryeh?" she said, grateful for his tact. "I do; it's homelike somehow. *Heymish,* is that the word? What about Ari? Would you hate that as much?"

"I don't hate it," he said. "It just feels like another life. The only time anyone used it was when I was called to the Torah, which hasn't happened since—well, since David's bar mitzvah, actually, but I haven't made a habit of it in a good thirty years. You can try Ari if you want, and see if I'll answer to it. Though it's fraught with association: notably *the* Ari, the great kabbalist Isaac Luria, who's well out of my league. That's wordplay too—an unusually exalted acronym meaning *the godly Rabbi Yitzchak,* and I don't know what that has to do with me."

"We'll find something else for it to stand for—something ungodly if you like. But I'll know what it really is. Ari ben Mordecai, master of *daat.*"

She had actually rendered him silent: he shook his head with a baffled smile, and said nothing at all. Then they reached for each other again, and this time she found that the arousal was containable, that she could endure a long minute as they joined the tips of their tongues, neither probing further, and maintained themselves in slow play on the edge of the first circle of liquidity. Then her deep muscle throbbed once, and she let his mouth go, her head bending slowly away from him, her eyes blind.

"I'd better leave, hadn't I?" he said. "You really do need some time."

No, that's not it, she thought, *I need you to—*But she could not frame the words even to herself, so perhaps he was right. "It's not fair to you," she said. "Having admitted I want to, I should just—"

"Not till you're ready," he said. "Mim, I've been living for months in the hope of that very admission. I can wait a little longer for the thing itself."

She held his hand; ran her thumb over the little hairs on the back of it. "I've been waiting for years."

He tilted his head, trying to catch her eye. "Why?" he said. "You're an incredibly sexy woman, once you make up your mind to it. Why did you take all this time to make up your mind to it? You said you'd had opportunities."

"Oh," she said, unable to think quite coherently, "it was luck again,

I suppose. I mean not having the right luck. They all seemed so un . . . unformed, or uncomplicated, after what I'd been through with Alan." She tried to think back: the old friends, and the men from the library, the faltering conversations. "They'd start telling me their sad stories, and I'd start theorizing about sex, and there was always this moment when I saw they didn't care about theory, they just wanted sympathy, and to get laid if they could, and—and everything would shut down. And they'd be all aggrieved—you know, 'Hey! I thought you wanted to fuck!'—and I'd say, 'Oh my God, I thought you knew how to talk,' and it was all just so dismal. I mean, of course I wanted that, but I wanted both, and—"

"What luck," he said complacently. "I know how to do both."

She laughed explosively. "You know too much for your own good," she said. "I must say it's a nice change. The others were still adolescents; their whole notion of sexual reality was from *Penthouse*."

"Whereas mine," he said, "is from the business end of a curette. What a balanced, civilized perspective."

"Well, it cuts out a lot of the guesswork," she said. "There were explanations that didn't have to be made. You had, after all"—an edge came into her voice—"searched me out and known me; you knew how the bones grow in the womb of her that is with child. What's left after such a beginning but *daat?*"

Morgenzahl turned a little pale. "Good God, Zusya," he said, "you're a dangerous woman."

"I hope so," she said; "you're a dangerous man. And what are we to do about it?"

"I—" He looked distracted. "That's what I came to ask you. Good God, I hope they don't all think of it that way."

"I hope not too. It's not easy thinking." But she could arrive at no thinking at all about the future. "Look—Ari?—I don't know what we ought to do. I don't want to set terms. You don't really want me to say Let's get married and have babies and live happily ever after."

"No," he admitted, "I don't. I wouldn't believe you. No, I don't know either; I just want to be certain, and I push it off onto you because that would be certainty of a sort, to do what you wanted. But one can't have certainty really."

"No."

They stood up by unspoken consent and moved toward the door. She got his coat from the closet; she was embarrassed to handle it, as if it went next to his skin and not over his clothes. "So . . . did you get what you came for? Or some semblance of it?"

"A very convincing semblance. Mim, I didn't come here expecting—it's enough that we're still talking."

"I will do anything," she said, "that doesn't stop us talking." A parting kiss, which momentarily did.

What did one do after such a conversation? She washed the dishes; she went back to the children's book; she fell asleep on the couch. In her sleep her body caught up with itself, in an incoherent dream of buying a house with Ari but making love there with Alan in a blue naugahyde reclining chair like the ones at the clinic; the pulsing woke her. She looked at the late afternoon light on the books and the floor, and tried to return to consciousness.

The effort of maintaining the conversation—combined, perhaps, with the reversion to childhood reading—had sent her into a compensatory state of stupid quiescence; she could not think at all. She listened to herself breathe, and wondered vaguely what she would tell her mother. In some sense she thought of this as her true self: a dim wordless consciousness that observed without acting. It was not her whole self—there were these anomalous attacks of public eloquence—but it was the earliest state she remembered, with vague associations of a yellow room and a porch looking out into treetops. That she should be willing to sacrifice that inertia, even for the sake of being intelligently seen, for the moment astonished her. Would it go underground, not to surface again until she was old and slow? Could it be driven away entirely? Would she cease being herself? Lately, as she had worked on her speech for the conference and talked to Ari and listened to the patients, she had had a sense of becoming a person at last, as if the missing parts of her soul were finally grafted on in middle age; now she wondered if she might be happier incomplete.

She got up and put on her parka and boots and went for a walk;

physical activity might cure mental inertia. She avoided, as usual, the west side of town, with its winding streets and genteel faculty ranch houses, and went to the square blocks of the east side, where the townies lived. She liked the small, lovingly built 1930s houses; there were a few very small ones that she kept her eye on in case they should ever come on the market. Just enough room for an eccentric old woman and her books, and maybe a cat or two; she would plant up the front yard in herbs, and not have to mow it. Would that ever happen now? Would Ari spend nights with her in a house like that? Like the little dark red one on Spring Street with the patch of side garden and the bit of low stone wall? Would he pull up in front of the house and walk up the path, foxglove and rose campion brushing at his coat, and come in? She could not imagine it; there was something impenetrably goyish and female in a house like that, and surely he would not feel at home.

She could not imagine the relationship lasting long enough for that in any case—for five or ten or twenty years; she imagined herself having lost it, looking back and trying to place it in the pattern of her life. A more apt activity for a woman in a house like that anyway than receiving a lover. The time would come when she would need to be alone again; something would encroach too far upon her inertia, and she would do something unforgivable in response to it and drive him away. Would that have to happen? Was it easier to detach herself (now or later) from a friend and lover who knew the suffering of her past, or to alter her sense of the future? Which would result in less pain? And why should she want that badly to avoid pain?

Irrelevantly, she thought of a moment from early in childhood—perhaps she was four or five, old enough anyway to take a bath by herself—sitting for a long time in the tepid water, looking at the pretty soaps (pink, peach and lavender in small oval bars) that Grandma Hearne had sent, floating in the water the delicate silver plastic swan that had held sugared almonds at a wedding; reflectively pushing a small finger up her vagina, where she had put it before sometimes for comfort. This time, for the first time, there was a moment of mature consciousness; she thought sagely in her flat intelligent child's voice *You might hurt yourself,* and she took the finger out and did not put it back for twenty years. Good Lord, what would Reb Sigmund say to that? She had made up for it since—in the years since Alan she had learned the inside of her body pretty well—but surely the moment was symptomatic, if not actually causal, of her general malaise in love and work. What kind of child decided, all on her own, to avoid the possibility of pain when she felt no pain? Was it something her mother had said, believing it or simply embarrassed to see her explore? Why on earth had she listened? How had that caution transferred itself to all her other evasions?

And why, when she looked for liberation from that excessive caution, was it only to men older than herself? Why never to men her own age? Why never to women? Why, of all men older than herself, only to those with an overwhelming personality and an overpowering religion? Reb Sigmund doubtless would say that she was still in search of her father, or for a version of her father that she could sleep with; doubtless she was trapped in the replication of her traumas, the compulsive reproduction of her own misery. It took a whole crowd of women to replace one man: she had to speak to a hundred of them from a platform to feel she was being seen at all. Sarita and Laura and Terry Treviso had all listened gladly, but Sarita's and Laura's and Terry Treviso's eyes did not supply the necessary light. Contemptible! She had to be some man's clever daughter still: nothing else was quite real to her, nothing quickened her blood like the thought of his praise. Why else return to a man, and to a male God, for the express purpose of being judged, of enacting her life before a critical witness?

She stood still on the sidewalk; she was trembling with rage. Well, was it capitulation or was it remedy? If you needed a critical witness, were you to starve for one all your life because you disapproved of where you found him? If you were stuck with some shameful neurosis, did you just have to live right into it, making your desperate mistakes and wrecking your life, because otherwise you did not live at all? Did the universe just keep handing you your self *(Look, I told you, this is you: do it until you get it right)* and expect you to learn how to use it? Maybe there was nothing to do but accept it: embrace it down to the bone and be damned to the shame.

She walked home, fast; her face was set, and as she went through the glass door of the lobby she thought she looked fiercely beautiful. Did Ari think she was beautiful? His hands did; his mouth did. She ran up the stairs, every muscle charged with lightness. She let herself in, marveling at what had taken place there a few hours ago, marveling that she was going to take a lover. The sun was setting; she pulled the shades against the oncoming dark.

Te lucis ante terminum on the record player: the yearning, bloodless male voices soaring into the twilight. The words of the middle verse registering for the first time: *Procul recedant somnia et noctium phantasmata, hostemque nostrum comprime ne polluantur corpora.* May dreams and night fantasies draw far away; subdue our enemies that our bodies not be defiled. The sad strife of men with their bodies. Why was it so difficult to forgive themselves the involuntary spasm, or the few reluctant motions whereby the involuntary and the voluntary briefly joined forces? Was the thousandth spilling of seed, or the ten thousandth, as confusing and disorienting as the first, that it needed such prayers? Little groups of men all over Christian Europe, under the luminous sky, pleading with God together not to let them touch themselves when alone. Why not instead be thankful that they were committing no violation, begetting no unwanted child?

On the cassette player—in the complicated arrangement of wires and switches one needed to play music these days—was a tape of Hasidic music. Men singing, again, but this time with a kind of alacritous joy that was anything but bloodless. *Ki eshm'rah Shabbas Kel yishm'reni,* when I keep the Sabbath God keeps me. The lead singer's nasal baritone was something like Ari's; the tune was minor and syncopated and seductive. A fifteen-second course in the difference between the two religions: once hear that shift between vocal styles and you would never forget. The Talmud enjoined couples to make love at midnight on the Sabbath; there were old texts with detailed instructions on how to satisfy a woman, her consent and her pleasure being necessary for the holiness of the act. The superstructure was repressive (and the texts always written to the men), but the substrate was molten; repletion and contentment, unconstrained masculinity, rang in every note of the song. Mim tested where the music went in her body, as an electrician tests for current in every soldered joint, as she had learned to do in yoga with her breath. She began to dance.

How had she learned to move this way? In no dance class she had ever taken were such movements taught. She was caressing the floor with her feet as if it had skin; she was dropping and shaking her hips, rippling her belly, arching her back. In high school she had learned Martha Graham's pelvic contractions, but in high school they had been denatured of sexual meaning, made tame and mechanical; later they had been enough to make Alan blush and swell as he watched her exercise, but till then she had not quite made the connection. She felt she had barely known what sex was till this hour; making love was only a tenth of it. It was as if the voices occupied space, as if sound and muscle could conjugate, as if every cell of her body lit with a smile as the music tumbled within it. *So this was what you meant by my self*, she said to the universe; oh, she could do *this* till she got it right. At least she could do it until the tape ran out, and she leaned exhausted and happy in the kitchen doorway, her breath coming fast and her heart pounding.

The man in the next apartment was sneezing. He had an odd sneeze: it began with a moan, a nasal, long-drawn "nnnnNNNN" that might have been prelude to a cough or a fit of vomiting or perhaps a bark. Five, ten, twenty years of the same exasperating habits. Five, ten, twenty years of Ari's dry little laugh: could one ever get tired of it? She wished she had something to hug, some piece of his clothing, or that one of his messages were left on her machine to recall with the intimacy of his voice the promised intimacy of their bodies. For the moment she made do with his book, inhaling its scent *(the most civilized of all smells,* Paddy Chayefsky had said somewhere, *the primordial musk of doubt)* and kissing it and pressing it to her breast. She thought of the morning service, and laughed: all those people kissing God's book in his absence. A terrible case of allegory. Still holding the book, she turned the tape over and danced.

CHAPTER 9

A clever father of a girl once told her:
'Say something interesting, and then they'll stop.'
She soon grew wise before she was much older
And left off talking once I'd climbed on top.

—John Hollander

"Sarita, do you still have that dress? The Rembrandt one?"

Sarita, Todd and Edith looked up from their work. Todd had been expounding, half-seriously, a complicated theory of spatial psychology which attributed housewifely despair in the 1950s to the low ceiling heights in ranch houses, and the urban unrest of the 1960s to the death of the tall cathedral elms. He had paused to negotiate a difficult sleeve setting when Mim appeared in the doorway. He glanced at her, preoccupied. "But of course that's provincial, isn't it," he went on, crestfallen: "they must not have elm trees in Watts. Do they? Does anyone know? Can't we ever blame anything on subliminals, or do we just have to keep coming back to the damned oppressor?"

Sarita smiled at Mim, pushed back her chair, and rummaged leisurely among cloth bundles on a shelf. Edith replied. "Todd, why should you want blacks and women to be ruled by subliminals? Is this some nonsense about intuition and rhythm and the cycles of the moon? Isn't oppression enough to explain—"

"No, it isn't," he said. "It's enough for economic and legal reform, but it's not enough to explain tearing the drapes down or setting your streets on fire. Violence is queerer than reform: it's what happens when you know there's really no hope, and the subliminals all conspire to make you just that little bit crazy. Sarita, isn't that right? Look who the real experts in subliminals are. It's not about rhythm and the cycles of the moon: it's the manipulation of space, the inversion of gender, Quentin Crisp in eye shadow on the London streets in the 1930s—"

"Here it is," said Sarita, tossing down a dark red bundle. "I knew you'd want it someday."

"Did you?" said Mim. "I didn't." She moved gently over to the table, stroking the cloth with a hand that seemed to float.

Sarita took it all in. Her eyes relaxed in a look somewhere between tenderness and sorrow. "So."

"So."

"I sense a subliminal in the air right now," said Todd. "Ssh!"

"Did you know who?" said Mim shyly. "Have I been obvious to everyone but myself?"

"Pretty obvious. But these things are never certain until they happen." Sarita shook out the dress and began to press it. Mim picked up the unhemmed head wrap from where it had fallen on the floor.

Todd could not stand it. "Did we know *who* who?" he said. "You're glowing; it must be love, whoever it is."

"Oh, Todd, really," said Mim a little unsteadily. "Who do you think it is? One doesn't go throwing oneself in the path of a connoisseur of women for months on end without some kind of result."

"Leave her alone, Todd," said Edith. "It really isn't our business."

"I don't mind if you know," said Mim. "It's not the kind of thing that stays secret. But it's all new since—really since yesterday."

"The dress was too long, wasn't it?" said Sarita. "Better try it on again, and we'll see what you need."

Mim escaped gratefully behind the curtain. When she emerged they all exclaimed, Todd with an exaggerated "Ooo" and Edith with a sincere one, and Sarita with a quiet nod of satisfaction. Mim looked ready to flee, so Sarita said, "Come in here. Let's get you away from these people."

She opened a door and showed Mim into the laundry room, where plastic jugs of procion dyes stood on shelves and wadded lengths of dyed satin waited on top of the dryer. "There," she said, shutting the door.

"They'll be going home any minute—we're just catching up on some work—but you don't need all Todd's foolishness. How are you, really?"

"Terrified," said Mim. "And so happy. It's been so long, I have no idea how to conduct myself. But he's so kind—and so funny—and it's so astonishing to be loved in the way one wants."

Sarita smiled widely and hugged her. Then (as if performing some medieval act of obeisance) she knelt at Mim's feet and began to take pins from the little pincushion she wore at her wrist. "Do you want it to trail in the back?"

"Do whatever you think," Mim said. "I really can't think." As Sarita pinned and turned her she felt the stiffness in her muscles from dancing, and smiled inwardly as if sharing some secret with the universe. "There's a blessing for new clothes," she said. "*Mal'bish arumim,* who clothes the naked. Of course there's a blessing for nearly everything. Various kinds of food, and various kinds of good fortune, and an extraordinary one for just having been kept alive. And some for wonderfully odd occasions, like seeing a strange-looking animal."

"Like saying grace before everything," said Sarita, behind her now. "I think that would drive me wild. Always having to drop God's name between yourself and the object, as if you might fall into idolatry by appreciating it in itself. Like putting everything at arm's length."

"Is that how it strikes you!" said Mim. "To me it feels like this marvelous change in the light—like being at work or anywhere ordinary and suddenly remembering you're in love. The descent of this wonderful confusion, a sign of this passionate connection that touches you at the quick."

"But you have a connection to the thing itself," Sarita objected. "I've said things to trees, or to food I was cooking, or to things I dropped on the floor. It's *recognition*: that here we both are, that the other one has its claim on my existence, which I acknowledge; that I don't have to have my will of it all the time. That we should live courteously together. Who can imagine that God wants to be mentioned overtly at moments like that? It's dull-witted, it's obvious—as if every time you saw a child you were supposed to say *It got here by fucking, it got here by fucking.* How else would it get here?"

"How indeed," said Mim, with a peculiar mix of responses: the layers of reality and allegory were shifting too rapidly. "There isn't a blessing for—for sex, you know; and there's even one for relieving yourself, quite a nice one about all the miraculous ducts and cavities. Perhaps even the rabbis thought it was a bit much to drag God into their beds."

"Or they knew they couldn't keep him out," said Sarita, grinning up from the floor. "Just try to stop him watching at that point." She put in the last pin and stood up, backing away to see the effect. "The clothing of the invisible God," she said, "there's a project. How soon do you need this done?"

"Oh," said Mim, suddenly blushing, "I was hoping to have it for— I mean, I don't know. Tell me when you can do it and I'll try to hold out until then."

"Good heavens," said Sarita. "Don't make a thing like that depend on *my* schedule. I'll do it right now. Edith," she called, opening the door, "Is that brown thread still in your machine? That'll blend, I think."

"No, no, Edith wants to go home. You all do. Let's say the end of the week. Let me pay for it now, and I can just rush in and pick it up on the way to—to his apartment, or wherever we decide to accomplish this. It's really all right."

By the time Mim changed out of the dress Sarita had already begun to close up the shop. Andrew's voice came floating up the stairs— "I dreeeam of Jesus with the light brown hair"—and he wafted into the room looking for Todd.

"Drewska," Todd said to him, "Rejoice and be exceeding glad. Mim's in love."

"*Mimmin in Love*," said Andrew promptly. He was growing a beard: a three-weeks' growth of dark stubble, trimmed low on the jaw. "Who's the lucky—man, I'm assuming, or are you going to surprise us?"

"It's the doctor, of course," said Todd. "She's been buying a dress to celebrate."

"Oh, which dress?" said Andrew. "Oh, beautiful. Just right for you, Mim. Do be happy. And do be *careful*. There are awful people out there."

"I know," said Mim hesitantly. "It hit me at work today. It's like falling in love with a cop, or a political dissident, or someone with a volatile illness: there's this sense that things could blow up in our faces at any time. I keep telling myself to remember to be on edge. But it's still not quite real."

"It's never quite real," said Todd. "It would paralyze you. If we went into shock every time we heard of a gay-bashing . . . though it's different, too, no one expects that a *doctor*. . . . I don't know, you live with it however you can. He's right: be careful."

"I will."

They left, and Edith left with a gruff "Good luck," and Mim wrote a check to Sarita. "But I can't be afraid," she said. "It's extraordinary. He's an utterly protective person in an utterly unprotected situation, but I feel safer with him than with Alan. We could be harassed or hurt or blown into oblivion, but when I speak he knows what I'm saying; that's better than a quiet life in the suburbs with someone who doesn't."

"I'll put in a word with oblivion," said Sarita: "not to receive you, not to have anything to do with you for a good long time."

"I think you could," said Mim curiously. She handed over the check; and then, with a directness and vibrancy that quite undid Sarita, moved close and kissed her on the lips. "Thank you," she said. "For the dress and for everything. I really owe this to you."

As soon as it was determined that they would be lovers, Ari went into action at unprecedented pace; a less sympathetic woman than Mim would have called it overdrive. "There's not a good Indian restaurant in this town," he said. "The only way to consummate one's midlife crisis is after a perfect Indian meal. No one else knows how to represent a complex passion in spices." He knew of several places, the best over two hours away (unless they wanted to go to New York, but there was too much to do in New York; there was no point in putting themselves in the way of distraction). They should go away together for the weekend—or for the Sunday and Monday that were his weekend, when he could manage to get one—to a place with no distractions at all, unless perhaps a bookstore or two. He pestered Mim to find out about accommodations in the town with the restaurant (there were guidebooks in Reference). Then he was unsatisfied with what she found. They sat on his living room couch as he ruled out one place after another. "Motels are sterile. Bed-and-breakfasts are oppressively cozy, and you have to look the other guests in the eye at breakfast after what you've been doing in bed. I wish I knew somebody out that way who'd like to trade houses for the weekend, but I don't."

"Calm down," she said. "Why can't we just stay here? Choosing between your place and mine is much easier than this."

"No. The Indian meal is essential. I think neutral ground is essential too; it's, I don't know, the power differential, it *means* something if I come to your place, and it means something else if you come to mine, and it's all too political."

"Whereas it means nothing at all if we go to a motel," she said. "That's not political, it's just sleazy; one can do it with a perfectly clear conscience."

"You know what I mean," he said. "If I come to your place I'm invading your inner sanctum, and you'll clean house all week and feed me something expensive and hope you're doing the right thing, and it's all disastrously tense and a terrible letdown. And if you come to my place it's worse, because there's no trace of your life around you and mine is all here, and you'll feel alienated and wonder why you ever thought you liked me. I suppose all that has to happen anyway, but if we can just begin to get used to each other first—"

"Ari, you're afraid," she said. "Oh, my dear, don't be. There are bound to be these moments of strangeness, but we know each other better than that."

"Mim, this is the most dangerous activity in the world; it can hurt you so badly. Of course I'm afraid. Aren't you?"

"Not about that part. That part least of all. Damn it, you're going to be in my body; why should I care if you're in my apartment? One has to have a sense of proportion in these things. Oh, you're blushing," she added delightedly. "I can embarrass you too."

"I embarrass quite easily," he said. "You just have to get me at close range, which most people don't. It's a question of boundaries; I was brought up to be anxious about boundaries, remember? One reverts to type in a moment of stress."

"One does, at that," she said. "I was brought up to transgress boundaries. But I won't. I will put the guidebook between us as it were a naked sword, and stop saying suggestive things and be very sedate. Look, here's an eighteenth-century inn right in the middle of town. What about that? It's not cheap, but I don't see why we should skimp."

"All right," he said, reading the listing. "Let us spend lavishly. I'll call them right now—no, I won't; I've got to find out if Sanders can be on call for me. He owes me; I took his side at a meeting at the hospital last week. But I'll call as soon as I know."

They beamed at each other; everything seemed to be settled at last, and the tension was gone. A few minutes later, without either of them being quite sure what had happened, they found themselves untangling their arms and their tongues and retrieving the crushed guidebook, with a hazy impression that each had encountered a few more parts of the other's body than before. Their ears were full of each other's breathing, and of the catches in breathing that registered each nuance of response; it was the breathing more than anything else that had compelled them to go on, each rising on the other's exhalations to a higher level of desire, till suddenly they seemed to have risen too high and run out of oxygen. "My God," said Mim, "we'd better stop this; there won't be any boundaries left to cross. Oh, you're lovely. What are we going to do?"

He gripped her hand. His face was nakedly joyful. "Well, we have a choice. In fact we have a whole range of choices, which I know you know all about. Various heresies. There's right here and now, right on this very couch or anywhere you want, with what's delicately called, these days, a glove—you know, rappishly, *No glove, no love*—I'm afraid I'm calculating enough to have procured some nice new ones against this very eventuality—"

His syntax was growing more and more tortured. "Hope springs eternal," she said, stroking his cheek with one finger.

He turned and slid the finger into his mouth. Mim made a sound she had not made in another person's presence in ten years. "Mmf," he said indistinctly, letting her go, "better not, or neither of us will care what happens, and there we'll be. Or we could run for the cold shower—severally, not jointly—and try to stun ourselves into propriety. I'm not sure that's reliable, though; two cold naked bodies want nothing so much as to get warm. Or we could go stagger around outside, where it's cold but at least we'd have clothes on, and then you could get in your car and drive home a maid."

"Or we could sit here and say silly things to each other until that becomes even more irresistible," she said. "If I really were a maid there would be no problem. The trouble is that once you're not, you have no preliminaries; you know just what you want."

He sat back, laughing and agitated. "You can't depend on preliminaries either. Ilene told me once—oh, damn, I'm going to commit the unpardonable sin and talk about my ex-wife. But it's a good story. Ilene's mother told her—back in the bad old days, I suppose it must have been about 1960—to be careful when she was dating because there came a point of no return, when a woman just couldn't resist any more. A man can never resist—no news to anybody—but the woman can always fend him off until she arrives at that point, when she simply stops trying. Ilene said that once they'd had that little talk, every time she went out she was like a kid on a road trip: *Are we there yet? Are we there yet?*"

Mim laughed helplessly. "Didn't her mother *know?* It's like telling her not to put beans up her nose. Parents are fools. My father made sure I read a lot of Yeats; I suppose he wasn't thinking about how it would strike a young girl, or else he was trying to tell me, in the only way permissible to a father, what sex was really for. *Love is all unsatisfied that cannot take the whole body and soul.* I was dying to lose my virginity from the time I was fourteen, and I had to wait until I was twenty-two because there was no one around I could imagine losing it to."

"And then you found someone who—! Well, I suppose he could think of body and soul in the same breath, but not very sensibly. You wait: I can do better than that."

"I know it," she said. "I know it already. Ari love, please: I can't wait, I quite literally can't wait, but I don't even get in to see the doctor till tomorrow." She caught his hands as they reached her; she got up, intending to leave, but could not take a step. "And I don't want you with gloves on," she whispered.

"Jesus," he said. "Mim, don't say things like that if you don't want me this instant. Are you sure—"

She was not sure enough; this would have been the moment to be brisk and quenching, but she had no spirit for it. She could not pretend to indifference; the prolonged unconsummated intellectual seduction of her youth had not prepared her to lie. *I was bred up in nae sic school.* While the girls in her Nana Como's Catholic neighborhood had been carrying little tracts on How to Say No to Boyfriends, she had been reading *Lysistrata*. But her mind stalled at the boundary, at the incalculable difference between saying they would be lovers and being lovers. "No," she said, her throat dry, "no, I'm not sure at all. Oh, my God."

The look he gave her was as intimate as if they were already lovers, serious and quiet. He put his hands on the sides of her hips and held them quite still. If he apologized she would not be able to bear it. "Mim, look, this is simple," he said. "Either we do something short of the obvious—which is perfectly possible, people do it all the time just for fun; or we do the obvious, with the protection we have at hand—I have some foam, too; or we do nothing, in which case you'd better make a run for it before we change our minds, but that's also perfectly possible." The faintest glimmer of a smile. *"Was will das Weib?"*

She squeezed his hands, laughing painfully. "You really could stop, couldn't you? If you can talk like that in this state, you really could stop." She could have too, at that instant; his eleventh-hour rationality had returned her just enough to her brain to make a decision. So it was decisively and slowly that she brought his hands to her waist, and stroked his head as he unbuttoned her jeans, and said, "Don't stop. Not the obvious. But don't stop."

His face against her belly; his hands moving greedily over her skin; his breathing lengthening again, heavy and trancelike. She sank down beside him and reached for his mouth; such solace in the way he gave it, with a little grunt of pleasure in mid-breath, and put one arm around her as the other hand moved down. *Are we there yet?* Alan had had a habit of teasing the thick dark hairs apart with a faint inflammatory touch; Ari was quicker to search between them and offer pressure, which she found she wanted badly. He gave a soft purposive moan and moved down her body, his knees sliding to the floor and his tongue to the place that had swollen for it; she could barely move except to give him better access. One part of her mind looked on, incredulous—can this be real, it's cold, will I spoil his upholstery—but the rest sank toward unknowing as he became engrossed in his task, until thought and observation became impossible and she rocked crying with bliss against his face. At last he moved up again, smiling victoriously; his beard was damp and fragrant with her juices.

She had thought that at the last boundary she might be shy, but it was easy to move her own hand downward; his desire and her curiosity must both be satisfied. "I haven't done this in a very long time," she said; "I hope I remember how."

"It's not difficult, woman," he said, his voice going hoarse. She freed the strange pink apparition, half animal and half mushroom, from the layer of underwear it had become involved in as it rose; it stood blood-warm in her hand. She laughed at its odd beauty and hoped he would not misconstrue the laughter. He did not; he moved, and she felt the traction of the flesh within the skin. She remembered how that double action felt in one's body, and her pelvis shuddered again; as a substitute for the full act she slicked both her hands between her legs and transferred the wetness to him. He expelled a harsh sigh, as much amazed as aroused. As he drew the next breath she bent down and closed her mouth around the velvety head. No, it was not difficult; from his movements her own movements and rhythms came back to her, and she made him twist beneath her as she found his sensitive places. She laughed again, deeply and with relish; what she had forgotten was this freedom, this power to compel another's gratefulness. His muscles relaxed profoundly as he let her work, and a slow moan sang in his breathing. Then he could not hold himself still any longer: he gripped her head and cried out, and the warm liquid spurted into her mouth. The indescribable taste. The pride of making him shudder as the flesh went slack, till he put a quick hand on her forehead to make her stop. The luxury of another will to encounter hers. He pulled her up along his body; they lay curled together, their eyes bright.

They were reduced to monosyllables. "Oh, what a good idea."

"It was your idea."

"Not in the details."

"I like some of your details."

"I still can't wait for the rest."

"Well, now you'll have to," he said equably. "Here, don't get cold. Yitzie, babe, no"—this to the cat, who, having observed the scene with some curiosity, was climbing to Ari's chest. "Some day very soon I hope Mim will spend the night, and then you can sleep on us. Not now." He sat up—Mim slid away to accommodate him—and Yitzie leapt down with a thump. "Poor kid: he has to get it vicariously. You've given him a lot to think about."

CHAPTER 10

> Holy Mary, queen of women
> Who conceivèd without sinning,
> Help thy little child believing
> How to sin without conceiving.
>
> —The "Maiden Prayer," as sent anonymously
> to Marie Stopes

The next day at work she looked at everything as if to see whether the atoms had perhaps rearranged themselves overnight, if the books in Cataloging had put on festal jackets or the dracaena marginata in Reference burst into bloom. Nothing had changed. The Acquisitions clerks did not look at her knowingly; Cedric did not revile her; even her friend Carolyn did not notice anything strange. When she asked for the Monday off her voice shook a little, but Cedric asked her no questions. She decided she liked secrecy.

On her morning break she wandered the first floor, seeking signs. At the copy machines a large young man in a FOLLOW YOUR BLISS t-shirt was pawing a thin young woman with permed hair. At the exit two children were going through the security gate while their mother checked out her books; the little boy, perhaps four, was walking right under the swinging bar of the entrance while his slightly older sister went through the exit, gesturing frantically at him the while and shouting in a loud whisper, "That's the In door, Brian! That's the In door!" (What did it say about men's and women's comparative moral development that girls were so unnecessarily good, so early?) In the bathroom, a woman's symbol written on the steel door of the stall in what could only have been internal juices; there was no soap within reach.

"It's all so relentless," she said to her doctor later. "Woman against nature. Men have their Jack London and their Hemingway; we don't need to survive in the frozen north or hunt wildebeest, we can get the full effect without ever leaving our beds. What if I don't *know* half an hour in advance?"

"Well, you still use it, obviously; it just takes about half an hour for the cervix to form a tight seal against the cap. Use a condom along with it."

"Oh, God. What I was hoping to avoid in the first place. I've been on the sidelines too long. Last time I did this, we still hoped the Pill would solve everything." Actually she had a deep aversion to taking the Pill again: the very thought of it brought back a desolate loneliness, the once-a-day correlation of honesty and dishonesty in her relations with Alan. Better to have something obvious, clumsy, cooperative.

"Well, it didn't. You're not at high risk—you could use it again if you wanted—but barrier methods really do become routine, and they're pretty effective. And when they're not—well, there's backup. We're lucky to have a good clinic nearby."

Mim opened her mouth and said nothing.

"If that's an acceptable option," the doctor said hastily. She glanced surreptitiously at Mim's chart.

"I volunteer there on weekends," Mim finally managed.

"Good for you," said the doctor. "No, nobody likes to think about accidents. But if you have one, there's help."

Mim did not explain that that wasn't the problem. "May I ask," she said, "what do *you* use? Have you found anything more or less tolerable?"

The doctor smiled. "Had my tubes tied after the second kid," she said. "I'd tried everything. It's all more or less tolerable, but only more or less. It's nice not having to think about it. But—short of that—?"

"I think," Mim said, "I'll take a cervical cap *and* a diaphragm: one for planning ahead and one for impulse. And each in case I get tired of the other. We can keep an array of things all over the house, and use them by turns: condoms on the coffee table, and sponges in a jar on the kitchen sink, and little shots of spermicide in the desk drawer."

"That's the way," said the doctor. "It's a comedy; might as well treat it as one."

A shy phone call. "Um, Ari, do you feel strongly about the question of leg-shaving?"

"Mim! Don't be silly; I've seen your legs. Why even ask?"

"Why not? After all, you are going to be—I mean, it seems to matter to some men, and I thought I'd better find out. It mattered to Alan."

"Oh, God. It would. Let me guess: he thought hair was masculine. He hoped if you shaved it you'd lose all your power, like Samson."

"Stop that. I think he just found it embarrassing. He had three teenage sisters when he was little; I think female grooming left him with permanent scars."

"Under what rock did you find this man? I've never heard anything about him I liked."

"Oh, Ari, that's too tempting. *Thou art Peter, and under this rock* . . . you're making me very ill-mannered."

"Mom? I suppose it's time to tell you—if there is any good time for these revelations—I'm in love."

"Oh?"

Her tone was perfectly neutral; Mim quailed. "With Bob Morgenzahl, from the clinic?" she went on irresolutely. "We've been going out for a few months; we've just come to the point of, of declarations and all that, this week."

Her mother was inclined to long silences at moments of revelation; Mim imagined her searching her database of maternal advice, looking for the most helpful words. By the time she found them, they tended to be the most nullifying. "Well, you're a grown woman," she said now. "I presume you know what you're doing."

"I seem to," said Mim, thinking that debauchery on the living room couch must be some sort of evidence. "If—if I am a grown woman, perhaps you could just be glad for me? You've been very nice about not asking if I was seeing anyone all this time; now that I am, would you rather I weren't?"

"No," said her mother, "of course I'm glad for you. It's only—the ones you pick. You never do make it easy on yourself."

Good God, she thought, *did you raise me to make it easy on myself? I have my pride.* "What do you mean?"

"Well, it's either no one at all or some saint. There's no happy medium. What's wrong with someone who's just pleasant to be with?"

"Bob's pleasant. We're very happy. And he's no saint, in the usual terms."

"No, but in your terms . . . mine too, for that matter. Practically a martyr. Don't let him use it against you."

It took the breath out of her. "Mom," she protested, "he's a person; we're friends. How could he use it against me? Why should you suspect, just like that—"

There was another long silence. "Look," her mother finally said, "you've never told us what went wrong between you and Alan. You said he wasn't unfaithful, and you said he wasn't violent, and you said he wasn't gay, and I've always thought it was really his damned perfection: you just couldn't live with a man who was right all the time. You don't have to tell me whether I'm right or wrong, but be careful. Don't pick another one from that mold."

Of course she was right; like Alan, she always was. Mim couldn't live with that either. "Don't worry," she said. "Bob's perfect, but not in that way."

"All right. But take care of yourself. Stay out of the way of those zealots." *Zee-lots,* she said.

Mim supposed it was at least a draw, but she felt scathed; it all felt like another version of *You might hurt yourself.* With her father it was easier; he didn't expect it to hurt. He might even be wrong, but he trusted her to find it out for herself. "Dad, I'm running away for the weekend with a man."

"Is he good enough for you?" he said at once, mock-severe.
"He's the first one in ten years who's worth it. I think he is."
"Christ, has it been ten years? What took you so long?"
"Oh, Dad, do all men want to know that? I'm discriminating; I'm a connoisseur of fine men. I was carefully brought up."
"He's not another ex-priest, is he?"
"He's a Jewish atheist. I will be perfectly safe." Strictly speaking, Alan had not been a priest—he had not taken final vows—but this was no time for quibbles.
"Well, calm seas—auspicious gales—all that sort of thing. Don't take any wooden nickels." She was left to ponder this mystifying blend of benediction and sheer inanity, typical, she supposed, of all fathers' helplessness with their daughters' sexual lives.

Friday night service, with the campus group she had discovered; the intensity of the song for the Sabbath Bride. Awake, awake, your light is come, rise, shine; the glory of the Lord is risen upon you. Why a fancy hotel, on a Saturday night? Why not now, on the Sabbath eve, as the rabbis ordained? But she did not have the courage to get in the car and drive down, and present herself before Ari. She talked to him on the phone afterwards, breathless and thoughtful.

"You're Mira Lonigan."
A tall, chunky man about sixty, in a plaid hunting jacket and a grey earflapped cap. Mim, who was waiting just inside the fence for patients to arrive, looked up in surprise. "I was," she said, "quite a long time ago now. Should I know you?"
"Benoit LaGrange," he said, "from Our Lady of Sorrows. I used to see you and your husband at Mass."
"Oh, of course," said Mim, vaguely remembering his face. She was preoccupied or she would have spoken first, just because he was new; she had better get through the morning before thinking about the night.

"What a memory you've got. It's nice to see you again; how are you doing?"

"Can't complain," he said, a little nonplussed. "Retired from the post office; have a little retirement business, selling stamps to collectors; five grandchildren. And yourself?"

"Doing well," she said. There was not much to add that he could hear comfortably: have a new lover, starting a new career in public speaking for the cause you're here to protest, doing a little volunteer work on the side. A little retirement business, making angels. (The delicate Catholic term for the abortionist's work.) "I'm very happy; life's good."

"Your husband—?" he said, glancing toward the clinic in some perplexity, as if wondering how it and Alan could inhabit the same universe.

"He's no longer in town. We were married for just a short time."

"Aw," he said, hurt, "a nice young couple like you? I'm sorry to hear that. What's got into people these days? Some little problem comes up, and *Let's call the whole thing off*. They don't learn the art of compromise." He gestured with his gloved hands; he was holding some glossy leaflets with pictures of fetuses.

"Some problems don't lend themselves to compromise," she said, with a pointed glance at the leaflets. Behind Benoit the other protestors were chatting and drinking coffee. There were seven or eight of them, and two children; they carried a lurid crucifix and a large American flag. "What brings you here, by the way?"

"Well, that should be obvious," said Benoit. "Anybody on this side of the fence is here to save babies. I'm more curious to what brings you here."

Oh, surely that's obvious too, she said to herself; anybody on this side of the fence is here to—but it was treacherous to adopt the other side's language, even ironically. "Benoit, look," she said. "I'm very tired of this argument. I'm sure you are too. I'm here, really, to help the doctor; why don't we leave it at that? When that man shot him last year, I had to do something."

"Now that guy was a wingnut," said Benoit expansively. "He took the law in his own hands. What was he trying to prove? Here we are telling *you* people not to kill; we have to set an example."

Mim sighed. "Maybe you could set an example of moderation? What we're doing isn't equivalent to what he did. We're only helping women who don't want babies not to have them; how is that the same as shooting a man in his forties who's loved and appreciated? And shooting him in order to *force* women who don't want babies to have them?"

"But," said Benoit. "That's a new little life growing in there; you can't end it, just like that."

"But you can," she said. "Women try it themselves when they don't have doctors. In the old days *they* used to die. How is it being pro-life—" She was sick of it, sick of it, she wanted to go out of town and screw, she wanted to lose her rational mind in the raptures of Ari's body. Ari. Birth control. Damn.

"God puts those babies in there," Benoit was saying. "The minute that egg and that sperm unite, that's a baby, and—"

"It's not," she said. "It's one cell. Stop calling fetuses babies, as if they could walk and talk at two month's gestation, and look at what really—" She was losing her temper, she was arguing very badly; this man could have been an ally of sorts, and now he would not be. Thank God a car was driving up; she would have to stop soon.

"Now there you lose me," said Benoit affably. "Calling fetuses babies—jeez and crackers, what would you call them if not babies? They're not bunny rabbits."

The car had parked; the other protestors were going into formation. Mim went through the gate. "Bunny rabbits can reabsorb their pregnancies," she said bitterly over her shoulder. "I wish we could."

The woman in the car was eighteen or twenty; her boyfriend was with her. She looked miserably at the protestors, one of whom had a video camera. Mim gave her a towel to put over her head—the clinic had devised no more elegant means of concealment—and she took it, muttering, "I don't believe this. I don't believe this." As Mim brought her to the gate, the protestors—now singing "Jesus Loves the Little Children" to a rousing beat—marched up and down before them on the sidewalk. Ari had sought and won an injunction requiring them to keep moving and not block the way—before that they had mobbed cars—but there was still some feinting and dodging, and Calvin Hardy, the minister, stood by the gate calling out in a high hoarse voice, "Miss, you're *ashamed* of yourself, that's why you hide your face. If you feel like a criminal now, how are you gonna feel after you kill that baby? Why, Jesus loves that little baby. Sir, how can you let her do this? She might be carrying your son. Don't go into that death camp. Come to Jesus. Come to Je-sus." And the little girl who marched with them—she might have been eight—shrilled out with narrowed eyes, "Mommy, don't kill me!"

Mim got the couple through the door. She waited on the steps for more patients; she did not want to talk to anyone. She was losing her grip: she had never argued at first. She had tried to choreograph the process, as if even moral struggle could be a dance, the protestors having their say and giving way before the patients' unwillingness to listen, a sort of political t'ai chi in which she expended very little strength while the protestors squandered theirs. She could not do it any more. As Ari's lover she simply wanted them to go away. The fight had come too close to home, and the combination of passion and detachment that had brought her to this point was catalyzed by fear into a different substance. Fear was the only constant in the situation: the protestors were terrified of a world in which women could refuse pregnancy, and she and the patients were terrified of the protestors. Would fear keep circling between them till nothing else could be felt? In the widening gyre. Mere anarchy is loosed. Why had she not talked to Benoit about God?

Ari drove up. She wished he would get there ahead of the protestors, but he seldom did; the intake and counseling process could start without him, and in any case he refused to be ruled by fear of further assault. Probably he was right—probably the only way to stop fear was by simple refusal—but she wished, as he took in the scene rapidly and carefully and nodded to her from the car, that she had gone to his house last night. If they did anything to him now, if they prevented her from his body—she began reciting the Yeats poem to herself, from the top. Stop thinking. Stop thinking.

The guard who had worked there since the shooting came out to walk him in by the side door. The protestors were singing again. "Where have all the babies gone," they moaned as the two men disappeared around the corner. "Doctors killed them every one." And the little boy who marched with them—he looked to be about six—broke from the line and ran to the corner of the fence, where he knelt and pointed. "Bang! Bang!"

"Now, Tyler," called his mother indulgently; but Mim, trembling, turned and met Benoit's eyes. She was not sure she saw contrition, or comprehension.

CHAPTER 11

For by stroking of him I have found out electricity.

—Christopher Smart

They stopped briefly at Sarita's shop for Mim to pick up the dress. The rise into peacefulness was like getting the bends: the beautiful swatches on the walls like works in museums, the garments in progress like elegant ladies asleep. The last of the opera on the radio, Papageno and Papagena earnestly stammering. Astonishing to the point of pain that such a world still existed.

Behind the curtain, Mim undid her clothes. Ari chatted with Sarita, who had given him tea. He knew quite a lot about sewing: his mother had been a dressmaker in Prague before the war, and he still had a few of her pieces stored away in a box. Of course Sarita could see them; of course she could study them; he and Mim would invite her over sometime. Mim decided against her underwear. She whispered the blessing as she slipped the dress over her head.

As they drove—first on an eight-lane superhighway that handled all the fast traffic on that part of the coast, then on a more modest highway that was one of its tributaries, and finally on a series of quiet back roads—they were mostly silent. Sometimes a hand reached across to hold another hand or to rest on a thigh. The last of the day's distresses ebbed away. Mim thought silently on the metamorphosis taking place: each of them relearning how to belong to another person, how to be belonged to, how to ride in a car without even quite noticing each other. Trust was the frailest thing in the world, it could be destroyed after any number of years of marriage, yet here it was trying to form again: as if it were the equilibrium, the resting state toward which every soul was drawn, as if love were a kind of gravity that compelled two people at last to settle in constancy.

At last a crowded town full of cars and people; the restaurant, in a squat New England house, its windows and inner doorways dripping with beads and the air swooning with the smells of turmeric and cumin and twenty other spices. Painted silks of Radha and Krishna on the walls; under the glass tabletop a square of silk with some other amorous couple—the man not blue this time—their fingers dipped in red dye, the woman bending deeply back over her lover's lap, their eyes locked in a perpetual soulful stare. The remoteness of the whole atmosphere from anything that Mim knew—from the library and the clinic, from America's frantic well-meaning mindlessness and Europe's wars, from religion whose God had no eye for beautiful women, from food whose ingredients and preparation she understood. As if the lamb and spinach and lentils and rice were each infused with a distinct flavor of incense, not the cheap cloying head-shop incense of her youth but the serious and significant blends of the Vedic masters, some healing property in every spice. The heat of cayenne spreading from mouth to stomach to brain, a shock slowly changing to a sustained and introspective pleasure: if she trained her consciousness on it she could rise on the heat, hover above it like the air at the top of a flame. ("They say it knocks out your pain receptors. We weren't using them anyway, were we?") Then a smoky spiced tea with sugar and milk, and what Ari promised would not be rice pudding: thick milk boiled for nearly an hour with cashews and raisins and whole cardamom pods and a few grains of rice, and a crunch of pistachios sprinkled over the top. "My God, Ari, it's the mother's milk of the universe; surely I'll disappoint you after this." "No, you won't."

They spent an hour in a bookstore, digesting and showing each other lines of verse; Ari bought two books of poetry and a new study of Kafka, and Mim spent thirty dollars on an Indian cookbook. When they registered at the inn, a wedding reception was in full swing: very young men in tuxedos hovered around very young women in formals, and oleaginous piano music came sliding out the door of the dining room. Mim shook her head, delighted to be illegal, delighted to be middle-aged. They went upstairs on plush postmodern carpet—even the eighteenth century was not exempt from such revisions—to a large narrow room with brass wall lamps and a white chenille bedspread and old prints of horses on the walls.

"Oh, dear."

"Quite a temperature drop from the restaurant, isn't it? Good Lord, look at that wallpaper." It was pale yellow with a thin green stripe at four-inch intervals and a line of medallions, or perhaps they were stylized flowers, between the stripes.

"We could have had your place or mine. You were the one who wanted—"

"We will from now on. We'll learn how to cook that food for ourselves, and stay out of these places. Meanwhile"—he experimented with a few switches—"there's a sort of bleak Yankee coziness about it, if you keep the lights low enough. There, is that better?"

"Soon we won't care," she said. She began to take off her parka, but her hands shook: she was suddenly trembling violently. "Elegant hotels are so strange," she said, to distract herself—her teeth chattered a little—"I've been to one other, in Florida, when Alan and I got married. That was his father's idea of an exotic honeymoon, and he was anxious to do the thing right. The place had the same combination of antique luxury and chill. And stateliness and tastelessness."

"It can't have been in this style."

"Pink stucco arches. But the same blandness of imagination, and the same smooth music, and no doubt much the same drinks. The names of mixed drinks have always struck me funny: Mai Tai, Manhattan, Old Fashioned. People are so earnest about them—even the silly ones—as if even losing your inhibitions has to be pursued with just the right invocations and measures."

"Would you like a drink?"

"No."

She could not sit down; she kept fidgeting with the leather pull of her overnight bag. The head wrap itched. She pulled it off and fluffed out her hair, and realized that she had made the first move. The trembling intensified. She kept talking: if she showed no confusion perhaps she would not be confused. "The astonishing thing about Florida was being out at sunset one night, standing on a dock and watching the birds come in. Two of them passed so low we could hear their wings beat—a pelican with this slow rotating *vvvmm, vvvmm, vvvmm,* as if someone were turning a crank, and a cormorant with a much quicker *ff ff ff ff ff.* It was—"

"*Ff ff ff,*" he said, coming close. They held each other quietly, not speaking. Without seeming to think about it he began kissing her hair, swaying with his arms round her shoulders. "You're shivering," he said.

"I'm afraid."

"Ohh," he said soothingly, rocking her. "The moment of truth. Scary, scary stuff. Want to talk?"

"No," she said, and laughed nervously. "I mean, talking would only postpone . . . Why should this be any different from the other night? We've already done all the rest. Why is crossing this line so uncanny?"

"Why is this night different from all other nights?" he said. "On all other nights we maintain a boundary, but on this night we smoosh together till we can't tell where one leaves off and the other begins. Why do we do this?" His hands moved over her, discovering in two soft but economical strokes that she was naked under the dress. "Ooh. Because it's irresistible. God, you're a beautiful woman."

She laughed again, with a different intonation. "God, you're a nice man." She reached up for his mouth and the trembling began to subside as her body was overtaken by a slower rhythm.

It became difficult to stand up. They moved, not quite disengaging, toward the bed. "Look," he said as they took off their shoes, "there's no good way to ask this, but do you need any help with your, ah, family planning?"

"No," she said. "It's the cap; I put it in in the restaurant. Didn't I look well defended, coming back from the bathroom?"

"As an army with banners," he said.

They lay down; for the first time the full length of their bodies moved tightly together, for the first time they twined legs. Her legs were so hungry for that action that she could barely unlock them again; it was only when she wondered if she might be staining the dress that she disengaged. She lay back and let him undress her, noting thankfully that Sarita understood fastenings that unfastened easily; people who made men's clothing did not, and she fumbled with his shirt buttons till she sank back under the complexity of feeling such lust and having to use her hands rationally. "You're wearing too much," she said, and he got up to shed it, laying jacket and trousers more or less carefully over a chair and dropping the rest where he stood. He undressed hastily, with his back to her.

"My dear, no, let me see you."

A lumpy, middle-aged body, robust and vigorous, the belly bulging a little, the skin clear and pale. Everywhere furred with black hair, or hair going grey—the chest, the belly, the arms, the thighs, the back between the shoulder blades. The broad dumb expanse of the chest, breastless, a stone wall with nipples. The scars on his shoulder, still livid after five months' healing. His penis crazily poking itself toward her, leaning a little to the right. His whole body charged with energy, without loveliness and radiant with beauty.

"You look like a Leonard Baskin."

"Which one? That one that's sort of in tatters, the Hydrogen Man?"

"The Yom Kippur Angel, with a damaged wing. Only, as I remember, he's androgynous, or ambiguous, or at any rate modestly covered." She turned down the sheets. "And you're not."

When she was fifteen she had watched a Lorca tragedy on television: there was a dance in it, with a woman in a long ruffled skirt and a man in black clothes, and at the climax of the dance the woman had bent backwards from her spread knees till she touched the ground and the man in one motion fell slimly into the ruffles. *So that's how it's done*, Mim had thought, and been glad to find out. But what cannot be shown in a picture is how it feels: the simple strangeness of naked flesh against flesh; hands everywhere on her and her hands everywhere on him, and the penis independent of the hands seeking its place, intent; the liquefaction of her nerves as he began to slide along the central one and found her body penetrable. The moment of her first opening to him, resolute and tender, all postures farcical yet a regal elegance in opening her knees and reaching for him, their eyes holding mutely as he pushed in. His voice sounding once, half moan and half laugh, as he was engulfed in the wet heat. Her own voice, unfamiliar and female. Her body miraculously split, and he in its middle, buried up to the root; the layers of slippage, the thick pressure plumbing her entrails, the slow seizures of gratitude. The equilibrium of the last moments, as he shrank within her and they became themselves again. The awkward, comical moment of pulling apart, liquescent and soft. At last two insatiably talkative people lay without speech, except for small sounds of affection. Snow was falling outside; she could hear it under the wheels of one slow car that passed by.

The dislocation of the morning: waking to a new concatenation of smells, and a wet spot beneath her on the sheet. Male socks and underwear on the floor, peculiar in their angularity; from the bathroom the torrential sound of urine falling from a height. His voice, humming something: its low resonance made her muscles grip and her back arch a little (for muscles are strings, she thought, and vibrate to their own frequency), but her mind meanwhile was running on something close to xenophobia. She had lived alone too long to find maleness entirely natural; she was at once moved and unnerved by it. How much you got, in getting what you wanted, that you had not bargained for: aftershave, and beard trimmings in the sink no doubt, and these dreadful boxer shorts; shirts that came wrapped up in plastic, not requiring to be tried on; baritone coughs that sounded like proclamations. Twenty years ago he would probably have smoked cigars. Would he leave the seat up? She hoped so; she would be charmed, remembering why. She supposed any one of these things might serve as a similar reminder, the shirts or the coughs becoming as eroticized as skirts or perfumes or (good Lord) brassieres were for men. It might be a question of how you disposed yourself toward them. She sniffed experimentally at the shorts; she put her head on his pillow.

He came back into the room and saw her awake. His eyes lit as she looked into them: immediately there was contact, concord, beyond the obsessional trappings and even the bodily distinctions of male and female. *Daat:* comprehension: they had been where none of that mattered. She had never much liked the dogma—whether propounded by men or by women—that the sexes completed each other, that the jigsaw mechanism of penis in vagina meant anything but itself. But it was dogma because it was imponderable; the experience did mean itself; like God's name, it could not be said or even euphemized without being misrepresented. Was it fusion or solitude? Was it polarity or union? Their bodies did not need those answers: obscure, inaccessible, their junction took place, nothing mediating between the one part's pleasure and the other's, and the mind knew its limits and gladly immolated itself. A Zen koan: Like a fish needs a bicycle. *Look, Ma, no hands.* She gave a conspiratorial smile and held up the sheets for him. He came back to bed.

The white light through the curtains was unfamiliar and flat: inland light. In it every hair was defined against his skin, every line of the fine skin around his eyes was fragile and beautiful. She sat astride him, savoring his movements as he pushed upwards, riding the line between delicious stress and discomfort. They were calm; they could take a long time. They even talked a little as they moved, about hunger and breakfast, and her hands played with his chest hair and his with her breasts. Then she closed her legs between his and tried a new angle of declination, and at once was struck silent: her mind made a profound retreat into itself, following a sensation she could not quite place. Were there nerve endings that far inside her? It was something more subtle: a presence, a web of perception. She floated her weight on his thighs, circling gently. Perhaps one got used to it; perhaps she would take it for granted once she could have it every few days, but—oh God, every few days. Her whole inside tingled with consciousness; it *thought.* In astonishment she stopped moving altogether, wincing into his eyes, feeling in the absence of motion a perfect balance, an absolute tension she did not want to resolve: desire and satisfaction at once, longing and satiety, an unknown extremity of loveliness. He moved just slightly and the contractions came on, collapsing her wonderment into the more accustomed cries and flexions, but it was a loss: she could have stayed forever in that penultimate state, the purely physical sweetness piercing her soul. He took a long time to finish; her body went in and out of climax, but that moment was gone. At last he tensed and released with two shuddering cries, and it was over, and they lay side by side entangled and sweaty. Someday when they had evolved language to speak of all this she would try to say what had happened; just now she could speak of nothing, and fell again into sleep.

He went out; he came back, bringing bagels and whitefish, coffee, the newspaper, and (unaccountably) a large bottle of cranberry juice. They ate and read, and stroked each other's bodies under the newspaper, but only for comfort: they had no energy left. "Shall we do anything else while we're here?" he said.

"I thought the whole point was not to. What shall we do?"

"I don't know. Church? There's a big one down the street with Mary in marble on the lawn; I saw it when we drove in."

She tried to roll him out of bed. "*You* can, if you want. I suppose you wouldn't lend me this while you're gone? You won't need it there."

"Sorry, it's attached. And in no state to do you any good. If you'd like to go out, it will follow you anywhere; church wasn't its notion. I just—this is a nice little town, and it's so pleasant to be where nobody knows who I am."

"Oh, of course," she said instantly. "I should have thought of that. Where shall we go? What time is it?"

"11:06 by the village clock," he said, nodding toward the digital display on the television. "I don't know: more bookstores, more food. Let's just see what there is."

There followed a long shower—neither found it quite possible to refrain from trying again, though it was slow and inconclusive—and at last they emerged from their room damp-haired and holding hands. It was noon; in the streets the shops were beginning to open, and the light fall of snow was shoveled into neat piles. Mim found herself moving differently: as long before, when she lost her virginity, she felt herself made distinctly of two sides and a center, and wondered if the change were visible. And he, beside her, glowed with potency fulfilled; he radiated happiness, and kept finding excuses to touch her. "I think," she said suddenly, "I'll buy a coat; I've been thinking I wanted one, and it will give you a chance to use your good manners. I see now why men help women with their coats: it's sublimation."

"It's indulgence," he said. "Mim, you wouldn't really—it's a step back into the dark ages, it's a sign of possession. Nobody's let me do that since about 1972. You're going to tear down all the gains of the women's movement."

"No, I'm not. It's not possession like property, it's possession like— like what we've been doing all these hours. It's indulgence for me too: I don't want it to stop. God, how clinging it makes one, being well satisfied." They had stopped at a traffic light; she leaned on him, molding herself to his shape.

"Know what that is? Oxytocin: same thing that makes labor not quite so laborious, and nursing so blissful. Sex is the third thing that releases it. Men get it too, a big shot of it. Really," he said as she laughed at him, "it's all chemistry. Let me put you into your coat and my mind will be pickled in testosterone, and I'll start opening doors for you and trying to keep you out of the Senate. You may call it consent today, but five years from now you'll be calling it phallic oppression."

"Phal/logo/centrism," she said as the light changed. "Well, what shall I do about it today? Stop seeing you? I don't want to stop seeing you; oh, love, I squish when I walk. How is it feminism to lie and say I don't want you?"

"Sweetie," he said, "where've you been? How is it feminism to gloat over having a man?"

The first coat she tried on was the one she wanted: it had a good line, like a coat in a '30s movie, and she thought Sarita would approve. For amusement, since she had expected to take more time, she tried on a hat with it: it was a strikingly handsome hat, and turned out to be shockingly expensive. "I'll buy it," said Ari, "oh, Mim, let me give it to you. If you're going to capitulate, let's have it be real first-class degradation."

"It's the calf-leather shoon," she said in a quiet shriek. The conundrum compounded: if polarity finally resolved itself into fusion, why not remind yourselves of your fusion by enacting polarity? It was a dangerous game, but she suddenly knew the rules: if you were not afraid of each other you could play it indefinitely. Could they keep from being afraid of each other? There was a song, a saying of the melancholy Rebbe Nachman of Bratslav: all the world is a narrow bridge, and the main thing is not to fear. She had the sense of propounding an enormous tease toward the universe: You try to confuse us with hormones and funny clothes, but I've found you out, and I'll throw the game back at you; no funny clothes can divide my lover and me. And when this soul, its body off, naked to naked goes—watch what I'll do for you, old dodger. "What shall I trade you?"

"You've already said. You'll let me handle you in public in these gorgeous clothes if I won't be stupid about it. I accept. I accept."

But as the afternoon wore on she felt a sense of annoyance, as if looking on through the eyes of her former self: who the hell is this complacent woman, strutting around in expensive clothes, oozing up to a man—what, thirteen years older?—as if all her bones had suddenly melted, and kissing him on the street? Transparently, grossly happy, as most people would never be happy, as the broken-hearted and those who could not kiss their lovers on the street must even now be snarling inwardly to see. This wasn't the sort of thing a woman with a mind did anyway: one paid for the mind with the body, one wasn't allowed to sit in a bookstore reading George Steiner while whiffs of one's own sexual perfume floated up through one's clothes, the mind and the body both humming with good exertion. That most of the women she knew (minds or no minds) had lovers—men or women, permanently or in sequence, occasionally more than one at a time—made no difference: *she* wasn't allowed. She would wake up and find it had been a dream, her mother would appear in the doorway to take her home, a papal nuncio would drop in and announce it. She crouched to get a book off a low shelf, and two flaps of her vulva pulled apart with a faint *plick;* oh, had Ari been near enough to hear it? She began to laugh: it was hopeless. She crossed the alcove to where he sat reading on a folding stepstool, and kissed the top of his head. She looked around surreptitiously—no one would see her—and pulled the sparse hairs with her mouth; she drew a line down his forehead with the tip of her tongue. It was a good sturdy stepstool: it held her weight too. He was blissfully brash, his tongue in her mouth, his hand in her sweater. "Let's go back," she said. "Love, we can't do anything here. Let's go back."

"Oh, Zusya," he said, recovering words after having been somewhere beyond them. They were submerged together, floating on a current of their own smells.

"Zisya," he said. "You know *zis?* Sweet. The German is *süss.* You might have heard that old song about the sweatshops, that ends *Makh mir zis mayn rue platz.* Make sweet my resting place."

She kissed the joint of his thigh. "All these names ending in Yah," she said indistinctly. "Batya is *daughter of God,* right? So Zisya would be *sweetness of God?*"

"From his place," he said, finding it. "Rose of the world, right?" He slid a finger down between the petals. "*Eros* and *rose* are anagrams, I suppose you've noticed."

"Mm," she said, too lazy to search for an intelligent rejoinder. "Love, wait; I'm not sure I'm good for much more at this point. I'm getting kind of sore."

The probe changed to a commiserating pat. "O rose thou art sore. That's too bad; you haven't had your turn."

"I had quite a few this morning. I'm not sure how to count them. Ari, we're not keeping score?"

"No. I guess I should say I want *my* turn. Here, let me try—softly softly—"

"Oh, love, it'll be interminable. It'll take me an hour."

"I have an hour."

CHAPTER 12

> That I should hear if we should kiss
> A contrapuntal serpent hiss.
>
> —W. B. Yeats

Fig leaves. The first clothing, filched along with the fruit (the rabbis said) from the twigs of the forbidden tree. Sarita was working on satin in green and dark gold. The dyes were subtle, coppery, spreading into each other in cloudy fields with blurred uncertain boundaries. The garments would be simple: kimonos, evening wraps, bias-cut dresses, so that the eye could follow the colors without distraction. Some she would use for the linings of capes and coats; imagine a staid suit-jacket whose inner unseen face recalled lost Eden. Women sitting in law offices and boardrooms all day, caressed in secret by those colors.

There was no way to impart to the garments the tomcat smell of fig tree—and no doubt that was just as well—but she gave the cloth a faint veining of dark red as the next best thing. The sexuality of trees and of people overlapped in some curious ways, nearly always through smell: the fishy scent of maybloom, which made it preeminently the tree of fertility in old England; the frowst of chestnut, which had always made her think of ripe corn till a friend said it was like semen (and she disgraced herself by saying so to an aunt who hated the smell); the redolence of plane-tree leaves, like a woman's heat grown cool upon one's fingers. But sight too—the sinewy upthrust of old beech trees, the intimate entanglements of birch and hemlock roots, the grooved folds of ash bark, the blatant tropical plants. Could smell be translated into sight? How strictly her work was determined by the narrowing of the senses: of the five she could use only two, sight and touch, with occasionally a faint rustle for the ears.

Sarita's profane humor did not extend to making the cloth into aprons; the wrong kind of person would buy them, the guffawing hopped-up tourist who would just as soon buy a shirt that said I GOT SCROD AT WAYNE'S WHARF. But when she found she had a long coil of satin left over from a circular lining, she did back it with muslin and roll it up, and stuff it with mung beans, and give it a high crested head and a forked tongue of wire wrapped with dark red embroidery floss. Too late she remembered the Gothic representations of the snake with a woman's torso and long golden hair; from such a snake she might have got straight answers. But as she worked—as usual, after hours, long after Mim and Ari had left the shop on their expedition—she was gratified to observe the quiet hiss that twisted its way across the room to her. Saurus, sussurus, sibilance: a chance to question.

"Eve was working too, wasn't she?" she said, not looking up. "She was presumably a gardener. Was she learning the uses of herbs?"

The hiss broke, as with laughter. "A curious thought! What labour should she do, mother of all, before her motherhood?"

"Adam named the beasts; perhaps she named the plants. They were put in the garden to keep it."

"A little pruning, twining wayward vines, gathering myrrh-drops. Nothing to confound her. Love was her work. Once differentiate—rib pried from rib—the Adam longed to join, and all Eve's garden blossomed toward that end. Their task, as trees' to flower, was to embrace, by high command assigned: nor turn'd, I ween, Adam from his fair spouse, nor Eve the rites mysterious of connubial love refus'd—but there I quote. My noblest chronicler, having suppli'd such words to tell the tale, surpass'd all other tellers. Since that time—my debt to him being great—I speak blank verse. But what would you, Eve's daughter, know of me?"

"What I asked. It can't be that Milton was right, that Eve was a vapid beauty hanging on Adam's every pompous word." Oops, pentameter was hard to resist; she had better be careful. In this interview it was necessary to keep one's wits. "After all, the mind seeks its own labor, as the body does; there's intellectual fruition too. Wasn't she in search of that?"

"She was when she accepted fruit of me. But there is doubt—some readers have discern'd—whether her fruit could fall before she did.

Opinions vary, but (you will observe) the pair did not conceive their firstborn son till after they left Eden."

"Oh, you mean—" She tore herself out of its rhythm. "You mean the stasis of paradise. Where everything is perfect, nothing is necessary: no art, no invention, no skills. And no need to reproduce, because there's no death."

The serpent's eyes—opal buttons—glowed with an inward pleasure. Apparently it found Sarita an apt pupil. "But on that point some differ. Death, 'tis said, might have been chosen freely—time and means—had man not disobey'd (though mortal still). Just so conception—had not your mother Eve so pliant prov'd to my fork'd reasoning—might have been chosen, subject to the will; and then had fruitfulness not been disgrace, nor accident made parents of the young, nor Adam's children, wild, o'ergrown the world."

Sarita stared. "But that's what we're trying to do now: make conception subject to the will. My friend Mim—who must even now be doing something to avoid conception—is in love with a man who prescribes birth control and does abortions. Someone tried to kill him for it last year. Why is it wrong to limit birth on purpose, if in Eden it would have happened by nature?"

The stone eyes flickered. "I said not *would*, but *might*: I deal, my child, in doubt, not certainty. Certitudes are the care of heav'n, and thence I was cast out. Say that Eve nam'd the plants: how would she learn the properties of Savin, or of Rue? Of Aloes, Tansie, Parslie, Pennyroy'l? Or Jesuit bark, whence Quinine is distill'd, that calms a fever or rids out the womb?" It looked at her sidelong, shifting its satin coils. "Did Ergot grow on Rye in paradise? And was it nature, or a blessèd art—though cursèd, outside Eden—if Eve learn'd, her courses late, to taste of such a plant, and sinless bring them on?" It was smiling now, swaying to the beat of its own words. "How many months did she dwell barren in lost paradise? Did her dominion over beast and fowl extend to water-dwellers of the womb?"

"It does now," said Sarita slowly. "In practice if not in everyone's theory. And in Eden . . . one hardly dares put anything past God."

"Whose name she prais'd," the serpent added meaningly. "Till I with subtle speech did wean her from that crazy salad's bite with sweeter taste beguiling. Then forlorn, impoverish'd of her garden, mute of praise, with Adam her companion forth she stray'd, to his subjection sentenc'd and to pains. Desire unhappie, desolate desire, drove them to couple; sorrow multipli'd, and she conceiv'd their firstborn son, call'd Cain."

It seemed to feel for Eve; Sarita found herself moved. "Do you regret your part in her fall?"

"My chronicler's compassion," it said modestly. "Not my own."

She should have guessed it; the spell was a little broken. "So," she said, briskly trying to conceal her emotions, "you're casting the fruit of knowledge as fertility drug—at least by default: the thing that interrupted the *in*fertility drugs. Is that something to lament or celebrate? Is fertility curse or cure? Is this another version of *felix culpa?*"

At those words the serpent sat up, as if a password had been given; its hypnotic swaying ceased, and it actually frolicked on the cutting table, rumpling the muslins and knocking an expensive pair of scissors to the floor. When it spoke again it almost giggled:

> Tohu va-vohu! *Mil-*
> *tonic/Newtonian*
> *apple of Eden, good*
> *lost, evil got:*
>
> *poison or medicine?*
> *Homeopathically,*
> *what is the curative*
> *dose of* daat?

Sarita jumped. "Your blank verse has fallen off considerably since the seventeenth century. Milton, thou should'st be living at this hour." She tried to untangle the meaning of the rhyme. "It's very clever, but you've only restated the question, you know; it isn't an answer."

It shot her a sly look.

> *Eva to Ave, the*
> *search for the antidote—*
> *malus to* bonus *and*
> *life from the dead—*

> *surfeit of sanctity*
> *cannibalistically*
> *changed (hocus-pocus!) from*
> *apple to bread.*

"Oh, *that* answer," she sighed. "Well, it's a novel use for it, if you mean what I think you mean; no one else has proposed the Host as a form of birth control. It must work as well as rhythm. I shouldn't have asked; I suppose you're locked into Pauline theology, and it's not fair to ask you to function outside it. I was hoping—you know, one reads all this new writing about the alliance between women and snakes, not as the original sinners but as the givers of wisdom. I hoped—" She was overcome by a sense of embarrassment, degradation, futility. This supercilious creature could not help her with its theological games. What was she doing, she who in profound loneliness had lain with an angel? "I hoped," she said, forcing the words out—when you became connected to other people you had to do these things—"we might hit upon some form of protection for Mim and her lover."

The serpent considered. Its eyes were unreadable, and she was not sure they were pleased. Perhaps it did not want an alliance with women. Perhaps the protestors were already its allies, and it did not want a conflict of loyalties. Or perhaps it simply could not think of a strategy. At last, as if buying time, it darted its tongue at her and offered:

> *Venus's penises!*
> *Aryeh ben Mordecai*
> *with his Miranda now*
> *revels and plays;*
>
> *but when confronted by*
> *innocent fetuses*
> *gynecologically*
> *numbers their days.*

"Oh, don't be frivolous," she snapped. "Can't you stop spouting these jingles? These people are in real danger. You know the kind of zealots that are at large. Are they yours or God's? Can you do anything about them?"

The serpent shuddered all over. It retreated to the farthest corner of the cutting table, where it coiled itself decorously and tried to recover its hauteur. It looked ruffled; its crest was in disarray. "What powers of desecration or despite you have employ'd upon me I know not, to cause me such unseemlie lapse of speech," it said. "The which has not occurr'd since Hell began, and Pandaemonium rear'd its mightie gates and thrill'd to martial music."

"It's the twentieth century," said Sarita. "It's been rough on us all."

It snorted. "As you say. And I, of fallen hosts acknowledg'd lord, who made great wars, am to these straits reduc'd—these derelict wombs and vex'd nativities." It eyed her impatiently. "You ask my aid, but for what due return? Your soul is in your work—nor God's nor mine—not free to sell. Do not so far presume, belated daughter of o'erweening Eve: who may with gods and men betimes prevail, but shall not with God's Satan, sterner made."

Sarita took this in. "I see," she said; "you only take cash. Or rather, you'll extend credit—you'll take a bequest—but you don't work *pro bono*. Or *pro malo*, as I suppose you'd have to call it. All right; I'll find another way. I doubt you would want my soul anyway; God doesn't seem to. But what do you mean, *God's Satan*? That's a curious notion. Can it be that under all the stale Miltonic bombast you're still making bets with God? Are you seeing how far you can drive Bob Morgenzahl before he caves in, like you tried to with Job and Faust?"

"Speak not so lightly!" it said. "These are mysteries. Dare not to search God's purpose." It grew less bombastic; its tone was almost hushed. "He it is alone forms light and dark, makes good and ill—no evil in the city but is his—and storm and wind, *and Hell*, fulfill his word." It stretched its head up, proud and cobralike; a quaver of emotion came into its voice. "His left hand, his mightie arm outstretch'd, do without thanks what yet his right knows not; and will while this earth lives, till he my author look from high heav'n on me so long estrang'd and say, 'Well done, thou good and faithful serpent!'"

Sarita flung back her head and laughed. "Oh, that was worth the wait. I've always thought there was more to 'Evil be thou my good' than met the eye." But quickly she sobered. "I suppose that's my answer, isn't it? The zealots are yours *and* God's; they can't lose. And in another sense Mim and Bob are yours and God's too. It's a sort of dual sponsorship, or else no sponsorship at all; as if you're both just waiting, as if all heaven waits quite passively to see what poor mortal flesh will do next."

"The earth hath he bequeath'd to Adam's brood," said the serpent with a moping shrug of one coil. "And much luck may they have of it. For me, I will retire—if you are answer'd now—and think on him in contemplation calm whose mightie works sustain and taint the world." It flowed gracefully down a leg of the table and toward the anteroom, beginning to chant something inaudible to itself.

Sarita started up in alarm: what would it do if it got outside the shop? Could it open the door? Why hadn't she locked the deadbolt? It was in the anteroom before she was out of her chair; she seized her shears and ran after it. The doorknob had delayed it only briefly: its head was already through the door, and the chanting was louder. "Plague, inquisition, warfare, woe, pogrom," it was saying in tones of uncontainable worship, "bomb, gun, grenade, blind hatred, ignorance. Apartheid, empire, revolution, rape, *Sonderbehandlung*, gulag, torture, lies." It undulated in rhythm with its words.

Sarita sprang after it. The tip of its tail was just going through the door; she snipped it off, and the serpent went coiling down the hall, scattering beans from side to side behind it. It was shouting hysterically now: "A kinder, gentler nation! Right to life! Diet delight! You've come a long way, baby!" But when it got to the head of the stairs its strength failed; it lay limp, depleted, moving ineffectually on the grey linoleum. She caught up with it and knelt by its head, uncertain what to do. It raised its head with great effort: the opals were milky, their lights hidden, its voice was a hoarse gasp. In spite of herself she leaned closer to hear it. "Trust me," it said, and died.

"Oh, Lord," she said. Then, against a certain distaste, she took hold of the wrapped wire and yanked it from the mouth. With the shears she tore the length of the satin body, wadded it into a ball, and took it back to her trash. She brought a broom and swept up the three pounds of beans it had taken to stuff the creature. What could she do with the beans? They were probably contaminated with floor wax, or for all she knew with cockroach spray; they couldn't be eaten. A waste entirely. Tears sprang to her eyes. Perhaps if she washed them carefully—but with what?—Todd would take the beans for his compost; they could sprout there and be turned under, and surely whatever had spoiled them would be dispersed there and not do harm. She tipped the dustpan into a paper bag. And then she sat at the top of the stairs and wept, for her failure and for her loneliness; for the impossibility of protecting any friend against danger; for her first memory of Mim, magniloquent and so strangely fearful, and for Mim's new courage. And because Mim had a lover, because she was giving the best of herself elsewhere, because anyone but Sarita herself should have the enjoyment of her body and of her mind.

CHAPTER 13

... the canny (uncanny) way that daily life continues, like parts of a severed worm ...

—Geoffrey Hartman

Mim's defenses were breaking down; she had not realized how good they were until she lost them. One forgot in love's absence—so as not to die from its lack—the mere elemental compulsion toward kindness and warmth: the idle caress done in passing, the silly face, the private mispronounced word. She began to miss Alan, with whom she had first done these things. There had been too much danger in missing him when she left him, and even later when he had moved and remarried—even when she had signed the annulment papers—she had refused to explore too much the shape of her loneliness. Now that Ari had filled it, she sensed the echo of Alan around the edges.

Not where she most expected to, in bed: there was too much distraction. She and Alan had barely found words for their acts; they had slowly evolved a rough code, but neither was quite easy with language for all those conjunctions. But Ari—the first day or two of wordless discovery gone by—was full of capricious metaphor and outrageous slang; he could not let a good line pass, and once on the point of entry he whispered wickedly in her ear, "A man, a plan, a canal—" There was something a little uncanny about their encounters: both of them swore that one night, when they had been kissing in a doorway with their legs twined, they had been balanced on one of Mim's feet. She had thought to herself through a stupor of lust, "No, I can't pick this other foot up: Ari has both *his* feet off the floor, and we'll fall if I lift both of mine."

"Next time that happens," he said, "we'll just ascend; now we know how Chagall's lovers got over the rooftops."

When he went to work she would say, helplessly echoing generations of anxious women and trying not to quaver as she did, "Don't let them do anything to you out there, will you?" And then she would go to work herself, and the familiar routine would lull her into trust, and soon she would find that every ordinary movement—spinning in her chair, opening her legs to get up, squatting at a low file drawer—stirred up her desire. Her pelvis was made of fire and water; she had only to think of him and a stab of joy would travel up from her perineum and into her breath, and her eyes would blink like overloaded circuits. The place between her legs (and it seemed vast, every centimeter of it a different neural territory) was a flood plain crackling with electrical storms: sometimes, instantaneously, it would pulse at the thought of a word or a touch he had given. He taught her how to exercise the muscle of the pelvic floor, and her pleasure became prolonged and profound; it was absurd to be learning this at the age of thirty-four and from a man, but she was glad to learn it at all, and glad to learn it from him because it was another excuse to think of him. O brave new world, that has such people in it. She smiled secretly as his seed came slipping out of her all day, onto the white pad. She would not wash it away. Two to four hundred million sperm in each spoonful, some of them viable and some not: some with two heads or two tails or heads oddly shaped, others ready right now to marry an ovum. *As the stars of the sky, as the sands on the seashore.* Would not one of those seeds be planted? For the first time in many years she imagined not fearing pregnancy, incubating with curiosity and trust a child of her lover's, sending her own blood into the stream of his people's life. *Abraham et semini ejus in saecula.* Had she simply first encountered the wrong people? The *brit*, the covenant, was in its first form nothing more than the circumcision, which Ari pronounced in the softer Ashkenazic, *bris:* "Put your law in my inward parts," she said to him once, in revenge for the palindrome, and he laughed and was shocked. (Alan had been circumcised too, by American medical custom—Mim had never seen a foreskin except in Greek art and pornography—but it had not mattered in any metaphysical sense.) She knew that these exalted ravings were no warrant for actually conceiving a child, but it enchanted her to know that she had time to think it over.

But that was when Alan insisted on being missed: quiet and bitter, his voice would sound in her ear. "Brittle repartee and sex on the floor, is that what 'choice' is making the world safe for, Mira?" She found herself struggling to make the case for frivolity. It wasn't mere shamelessness; surely even Alan knew that by now; it was relief, consolation, the play of intelligence between two bodies made happy: sprung rhythm.

There was a bare patch on Ari's back, low down on the left side, the skin white and puckered with old scars. "Oh, that's my war wound," he said. "I got that in London in the Blitz—really; I was just a baby, not even walking yet. Kind of like Yossarian, isn't it? They're trying to kill me."

He had been born in London, in '42; there was an older sister, three years old at the time of the bombing, who had died of her burns. He had no memory of her. "It's as if I did, though," he said, in a puzzled tone that Mim was hearing for the first time, "because my mother would talk about her. There are these little Ur-narratives running around in my head about Anna's first step and first word and the music she liked. And of course the night of the fire. Much later—toward the end of her life—my mother said she talked about Anna so much to me because there was nobody else she could tell. She didn't mean my father, who was right there; she meant her mother. She hung on to the end of the war just hoping to tell her mother."

"But her mother—" said Mim: not quite a question.

He nodded. "Even before the fire. Before I was born."

Mim pulled the quilt closer. "I get spells of having to read about it," she said. "Every time there's this moment of absolute disorientation, and I say my God, they did *what*? It's as if everything I know about it keeps rolling off. As if I never know anything about it. I know what it's like to read about it in a warm place with hot and cold running water and plenty of food."

"Nobody knows about it," he said. "People who were there can't really get a handle on it."

They had gone on to New York after the war, when Ari was five and

Jay was a baby in arms. Their father, who had been a fabric importer, reestablished his business; their mother kept the books. She never made dresses again. At five, Mim had been at home in a placid town in Ohio—riding a miniature bike with training wheels, craving a Minnie Mouse lunchbox, helping her father burn the leaves in the fall. "My life's been so safe," she said. "Of course everyone wants a safe life, but it's so unconscionable to have one; you have it in total ignorance of other people's unsafety, and it makes you a fool. No wonder I can't seem to take hold. I grew up outside of history."

"Did you," he said without assent. "*Humanae Vitae,* that's not history; *Roe v. Wade,* that's not history at all."

"But that's not the equivalent—"

"No. But it's not outside history. History knows where to find you, ready or not."

"I was trying not to be findable," she said. "I put a lot of work into staying outside it. Killed for it, if you want to think of it that way. Nothing had ever happened to me, and the abortion was an effort to make damn sure nothing ever would."

He sighed. "Oh, Mim, don't. Lots of women have babies to make sure nothing *else* ever happens to them."

She sat up, taking the covers with her and stared out the window. He absently knuckled her spine. "Isn't it strange," he said presently. "Torturers know the body better than lovers do. There are innumerable ways to make a body suffer, and only a few ways to comfort it; pain's more convincing than joy. Enough pain will create a permanent deficit: there's no way to be happy enough to reverse it. We're really not all that strong."

She shook her head. "Maybe that's it," she said obscurely. "We goyim have to make our unsafety for ourselves, consciously; it's not given to us."

Perhaps that was all it was, to convert to Judaism; perhaps she was only saying with foolish solemnity, in a useless and belated gesture of solidarity, *They're trying to kill me too.* They weren't; and even if they should be, her job would not be to let them, to go courting danger out of some fraudulent heroism, but to do what those who had died would rather have done—what those who survived had managed to do, through luck or self-discipline or lack of scruple: to resist and evade and scratch out interstices in the system where they could survive. Nothing in her education had prepared her for that. (Except perhaps lying to Alan: her one moment of emergency, which she had half brought on herself.) She forced herself to speak plainly. "Is it presumptuous, is it silly, to try to become a Jew?"

"I can't help you with that, sweetie," he said, not unkindly. "Ask the rabbi; he's the quality control officer."

"He doesn't know either. Or at least, he's in favor of chutzpah; humility makes him uncomfortable, he doesn't like my grovelling around being worried about my presumption. He'd rather I just presumed. I think he thinks my quality is all right. But I'm not sure my motives are."

"That's so Catholic," he said. "Don't worry about your motives. Secret things belong to God, who's probably not even there. What matters is what you do."

"It's a killing machine," said Del Marlin. "I don't know what I could say to make it any clearer. It's a pretty sad day when one of God's chosen is in charge of a killing machine."

Jerry Kaplansky stopped himself—barely—from rolling his eyes. He had been checking in on Del every few weeks, and had started writing a long piece on him; the man held a weird fascination. "I wondered when we would get to that," he said. "Are you of the Jerry Falwell school, that says God doesn't hear Jews' prayers?"

"Look," said Del, "I want to make one thing clear. You media people, you're always trying to make decent Christians out to be Jew-haters. I have the greatest respect for the Jewish people. I have no problem at all with the *real* Jews, the ones that follow the Law: they're good religious folk. You can tell it by the size of their families, eh?" He laughed and wheezed. "It's these turncoat, half-assimilated ones that are causing all the trouble. They're not following God's plan for them. They've strayed. This Mergenzole, do you think he prays anyway? Don't bet your life on it."

Jerry, who had consumed a cheeseburger on the way to the prison without a pang of conscience, could not forbear to raise an eyebrow. This was a new twist. He had been expecting to hear something about the apocalypse, the Rapture or whatever they called it, mixed with warmed-over conspiracy theories from the *Protocols of the Elders of Zion*. Perhaps interfaith dialogue, in spite of itself, was having some good effects. Jerry had himself done nothing resembling prayer since his bar mitzvah—his kid brother, now a junior in college, was causing consternation at home by his fascination with the campus Hasidic movement—and the thought of the fundamentalists of one religion defending the fundamentalists of another struck him as ominous. Still, he was relieved at Del's apparent innocence of the nastier forms of anti-Semitism.

Del, having digressed, returned to his subject. "No, it's a death mill. A disassembly line, right? Do you know there's one kind of abortion where they go right in and tear the baby limb from limb, with pliers? Dilation and execution, I think they call it. What kind of a person would be willing to do such a thing?"

Jerry—not being interested in these elaborations, which struck him as pornographic—decided to try him. "What about the Holocaust, Del? Did it happen?"

Del puffed up, outraged. "You wait just a minute! Don't you go putting in your newspaper that I'm one of them bigots, who deny the whole thing. You want to discredit the whole prolife movement. Of course it happened. I was stationed in Germany in the service, just a few years ago; I bet I know more about it than you do. I drove some American diplomats right into Poland, *behind the Iron Curtain*, to see some of what was left over. I seen Auswitch with my own eyes, mister—the gas chamber and the ovens and all, and a whole room full of suitcases, and a room full of hair, did you know that, that they cut off before they sent them to be gassed. Why do you think I want to defend the babies?" He stared through the glass in mingled grief and indignation. "No, you don't see it; you think it's two different things. But it's not. There was a lady on the trip—a lovely Christian woman, a senator's wife—who just about summed it up. She'd been real quiet and brave—we were all kind of stunned, I don't think I even remember anybody crying in there—but on the way back her face kind of quivered and a tear spilled out, and she said, 'What an evil man. I just don't understand it. But you know, even a man that evil—even a man who could do *that*'—she waved her hand back toward the camp—'wouldn't sink so low as to countenance abortion.' Her husband said, 'Oh, for God's sake, Fayrene,' real disgusted, but it changed my life, I can tell you."

Jerry thought it might change his too. The conversation was becoming surreal; perhaps he should try to pitch this story to the *New Yorker*. Certainly he was right to keep coming back for more. "I don't think Hitler had the fetus's well-being in mind," he said, trying to keep his voice steady. "He was trying to produce a super-race, remember? He wanted blond, blue-eyed fetuses. Being Jewish and pregnant was a sure way to get yourself killed."

"God works in mysterious ways," said Del. "Who's to say He didn't see an opportunity there, at least to save some babies of the Arr-yan race while Hitler's mind was elsewhere on those terrible things?" He lit a cigarette pensively. "Oh, it happened all right. There's never been anything like it in the history of the world. Besides," he added practically, "it had to have happened, or we couldn't be saying abortion is just the same."

In April, a seder at Jay and Lisa's apartment on the Upper West Side of New York: hours of ritual and quantities of food and an air of barely controlled chaos. There were twelve adults and what felt like eight or nine children (one in the womb, at fifteen weeks); the younger children thundered from room to room while the adults tried to concentrate. Dina, daughter of the house, changed midway in the seder from her blue dress with the white pilgrim collar to a pink tutu ("Tu. Tu." she said reflectively when Ari remarked on it) and emerged from her room carrying by the hair a clutch of Barbie dolls. She must have been about four, with delicate springy limbs and fine brown hair. "Wanna see something pretty? Wanna see something pretty?" she kept saying, and doing gymnastic stunts; she would do a backwards somersault and pose, her arms outstretched, one foot placed in front of the other, her face tilted downward as her eyes looked up and lit in a seductive smile. Did she know what that look conveyed?

There was a three-year-old, Tal, with angelic blond curls and a face like an English choirboy, whom Dina pulled around protectively and addressed as "my little boy"; there were some six-and seven-year-olds whose names Mim never got straight; there was Evan, Dina's brother, a sardonic ten-year-old with glasses who by the third cup of wine was muttering frank insults at the little ones. The child in the womb was called BIV, for Benjamin Isaac (or Barbara Ilana) Vigder; its mother was a children's book illustrator, and was making it a book. ("When I'm done with the paintings, *then* they can tell me its sex.") Maybe that was all the children—Mim was unable to gauge the number of six-and seven-year-olds—but the air split with high shrieks from time to time as if they were increasing on the spot.

Ari's daughter was there, flown in from Berkeley; Mim had an impression of energy and discontent, but Marcie was helping Lisa with the meal and there was not much chance to talk to her. As they ate between sections of ritual Mim heard bits of her conversation, but she was simultaneously hearing bits of everyone else's:

"—this little bulletin board you're on is nothing, Daddy. It's just a nice convenience to save people from mailing letters. In five years we're going to see interactive linkups with people all over the globe; if you want to find out about abortion providers in Russia or Japan, or even Romania or say Thailand, where there aren't supposed to be any, you'll be able to do it. There'll be all these squirrely guys like ham radio operators just living to set up these networks. We'll have them for ecology and human rights—"

"—and the antis," said Ari.

"—and terrorists and neo-Nazis and right-wing vigilante groups," added Lisa.

"Jeez!" said Marcie. "You've got it all figured out. Listen, what progressives will be able to do will surpass—we're talking about a world civilization, where people have access—"

Somebody asked Lisa about neo-Nazis, and she began describing her book: "—comparing the types of hysteria, and the libels and actual methods used by various kinds of extremists. They're remarkably similar, even across groups that are unlikely to have contact with one another, and between groups that advocate violence and groups that are just disaffected. My working theory is that the similarities are due to the nature of the human body—which is always vulnerable in a particular range of ways—and to certain fears of conspiracy, witchcraft, blood, uncontrolled sex, contagion, poisoning and so on that seem to be latent in the human mind."

"Like what Cohn said in *Europe's Inner Demons*."

"Yes, I'm building on that. There seems to be a certain state of mind you slip into when you feel free to hate; I'm trying to find the connection to brain research, where they tickle a certain area with an electrode and the patient sees little grey men—perhaps there's an area, or a neurochemical mix, for paranoia and persecution, even in the nominally sane. Causeless hatred, the rabbis called it. Hatred brings out the urge to mutilate; if you don't dare do it yourself, you'll project the urge onto the Other, or you'll formulate your cosmology in a mutilating way. You find the same fears in astonishing places, totally unselfconscious. From white supremacists to prolife fanatics to—radical feminism is an incredible source. I hate to say it, but it's true; it's one of the things that got me started on this. They even have racial pseudoscience. This notion that parthenogenesis is the natural form of human reproduction, and that since all fetuses look female at first, men are mutants—"

"But how do they—the fetus has a Y chromosome all along—"

"Ah, but the Y chromosome is sinister: it's a damaged X. Metaphors of crippling—"

Jay, who had heard it all before, was talking Israeli politics with Ari and Marcie and BIV's father Mike. "—Papa having had the bad judgment to be *anti*-Zionist," he was saying.

"Or the foresight," said Ari darkly.

"Jay! Dad! I can't believe you never told me this. I didn't think he was that religious. Was he waiting for the Messiah to come before—"

"No, no; it wasn't that," Ari said. "It was more a mistrust of nationalism; he didn't like what he saw of it in Germany, and he didn't relish the thought of Jews having to get good at it to survive. Even pragmatically he thought it was safer to come to the States in '47. He said *Why should it be any different in Palestine? There they've got us all in one place.* He watched what went on in Israel as obsessively as anyone else, but every time there was some altercation with the Arabs he'd say *Make us just like the nations,* and go into a depression about it."

"—song about a man poisoning the well in this utopian women's village," Lisa was saying. "*Jewish* women. Totally unselfconscious."

"Look at me! Look at me!" Dina shrieked, going into a handstand.

"Sweetie, do you want to do that on a full stomach?" said Jay. He patted his lap. "Come on up here. Want some soda?"

Dina climbed up. "Okay." She sipped noisily and looked across the table at Mim. "Your dress is pretty."

"Thank you."

Dina considered. "I know you're Uncle Bob's girlfriend," she said, "but I forgot your name."

"Mim."

"I'm Dina."

"A master of the obvious," Evan muttered through a mouthful of chicken.

"Uncle Bob got shot," she confided.

Mim nodded seriously.

"Were you scared?"

"Yes, I was."

"A crazy man shot him. To make him stop helping women."

Mim nodded. That was one way of putting it, for a four-year-old.

"Are you going to marry him?"

There was a slight stir of discomfort; Mim and Jay both opened their mouths and said nothing. Marcie's face was unreadable. "Well, you should," Dina said. "You should take care of him."

"These are sensitive questions, Dina," said Ari calmly. "You'll be the first to know, okay? Would you pass me the *maror?*"

"*Maror,* eww," said Dina, reaching carefully for the bowl of beet-stained horseradish.

"Eww," said her brother mockingly.

"——*sacrificing male babies in the back of the women's bookstore,*" said their mother with animation. "I kid you not. These women were making phone calls all over town, accusing the bookstore collective of slitting throats in the sink, and meanwhile the pro-lifers—"

"*Mom,*" said Evan in anguish.

Lisa broke off. "Sorry, kid," she said with obvious affection. "It's my work; I get carried away. Like when you're on the computer? It's compulsive. Anyway, it's no worse than what we've just been reading. The Egyptians lost their firstborn?"

"Yeah, but this is real," the boy said. There was an assortment of lifted eyebrows and soft explosions around the table.

"But it isn't; that's just what I'm saying. It was a hysterical rumor. Mom collects hysterical rumors. But they're never true."

"Why don't you just read Stephen King," said Evan, oppressed.

"There is a reason," said Lisa, "but do you mind if I explain it later, tomorrow maybe? I want to get the desserts."

There followed a short interval of table-clearing and trying to find space in the kitchen for all the used dishes, during which Mim overheard Marcie interrogating Ari in the kitchen in a fierce, carrying whisper:

"Dad, is she interested in you?"

"At what level are we using the word *interested?*"

"She is, then. Oh my God, I can't believe you're doing this."

"What exactly am I doing? Your mother and I are, after all, divorced."

"Dad, do I have to say it?" There was a meaning pause. "That trophy thing, that whole pattern of dipping into a younger generation. My own father. At least she's not in her twenties; that would be worse." Then, spitefully and eagerly, as if it were just occurring to her, "You can hear her biological clock ticking away."

"Masha! I will not listen to this kind of talk. I don't tell you how to run your life, and you will not tell me how to run mine. Go out there and be civilized."

"You're going to make me say it, aren't you? She's not Jewish. With all the Jewish women your own age who are looking for someone. Not only the mid-life crisis but the eternal pursuit of the shiksa."

"You wouldn't understand. Out."

Mim escaped to the bathroom; she was not up to explaining her relation to Judaism at a Passover seder, and had a feeling that Marcie would not take it seriously in her father's lover. When she returned Ari was back at the table, expounding the rabbinic responsa on abortion to the father of one of the seven-year-olds, a man named Earl. "—never took that crucial last step," he was saying. "Yes, always to save the mother's life; yes, even to spare her mental distress; but not just because she judged it was the wrong time to take on that responsibility. In these late responsa they come very close to seeing what it's all about for women, but they shut their eyes at the last minute: if economics and shame and the overwhelming demands of life are sufficient reasons, then the world is a very different place than they thought it was, and women's lives much more painful. A matter of profound guilt for compassionate men, as you may imagine."

"But in practice, were they more liberal?"

"Some were, I would guess; of course there's no way to know what they said in private. The important point is that on paper the choice is still not up to the individual: the choice is up to the tradition. As interpreted, of course, by the current generation of learned men."

"If there had been more learned women—" said Mim, sitting down.

"Yeah, well, that's why they kept the women so busy having babies," said Ari. "My friend here," he continued to Earl, "is smitten with talmudic debate: it looks so much better than a papal encyclical. Good Lord, people deciding individual cases, paying attention to nuance: it's raging pluralism. But it's not; it's a more attractive form of authoritarianism, but it's still authoritarian. Hi, sweetie."

"Hi."

"But does it have to be?" said Earl. "After all, there's that business of the Torah having a different face for every person who stood at Sinai; subjectivity is built into the tradition."

"Not reliably," Ari said. "When I was still here in the city I used to see ultra-orthodox women occasionally; they'd come in extremely discreetly, usually having asked their rebbe's permission to abort the previous pregnancy and been denied, and having learned not to ask this time. These were women with six, seven, eight, ten kids. Even more occasionally, we'd see woman who actually *had* the rebbe's permission, usually for health reasons; I won't say which rebbes, but some were more elastic than others in their definition of health. And from our point of view it was all rather arbitrary. The women who had permission, nothing could touch them—oh, did they snub the counselors—it was like having divine sanction, though of course they weren't happy to be there. The farthest anybody else got was the raw wind of existential freedom."

"But at least somebody got divine sanction," said Mim. "I don't say that's enough, but at least sometimes, under some circumstances, the woman's needs do come first. Compare—well, a papal encyclical. Earl, do you know what Paul the Sixth based *Humanae Vitae* on? The minority report of the Papal Birth Control Commission. The majority was ready to go for divine sanction on the Pill, but the minority said—wait, I can quote it verbatim—" She shut her eyes and put her hands to her forehead. *"The Church could not have erred through so many centuries, even through one century, by imposing under serious obligations very grave burdens in the name of Jesus Christ, if Jesus Christ did not actually impose those burdens.* In other words people's needs simply don't matter, we have a reputation to uphold. Can you—" The two men were laughing, with the manic delight of inveterate church-watchers. "No, really, it doesn't *matter* that Jesus never said a word about birth control. It's another tradition of interpretation and accretion; he can say it retroactively, for all time."

"In 1960 something," gasped Ari.

"In 1966. But anyone with an ounce of logic can see—"

"Or a semester of history," said Earl. "My God, Galileo? They erred that way all the time."

A woman in purple and crystals (was her name Leah, and had she said she did some sort of New Age body work?) leaned across the table intently. "Have you ever wondered, Bob—why do you do this? Why have you chosen this work that makes you so many enemies?"

He was startled. "Nu? Life is real, life is earnest. Why should I not make enemies?"

"Most people find it very stressful," she said. "To be that close to such hatred—"

"That's an epiphenomenon," he said. "It's not why I chose the work. Those people weren't even on the scene when I started."

"But they are now. And after all you've been through, maybe you need to ask yourself—why are you seeking this non-pleasurable thing to do? Why do you keep going back to it?"

"Because other people aren't clamoring to take my place," he said. "It's not, of course, anyone's business to do an unpopular job."

The woman gave him an understanding look. "A lot of our generation think we haven't suffered enough."

Irritation shot out of him like spikes. "You know," he said, "I believe in psychoanalysis as much as the next man, but somehow one still has to act. What if I am walking around with a survivor complex? These women need help. You want me to help them and have mental health too?" Marcie looked on, deconstructing his scorn for the woman; Mim noticed a family resemblance in the tilt of her head.

At Mim's left, the three-year-old was standing in his father's lap, much occupied with a cup of coffee. "Ooh, it's going to be so sweet now it'll be awful," said his father encouragingly. "How is it? Is it good?"

"Yes."

"Is it sweet?"

"Yes." A considering pause. "Needs more sugar."

"No it doesn't. No, Tali, put it back. If you want more sugar, you've got all the sugar you need on your placemat." The child scraped some of the grains into a handful and let them sift slowly into the cup.

Lisa swept through the room, calling children. "Kids? Kids? Dina, where are you, sweetie? Who's going to find the afikomen?"

CHAPTER 14

"It was an *accident*. I was exhausted from running after the other two all day and I missed a pill. How is having a third one going to help me be any less busy? Those people out there, would they like to stop marching around and come clean my house?"

"If they were serious about stopping abortion they'd spend all their time being chaperones, wouldn't they? Where were they when Denny was all over me at the party, totally shitfaced, and I kept saying No no no and he just kept going? What gives them the right to show up *now* and say that stupid five minutes determines my life?"

"Why would I be taking pills? I wasn't expecting to—I mean, I never let him get that far before. He used to call me the Ice Maiden. A couple of times when he really whined about it I gave him—you know—a hand job, but that was it. I'm probably the only virgin at Regional.—I mean, I was. Oh, God, I never thought I would have to do this. I started a rumor in tenth grade about this one girl, that she'd been here. God, I'm so sorry now."

"Don't make it easy on her. I don't want her thinking she can just do this, get herself knocked up and then come here and get rid of it. This should be the worst day of her life. Make it hurt."

"My God, I thought it was menopause. I haven't had a period since August. I'm forty-eight. I can't imagine having a baby now. It takes us two days to recover from seeing the grandchildren. Isn't this crazy?"

"I said to one of those women outside, Now be honest: do *you* come from a family where nobody's ever had an abortion? Do you know for sure, for all the generations of your family, that no one ever ended a pregnancy? Don't talk to my daughter like that. She's doing her very best, and I'm proud of her."

"Stupid, stupid, stupid. We didn't want anything to interfere with the sacredness of our love. Well, this interferes with it big-time. How dumb can you be?"

"No, he doesn't want me to have the baby. But he's real disgusted with anybody who'd have an abortion. You've got to do one or the other, don't you?"

"If his two sons don't make him a faithful husband, why should this baby? I just don't think I can take the risk."

"No, I don't need to talk it over. I thought about keeping it—I really hate to do this—but I'm not in a steady relationship right now. It was sort of a . . . well, I wasn't planning on it. If I had it to do over again I'd say Nothing doing, mister, not unless you wear a condom, but—but you know how it is. Or maybe you don't."
  "No, I do."
  "When I was pregnant for Jamie, my first, I was against abortion, but I guess I learned something. It's a lot of work being a mother. I don't

want for us to be poor all our lives. If it was just a question of what I was for or against . . .

"One of those people out there said to me, 'You know that's a baby you're carrying.' That's kind of the point, isn't it? I just can't have another baby right now. I just can't. Last night I was talking to it," she said, suddenly breaking down, "to that little person in there, saying I was sorry, saying I have to do right by Jamie, that she was an accident too . . .

"Jamie? She's four. Yeah, I was pretty young. This is her. Isn't she darling with her hair in those two little ponytails? I just love her to death. That little girl is the center of my life. Did you hear about that woman who drowned her two-year-old in the bathtub? I cried my eyes out. That woman should rot in hell. They say she was abused as a child, well that's no excuse for killing your own baby. I just picture his little eyes opening under the water, looking up at her like 'Mommy, why are you doing this?' The death penalty is too good for her. She should live a long time and suffer every day of her life.

"I'm sorry, I'm running on, it just makes me so mad. Listen, I really appreciate that you would reduce the fee—when you live like I do you have to count every penny. Listen, when I'm a nurse—and it's when, not if, even if it takes me ten years—I'll pay you the rest of the money. Is that okay? Where do I sign?"

"Amy, please, are you okay? We can go if you want; you don't have to go through with it. Amy, you scare me when you just sit there so quiet."

"Brian, shut up."

"My mom doesn't believe in this at all. She's been out there picketing before; she has these gross little pictures of fetuses stuck to the fridge. No, of course I didn't tell her; my boyfriend is with me. She says a girl who has an abortion spends the rest of her life trying to justify it—she gives you one excuse after another for why she had to kill that baby, and that's all they are, excuses. Do you think she's right? Do you think I'm going to hell for this? Kendall, that's my boyfriend, says religion is all bullshit. Do you think he's right?"

"All I keep thinking is *Now I'm not a nice woman.*"
She was a fifth grade teacher; they had opened the side door at six a.m. to smuggle her in before the pickets arrived. (They were out there now, marching with two-foot white-painted lath crosses, chanting some half-audible parody of "M is for the many things she gave me.")
"Look, it happens," said Ari gently. "How many chances do you have to get pregnant in a year? Do the math: you ovulate thirteen times, and that accounts for a few days each cycle; multiply that by even ten years of sexual activity and you get somewhere between five and six hundred opportunities. The odds are all for it. It's not a sin, it's biology. Don't beat yourself up for failing. You're still a nice woman."
"That's nice of *you*. But I still think that if I were really determined I could get on top of it all—my other kids, and my work—I was reading the *Spoon River* poems to my class the other day, and there was old Lucinda Matlock, cheerful, indomitable, raising twelve children. My grandmother raised eleven. Did she ever feel such dismay at finding herself pregnant again? Or did women in those days just take it? *Degenerate sons and daughters, life is too strong for you.* I can't help but feel I fall short."

"I just feel so guilty." The girl's friend, in flowered leggings and a pale-blue babydoll top: she sat twisting her purse strap in her lap. "See, I was the one who said it. I'm the only person she's told: she won't tell her parents, she won't tell her boyfriend. She won't go to anybody who could really help her out. So finally I just looked at her and said, Have you thought about an abortion? And she said Yes, I have. It was like I was giving her permission, just by saying the word. But the thing is, I don't think I believe in abortion. But I had to stand by her because I said it first. If that's what she really wants, and I don't try to stop her, does that mean I have to believe in it?

"Her mom thinks we're at the mall. I wish we were."

"Her dad has become serious about his religion at this late date. What would he say to her if he *knew* she was pregnant? Her life wouldn't be worth living. It's so hypocritical: abortion's a sin but pregnancy is a disgrace. Me, I don't have to run around proving how Catholic I am by putting my daughter through hell. Bless you for being here."

"He wants to get married. He has this quaint old-world notion that the first woman he did *it* with would be his wife, so now of course I've got to be. And I don't think I want to. I'm so scared. I'm out of my depth. I absolutely can't have a baby. That's not something you do without being sure of the man. We had sex because . . . because we were curious; I don't think you could even say we made love. I'm not sure I've ever met somebody I could *make love* with, in that sense. I can't see us being together for the rest of our lives. Does that mean I'm too choosy? How far do you have to lower your standards to get married and stay married? When will I know what I'm doing?"

"I said she should do whatever she felt she had to. But I don't want her to do this. No, I didn't mean to get her pregnant, and yes, I'm scared too, but . . . but I'm proud; I'm so amazed that plain ordinary, uh, *come*, can actually do this. I mean, I don't think I really believed it. And I think it would be great to have a baby. You know, teach it words, and watch it crawling around . . . buy it computer games . . . we used to make jokes about it, how soon we would get our kids on line. But it was all kind of facetious, and I guess she was more facetious than I was. She could always go back to school later, couldn't she? Or keep going part time? But she says she doesn't want the baby at all. She says I'm not serious about working. I think I'm pretty serious. I want to be a comic book artist; you can make a real living doing that. I want to do the right thing. I don't think you should destroy life just because it's a bad time, or you're not sure where the money will come from. You should trust in God, right? She says she's worried about the future, but the future's not even here yet. She's the only person I've ever loved that would love me back. Why doesn't she want my baby?"

"I'm not meant for motherhood. Nobody should walk the earth that's a product of me. If it had to stay in my body for nine months I'd poison it with my blood."

"My God, I don't *know* what to do. That's why I missed my appointment before—I thought I'd decided to have it, and now I don't know again. How will I feel if I kill it? But what if I have it and have to go on welfare? I think people who do either one of those things are scum. How could I end up in a situation where whatever I do, I'm scum?

"Adoption? Oh no no no. It's my baby. If I have it I keep it. It's my fault, I got pregnant, and nobody's going to take that responsibility off my hands. I think it's sick, people hanging over you saying *Give me your baby*. When my sister was pregnant she got that all the time. Just because she wasn't married. Like you wouldn't love your baby just because you weren't married. I mean, I would love my baby even if—even if—does it sound weird to say this?—even if I decide, um, not to have it?"

"You know how I look at it? It's as if one of my kids wanted something that wasn't good for her, or that was harder to do than she realized: here she is flinging herself on the floor in a tantrum, or just tugging on my skirt and gritting her teeth and saying *Mommy, can I please, pleease*, and I just have to hold firm and say *No, dear, I'm sorry*. The poor kid is suffering: there's an agony in knowing how she feels and having to deny her. But, damn it, it's my job to know best. And in this case one of my kids wants to be born, and I just have to hang on to myself and say *Honey, I'm sorry, no.*" She could not hang onto herself: she was weeping.

"This is our *authority* as mothers," she went on in a pinched voice, "to order our children's lives. We don't do a perfect job of it, but we try very hard, and who else can do any job of it at all?"

"Elsie, for God's sake will you stop being so silent. I said I was sorry; I don't know what else I can do. I mean, besides paying for this. And sitting here with you, my God, how long is this going to take.

"Honey, I know I have a temper. I said I was sorry. You're not doing this just 'cause I lost my temper, are you? I guess I could deal with a baby right now if I really had to, but it's just such a shitty time. I didn't really mean you did it on purpose. You can always have another one later, right? Right, honey? A couple of years down the line."

"Robby, shut up."

"Please, don't even say that. I put the first one up for adoption, and it almost killed me. I can't do that again. They tell you it's such a noble thing to do, and then they treat you like trash; my family will throw it up to me for the rest of my life. When the nurse took the baby away I thought I would die. She gave me this innocent look and said, 'But you *chose* to do this.' Hell can't be worse than what I went through for that baby. God owes me for this one."

"I'm sorry, I can't do this. It's wrong. It's wrong."

"But it's wrong to put unnatural substances into your body. We're trying to live a really pure life. We're vegetarians, and we don't do any alcohol or dope, and I was keeping real careful track of my cycle. The wise women of ancient times used to be able to conceive or not through meditation alone. No, it's just the wrong time: financially we're not real stable, and we weren't asking for a baby to manifest, which is why I can't understand . . . I keep asking myself, why was I chosen to have this experience that I don't want? What am I meant to learn? I've really bonded with this little being inside me; I'm sure it's a girl. We've named her, Michael and I—Tiffany Bright. Tiffany is such a sweet name, and it comes from this word *theophany,* that means when God manifests, you know? So it just seems so perfect. We wrote her this little prayer . . ."

Dear Tiffany Bright, she and Michael read together in the procedure room, a candle burning before them. *We thank you for gracing our lives with your innocent presence. We understand that you wish to leave the earth plane and return to a place of pure light.* ("Oh, Ari, it's awful, it's cant: the fetus doesn't wish for any such thing." "You're not, I trust, suggesting we hold off till she can recognize cant?") *Go in peace, to return to us at a more appropriate time or go to other parents who will love you just as much.* But in the recovery room she cried, and Michael clung haplessly to her hand with his large pale one and said, "Jenna, please don't. Jenna, you said you felt peaceful about it. You said you meditated and got her consent and she didn't want to be born. Please look at me. Jenna, I think they're right, you should go on the Pill. Can you please look at me, Jenna?"

"Michael, shut up."

·

CHAPTER 15

Mature religion as well as mature politics requires solitude.

—Thomas Merton

Mim had expected pickets at the conference, and was surprised when there were none; but then she had expected the conference to be in some interesting historic quarter of downtown Boston, and was disappointed to find that it was in a nondescript chain motel near the airport. Perhaps the price of anonymity was dull and depressing surroundings. But there was a charge of excitement in walking into the lobby, seeing the discreet little sign that said *CLCC* at the top of the stairs, hearing the buzz of talk that floated up from the registration table. She felt—ridiculously, since it was only a little regional conference—that she was about to make her mark on the world.

She and Ari had talked about what they were going to say, but they had decided midway not to show each other the drafts; they wanted to surprise each other. Sarita had listened to Mim's speech, and no one had yet listened to Ari's. She liked this idea of presents: flowers and candy would have annoyed her, an expensive hat was good for a laugh once, but words would endure.

His hand in the small of her back as they waited for the elevator: the proprietary gesture, in spite of himself. Just the fingertips touching her, the palm cupped. *Oh God, never let him steer me by the back of the neck.* But the touch heated her, and when they were closed in the elevator box she kissed him insistently; he walked down the hall holding his jacket in front of him like a fig leaf. It took them some time to unpack.

At the registration table, when they arrived there at last, M.C. O'Connell was carrying on three conversations at once and only had time to shake hands; Terry Treviso hugged Mim, shook hands with Ari, and gave them their registration packets and name tags; a succession of people, seeing who Ari was, admired him and asked him questions. Mim retreated to the literature table. There were sheets of statistics, newsletters, informational fliers about other groups, pamphlets to help women think through their decision, insouciant bumper stickers. She took copies of everything free. She studied the schedule: Ari would speak that night, after the opening ceremonies; there would be a panel discussion next morning, and some small group discussions with names like "Mobilizing for Choice in the Religious Community"; Mim herself (she felt a thrill of fear when she saw her own name) would be speaking at lunch, a placement she could only attribute to an overly hard sell on Terry's or M.C.'s part, or to their having run through the better qualified speakers in previous years. More group sessions after lunch: "Reproductive Rights Issues for Women of Color," "Global Issues," "Dealing with the Media"; social hour, dinner, a screening of a new documentary on clinic violence, next morning another panel. She marveled at people who could organize programs, and wished they could come up with more adventurous titles.

The opening ceremonies, led by M.C. in a piercing soprano, turned out to be religious in nature: several nondenominational prayers read by denominational clergy, and—horrors!—some hymns, from which the name of Jesus had been thoughtfully expurgated for the sake of the few Jews in attendance, but whose Protestant cadences could not be revised. Mim muffled her tone a little so as not to be actually heard participating, but Ari sang in his strong untrained voice in a manner both enthusiastic and faintly supercilious: she was reminded of a political parade she had marched in as a child, her friend Zoë Raskin swinging along beside her chanting with exaggerated fervor and deadpan eyes, "aaeL! B! J! For the ewess—A!" One ought not to laugh at anybody's devotions—her own, no doubt, were just as naïve and clumsy—but there was something so undevoted in these, so approximate to the essence of worship, as if the people had been told about passion for God but had never experienced it. Surely that wasn't true in their private lives. The prayers were a show of allegiance, not a flight into love; why was it so difficult to admit that love in a public gathering?

M.C. introduced Ari with adulation: it was clear that she thought him well on his way to sainthood. Mim was struck by the list of his achievements: he had written a lot of articles, had held office in the National Abortion Federation, was on a task force to find ways to train more doctors in abortion procedures. But the fact that he was alive was of course the real point; the group rose to their feet as he went to the podium. He thanked them inaudibly, nodded acknowledgment several times as the applause wound itself down, spared a quick glance for Mim. At last they were quiet.

"When I was convalescing after the late unpleasantness," he began, "one of the books I read was Elias Canetti's *Crowds and Power*. You may not have heard of Canetti: he won the Nobel for this book in 1981, but that doesn't put one's name before the public in quite the same way as (for example) being murderously assaulted. He was born in Bulgaria, raised in England and all around central Europe—ended up back in England, actually, because of the war—and in the 1920s in Frankfurt, as a young man, had a striking experience of almost being swept up in a political demonstration. It wasn't so much the ideology as the atmosphere of this demonstration that compelled him, and the compulsion seemed to him so peculiar that he spent the next thirty years of his life trying to understand the phenomenon of the crowd.

"Obviously there were some crowds worth studying in Germany in the thirties, but Canetti didn't confine himself to current events: he read a great deal in anthropology and classical literature, and put his own spin on it all—fatally Eurocentric, of course, but also quirky and interesting. The book is an extraordinary mess of allusion and speculation, hanging everything on this notion of the crowd, and it's one of the most intellectually haunting works I've ever run into. I know this isn't what you were expecting to hear about, but my reflections on being the target of a crowd's displeasure became so bound up with this book at a crucial moment that I still find myself filtering my experience through its concepts. I hope you'll indulge me."

Well! thought Mim. They had talked about the book on and off once she had read it too, and she was not surprised it had turned up here, but she wondered what the clergy would make of it: it certainly wouldn't fit their notion of what an abortion doctor thought about.

"Canetti says we have a crowd instinct as elemental as the sex drive. We love to be in a crush of people, to have a common goal, to feel the crowd growing as it attracts more and more of what looks—for the moment—like *us*. He says it's the only place in social life that we find real equality, and the only time we don't hate being touched by strangers. A crowd is by nature impermanent—it can disintegrate as quickly as it assembles—but while it coheres it's a Dionysian force. We cede some of our judgment to it. You may remember that Stanley Milgram, in his famous study of obedience—the one where ordinary people were willing to administer supposed electric shocks to a subject in the next room—said that when we enter a hierarchy we cede some of our conscience to it. The crowd is like that, but more egalitarian, more visceral. We obey a boss or a commanding officer or a scientist doing research because our job's on the line and we want them to think well of us; we go along with a crowd because it's *fun*.

"Canetti's a great classifier: he categorizes crowds according to their purpose, and comes up with things like baiting crowds, flight crowds, feast crowds, prohibition crowds like strikers, reversal crowds like revolutionaries; war, he says, is essentially a conflict between opposing crowds. There's the slow crowd, which defers its gratification: the classic slow crowd is religion, which defers it right into the afterlife, and which generally begins as a popular enthusiasm but is deliberately slowed down by its leaders, who fear—with some reason—what enthusiasm can do. One could call the crowd that gathers in front of a clinic a slow baiting crowd: it's not, at this point, officially out for the kill, it's there to shame the women and intimidate the provider. Of course that crowd would define itself rather differently: it would think of itself as a prohibition crowd, on strike against murder, and entitled to *say* anything at all precisely because it's slowed down just enough not to act." Mim thought of Benoit: all innocence as he called them killers, wholly detached from Del Marlin's murderous will.

"Now the categories I've mentioned so far are all literal, practical ones," Ari went on, "but there are some impractical ones too: metaphysical crowds, or crowds which may not actually congregate but which exist in the collective mind as if they did. Canetti gives men and women as one example: they don't have to gather in groups to be imagined as very distinct categories, sometimes at war with each other. The dead are a crowd, he says, though they can't congregate or do anything at all: they've all gone where we're going. It's irresistible to imagine them all in one place, having intentions towards us. And it's irresistible to imagine those who come after us, too, and to have intentions towards them; and here we begin to piece together something of the present emergency, and to see what application Canetti's thinking may have for our own.

"Let me read you a little of what he says about posterity." He took up the large grey paperback. "'For most of us, the hosts of the dead are an empty superstition, but we regard it as a noble and by no means fruitless endeavor to care for the future crowd of the unborn; to want their good and to prepare for them a better and juster life.' His eventual point in this passage is nothing to do with abortion—he's worried about the Bomb—but these days we hear the word 'unborn' rather differently, and it's instructive to read the passage while keeping in mind all those people who insist that the unborn be born even when their mothers don't want to bear them."

He had let the book close on his thumb; he spread it again. "And the real curiosity is that Canetti classifies *spermatozoa* as a crowd. 'Two hundred million of these animalcules,' he says, 'set out together on their way. They are equal among themselves and in a state of very great density. They all have the same goal and, except for one'—and that's under conditions, I might add, that are rather uncommon from a sperm's-eye view—'they all perish on the way. It may be objected that they are not human beings and that it is therefore not correct to speak of them as a crowd in the sense the word has been used. But this objection does not really touch the essentials of the matter. Each of these animalcules carries with it everything of our ancestors which will be preserved. It contains our ancestors; it *is* them, and it is overwhelmingly strange to find them here again, between one human existence and another, in a radically changed form, all of them within *one* tiny invisible creature, and this creature present in such uncountable numbers.'"

He looked around. Mim wished she could; she would be conspicuous turning around in the front row, but she would have liked to see the clergy's expressions. "Remarkable stuff, isn't it? And where have we heard this before, or something very much like it? In the antis' rhetoric, which combines solicitous care for posterity with awe at the miracle of fertilization. Canetti draws on the same emotions with this business of the one chosen spermatozoon that survives that death swim up the Fallopian tubes. Of course there's the ovum too, of which Canetti says nothing; perhaps since only one of these matures at a time it can never be part of a crowd. We may want to keep that in mind." It was an odd shift; what was he doing?

"Canetti of course was writing before abortion became a question of political moment; the book was published in 1960. So his categories, commodious as they are, do not include the crowd of the aborted. I wonder very much what he would make of all this. But he's assembled all the components, and we can take it from there; he gives us a way to understand the antis' perceptions. Of course he has a sense of humor about it and they don't; that's why he wrote a book and they stand in my parking lot screaming. They've found their crowd: they've got their thinking all laid out for them, they've got their common goal, and they've got that Dionysian charge of seeing their numbers grow. And their numbers *are* growing. It's a very bad time for abortion providers, and it's going to get worse. We in this room are a much slower crowd than they are.

"Now this excursus has been rather unusual," he said; "it's a kind of language and a train of thought we never run into in public discourse, it's not crowd language at all. But you see well enough how it applies. Here's a mass movement, a literal crowd, that bases its appeal on the supposed protection of a more conceptual crowd, which they hyperbolically call 'the babies.' What's really curious is that the protection is conceptual too: except for a few diligent people who take in unwed mothers and insist that they have those babies, most clinic protestors just make the gesture of protecting the unborn by vilifying providers and patients. Their task isn't creating better conditions for mothers and children; their task is forming the crowd. One of their big *machers* recently compared his flock to the righteous gentiles during the war—quite a weight of vicarious glory—and it was a curious comparison: his point was that it's so much *easier* to 'rescue' in this situation. Hell, you could get yourself killed hiding Jews from the Nazis, but all you have to do to save babies is be willing to be arrested and maybe get your name in the paper. You don't even have to adopt the babies. What's the matter with this man? Never mind Europe during the war, the mere invocation of which is so frivolous as to take one's breath; how does he understand the activity of rescue? Would he be willing to pay for the prenatal care of, let's say, fifty babies a year, let alone feed and clothe and educate them until they're eighteen? How about forty-five babies? forty? thirty? twenty? ten?" A slow ripple of laughter as the audience got it: Abraham's dickering for the possible righteous in Sodom. "Would he be willing to see that some women simply want to be rescued from the pregnancy? Would he bother to take any moral stand that didn't get him publicity? He has to make a loud noise; he doesn't know how to help. His only hope of looking righteous to anyone is to stir up some public hysteria about sexual conduct, which is so easy to do in this country that it shouldn't even be news. I sometimes think the whole movement is a sort of right-wing *hommage,* half unconscious and half parodic, to the liberal causes like the union movement and the civil rights movement and the antiwar movement that these people were born too late for or didn't get in on. Never mind that they'd have been on the wrong side of every one of them; they want their day in the streets.

"Now the critical thing in all this is that the woman who aborts is alone. She's as far as she can get, at the moment of her decision and at the moment of the procedure, from being part of a crowd. There's a crowd that supports her right to do it—which can be as euphoric and noisy as the crowd that opposes that right, and which when it marches on Washington gets a whole lot bigger—but they're one step removed, they're not with her when she goes through with it. She wouldn't even want them to be. She's refusing, at that point, even to be part of a dyad—

of course that's what enrages the antis, that the presence of the fetus seems to her not companionship but invasion—and though in another sense she's part of a dyad by definition, through having a sexual partner, who that partner is and how helpful he is will vary enormously, and even the most helpful man can't experience it in his own body. In a fundamental sense she's alone. If we're going to keep using the notion of the baiting crowd, whose whole intent is to shame her, this is part of her shame: isolation is the most abhorrent condition they can think of. And what's worse is that she can take care of the problem pretty much on her own. If she knows where to find a doctor who will do it, a first-trimester abortion is a simple medical procedure and financial transaction. It's the most common minor surgery in America today. And that's what drives these people over the edge, the simplicity: the fact that preventing a fetus from becoming a full-term baby is minor surgery. As soon as it becomes legal, it becomes easy; as soon as it becomes easy, it appears to be *too* easy. You should have to do penance, you should have to wear a big scarlet A, you should have to walk through the valley of the shadow of death if you're going to do such a thing. At the very least you should be screamed at on your way into the clinic, where you wouldn't be if you weren't pretty certain of what you were doing, on the theory that you haven't thought about it enough. Why do they think she hasn't thought about it enough? Because she's thought about it beyond the reach of the crowd.

"Now as you and I know, very few women make the decision either to abort or to carry to term without the most rigorous assessment of their situation and their character—or the most rigorous they're capable of at the time, which may not satisfy their severest critics, but then it's not the critics who will be faced with bearing those children. But watch what happens as soon as you acknowledge that the woman does think about it. You've acknowledged her isolation. You're not trying to reclaim her for the crowd. You leave a space in which her conscience can operate. Conscience doesn't operate in the crowd: you may go there at the promptings of conscience, but the minute they start chanting in unison and you join in, you forfeit your conscience for the duration. By holding aloof from all that, you preserve your conscience and hers, and that *is* rescue. You're actually in a better position to help her think about it because you're willing to let her think. You know you can't cancel her isolation; you're trying to minimize the *risks* of her isolation, you're trying to maintain her ties to a civilized community that will help her, but you recognize that her plight removes her inward to a place not quite accessible to the community.

"I want to pause on the word *civilized*," he said with a sharp look. "The antis will go on about the decay of civilization, they'll talk about SS men who played Mozart in between shifts on the ramp, but I insist that legal elective abortion is civilized in the most legitimate sense: it's the safest way we have to deal with a situation that makes women completely vulnerable and desperate. It's not a happy act, it's not in any absolute sense a good act, but it's an eminently civilized act, because it tries to contain suffering. The antis like to represent themselves as the last holdouts of civilization, America's superego, but they give themselves away when they behave like the unleashed id. They're one of civilization's discontents. In a crowd—or in a legislature—they're barbarians: they don't give a damn for the future or for the social order or for the real needs of a pregnant woman. They don't care what happens to her as long as they're righteous. How is that righteousness at all?

"I'll agree that abortion is sad. I can't tell you how I would love to do fewer of them: how I would love to have a world where birth control always worked, and people always had the presence of mind to use it, and there was always money and energy enough for another child, and lovers were always good to each other. I'd love it if my patients got pregnant only when they were financially stable and domestically tranquil. But human biology and human emotions and human economics not being very dependable that way, it's not going to happen. Abortion is going to continue to be extremely common whether anyone likes it or not. There's a great need for mercy here. No religion, no politics, and perhaps we should add no Supreme Court ruling can translate mercy into policy; mercy is too specific, it has to be given from one person to another, and policy can't accomplish that. But policy can leave space for mercy to operate, and if religion is worth anything—I speak, you understand, as a skeptic to clergy—it will honor a policy that allows for legal abortion as one of many necessary ways of leaving that space. I thank you, entirely without skepticism, for being willing to entertain such thoughts—and I hope that you can prevail."

They sprang to their feet again, for the moment a crowd themselves. Ari came back to his seat, and Mim squeezed his hand; they had decided beforehand not to behave too visibly as a couple, but she had to make some gesture of delight and approval. M.C. made a few last announcements, and the evening was done. People came swarming up to Ari, bursting with things to say; Mim relinquished him. He talked with them, lit with well-being; *he* wouldn't be instantly swept with shame, his hands wouldn't be cold, no doubt he would come to bed triumphant and lively. What gave him such freedom? Probably it all went back to his bar mitzvah speech.

The panel next morning consisted of three local ministers and an ex-priest, who spoke on referral counseling before and after legalization. Mim learned things about the illegal days that she had not known: there had been quiet arrangements between college chaplains, infirmarians and local doctors (some of them associated with Catholic hospitals) to help women students get abortions. There had been a humble ambivalence even among fundamentalists about the morality of abortion: they had squirmed and equivocated and finally, when forced to a statement, said that it was a terrible choice but it must be the woman's—after all, it was *her* life. On the standing of the fetus they had said that the first breath was decisive, citing the second chapter of Genesis as their proof-text: "And the Lord God formed man of the dust of the ground, and breathed into his nostrils the breath of life, and man became a living soul." *Nefesh chaya,* Mim whispered to herself, the numinous beauty of the words seeming to diffuse itself through the room; she meditated on the three Hebrew words for breath (or spirit or wind), *nefesh, ruach, neshama.* It was Saturday morning; she wished she could be in shul. There were two lines about breath that came near each other in the morning service; she sang them silently to herself. She was, as Ari had predicted, exhilarated: she would be able to talk to these people.

She spent the next hour, when she should have been in a small-group session, going over her speech one more time: she was getting anxious about it. Next to Ari's it seemed thin and reclusive, uncosmopolitan; of course that made sense if the salient feature of being unwillingly pregnant was isolation, but then isolation was clearly a handicap. Her exhilaration faded. She could see new flaws in her logic; she could hear her father and Alan, from their incompatible viewpoints, explaining why she was wrong. How had she done so badly? Had she been too flattered by Ari's confidence? Addled by too much sex? Or simply inhibited by not knowing her audience, having to write a set piece rather than sensing the needs of the moment and rising to them?

Lunchtime came. Mim would speak during dessert; for the meal she sat at a round table, front and center, with several of the conference's organizers. Ari was on her right; on her left—rather to her annoyance, since she would have liked to talk to M.C.—was a chirpy little man in a black short-sleeved clerical shirt with a white dog-collar. Episcopalian? "Fascinating talk last night, Dr. M.," he said, crunching his lettuce and talking across her to Ari. "This man Canetti, I'll have to look into him. And to take it in the direction you did—an unusual train of reasoning. What's your Myers-Briggs?"

There were moans from around the table. "Oh, Kirby, don't start. We'll spend our whole lunch playing Myers-Briggs." Ari looked blank.

"Oh, I know about this," said Mim. "It's one of those personality tests, isn't it?—something Jungian. I have a friend who knows all about it."

"Jung according to Myers and Briggs," said the little man. "In brief, Dr. M., there are four psychological categories, each one of which divides into two polar opposites. There's the source of your energy: are you an Extravert or an Introvert? The source of your knowledge: are you Sensate or Intuitive? Your method for decision-making: Thinking or Feeling? And your preferred *modus operandi:* Judgment or Perception? Once you know which you are—of course there are sixteen possible combinations—you can begin to see fascinating things about why you do what you do."

"I vaguely remember this," said Ari. "There was something they put us through early in med school. I don't remember what I turned out to be."

"Now me, I'm an ESFJ: outgoing, pragmatic, methodical, and pretty good at rising to an occasion when someone needs help. ESFJs like to give." The little man beamed. "You, I'd guess—well, it's tricky. You're a versatile man. I was trying to figure out as you spoke whether you were an S or an N. S, I would say—very grounded, very keyed in to your surroundings—but an S tends to accept reality just as it is, and you're very much the idealist. When you said—"

"Wait a minute," said Ari. "The S and the N stand for what?"

"Sensate and Intuitive. Oh, of course, Intuitive is really an I, but we've already used I for Introvert, so we go to the N instead. You're an ESFP, I would hazard: lots of energy, a people person, great in a crisis. Although ESFPs tend not to be intellectuals. ES*T*P, maybe: outspoken, gravitate toward high-risk, high-action professions. Again, good in a crisis—your work is nothing *but* other people's crises—but still, it's another type that tends not to prefer demanding reading. *I*SFP? That's a toughie. I don't think you're really an introvert." (Mim stopped chewing, horrified: how could she have ended up with someone who wasn't an introvert?) "And again, the intuitive side . . . not an ENFP, though; you're too steady. Twenty years at the same work. Still, the leadership qualities . . ."

The entrees were being brought out; Mim gratefully let herself be distracted by a slab of boned chicken breast and roasted peppers in the Southwestern mode. As soon as she let go of the conversation, she felt a stab of fear: her turn to speak was next, and what would she do? Her speech was in a folder under her chair, seeming to radiate a malevolent imperfection toward the skin on the backs of her thighs. She inwardly shuddered away from it. She must not get into a state of paralysis; even the conversation was preferable to that. She looked up; the little man was still at it.

"But the Ts and the Fs can get tangled up," he was saying. "Funny, because thinking and feeling couldn't be more different. Somebody gave me a quote once from a poem, *her body thought,* but of course that's poetic license."

"Perhaps the system needs improvement?" Mim ventured.

"Now there speaks an INTJ," said Kirby. "It's written all over you. Look at those intense eyes."

"But bodies *do* think," said Mim. The man was patronizing her; she would give him a run for his money. "I wonder—perhaps the whole scheme was derived from a rather limited sample? Perhaps in other cultures there'd be other categories? Jung was Christian, or postchristian on a good day; perhaps there were other patterns he couldn't make sense of?"

"Aha," said Ari. "That's it: you have to allow for the Flatbush Factor. Subjects with this variation can be extraverted, high-risk *and* literate, owing to a tradition of group study under intense external pressure—"

"I refuse to let this go on," M.C. called across the table. "Kirby, let us have him now. You can talk Myers-Briggs to anyone, any time; use it on your parishioners. Dr. Morgenzahl, I was struck by—"

"What was Alan, I wonder," Mim murmured. "Kirby, where would you place a man who was strongly idealistic—even rather dogmatic—very inward, very serious, rather easily hurt in love and religion . . ."

"Well, of course I'd have to know more," he said. "Being a sensate, I can tell a good deal by interacting with a person. But just as a guess, I'd say investigate INFJ. This is someone you know?"

"An old friend," she said. "Ex-husband" seemed merely petulant. She picked at her baked potato.

"Hmp," the third man at the table was saying. "Funerals for fetuses. I don't think that's the direction we need to go."

"But these women needed a sense of *closure*," M.C. insisted. "They still hadn't come to terms with the experience, even after ten or twenty or thirty years. They still felt the need for a healing service, something to reconnect them to the Church."

"The Church should have no trouble with that," said Ari. "They used to be experts. One of my history professors was an authority on the parish records of medieval England, and he said there was a good deal of infanticide among the poor back then, to judge by the number of penances given out for what was called 'overlying.' What that amounted to was the woman rolling over on her baby and suffocating it, ostensibly in her sleep; it was clear to everyone that maybe she wasn't asleep, and yet the penances as a rule were rather mild. It was treated as some sort of shadowy thing, not really an accident and not really full-blown murder. I don't know where they get off these days, excommunicating for abortion—and not only the woman but all the accessories, the doctor and the counselor and the taxi driver—when in the old days they used to handle the finer points of *real* baby-killing with such finesse."

"Imagine a Church where—" said Mim, and laughed suddenly at the audacity of the notion: "imagine Catholic women today memorializing the fetus, lighting candles for it, creating some ritual, perhaps utterly openly—making an outright cult of it. Wouldn't it drive the priests wild?" She caught M.C.'s eye and wished Terry were at the same table: both of them would know priests who were repulsed by the lighting of candles in these postconciliar days. "And wouldn't it in fact provide the necessary outlet, the sense of penance or closure or responsibility that Catholicism has encouraged all along? If they're going to say it's a sin, you know, *that's the sinner's recourse:* that's what absolution is for, to let you atone and amend and keep living. They can frighten you all they want, but at some point they do have to accept that it happens."

"They do something like that in Japan," said a young woman who had not spoken before. Her name tag said *Nadine Gilchrist, Harvard Divinity.* "They put up a little statue for an aborted fetus or a dead child, and they visit it and propitiate it with toys and write it letters saying *We're sorry, thank you.* The whole family signs them. They admit outright that the family's well-being is bought at the sacrifice of the fetus, which they imagine as more or less voluntary, or at least cooperative as long as they render the proper thanks. It's all perfectly open; extraordinary."

The third man made an explosive noise of rejection. "Isn't that just what we need! Creeping guilt, revealed religion getting its clammy tentacles in there. Little statues, my ass. I've been saying it for thirty years, I'll say it again: *Women shouldn't have to apologize.*" Bert Cray was his name: Humanist Assn.

Nadine Gilchrist looked startled but not offended. "Is it an apology, or an attempt to incorporate the abortion into the whole context of their lives?" she said. "It's a liminal act: people want to place it in their ethical system. I've wondered about this in relation to the child sacrifices that are so fiercely condemned in the Bible. Did they begin as a way for Canaanite women to reject an unwanted child while still maintaining a sense of sacred connection?" Eyes popped open all around the table, but she continued, "Think about it. Their techniques of birth control and abortion were much less reliable than our own; more unwanted pregnancies would have continued to term. Generally it was the firstborn child, the one that 'opened the womb,' that belonged to the gods—the one most likely to be unplanned. And sacrifice in all these societies was considered a crucial and deeply responsible act: it was thought to sustain the world. They wouldn't have thought it selfish to make a place for the unwanted child in the sustaining of the world. Besides, this wasn't a patriarchal society: paternity wasn't the primary issue, and in many cases was probably not even known. Did the Yahwist religion, which was bent on harnessing and controlling women's sexuality in general, accurately sense that—"

People were beginning to stammer. "Oh, no, not child sacrifice, that was an abomination—" Kirby was saying. "Don't even breathe this in Peoria," said Ari. "You're suggesting it evolved from there into an institution, like the Mayan—" said M.C. "Damn," said Mim, "now do we blame the Jews for—" But the voice that won out was Bert's, which trumpeted, "Supernatural hokum. Why not get rid of it all? Why should women have to grovel before some god to justify their decision? If you absolve them through religion, you keep them dependent on religion."

Mim tried to get a grip on herself. "Bob," she said, "you've been to Japan; did you see these shrines? Did it look like groveling, or was something more complicated going on?" A waiter reached between them to take Ari's plate, and she jumped: how much of Nadine's speculations had the man heard?

"There was a temple in Kyoto," said Ari. "I couldn't quite follow the details. Groveling, not at all; I didn't sense any fear, though of course I was an absolute stranger. It was sorrow somehow categorized, made cheerful and manageable—made into generosity, almost. More groveling goes on in American clinics: I get patients asking me for what's essentially absolution."

"But don't you see," said Bert, "revealed religion insists on setting the terms. Why should sorrow have to be managed? If you feel sorrow, why shouldn't you just feel sorrow? Because then you wouldn't be controllable: you'd just feel it as long as you needed to, and then stop, and you wouldn't have to go to some temple, where no doubt the priest is collecting a few yen every visit—"

"ISTP," murmured Kirby.

M.C. looked at her watch. "Oh, mercy. Look at the time. Mim, we'll have to get started. You'll be bringing the coffee soon?" she said to the waiter. And as coffee and cake were brought out she got up, made a few new announcements, and finally introduced Mim, leaving her to walk the few steps from the table to the podium with the applause like a wind at her back, propelling her too fast toward her fate as if toward a rock.

CHAPTER 16

A voice is louder, i.e. more audible, in the physical world, the more intense the vibrations are that it produces in the air. It is otherwise in the spiritual world. There a voice is more audible, i.e. "louder," the more it expresses underlying *effort* and *suffering*. *Work* and *suffering* are the things which render our voices audible in the spiritual world.

—*Meditations on the Tarot*

The public speaker, in the urgency of his task, is no longer restricted to the vague, hovering realm of the linguistically possible, but often will conjure up the shades of the linguistic underworld, and, with the blood of his imminent need, bring them to speech.

—Franz Rosenzweig

She took her place at the podium. *So Zusya arose and went unto Nineveh.* There were perhaps sixty people, quietly eating their cake, sipping coffee and carefully putting the cups down with unobtrusive little *tink*s. They looked at her with polite expectancy.

"This is the first occasion," she began, "that I've been able to speak on the subject of abortion in a slow, considered way and in quiet surroundings. Before this I've spoken only at charged political moments, and most recently I've counseled women in the time of emergency as they made up their minds to have an abortion or have a child. I thank you for this chance to think long and carefully in a place where no action need follow from what I say." She shot them a glance, and they laughed quietly. She was calmer already: there was something about an audience that gave her at least the power to address it with grace.

"In charged political moments everything has to be answered quickly and simply: adrenalin shortens the attention span. One's in the position of a parent whose six-year-old child has just asked piercingly in the supermarket line, 'Mommy, what's a bortion?'—everybody's listening, and there's no time, and the questioner's understanding can only hold so much. We have to simplify in order to answer at all. Sometimes I think our opponents are happy enough to stop at the six-year-old level—'It's a bad thing ladies do to kill their babies'—because at that level there's at least a reassuring sense of right and wrong, and one can believe that the center holds. But surely most of us long for the time when the child is twenty or thirty, and we don't have to fish for a way to explain how a woman can start growing a baby when she doesn't want one to someone who's never felt sexual need, and we have a certain range of understanding in common. We long to acknowledge the delicacy of the question, and not to reduce events to slogans, and not to pretend either a horror or a complacency we don't feel." Their attention was friendly; she could get through the twenty minutes.

"We can't consider unwanted pregnancy without considering the act that leads to pregnancy. The cause-and-effect process is obvious enough, and yet saying Yes to sex is not always saying Yes to pregnancy, and saying No to pregnancy is not always saying No to sex; we get nowhere if we look at it in simple binary terms. It's an act, or a process, for which there really is no word: we call it sex, or intercourse or lovemaking or one of the vulgar synonyms, but those are all ways to avoid saying what it really is, because it exposes and chastens us and we can't bear to know that in public speech. We can barely manage to talk about it to our lovers. Whether it's an epiphany or a violation, it's always a convergence of body and spirit, and that's why it's so compelling and so fraught with difficulty. Our opponents know this: they tend to approach it in the simplest and most punishing manner, but they know that sexual conjunction has something to do with the soul. We have to know it too: we have to be quite clear that sex is not simply physical in the narrowest sense, that nothing we want so badly and pursue with such a peculiar mixture of self-interest and self-sacrifice can ever be simply physical in the narrowest sense." She felt a qualm: what she was about to do next would probably shock them, but it was fatal to show any doubt. Something happened in her face that she had seen happen in her mother's, in the moment before a concert, when she changed from a frazzled faculty wife to a lightning-rod for Bach's music: a subtle intransigence.

"I won't ask your pardon for reminding you, in a place where we all prefer not to think of it, that the act of generation is the intersection of male and female bodies at one of their most vulnerable parts, through the rubbing of the one part within the other, at best with profound affection and unwavering attention and extraordinary nuances of rhythm; that it generates heat through friction, that it causes the discharge of fluids over skin made even more sensitive by fluids, that it rocks flesh against bone into an explosion of feeling and motion that's fierce and incomprehensible and intensely sweet. That it's our pride to give another person that sweetness, to discern from another person's body and breath and voice some news about their life—their desires, their disappointments, how easy it is to surprise them into hope. That it's at once dignity and indignity, surrender and mastery, exposure and amnesty. 'The force that through the green fuse drives the flower'—it's our share of that force, whether or not it makes a child, and whether we think it's sacred or profane. It's so strange," she said, suddenly departing from her manuscript and staring intently into space, "because one's just a person, and people are funny-looking and inadequate and not likely conduits for such splendid energy, yet when we feel it we become beautiful and royal, and we'll risk almost anything to have that feeling. We don't want to believe there might be drawbacks to it. We don't want to believe we might be discovered, we don't want to believe we might get pregnant, we don't want to believe we might die. We just want to feel fully alive in another person's arms."

She paused and looked round. No one was drinking their coffee. They were listening, but they were unearthly still. Some eyes were lowered, others carefully neutral, others abstracted as if in some powerful recollection of their own. A young woman near the front was nodding fiercely, utterly attentive. Ari, at the head table, played decorously with his coffee spoon, but he was not missing a word, and his eyes were sharp and approving.

If she said *Your coffee's getting cold,* she would get a laugh: she would shatter the tension, acknowledge that she had gone too far, admit she was really just one of them, a nice human being who could apologize. No.

"When a child is conceived inadvertently from this process," she went on, following her manuscript carefully, "—whether by carelessness or contraceptive failure or simple inability to face the question—the shock is profound and of a whole different order of reality. The moment of understanding that our bodies can do this, without our knowledge and against our will, is a moment of such radical realignment that we're never the same again. At that moment another life is grafted onto ours, in an indissoluble bond to which we have not consented. No, abortion doesn't dissolve the bond. Abortion relieves us of the years of raising the child we didn't expect and didn't invite, or the years of distress over how someone else may raise it; it doesn't cancel the fact that for a few weeks a separate genetic code was repeating itself within us, a body was growing. What we call that body—a fetus or a baby or tissue or human life—is a rhetorical matter; what's true, no matter what we call it, is that it grows. The essential question isn't when life begins: it's whether we have any defense against the overwhelming claims of that growing body on ours, the insistent claim on our love of a child that arrived because we were trying to love someone else." *Mira, of course not.* She ignored the voice and went on.

"Our opponents sometimes talk as if the trauma of abortion could be avoided by simply not having the abortion, but that's either disingenuous or witless: the trauma is the pregnancy itself. If we have the child we rearrange absolutely the life we thought we would have; we allow a chance occurrence to become a central determinant of our life. If we give the child up for adoption the trauma continues, somewhere detached from us but capable of reappearing at any time; women search the faces of strangers the right age, hoping or fearing to find the face of their child. Abortion is the least traumatic of the alternatives, which is why in the same breath that they call it traumatic our opponents call it too easy. But whatever we choose, the choice is forced by a condition about which we have no choice at all at that point: the pregnancy. Our real choice is to be what we were before that—'Renew our days as of old'—but that's the one thing we can't have."

She looked out again. The attention was holding: she could feel it stretched between her and the listeners like a woven fabric. Like folding up sheets: you got into a rhythm together. "I've been struck," she went on, "by a phrase in Primo Levi's last work, which foreshadows the course he eventually took with his life. 'Suicide,' he said, 'is an act of man and not of the animal. It is a meditated act, a noninstinctive, unnatural choice.' I suspect that abortion is somewhere on that same continuum. Of course our opponents say that abortion is the very opposite of suicide, that it's murder, but I think it may be somewhere between the two: a kind of half-suicide, the cutting out of oneself something that's scarcely a separate being yet, the forcible removal of something one's whole body is designed to protect. Like suicide, it's evidence of some absolute breakdown of trust, a disbelief in the fitness of our surroundings to sustain life—a disbelief in ourselves, as the fetus's surroundings, as fit to sustain *its* life. Whether we can apply the words *noninstinctive, unnatural* to it, I'm not sure: the distress can be as instinctive as anything we'll ever experience, though the procedure has to be meditated. What's certain is that the fetus's life, like the suicide's, doesn't seem a self-evident good: if abortion is a kind of half-suicide, having the baby would be the other half. There's no choice that isn't destructive.

"The fetus trusts *us*, and that's what we can't comprehend; how did it make this mistake? How did it settle on *this* womb, this month, to try to become? How, if these things are chance, did this egg and this sperm unite into this relentlessly purposeful creature that will want love and meaning? How, if these things are God's will, can God hate us so much? The fetus's trust in us undoes all the other trust in the universe: it's a cosmic slip, the dropped stitch that starts the whole moral fabric unraveling.

"Our opponents say we dropped the stitch: in their view sex for pleasure is already immoral, and our duty is to atone for it, to knit up the moral fabric by rising to the fetus's needs. Its trust in us requires us to become trustworthy. They're deeply serious about it: they believe duress is a holier state, they believe God speaks through our suffering, they're trying to bring God into the world by main force. Can it be done? We know that we can become trustworthy when we're trusted—that as children when we're given a new responsibility we try hard to live up to it, that as lovers when we're trusted to have integrity we develop integrity, that as parents we become dependable because our children depend on us. We know it doesn't happen for every person in every case, but we know that it happens. Does God also develop trustworthiness through our trust? Can trust be, in Levi's sense, unnatural, meditated? Can trust be called into being *ex nihilo,* arranged as methodically and cold-bloodedly as a suicide, but arranged for life and for peace? Do we delay the healing of the world by refusing a pregnancy? If we treat it as an evil, do we deprive God of the opportunity to become good?"

The atmosphere clouded; she could feel the doubts gather, like moisture toward condensation. They were wondering, *Is she on our side?* It was the moment she waited for: like the penultimate moment in lovemaking, it was an emergence of certainty, the first stage of an irreversible process of which she had full control. Anything she did now would get the desired result: the poles were aligned, positive to negative, the current was flooding through them. She felt her weight on the soles of her feet, and the energy of her body coursing upwards, as if straining to gather and concentrate all the doubt in the room; she gripped the sides of the podium as if she might be torn away from it by the force of a thought that was coming. From the corner of her eye she saw Ari watching her, motionless. She spoke without notes.

"That's the most damning argument against my own position I can think of: that a woman who aborts doesn't have the *imagination* to see how she might have and love the child, can't rise to an occasion, can't shift her spiritual gears. That she doesn't want to become trustworthy. That the unfortunate women who come to us so badly prepared to think, so unlettered in every moral and spiritual sense that nothing I've said here would make sense to them, are the common denominator toward which all women who have abortions sink. But it's not true: there is no one paradigm, and there is no one condemnation, for all women who make this choice. And there's no one paradigm for women who bear their children—some rise to the occasion and sink again, and treat their born children as if they were perpetually trying to abort them. Nothing can prepare the morally unlettered for either the abortion or the child. And nothing can prevent the morally literate from applying their literacy—which has nothing to do with either education or class, by the way, nor with religion in the ordinary sense—to either the abortion or the child. If we're looking for our right relation with God, we'll look for it anywhere; if we're looking for it we'll find it."

There were three pages left to her speech; she could not return to it. She felt her train of thought being twisted out of shape, her logic unraveling, her voice coming out of a place that was not quite her mind. "Because beneath the eclipse of trust that the pregnancy causes, there is a deeper trust: a dreadful, intimate trust that beats in our pulses and that we cannot avoid. Certain talmudists maintain"—she had seen this in George Steiner and not remembered that she remembered it—"that when we face God directly, and only then, the ethical dimension of life is entirely annulled. That is, God forgives: he makes a place for our sins. God, who is himself a destroyer, who repented that he made man, who struck out at the obedient and the disobedient, who has sent wave after wave of disaster against his own people—who put into the world the random and the uncanny and even the uncommanded—he has anticipated in the making of the world what we do in the unmaking of a child. Before this God we can maintain our ways, because we have seen his. And he will return us to mercy: severity and mercy are two limbs of his invisible body, two palpable presences of his absence, with which he encircles and maintains us in the absolute contradiction of good will and bad action through which we live out our lives. He does not abandon us. When we are least good, he most understands us. Maker of trust and mistrust, he wholly surrounds us."

She stopped; there was silence. She dared not look down at her speech. There was no way to return to it: no way to go back to the reasonable, personable tone she had worked for months to achieve. Inwardly she cried out some inarticulate syllable, half prayer and half curse; outwardly she said softly, "Thank you." She stepped down, to the crack of applause that signaled the release of extraordinary tension.

What happened was what always happened after she spoke. People exclaimed over her; they said glowing things, whose sincerity matched her relief but whose inanity made her doubt they had heard her right. "Beautiful. Beautiful." "You've just said everything I think, only I couldn't have said it." "INTJ, what did I tell you? And a wonderful specimen." A few tried to make points of their own, which were largely unintelligible because there was no time to make them slowly. "But we don't have to think of God as a punishing father," said Nadine Gilchrist. "God can be a nourishing mother, just being with us. *Imanu-el*, right? *Imanu ima*. The God that surrounds us, that's a uterine image." M.C. said, "You'll let us publish this in the national newsletter, won't you?" Someone else asked her to speak at a Unitarian church in Vermont. Bert Cray wanted to know what she thought of assisted suicide and why in hell she insisted on using the word *sin*. Ari simply held her hand and said, "You're a scary lady." The program quickly moved on; she sat dazed through the afternoon sessions, half-hearing about the coerced sterilization of black and Hispanic women, and about little makeshift abortion funds that were starting in states that had voted last year to deny public funding. Social hour, dinner, the video: Chester Ludlow of the militant Salt and Light Brigade (salt of the earth, light of the world, and—presumably—into the jaws of death) haranguing a mob outside a clinic in Florida. ("He's written me letters," Ari said to the group. "The cops found some of his pamphlets in Del Marlin's room.") Not till that night did she have time to relax; then she fell apart, weeping hysterically, showing Ari the real end of the speech, despising herself. "Undisciplined. Self-subverting. An enthusiast, with no strength to resist an impulse. A sloven, a failure."

"A failure? They're raving about you."

"Oh, that's nothing. They'd rave about anybody. They just want me to be on their side. I could have said anything as long as I stayed on their side."

"Mim, that's terrible nonsense. You're very good. You pushed them as close to the edge of their own side as anyone could; you even had *me* worried a couple of times. Who'd dare turn the antis' own language on them like that?" He gave her one of his full-length hugs. "And who'd dare to talk like that about sex. That little guy at our table, what was his name, Kirby, you could hear his heart palpitate. I think we should make a big show of being lovers, myself; I want them to envy me."

"You silly man. It's not enviable." She squirmed out of his arms and sat on the bed. "This always happens—this sort of divine afflatus, or some kind of afflatus, that takes over and makes me say whatever comes into my head. I can't seem to refuse it. And it doesn't have any political sense; imagine what the antis would do with that business of God the destroyer. M.C. should have unplugged me. Instead she's treating me like some great theological mind. Maybe she didn't follow it."

"She followed it. It's the people who can't follow it that would give you the trouble. She thought it was remarkable stuff. So did I. So did most of them."

"Don't praise me. I'm so sick of praise." She made a violent gesture, randomly aimed. "It went over all right. It always goes over all right. That's delivery; I'm good at delivery. It doesn't mean I can think."

"Ooh," he mocked, undisturbed, "just because I'm self-deprecating doesn't *mean* I'm not worthless. Really, Mim, do I have to come up with some criticism just because you want to hear one? I'm not going to keep you in psychological downers; it's a nasty habit. I've been waiting all day to tell you about this notion the rabbis had. They didn't talk about body and spirit, they talked about the lower body and the upper body—sex and speech. That's what we're supposed to unite, and that's what you did. Sound familiar?"

She gave a dry laugh. "Fucking and talking."

"That's right. Turn it and turn it, for everything is in it," he said, trying to roll her over and over; it was a line from the Talmud. She resisted him and sat up. "That's charming, but *listen*, Ari: I hate what I do. I hate what they want me to do. Who wants to be a professional

Voice for Choice, a dependable little thorn in the flesh of the body politic? And who wants to have lapses like this, into—what on earth would you call it—intellectualalia, where the words just start spilling out? It's not thinking; it's some sort of babbling. I should just go back to my job where I can't say anything. *I'm sorry, Mr. Post is in a meeting right now, would you like to leave a message?*"

Ari shuddered. "No, get out of the job. Anybody could do it. Go do something that not anybody could do." It was after midnight; he stood up and began pulling off his clothes. "Look, Mim, I don't know what to tell you. I thought you were fabulous. You gave them a level of honesty they're not used to getting; it's important to do that. God knows, the body politic—upper or lower—needs all the help it can get. Not to mention the erring people of Nineveh, who are out there without a clue, not knowing their right brain from their left." He disappeared into the bathroom. "And also much cattle," he called as an afterthought. "At least give the cattle a chance."

Half an hour later, as she was drifting into sleep with him curled around her, she felt his penis start to grow along the underseam of her buttocks. "Is that all it can think of?" she said, wryly comforted, glad she had not removed her cervical cap. "Oh, John Thomas, John Thomas. I suppose John Thomas wasn't circumcised, was he? Not in England in those days."

"Yonah Tuvyah," murmured Ari imperturbably. "Ay, lass, tha's got the nicest tuchis on thee . . ." And a brief coupling, which to all outward appearances would have looked quiet enough, but which gathered the distress of the day into an implosion of feeling that Mim found she could not bear. She felt dismantled, unstrung. She did not think Ari had heard her either, any more than Bert or Nadine; he was inside her, something hurt wonderfully far within as he sounded her, but he had not heard her. Or had heard her only with appetent admiration and not with full judgment. As if all the words of her speech—all the work of her mind—resolved itself finally into nothing but the naked cry *Fuck me, fuck me*. All she really needs. Why so much shame in that, if men needed it too. All talk, all thinking finally a sexual gesture, the subtler and more elaborate the more wanton: the blandishments of a girl who had first made love in mid-air, her words turning, brushing, thrusting against her father's. At the thought she convulsed, clinging to Ari's free hand. For the first time he was not her right audience; she had no right audience; even God, who had sent her the words, was not her right audience. They all looked on admiring—*beautiful! fabulous!*—without needing the words as she did. Intellectual voyeurs, God masturbating behind the one-way glass as he watched her. Ari clutched her and gasped: his poor lovely body, ignorant of her thoughts, firing its million projectiles. She reached down and stroked his leg. Poor Ari, not his fault. He patted her belly; she fell asleep, sated and grieving.

The loud laughter of the women at breakfast jangled her nerves: she was not ready for people. She wanted to sit alone with a book, staring miserably up from it at intervals until the words cured her. There was no time for that. They were passing around a magazine: a slick ecumenical monthly specializing in current controversies. "You've got to hear this," said M.C.

"No, please, it's too early." Someone was eating bacon; Mim smelled it and missed it and decided smelling it was enough. She hid herself in the menu. A mushroom omelette.

"But it's unbelievably backward. It's medieval," M.C. was saying.

"But it isn't," said Nadine, "that's the whole point. The earliest thing he quotes is from 1915. Where was it?"

M.C. scanned the page. "Here it is. John Ryan. 'The impelling principle of contraception is dislike of sacrifice.'"

"You're making this up," said Ari.

"I'm not," said M.C. "I've run into it elsewhere. And listen to what this guy does with it. 'There are two senses in which this statement may be true. The first is the obvious economic one: as the family becomes smaller it becomes more acquisitive. Children are weighed in the balance against commodities and found less desirable. But secondly and more profoundly, the contraceptive mentality dislikes the sacrifice of the spirit. And that, unequivocally, is the sacrifice the Church tells us to make. After all, there are compassionate reasons as well as selfish ones for urging the acceptance of contraception: poverty, the strain of repeated pregnancies on a woman's health and on marital harmony, the strain of the world population on the world's resources. All apparent common sense tells us that in these respects contraception solves problems. The Church says no. It requires us to sacrifice even our concept of problem-solving. It should be our glory to obey—not because it is convenient but because it is inconvenient, not because it makes sense but because it goes against the grain.' No, shush," said M.C. to the growing incredulous murmur around the table, "the best is yet to come. 'We are asked to obey as Adam and Eve were asked to obey in the garden. They fell, and condemned Christ to the Cross. When we fall, to what greater depth of suffering do we condemn Him?'"

The others erupted. Mim sank deeper into her menu. "Where did they dredge *him* up?" someone said.

"Even for *Christian Challenge* that's a new low."

"Maybe this is diversity: they had to pick one real throwback."

"He's younger than me, that's what's scary," said a woman in her fifties whom Mim had not met before. "I'm beginning to feel like Sisyphus. Does it say if he has any kids?"

"Nope," said M.C., peering down at the bio. "Oh! Did you see this? 'In addition to the Quik-Save methods of the televangelists, we now have the New Age fascination with "spirituality," that grab-bag approach to world religions and mystical disciplines. Here too the educated bourgeoisie is cannily keeping the numinous at arm's length. They want art, not religion: everything they want of the numinous could be satisfied by an afternoon's visit to the medieval wing of the city museum, or a tape of Gregorian chant.'" (Or the B minor Mass, Mim thought, reacting in spite of herself.) "'In the end this facile aestheticism mocks the numinous, which is not merely beautiful but demanding, which is not vague and nameless but active and personal, and which did not hold itself aloof from our pains.' Isn't he on a roll?"

"Who *is* this?" said Mim and Ari together, ignoring the arrival of coffee. "He's a jerk," Ari added, "but he's an interesting jerk."

M.C. passed over the magazine just as someone else said "Alan Lonigan," and Mim fumbled and nearly dropped it. There he was: one of four faces at the head of the article—two white men, a black man, and a white woman—and the headline "The Crux of the Matter: Four Christian Social Critics Consider the Modern World." He looked older: the pale, rather immobile Hibernian face was thinner, the sensitive twitch at the mouth was better defined. She read the last paragraph.

"Above all, modernity has made it less and less possible to speak the plain truth of spiritual development: that the human character is formed not by escape but by capture, not by the indulgence of our desires but by their interruption. That one must be nailed to the cross of one's life in order to be worthy of eternity. It sounds brutal to modern ears, it becomes the butt of a hundred 'recovering Catholic' jokes; but it remains true. Is it our ability to escape our sons and daughters—to evade their interruption of our desires by any means necessary—that has made us unable to listen?" The Catholic worldview stole over her like a cloud of frankincense: heroic, uncompromising, mind-muddling. She coughed inadvertently.

"So that's him," said Ari, reading over her shoulder. "Good Lord, he's the real thing."

"Duress as a holier state," said Nadine. "You said it yourself, Mim, yesterday; you might have been listening to him."

Mim murmured something deploring and wrote down the issue number; she took Ari's hand under the table. "He's very old-line," she said.

"He's a throwback," somebody said.

"He's probably a pillar of Opus Dei."

"He doesn't have the sense God gave a turnip," said M.C.

"As Tolkien once said of Beowulf," drawled the woman in her fifties, "he is a man, and that for him and many is sufficient tragedy. Pass the cream, please?"

Mim felt raw: it was too much all at once, while she was still in the throes of shame after a speech and feeling this uneasy disappointment with Ari. Hearing Alan's voice in her head at odd moments was nothing like encountering it full-strength in the public realm. Her concentration was gone; though they stayed through the morning—Ari was on the last panel—she could not keep her mind on the program, and at last she borrowed the magazine from M.C., left the meeting room, and sat reading out in the hall in the ruins of the registration table. Even then she could not follow the argument steadily; she kept having to reestablish herself, to feel her own mind form words, to see them emerge in her handwriting through a pencil (she began making notes on the back of a printed Fact Sheet on Clinic Violence). He had more spiritual force in half a sentence than most of the people at the conference seemed to have in their whole minds, but he was wrong: you could go against your own grain for the sake of obedience, but you couldn't compel other people to. But he didn't seem to care about other people: if solving our problems was disobedient then problems must by no means be solved, squalor must multiply, fetuses must be conceived and carried to term so abandoned babies could die in Mother Teresa's arms. If it took misery to make saints there must be an abundance of misery. Not only that, but our misery spared God misery: we hurt God directly by trying to order our lives. A few years ago Mim had seen scrawled on a bathroom wall *God loves you no matter how much you hurt him,* and this was the same sensibility—the Catholic version rather than the fundamentalist, but the same tacit assumption, and the same precipitous slide from severity into mawkishness. But she remembered the small flame burning under her heart as she knelt in church, enduring the aesthetic squalor of the vernacular Mass, yearning for the little dry transformative wafer: *For Christ, even this.* If you yearned strongly enough for your slice of God's body, you might worry about how you could hurt him.

The exhausting transit between another person and oneself. It would have been bad enough even if she were in perfect concord with Ari. When she thought of Ari her senses bleared, and she wondered why she was with him. She did not have many moments like this; there had been one in February, waking one Sunday at twilight with him sprawled diagonally beside her, and wandering stunned and hungry into his kitchen, where she did not know where anything was. The darkness outside the windows filled her with grief. A line from one of the Franz Werfel poems they had heard set to music ran through her head: *O Bett, du letzte Heimat, du tiefes altes Allgemein.* O bed, thou last home, thou deep old universe. Ari had found her frying onions and brussels sprouts and eating cereal in handfuls from a box. What if Ari were no longer her critical witness? What if her critical witness were, after all, Alan—not because he saw her intelligently but because he didn't, because he would be reliably obtuse until he dragged out of her all that she had to say? If the prochoice clergy were far too easy to please, he certainly wasn't. She heard Ari say something inside the meeting room, and heard his audience laughing, and her belly relaxed; she wanted to make love with him again, face to face this time, her shaved legs enclosing his hairy ones, the furred bone tingling against the risen and inreaching flesh.

Of course she could not; she stayed outside and had most of a letter to the editor down on paper when singing began inside the meeting room. The conference was over; this was the closing ritual. She had seen in the program that it would be led by Terry, who had acquired a name beyond Easy Landing for liturgical expertise. Against her will she could make out most of the words as they floated under the door:

> *Go in peace! May (something) your footsteps,*
> *May God's blessing (something) on your way,*
> *May love be brighter ev'ry radiant hour*
> *And ev'ry moment of your day.*

Mim sighed. This was the public realm: her absence was probably noted. She rose and went in—they were standing in a circle, swaying and singing shamefacedly—and unlinked the hands of two strangers and stood between them. She refused to catch Ari's eye so as not to laugh. For choice, even this. What was she doing here? How had this issue come to hold such a place in her life? How had it gotten into the public realm? The closer she got to it, the stranger it all became. The only real thing in it was what took place in the clinic on Wednesdays and Saturdays, Ari patiently wielding the cannula in that unhappy parody of the sexual in-and-out, the fetus meeting its end, the woman staring up at the ceiling—Ari kept a Barbizon landscape there to distract the eye—but seeing instead of it, surely, the face of God, the ethical dimension of life entirely annulled.

CHAPTER 17

Perhaps every breath you take is someone else's last.

—Elias Canetti

And I will make your seed as the dust of the earth.

—Genesis 13:16

Sarita negotiated with the bookstore downstairs for a corner of the display window. It was summer and the tourists were back, and she wanted street-level advertising. She set a mannequin in the window (the coppery one) dressed in a long gown in sea colors, and hung a blue cloth behind it. She bartered with the calligrapher for a sign with the shop's name and an arrow pointing upstairs. The mannequin was rather incongruous next to old nautical books and leatherbound copies of Dickens, but it would have to do; the upstairs window was high and the street was narrow, and she had always had trouble attracting walk-in traffic. Todd had suggested suspending the mannequin in a net with glass floats and calling it "Found Drowned," but she suspected the tourists were not ready for that.

When the display was done she paused in the bookstore, idly looking around. Among the remainders was a coffee-table book on the Canadian wilderness: deer and salmon and loons, green spruce and grey water. She turned the pages, half-hearing the background music, a sonata for violin and piano she could not place. Unexpectedly, as she took in the pictures, a voice came into the music: it startled her by its presence and by how modern it sounded, dropped in seemingly at random among the measures. It burst full-blown out of nowhere and stopped after two or three seconds, a rich mezzo note, its vibrato so regular even at the attack that Sarita was struck with admiration. How did the singer do that? Maybe Mim knew. The note came again after a few measures, beautiful, like a loon's cry, and Sarita looked at a picture of mist rising on Lake Louise and wondered if the composer knew the Canadian wilderness (but who *was* he? the style was so nineteenth-century) and wanted to preserve its voice. It came a third time; and someone in the shop said, "I'll get it," and it was the *telephone*—one of those warbling modern microchip-generated tones she had always hated. Now, hearing the loon's voice break through it, she was moved and bemused: maybe, if you listened right, there were only so many voices. She went outside, alert for strangeness: absolutely anything might turn out to be alive. Two cop cars coupling in a driveway across the street, nose to tail, the drivers conversing out the windows.

    She was invited to Bob Morgenzahl's for dinner; he and Mim had promised her an elaborate Indian meal, with crisped onions and homemade cheese and lime pickle and God knew what all. They were preoccupied with its timetable when she arrived. She leaned in the kitchen doorway and watched them work: Mim in her Rembrandt dress, moving with a confidence Sarita had never seen in her, and Bob in a garish Hawaiian shirt and a pair of khaki shorts. Why couldn't one get men into flowing robes? Sarita had put on the prototype of a new summer dress, and she and Mim looked graceful and timeless while he seemed hopelessly fixed in the most unflattering mode of the twentieth century. In college she had done some of her first professional sewing for the Miniver Cheevy Society, and *those* men had known how to wear robes: they had impersonated old kings and wizards as if born to move grandly. She had pictured them carrying the new style into their later work, restoring medieval gravity to professors and judges and offering it for the first time to newscasters and systems analysts. Of course it had not happened, and she had scaled down her hopes and merely gone into business. But she had been disappointed, and still sometimes sketched in her head the ideal garments of dignity for a man. A striped caftan, she thought, in this case. At any rate there was this much to be said for the ugliness of men's clothes: it threw the attention back to the face where it really belonged. Mim was looking there now, exchanging an impish smile with her lover, smudging with her thumb a little stain on his cheekbone. "How wonderful," she was saying. "To have cinnamon under your *eye.*"

"You work nicely together," said Sarita. "No impatience, no irritation. That's so rare in a couple."

"At home with the Palindromes," said Ari. "Well, I love domesticity. It never worked right before, but it seems to this time. Maybe I'm grateful enough."

"I resist domesticity," said Sarita, not wanting to think of his gratitude and at the same time resolutely wanting to let Mim be his. "I lived with a lover once, but I couldn't face dividing the air with her. When you're alone you take up the whole space; you have—what do mushrooms have—mycelia, sunk into all your surroundings. With another person around, you can't do that; you go back to being a spore."

"Will we become spores if we live together?" said Mim plaintively. "Can't people who like each other enough grow a joint system of mycelia? I'm sure botanically that's all wrong, but psychologically it isn't."

"Fungi aren't plants any more," said Ari, arranging sliced eggs and almonds on a large mound of fragrant rice. "The botanists threw them out. The word you're searching for is *mycologically.* But what we'd have to do first is find a big enough place for our books."

"Just go up," said Sarita. "Build the shelves right up to the ceiling, and get a ladder. Don't give up this gorgeous place."

"Condominium *is* an auspicious word," said Mim. "It really does mean joint dominion, and that's rather appealing."

"All right," said Ari. "We will condominate. Thy mycelia shall be my mycelia, and thy books my books. Sarita, want to take the chair by the window?"

She had thought it might be difficult to keep hold of her feelings, but it was not; she could sit in the presence of a woman she loved and the lover she had accepted, and the conversation was good and the food was miraculous and there was nothing in the atmosphere she would have changed. Civilization did kick in, some time in one's thirties;

jealousy was not worth disrupting an evening for, not even her own evening. Toward the end of the meal, as twilight began outside and the only light in the room was the pale light of sky and water, she even found herself emboldened to speak in ways she ordinarily would not: about her odd turn of consciousness in the bookstore, and about her own perennial questions. "—like what you once said, Mim, about the angel of transmigrations being so busy during the Baby Boom that he patched the souls to the bodies any old way. What if that sort of metempsychotic break has been going on all along? Who got Wilfred Owen? Who got Simone Weil? Who's walking around with pieces of extraordinary souls, perhaps mixed up quite incompatibly, and unable to make the pieces function in concert?"

"The question would be," said Ari, "whether Wilfred Owen and Simone Weil had finished their work. It's the soul with a job to do that comes back as a dybbuk. Owen and Weil both died young, but they'd done remarkable things. What about the unknown and uncertain—Rosetta Stein, Nemo Nachman—who, for reasons we might as well leave unstated, couldn't get to that point?"

"I know that's the classic view, that you don't come back unless your work is unfinished," said Sarita, "but I've always thought the universe was more thrifty than that. If a great person dies, why should the components of his mind, or hers, just be removed from circulation? Why shouldn't they go back into the intellectual soil?"

"They but thrust their buried men into the human mind again," said Mim, caught by the notion. "Maybe I should advertise in the world beyond. *DWF, intelligent, witty, clueless, seeks strongminded ghost for possible permanent relationship. Let me finish your work.* Would that bother you, Ari love?"

"Depends on the work," he said. "Maybe I'd like to read it. But see, if you have the person's works, her mind never *is* removed from circulation. You can just go read the books. The ideas she never wrote down, or her unfinished life, might still be floating around in the beyond, but most of her mind is still here."

"Until they burn the books," said Mim. "How much of Sappho was dragged back into potentiality as her poems were reduced to fragments?"

"So that, having done her work once, she'd have to come back and do it all over? Oh, Lord," said Sarita, "what drudgery."

"The rabbis said that if you teach something in the name of the one who taught it to you, his lips are moving in the grave," said Ari. "If the name dies out—still more, if the knowledge dies out—maybe he has to come back and reestablish it."

Sarita sipped her tea thoughtfully. "Would you have hints of it, I wonder. Having a dybbuk. Like having a different anatomy in dreams."

"Ooh, and then would you have to accommodate your real anatomy to the dybbuk's," said Ari. "And is that where we get transsexuals and anorexics and people who move as if they're not at home in their bodies."

"Hildegard von Bingen says—" Sarita began eagerly. "You know, the visionary twelfth-century abbess who wrote all that striking music? She was an herbalist and a medic too, and she said character formation was like cheesemaking: it all happened before you were born, and it depended on the quality of the raw materials. They didn't know how conception worked in those days; she thought of the semen as setting the menstrual blood, like rennet."

"That's what Aristotle thought," said Ari. "That's what everybody thought until Jan Swammerdam dissected the ovaries in 1670 something. What was Hildegard's take on it?"

"She said there were strong and weak cheeses. If you had good rennet, you'd curdle a noble cheese: a child with power and stamina and spiritual gifts, who'd take a great role in the world. If you had weak rennet you'd get a weak cheese, a shallow person who wouldn't seek God and whose work would come to nothing. And bitter rennet would curdle a bitter cheese: that was how we got cripples and mad people, so weighed down with adversity that they couldn't get free of it."

"This lends itself ineluctably to the image of a rennet-tasting party," said Ari. "Young marriageable women would have to inform themselves—"

"Ari, good heavens," said Mim, blushing. "So nurture has nothing to do with it?" she said to Sarita. "It's all set in the womb? If you can't finish your work, maybe you were just a weak cheese."

"Or nurture keeps running up against the limitations of nature," said Sarita. "And you handle your work according to the sort of cheese you are."

"Lowfat cottage cheese," said Mim regretfully. "Thin and runny, not worth a second sniff."

"Triple cream brie," said Ari, "with pepper. You'll finish your work."

After dessert he brought out the box of his mother's patterns; Sarita thought *she* at least had finished her work. There was a sleek 1930s tea gown and a crepe suit; there were several muslins rolled up and tied with ribbon. "Oh, look," she said softly, reaching, "they're tagged." She turned over the tiny cards, written out in a delicate hand. *Frau Schimmel—Bluse, Frl. Edita Birnbaum—Nachmittagskleid, Lotte Kaufmann—Mantel.* Like her own muslins, each was not simply the design in the abstract but the design fitted to a person, the record of a particular body. She said so. Mim looked stricken. "Who were they?" she whispered. Ari shook his head.

Sarita untied the first ribbon. The pattern pieces were pierced with old pinnings and bastings, and written on illegibly in German script and in Yiddish. "Oh, my," she breathed. "Look how the pieces join here. Imagine this in silk noil. Do these cuffs turn down at the corners, is that what this note means?" She sketched rapidly in a small notebook.

"I don't know," said Ari. "I don't know much about them. My cousin sent them after my uncle died; they were stashed away in a trunk in his place in London. My mother was dead by then too. Would you like to copy them and experiment? I suppose Marcie will want them someday, so I can't let you have them, but if you'd like to borrow them for a while . . . and if you see anything you think would look nice on Mim . . ."

She knew which one it would be: there was a dress ingeniously cut, which draped softly in the upper body but clung at the hips, and which would make up beautifully in a new silk twill she had found. Long ago in a revelatory moment in a department store she had proclaimed Bunge's Law: for any given piece of ready-made clothing, either the color, the cut or the texture would be all wrong. She felt freshly the triumph of having control of all three.

At home, at midnight, she drank a last cup of tea and made watercolor sketches of the dress in various colors; then she made a sketch of Mim's face. The heightened consciousness of renunciation warred with the joy of having a good reason to think of Mim. The Rembrandt dress had been loose, and had not been made for her; this one would need careful measuring.

She unrolled the muslin again. History clung to it: her own time had dragged itself steadily away from that time, and Europe of the thirties and forties had taken on almost the stature of myth. To have in her possession a dress pattern from those years was like having one of Zeus's dropped feathers from his struggle with Leda, or a shard of Pandora's box. A profane relic. But it was not myth; it had happened: squalid as a cesspit and drab as a train schedule it had proceeded hour by hour, not a moment of it foreordained or inevitable. *Die Nachgeboren,* Brecht had called her generation, those born after: those who could never know. This muslin had no little tag; who had it been for?

She looked away. A fashion magazine in the mail, on the table beside her: models posed invitingly against trees or straddling bicycles, long dresses unbuttoned up to the thigh. Sarita imagined them all five weeks pregnant, the deadpan bravado of their faces concealing dread. The post-prom rush, Mim had said they were in right now. That pensive model at the window, was she counting the days? The one in the plum beret, sitting with a stubble-faced young man on the steps of a brownstone, was she about to spring the news on him? How obsessed one became with this subject at the least provocation. Imagine being pregnant during those years. Imagine being pregnant upon arriving in the camps. Imagine arriving in the camps.

She could not, of course, imagine it.

She felt outclassed by Morgenzahl, really: it was uncomfortable to have to admit it, but wrong to deny it. He had upstaged her, made her invisible, merely by not being one of the *Nachgeboren,* as if Winston Churchill or Roosevelt should emerge from history and distract Mim's eye. It was unfair to object; she herself had not known Mim for long, and certainly had no claim on her, whereas he had taken an extraordinary role in her life many years ago and was the obvious person to answer her present needs. Ari the Archetype, she thought bitterly, and at once was remorseful; but she too could have answered Mim's needs, by a less direct route. Why did a woman of such gifts fear her own influence, speak and then doubt herself? What made her recoil from finishing her work? Sarita knew: it was longing, a longing so powerful to do the work right that she could not bear to do it sufficiently.

She laid the muslin out on the floor. Where it tried to curl up at the corners she weighted it with little stones she had picked up at the beach. She put the sketch of Mim's face over the heart. She twisted the pale-green nameless ribbon into an infinity symbol and patted it to the cloth just above the sketch. An unsatisfying visual image, a double halo that ridiculously suggested a propeller beanie. That was the hazard of this kind of searching: there were no tools except those at hand, which might be grossly inadequate. She was not even sure of what realm she searched, on any of these excursions: infinity, or the collective unconscious, or merely her own psyche. For the moment it did not matter: it had to be done. She looked steadily at the assemblage, slowing her breath.

The dybbuk Esther waits her turn. Her name in life had been Elena, but the Recording Angel speaks only Hebrew: for him, as for her tormentors, the only thing that counts is that she is a Jew. It is the mid-fifties: Czechoslovakia is a Soviet satellite, Russia struggles to recover from Stalin, there are no Jews left in her town. "Please," she says to the angel, "the one in America."

The angel frowns. He is having enough trouble with the logistics of matching the dead to the unborn; special requests annoy him. He knows God has trained this people not to acquiesce—and that the war put this training to the test in the most unimaginably brutal way—but he wishes God would consider the strain they put on the system. The higher-ups, the seraphim and the ophanim, suppose (if they think about it at all) that the refugee problem is solved by the development of the postwar baby boom; for the lower functionaries it is just a lot of work. His job is turning into a bureaucracy, the Office of Transmigrations; there are several minor angels on the intake side sitting at desks with lists. During and just after the war there were riots: the Jewish dead do not like waiting in lines.

Esther has seen it all before; this is her third time through. She suspects that she is getting to be a difficult placement. The first time she went to a woman in Rehovot, a survivor of Mengele's experiments, who had lost her first child in the camps and was trying to have another; Esther became her third miscarriage. The second time was to a sixteen-year-old whore in Naples; it was a healthy pregnancy, but in the tenth week the girl pushed a knitting needle into her cervix, sickened, and died, and then there were two souls waiting in line for new bodies. The girl seems to know that Esther was her baby: she has been giving her spiteful glances as they shuffle to the front of the line, and occasionally muttering an elaborate Italian curse.

Under her spiritual arm Esther carries a spiritual book: the manuscript she lost in the war and rewrote in London. The title is on the cover, *Philosophische Aufzeichnungen*, and her name, Elena Kleinova. In it is the philosophy she had hoped to be known for, unpublished and unread by anyone but her lover (who died, she now knows, in Riga in '42) and a London publisher who did not have enough German. It is a palimpsest of the lost draft and the restoration; she clutches it tightly.

Elena's grandfather was a rabbi, her father a lawyer. Her parents' house contained no Jewish symbol: no scroll on the doorpost, no Hebrew books on the shelves, not even a pair of candlesticks on a sideboard for Friday nights. Her parents were done with religion. But her grandparents taught her the blessings, and sometimes (not telling her parents) would bring her to the cramped little synagogue, where when she was very small she would toddle shrieking happily among the men, and as an older girl would sit behind the curtain with the women. She conceived a great love for the proceedings there, which translated into an acute sensitivity to all forms of Jewish ritual. In adolescence it became actually painful, like the stories one heard of the suffering Christian saints: every time she touched the mezuzah at her grandparents' door she received a shock, every time she blessed food her mouth burned as if with cayenne. Had she lived in a time when women could be called to the Torah she would have been scorched by its touch, would perhaps have slipped weeping from the room rather than approach and be burned. Her parents were mortified: this kind of thing was archaic, even disgusting. How could a thing so irrational have happened in *their* house? Had she been a boy (her grandfather argued) it would have been easier: she could have been sent to yeshiva, where the stringent texts of the Talmud would cure her of ecstasies. As it was they might *find* a nice boy, a religious boy, whom eventually she might marry, but not yet, not at fifteen. Her parents were enraged at the thought of the religious boy. He was not to be thought of. Elena was a cultured girl, not a *yiddishe mame*. Her obsession was dangerous; it could not be allowed to go on. They moved to Prague and sent her for psychoanalysis.

In line, with the prescience of the dead, Elena—or Esther—observes the conceptions taking place at this instant: anyone may see them as the angel surveys them. Four to peasants in China—but girls may be killed there at birth; one in Indochina, but she has a bad feeling about Indochina; two in South Africa to blacks living under apartheid; and so it goes on, one objection after another. A minute ago there was a Hasidic couple in Brooklyn—an unusual circumstance at mid-afternoon on a weekday, but the couple is much in love—and Elena had cried out in longing; but the angel had given it to a shy man whom she had not noticed, calling his name, Menachem Mendel ben Dovid, and she understood that he had lived righteously and had won the place on his merits. Well, she has no particular merits. Now, in Chicago, it is three in the afternoon and Matt Como has just come home from his lecture on seventeenth-century verse and found his wife doing laundry, and in their haste to tumble on the stripped bed they have managed the diaphragm badly and a squad of sperm have slipped through. "The father's Italian," shudders the little whore; "I know those Italian men. *Porca madonna*. No. Send me somewhere else." The angel tries to explain (but impatiently; he should not be taking the time) that the man has abandoned the Catholic church, that he is making himself over in the image of his Harvard-trained Shakespeare professor, that his wife is an Irish Protestant, that in America what really counts is education and these people are putting themselves through college (the wife by giving music lessons, the man on the G.I. Bill); but there is a commotion in the line as a busload of tourists goes over a cliff in Peru, and the angel is distracted and begins simply making assignments.

When Elena was nineteen she met a man. She had been going to evening lectures at the local Gymnasium and writing a paper, and there was a man at the end of one lecture who asked an interesting question. They had friends in common; she met him; they fell in love. Her parents, with much relief, encouraged the attachment; her sessions with Freud's disciple had weaned her from piety, but nothing was secure until she was actually married. They liked the man: he was lively, intelligent, stable—a promising surgeon—a bit too much attracted to Zionism perhaps but not a fanatic, and he was good for Elena. She was writing a book now, reading papers to a small group of intellectuals, becoming a young woman of substance. They would make a fine couple, and there was no reason she should not go on writing once she was married: women did such things nowadays.

No one had reckoned with Germany. They had all heard the rumors—among other sources, their clever little dressmaker had married and moved to Berlin, and kept sending her family dire news—but no one had understood the full terror of what was happening till it spilled across their own borders: till the invaders forbade them to ride the trolleys, abolished their jobs, confiscated their telephones, compelled them to wear the star. Early in '42 Elena's lover disappeared; he *was* her lover by now in the full sense, the stress of the times having dissolved their restraints, and they had met at his room when they could, until he was forced to move to a smaller place with eleven people crammed in three rooms. The next month he was gone altogether. Their wedding had been postponed again and again. Elena was frantic. Finally she heard that he had escaped the city and was with some of the Zionist men, homeless in the woods near Prague, filthy and stunned; she never saw him again. *Tell him,* she whispered to the messenger, *tell him I'm carrying his child.*

Her mother sighed heavily and went to a dresser drawer; she took out a strange object, a rubber bulb with a long metal tube. "You boil water and fill the bulb," she said, "and you put the cannula—let me help you, it can go wrong." Elena struck the thing from her hands; it rattled to the floor and rolled wagging from side to side. She was still pregnant three weeks later when she was deported.

They took her clothes and her book. They shaved all her hair: her head, her limbs, the places only her lover had touched. Her pregnancy had not yet begun to show; her new clothes were too large, and concealed it up to the end. Her mother, her father were cloud; her grandparents' whole village, she heard, had arrived and been turned to cloud. She began talking to God. *Who has not made us like the nations, who has given us a fate unlike theirs.* The baby came early, at seven months; a kind prisoner doctor strangled him. She stopped talking to God.

In London, after the war, she sat in a café with other refugees and tried to recover her mind. She was reconstructing her book; why, she was not really sure, except that it leaked out of her involuntarily now that she was well-fed again, rather as her periods had once more begun to do. A sickness, a folly, a reflex: nothing she wrote was as true as thirst and cold. She was twenty-eight. She spoke very little. She was there as the guest of a publisher and his wife, who were paying for a cheap room where she lived and wrote; the publisher was trying to seduce her while the wife did Red Cross work. In the café at least he could do no more than fondle her knee. He kept up a rapid patter of gossip by way of distracting her. "That's Canetti, the Viennese writer," he said, *sotto voce.* "He's mad; been working for ages on some heavy tome about mass psychology. Thought of it even before Hitler, he says. A sure moneyloser; fine work, no doubt, but I wouldn't touch it." (The wife was the intellectual; she had found Elena in the DP camp, seen a page of her work, and insisted on bringing her home.) "Gollancz may take it on as one of his charities. After he gets tired of cosseting the Germans; have you heard—"

Elena waved him away, eavesdropping on the wild-haired man at the next table. So as not to stare at him—soon she would find some pretext to introduce herself—she let her eyes wander over the tables. Just opposite was a couple with a baby and a boy of four or five. Not recent refugees, by the condition of their clothes and the relative composure of their faces, but certainly refugees and Jews. (Was the woman's face familiar? She was not sure. Her eyes had developed a trick of seeing a living face dead.) "—the extraordinary practice among Australian aborigines," Canetti was saying with animation, in excellent English, "of flinging themselves in heaps on whatever they greatly prize. Everything from sacred objects to dying men. The object or the person is so precious that it must be guarded with all one's might, and that means guarding it physically, piling themselves on it in a warm entangled mass—"

Elena shuddered profoundly. She had seen starved women pile themselves so on a piece of bread. "With all one's might"—one was commanded to love God with all one's might, and with all one's heart and soul, and she imagined the stiff-limbed heaps of the dead in Birkenau piled protectively on their most prized possession, the assertion of God's unity. She had spent all her effort on not becoming one of those bodies; perhaps she had spent it on not guarding the *Shema*. A folly, she thought, a reflex: when the body is well-fed it thinks, when it thinks it makes systems. The scene in front of her dissolved and she was back again with the dead, walking ragged and half-alive among them, smelling the ineradicable smell of ordure and death and burning.

She collected herself with great difficulty. The publisher, intent on his own end, had noticed nothing. But the little boy just across from them was staring at her. The eyes in his five-year-old face were troubled and wise, and uncannily like her dead lover's; his gesture was like her lover's, a certain trajectory, as he reached across the back of his chair to her. "Sheyne," he said.

It was a word that any child who spoke Yiddish would have known, and it was not strange (now that she had her health back) that a child should think her beautiful, but it was what her lover had called her; the endearment had escaped his Zionist contempt for the ghetto language because it rhymed with her name. The child was not describing her but addressing her. Elena fainted.

She was on the floor; the boy's mother was mopping her face with a napkin dipped in cold tea. The little boy looked on from a distance, gravely. The baby was in its father's arms, beginning to fuss. The publisher chafed her hand. "Like shell shock, you know," he said helpfully, to no one in particular. In the taxi on the way home he kept one arm round her shoulders. When he took her up to her room he did not leave; he talked confidingly to her as she lay inert on the bed. She did not reply. He lifted her thin rayon dress and unbuttoned his trousers—just enough unclothing to gain access—and panted in his soft tenor voice above her unmoving body. She felt nothing. Then, mechanically and from a great distance, she felt a weak climax ripple. Repelled by the man and by her own body's betrayal, she did not move or cry out. "I'll be damned," said the publisher, tucking his shirt in, "another cold fish. Thought you Jewesses were supposed to be livelier than our English bitches. Live and learn." He slammed the door of her room and thundered downstairs.

That night she wrote in her manuscript: *They know nothing here. He told me he wanted his ashes scattered in the wild when he died, somewhere in Cumbria. A place from his childhood. What innocence.*

My grandfather used to tell of the dybbuks, who return to finish their work. Our work is unfinishable. It was cut, dismembered: when we return we will only cripple the future. The vacuum of spirit will suck at the world's lungs, from the center of this century outwards in all directions. No work will be finishable. The permanent incompletion of the work is our task (Arbeit macht frei). *We are not free to desist from it.*

She read it over, tinkered with the prose. She kept seeing the little boy's face. At last—it was now very late—she carefully spread the book open upon the grate, with the pages fanning upward, and lit it. While it burned she carefully checked the room for cracks and drafts, and methodically stuffed them. She cut off her hair and tossed it on the embers of the book; it crackled and withered and exuded a stench like burnt bone, like bitterness of soul transcribed into a smell. When the fire died she turned on the gas, jamming the meter as she had seen other tenants do. When the publisher came by in the morning—determined to make amends by at least taking her manuscript—he found the house in chaos and that smell pervading her room.

The Peruvian busload jostles the line. The Angel of Transmigrations lifts his flaming sword. *Esther. Giulietta.* There is a crack of thunder and a rush of wind that ends in a muffled gurgling sound, and the two of them in a confused mixture of substance, Elena and the little Italian whore, settle ectoplasmically down around the egg, which has selected a vigorous female sperm and is already beginning to divide. Ricotta, romano, asiago, mascarpone. "Matt," says Libby Como, "I'm pregnant. I know it."

"Oh, my God," says Matt. "But you can't know it. You haven't missed, um, your—"

"It just happened. I know, you're not supposed to be able to feel it, but I feel it. A little spark. Stop laughing. Remember, Mama can see the future sometimes."

Matt does not believe in clairvoyance, but he believes in Libby's mother, who has striking symbolic dreams. He laughs nervously, with apprehension and excitement. "Well, Sparky," he says, putting his hand on his wife's belly, "you're a tough little kid to swim through all that goo. Let's see how you turn out."

CHAPTER 18

This is what is so immoral about the much lauded *conscious* procreation. The crime of *making a man*, of bringing more evil and sorrow into the world, is not committed unconsciously in dramatic ecstasy, in the darkness of copulation; it is coldly premeditated.

—Guido Ceronetti

Master of the Universe, this droplet, what shall it be, mighty or weak, wise or foolish, rich or poor? May it be thy will that what I am about to do is for the sake of heaven.

—Hasidic prayer before intercourse

Mim's mother, like Mim herself, had lived for a long time on the fringes of academia. In one sense she had lived right in the heart of it, but invisibly, as a faculty wife, and her work had gone on elsewhere when she could find it. She had a B.A. in music, but her prospects were limited by living in the smallish Ohio college town where the family settled when Mim was three; some jobs that she might aspire to would never be open, and no one was likely to take her seriously if they were. She had been visiting music teacher in the elementary schools, a thankless job in which it was never possible to do sustained rehearsing; she had been record librarian for the college FM station; she had led the summer youth choir one year when nobody else could. She had always given voice lessons at home to the college students, even before Mim started school, but her real interest was choral music, and it was nearly impossible to get steady access to a good choir. The high school choirs were led by a lazy, smiling man who liked Broadway shows—when Mim reached high school she openly despised him and would not join—and the college choirs were led by men with better credentials, and the steadiest work Libby Como could finally get was in the Lutheran church, where she had a wheezing pipe organ, five quavering sopranos, an assortment of reliable altos, three ear-peeling tenors and two basses, and a congregation suspicious of difficult music. She had pushed them all beyond their capacities without making them angry, but the work told on her: she was not really an organist, and the singers were not really singers. It did not help that Mim's father (now published and tenured) made fun of church choirs.

Mim's doubts about her own work might have begun in her fourteenth year, when her mother at last got her choir. Libby had fallen in with the arts crowd in town, which had been grousing for years about the high school music program; at last their exasperation took form, and she was suddenly put in charge of an after-school youth choir at the town's little non-credit night school. She gave it her soul: with twenty young malleable voices she put on a concert that astonished the town. Adults came out of the woodwork, asking to join; it appeared that all over the landscape there were people who wanted to sing choral music, as long as they did not have to get up early on Sundays and feign belief. The choir was reconfigured as the community choir, and kept growing till it reached about forty. Mim, of course, was a charter member; she brought some of her friends from school, including two of the black students; some black adults joined; the town council, which was nervous about racial mixing (and which to some extent subsidized the night school) decided after the second concert that too much expensive sheet music was being bought, and cut the choir's funding.

Mim had never, till then, seen her mother ruthless. Libby went before the town council and defended the choir; when it became obvious that the town council had other things on its mind than the arts, and would in any case have been just as happy with Broadway shows, she sought out private sponsors. She had coffee with Junior League women in houses with white carpet; she entertained, instructing Mim with relentless efficiency in what Mim now called "faculty wife tricks" of cooking and conversation; she entered the choir in a state competition, and won. As a young mother she had been soft, unflappable, easy; as she mastered the funding of the community choir she developed an implacable charm, not false but deliberate. Her down-to-earth confidence was now a means to an end; there was something perfunctory, sexless in it, like the motherhood of some of her friends with large families. Only in rehearsals did the mask seem to fall from her, and even then she was not herself but the force behind music: intent, impersonal, her mind entirely on entrances, tempo, blend.

Mim became deeply ambivalent about the choir. The town council's injustice, of course, was galling, and she worked hard at acquiring her mother's social graces for the sake of subverting it, but she did not like this glimpse of the struggles and compromises of adult life, and did not want to be her mother's apprentice. It was her father's world she was drawn to—words at their best, not words at the most persuasive; she felt unclean after a few hours' work at oiling the wheels of sponsorship. She began picking fights with her mother each week on the way to rehearsal. She resisted singing soprano, though that was what her voice naturally did; she said she wanted to harmonize, to understand the less melodic supporting lines, but when pressed she said truculently that she hated the sound of the human voice between E and high C. She refused categorically to be a section leader, pounding out phrases on a piano and counting rests. Once they arrived at rehearsal she liked the work, its alternating tedium and exhilaration, the hilarity of the backchat and the bad puns, but the next week it started all over: the rage of being her mother's daughter and bound to her mother's work. She went as far away as she could to college. She could have had free tuition at home, but it was a point of pride not to: faculty children with good grades all went somewhere else. But she had felt traitorous abandoning the choir—and her one small contribution to the racial struggle, whose terms were hardly so simple on the new campus—and that sense of treachery as much as anything else had held her back from finding and doing her work. She felt obscurely that she should leave the field (whatever field it might be) to people of greater conscience. She did not join the university choir.

What feminism could never seem to do for Mim it had eventually done for Libby: the college, after subsuming the community choir into its own night school budget and hiring her as a visiting instructor, and after passing her over twice for full-time positions, finally gave her a job. She was fifty-one. That was now seven years ago, and aside from the irritation of departmental politics she was happy doing her work. She rolled her eyes at Mim's lack of ambition, at her odd marriage and subsequent inertia, at her disgraceful job. But Mim, discouraged as she was by her low status in the library, did not know what else to do. Sophia in the brothel, Ari called her, when he wasn't calling her Jonah in the belly of the whale. She did have to get out of the job somehow, now she had Ari; it was simply embarrassing to be his lover and be doing a job like that.

But it was embarrassing to be his lover at all, given his history with women: Ilene had published (after their divorce, to be sure) a monograph on the woodcuts of Aaron Hacoen, Cleo was a meteor on the night sky of deconstruction, his most recent lover had been a very good painter. Of course Mim was willing to consider living with him and they weren't; there was that advantage. The painter had broken off with him over precisely that question. She had not wanted to cross the line back into the heterosexual realm publicly and quasi-permanently, but more importantly she had not wanted domestic life with an established professional man; she had been married at one point to a rising young history professor, and refused to become a doctor's wife who dabbled in oils. "But her work is so strong," Mim said, shocked. "Nobody would mistake—" "Because she protected it," Ari said flatly. "Who knows, she may have been right." He had kept two of her paintings—he had bought one before they were lovers, the other had been a gift—and privately renamed them the Minefield Duet, "to remind me to fear to tread." Could Mim, following after—though she did her work, such as it was, the better for Ari's presence—live up to these powerful precursors? If she couldn't, would he get bored with her and take up with someone more interesting (someone younger, perhaps)? If she could, would she in her turn become preoccupied and protective of her work and decide to leave him?

There was something unreal in these speculations, which felt nothing like their daily lives—the unfailing shock of joy each time they met, the flood of their conversation. But there was something unreal in their being together, when less than a year ago they had been motes in each other's past, had seen each other long before for maybe three hours all told. The strangeness of parting was a permanent possibility within the strangeness of meeting: if they had the freedom to get into bed together they had the freedom to botch their relationship and get out again. People joined at the roots and then disjoined as if it meant nothing; what was to prevent her and Ari from doing the same?

She managed, some Friday nights, to get him to shul; they would sit together and sing—people noticed their harmonies—and he would point out bowdlerized passages in the translation, and sometimes they would hint by soft looks and touches what they would do when they got home. Once, as the congregation rose and turned toward the doors to welcome the Sabbath Bride in the old kabbalistic tradition, Mim noticed a little girl who had not turned around: she was only two, perhaps three, standing in the aisle near the back and watching the others turn with wondering eyes. She was wearing a short sprigged dress, from beneath which depended incongruously a grubby grey plush head and ears: she had wedged her stuffed bunny between her legs so as to have her hands free, and appeared to be giving birth to it. Mim nudged Ari; he grinned in utter delight. A strong sense assailed her of themselves as a couple, capable of producing a child. The girl's sheer obliviousness to convention, to meaning, to anything but the newness of life, washed over her like a salt wave, cleansing: imagine such a refreshment emerging from one's own body. Imagine such a respite from the adult quarrels of politics and religion living right in one's house.

She caught the echo at once: it was a line from Alan's polemic in the magazine forum. "Fruitfulness preserves innocence—ours too." *Oh, wouldn't you just,* she said—to God, not to Alan—amused and a bit appalled to be thinking this way. Life imitates rant, she thought. It was an adult's view of childhood, but from that angle it did not look so bad:

what the child really had wasn't innocence at all but confusion, a muddle of permissions and prohibitions, of bliss and betrayal, but what the adult saw was its sweetness—energy, vulnerability, the drive to keep trying. Motherhood, she thought, is at once the most intimate and the most impersonal thing one can do, and somehow that was intriguing rather than frightening: it could be like speaking in front of a crowd, like those first conversations with Ari or those first times in bed, just knowing what to do by some grace. Once, years ago, she had seen a young woman whirling down the sidewalk with a very small baby in her arms, holding it up and dancing along between the library and the gym, oblivious to everything but her joy. Absolute liberty. Perhaps it wasn't something to prevent.

She imagined herself in the indolent arrogance of a happily pregnant woman, enclosed with the coming child in some intricate private world. *You wouldn't understand: I'm God.* Making a person, cell by cell, not even knowing how she did it. *Making my Ari's child.* And she remembered the revolt of her flesh against pregnancy, the terror of it, a foreign body, the fetus like a splinter in her womb. How could one feel both in the same lifetime?

They spent a Saturday night at her apartment and ambled along the street the next morning, looking for something to eat. Ahead of them a young father held his son's hand, inching along and talking in the super-audible way of parents with young children. "Taddow," said the boy, pointing downward. "Yes, that's a *nice* shadow," the father said, and the two of them paused by the parking meter that cast a diagonal shade across the sidewalk. "Ari," she found herself saying as they passed, "how do people decide? Is it self-doubt, that makes them feel worthless unless they're parents? Is it a fantastic self-confidence, that makes them feel as entitled as anyone else to have children? Is it sheer unconsciousness? Do they need something to do with their time?"

"Or they have accidents," Ari said simply. "A lot of them still don't *decide,* in that sense; it just happens along, and they say Oh well, we were going to do this sooner or later, we might as well do it now. You've heard all the ways it happens. You just see the ones who don't think they want to go through with it."

"It must certainly be easier to accept when fate does it for you," she said. "How anyone starts trying, in cold blood . . . how anyone dares . . . is there anything to it besides biology?"

"I don't know," he said. "Does there have to be? We're biological."

"I don't know," she said, with another inflection. "I think I understand the biology, up to a point. When I think of getting pregnant by you there's this wonderful sexual charge: it's as if pregnancy and motherhood are the production—no, the *extrusion* of this excruciating love into the world, the real *ex stasis* of the union of man and woman. But is that reason enough—? It's nice biologically—it's even nice metaphysically—but you still end up with another person, who won't feel that way about it and who needs endless attention and care, and is it fair to them to produce them just because you're in love?"

They were passing a real estate office, closed on Sunday; he leaned close to her in front of the photo display. "And people say intelligence isn't sexy," he said. "Extrusion, good Lord. Mim, I don't know: it's been so long since I had my own kids—or since Ilene had them, you know what I mean—that I really have no idea. The times were so different. We didn't *decide*; it was what people did, and we did it. But people do all kinds of things now. No, on the whole I'd say don't have a kid just because I turn you on."

She was looking at couples differently these days: she did not know how she had taken for granted so long that men and women touched each other. She read their affection with a surprised and knowledgeable eye: *Oh, she leans against him that way because he's pleased her deeply—not long ago, last night or this very morning.* Or *Oh, at their age are they still—? Good for them, so may we.* Or she read lack of affection: *She leans against him that way because she's drunk and afraid of him,* or *Look at the fury in that smile.* Now she began to look at children differently too. In the supermarket one evening she heard a small voice say severely, "*Veg*'table oil. *Veg*'table oil. Is that *veg*'table oil?" and looked around to see a girl of six or so reading labels. In the airport one night, waiting for Ari to arrive home from a meeting, she saw a couple with a little boy:

unpretentious people in their late twenties, the man with a scruffy blond beard, the woman dressed in a cheap cotton skirt and vest of some ethnic group not her own, the child in red flannel overalls and much preoccupied with a toy wooden dump truck. The parents talked quietly together, with no trace of discontent. The boy pushed his truck along the floor with quirky assurance; at one point he lost his balance, rolled comfortably over the truck and lay on his back beaming, drumming his heels contentedly against the carpet. As calm as lovers' play, she thought: he was the extension of the ease and charm of his parents' bed into the public realm, in a way that could not be suppressed or gainsaid by society. If his parents made love in the airport, that would be indecent; the presence of the child, the literal issue of their lovemaking, was not. She found herself thinking with a startled laugh, *Oh my God, Sarita, he got here by fucking.* It did make a difference to think of it that way: not that every child was the result of mutual love and profoundly generous coupling, but that every child was evidence of things not seen. Laura had said something like that a long time ago, and Todd and Andrew had been very funny about it once ("Hets flaunt their proclivities every time they take the kiddies for a walk; the rest of us can't afford modesty"). Pregnancy as a form of insouciance, insistence, a form of sexual display, so immodest it was taken for granted. Oh, she could do that.

But Ari arrived home tired and unhappy; he had caught a cold, and he had been hearing from his colleagues about the latest advances in protest. Between sneezes he told her the stories: bombings, blockades, people chaining themselves under cars or posing as patients, people squirting some putrid chemical into the walls. A doctor's children had been filmed walking to school. "This car crawled along behind them, one woman driving and the other with a video camera. Right out in the open. The kids were petrified. The oldest one did have the sense to get the plate number. Crazy people: I suppose they thought Jesus would make them invisible. Well, at least we're raising some gutsy kids in this movement."

Yes, Mim thought, unless the fear breaks them; unless they grow up simply wanting to hide, or spend their twenties and thirties writing exposés of their parents. (*My Life as a Pawn of the Liberal Agenda*, by Beth Como-Morgenzahl. No, not Beth.) Imagine the extrusion of your love getting out into the world and getting even: what better reason not to have children? But her immediate response was defiance, of a ferocity that astonished her and made her laugh: by God, they wouldn't stop her and Ari from making more of themselves. If she decided not to, she'd decide it on her own terms; she refused to be frightened out of it by people who wanted to force women . . . ah. To have children. Was she merely taking the bait?

"It's so circular," she said to Sarita. "And I have this terrible feminine sense of taking on the coloration of my surroundings. Alan believed in slavery and so I became a slave, whereas Bob is free so I have to approximate freedom. But then is it freedom, or slavery to a free man? Are women ever really brought out of Egypt? Or is a uterus a portable Egypt, that I carry around with me and that enslaves me whether I use it or not? On what basis can one possibly decide to have a child, given a really free choice?"

"I don't know," said Sarita. "I decided against it quite young. Don't maternal women often know themselves early in life? Like knowing whether you're gay?"

"If they do, then I'm not," said Mim. "Maternal, I mean. I never got any farther in childhood than making up names for my children. I remember deciding I wanted to have three boys, not realizing that in the matter of gender you had to take what came out; I didn't yet grasp the essentials. Even now all I have is a sort of wild surmise. I want to see what my body can do; I'm curious what it's like to be pregnant, to give birth, to give milk. Like owning a four-wheel-drive truck," she added apologetically, "if you never take it off the road—"

"You never flip it over," said Sarita austerely. "Is this the first time you've been curious? Is it just age?"

"Damn," she said. "Bob's daughter thinks that; when we met in the spring she was listening to me tick the whole time. I don't think so; I've always been vaguely curious about that part. It's *raising* the child that scares me. Though of course in the absence of opportunity I didn't think much about it. I suppose it is now or never, but that's not really the problem."

"What is?" said Sarita. "Opportunity? Is Bob leaning on you about it?"

"My God, no. That would be easy. He refuses to lean one way or the other; he leaves it all up to me. He said at the outset he'd do whatever I wanted, which I thought was just lust talking—the sort of promise men make on the edge of the bed—but he sticks to it resolutely: he really won't say. No one who really didn't want children would leave any doubt, but anyone who did would surely be happy to see I was thinking about it."

"Maybe he thinks it's essentially women's business. Maybe he just supplies, you know, the rennet, and the rest is your job."

"Well, it is, in a sense; *his* body can't do those things."

"You know what I mean," said Sarita. "I mean what goes on between feedings, and after weaning, and all those times when you just need opposable thumbs. Think of all the women you know who've had children for love and ended up raising them alone with no money. Or raising them alone with the father there."

"I don't think he would—" said Mim, and fell silent. "Of course neither did they."

The dryer, which had been humming in the next room, wound down to a stop. Sarita went out and brought back a long piece of satin in shades of gold and brown, shook it out and began to press it. "God knows," Mim went on hesitantly, watching her work, "there are too many ways of losing him anyway. Because he's older than I am, or because the relationship goes the way of all relationships, or because . . . because the next person aims better. It complicates matters. If I didn't have him, would I want at least the reminder. It stops sounding sentimental when you're faced with the possibility."

Sarita murmured assent. She still could not quite take it in, that half a mile from her shop there was a doctor's office in a perpetual state of siege. "If it's the protestors," she said, rather obliquely, "you might not lose him, but life might become so impossible—you might have to think of leaving *him* for the child's safety, if—"

"Oh, no," said Mim, stricken, "no no no. I won't do it at all then. I will not treat him as a liability. If becoming a mother shifts my first loyalty from him to the child—oh no, it's not worth it." She looked at Sarita wide-eyed.

Sarita looked back. It was a hot day—the smells of her customers' bodies, and their sticky warmth, had repelled her all day with a sense of unwarranted intimacy—but she wanted to hold Mim, to comfort her, to apologize to her, to distract her. Damn the man, she said to herself, I hope he knows what he's got. She did a complicated flip with the piece of satin and started pressing the other side. "It's the same as with Alan, isn't it?" she said. "You wanted his friendship."

"Of course," said Mim, wondering why she had not seen it. "And with Alan I thought having children would make that impossible. Of course *not* having children made it impossible too. But with Bob, I don't know—"

"You're afraid of how it would change you."

Mim nodded. *"Matris integritas post puerperium,"* she said. "That's why it's a miracle."

But even with Alan she had tried to dispose herself toward wanting children eventually; she had taken books on childbirth out of the public library and studied them cautiously. She had been curious then too. She had not made a secret of it; Alan had known. Once, shopping for a stuffed animal for some friends' newborn baby, she and Alan had found some amusing little toy hedgehogs with soft grey spikes and long snouts, and bought two for themselves and a teddy bear for the baby; several weeks later, on a whim, she had cut out some bits of old coat lining, rolled them into little conical shapes, and sewn a black bead on the pointed end of each one, and when Alan came home there were five infant hedgehogs, hairless and eyeless, suckling (right on his placemat) from the hedgehog they had designated female. It was entirely out of character; probably it was the one time in her life she had done something cute; it was not—or would not have appeared—the act of a woman ambivalent about pregnancy. No wonder Alan had felt so cruelly tricked. She had only meant to close some of the distance between her fear and his eagerness, but it must have seemed a calculated deception.

Had she had his friendship? Their eyes had met kindly; he had felt blessed to find her, and she had felt honored to be found. Living with him had been pleasant; there was bed and conversation and study and Mass and shopping and going for walks. (Ari didn't take walks; he swam at a health club for exercise, and Mim had started teaching him yoga.) The trouble was that in conversation she kept being blindsided: he trusted what she was suspicious of and was suspicious of what she trusted. Feminism, of all things—egalitarian as their relationship was in several practical ways—was by his lights a Marxist movement, or sometimes a gnostic movement, and didn't have women's well-being at heart as the Church did; feminism said women could be equal to men, but the Church said they could be saints. Marxist? said Mim, confused, and Alan said Yes! it comes from the Left, and that consciousness-raising technique is straight out of Marxism, self-criticism, look how that's used to make Soviet dissidents recant. But *confession* is self-criticism, said Mim, and he said Oh, Mira, one's secular and the other's religious, it makes all the difference. Mim had been red-baited herself as a child, apparently for nothing more than being a faculty brat, and was uneasy at this dismissal. Well, why gnostic? she asked, and he said as if it were obvious Because it abhors the flesh! It hates women's natural role, it hates motherhood, it promotes perverse sexuality, it aims to make even marriage as sterile as lesbianism. That's not because they think the body is evil, Alan, it's—but there was no talking to him, he was better-read than she was in both politics and theology, and she could only sneak off and swallow her pill and hope for eventual enlightenment. (A loaded word too, it turned out.) In one of the terrible letters he had sent her after she left, he had called her a Manichean, his worst insult: all totalitarianism was Manichean, there was no margin in any of these utopian movements for the unexpected or the imperfect, abortion was the "womyn's" equivalent of a Stalinist purge, eliminating people who were ideologically inconvenient. Even the rhythm method was Manichean originally—Augustine, who'd learned it there, had later called it the pimp's method—and maybe that had been their first step on the slippery slope; the Church had permitted it only slowly and grudgingly, and never to prolong childlessness at the start of a marriage. Yes, it was Alan's own fault; he had to admit it; he had made a concession to heresy. "And that was as far as he'd go," she told Ari. (They were at her place, and she had dug out the letter to show him.) "That was the only thing he could see he'd done wrong. Imagine fathering children for a reason like that."

"Imagine thinking it for five minutes," said Ari. "Refresh my memory: *how* did you end up with this man?"

"He could talk," she said shortly. "And I was tired of being alone, and tired of virginity, and so startled that anyone I could want could want me. And brainless. I knew rhythm didn't work; I'd read that over and over." She put the letter away and sat thinking restlessly. "The trouble is, my ethos is changing on me. In those days what I really thought was, Why have children at all? Why did there need to be more of me? There were plenty of white people, there were more than enough goyim, both the Irish and the Italians had done their share of proliferating—"

Ari snorted. "What, are we on a quota system now? If there weren't 'enough' white people, would you go join up with the Klan?"

"Of course not; I didn't mean—I meant I didn't see any necessary link between sex and pregnancy. And now I've begun to. Was I really a gnostic without knowing it, like Alan said? Like those ads for the Unitarians one sees sometimes? Am I getting sentimental in middle age? Is it my incipient Jewish soul, my *yidishe neshoma*, just waiting for me to cross over? Is it leftover guilt from before? I don't know what to think."

"Well, if it's Alan, don't let him get to you," said Ari. "His idea of the link between sex and pregnancy is *You wanna play, you gotta pay.* As if kids were currency. As if every time you went to bed you put it on your credit card, and nine months later you got the bill. Of course there's a link between sex and pregnancy, but it's not crime and punishment. You don't have to buy your pleasure."

"No, but—if you felt you owed something for it? If you were that grateful?" She saw a flicker of something behind his eyes, some deeper attention, and went on too quickly, "And if in the past you did badly, and want to repair—"

Ari jumped up with an exasperated noise. "Mim! Christ! Forget the past for a minute. You were young and stupid once; we were all young and stupid once. That's one reason the laws were changed. But it's just beside the point now. *You don't have a kid on principle*: not to punish yourself, or to prove yourself adequate, or to please Alan, or to please me, or even, God damn it, to replenish the Jewish people. You do it because you love seeing a little warm bundle of imperious instincts grow into a person; you do it because you want to see what happens, at the absolute risk of your private life to a relentless, exhausting, symbiotic job. And at the absolute risk that the kid will turn out to be somebody you don't like, and if he does you'll still have to love him and take care of him. Or, of course, her; I don't mean to imply—look, it's not rational. Birth control is rational; deciding *when* to have kids is rational. Deciding *to* have them is crazy. You only do it if you have so much trust in your own life that you can squander yourself on night feedings and sore throats and having a two-year-old follow you around saying everything twenty-five times. They're very sweet. But they're a lot of work, and you have plenty of other work, and you don't owe the universe a child, and I can't stand to see you imprison yourself in this tail-chasing self-doubt." He stopped pacing and sat down again, embracing her and talking urgently into her ear. "Sweetie, you run your whole life by theory. What do you *want*?"

She covered her eyes. "To be a tree. Not to have choices."

Choice as the central act of religion. A religion whose central imperative was to survive as a choosing people. Choosing to make more. Fructify, multiply. How could she be so ambivalent about having a child for love and still be drawn to having one for religion? And why now and for this religion, if not for the first one? (And if not now, when?) How could religion, which wasn't even real, compel one to want to care for the realest, most terrible thing in the world, a child of one's body? How was it religious at all, to involve oneself in that prolonged mutual invasion of privacy, to lay every moment open to interruption, to put oneself in a position to say to another person, several times a day for some years, "Do you have to go?" (Oh, in New York they said *make:* would Ari say that?)

But perhaps that was the attraction: in Judaism the biological patterns of the human body were the ground of religion. Sex and generation were not second-best, one could spend one's best efforts not on reining in the disobedient flesh but on raising up people to talk to. Surely one could arrive at that understanding in any religion, surely it was foolish to go all partisan about it; Catholics thought the act of love was an act of worship, which as a young woman she had found unexpectedly earthy. *But the manger got in the way,* she found herself thinking, not sure what she meant. It was as if Jesus Christ, singular as he was, were the paradigm for all Christian births: the manger, the magi, the angels, the mother fixed in virginity because he had grown in her, the Unmoved Mover helpless in the straw, all added up to a vision, again and again set before one in Christian life, of *baby as deliverance,* omnipotent baby, baby to whom one must yield. It was strange when you came to think of it, because every other baby acquired its own share of original sin, as it began acquiring its own bacterial colonies, the minute its head breached the cervix. Judaism, which did not think of original sin or accept the incarnate God—and which was extravagantly kind to its children—did not spend much emotion on babies' innocence: a baby was someone to whom in a couple of years one could begin to say *Zay a mensch!* And it worked: at least one could, with some effort, become a mensch, whereas one could never retain or regain the innocence of one's birth. As Alan's wife she had worried about how she might damage a child, as if simply by having grown up she had become its natural enemy; now she thought the world was a damaged place, but parents and children might be in it together, allies. Was that any more than theory? How would it look on the twentieth sleepless night, or in the seventeenth year? Could one be to one's child what it mattered most to be to anyone, a critical witness?

She awoke from a nightmare, weeping: Ari dead on a long table, and three men from the synagogue standing over him with white cloths dipped in warm water. They were washing him gently and thoroughly: the ears, the nostrils, the navel, the fingers and toes. They washed even his back, turning him on his side by crossing one arm and one leg over the midline of his body to shift his weight. She, heavily pregnant, looked on invisibly and wept. She knew the men: Morton Roth, Toby Sandek and Joel Sussman, Sabbath regulars and members of the burial society. They mopped blood from a purple wound in Ari's chest. They put the stained rags by to go in the coffin: blood was not discarded but buried along with the dead. They were singing prayers, lines from the Song of Songs: his head is finest gold, his hands rods of gold set with beryl, his belly a tablet of ivory; his legs are pillars of marble in sockets of gold. This is my beloved and this is my friend, O daughters of Jerusalem. Effluent trickled down the back of his thigh as they turned him. She could smell it: not the ripe rankness of warm shit but the thin cold smell of sewage. They washed it toward a drain in the foot of the table. Toby took a wad of cotton and impassively plugged the rectum. She remembered the sphincter dancing around her finger, the body leaping with joy. They lowered the dead weight onto its back.

She felt a long pull in her uterus. Through dull pain she saw each man take a plastic tub of cold water and move toward the head of the table. They would pour the water over him, pronounce a Hebrew formula, and he would be cleansed; they would dry him and dress him—the ritual garments were laid out, baggy and strange—and shift him into the coffin, where a sheet and his little-used prayer shawl were already spread. Her belly contracted. Joel raised his bucket. If the water spilled over the lip, if the amnion ruptured, the dream would come true. She knew it was a dream now, and labored to wake; swimming up to consciousness she lay on the hard mattress squeezing tears from her eyes. Ari snored gently beside her; her whole right side sensed his warmth.

"Ari," she said weakly, not certain she meant him to hear. He rolled toward her, folded an arm and a leg over her, and said clearly, "It's all right, that's not going to happen." On the next breath he snored again; and Mim, wide awake, stared into the darkness. How did he know that? How could anyone know that? What on earth had occurred? There was no understanding it. His chest rose and fell against her; his penis stirred at her thigh; his limbs resting on her were heavy and living.

Her womb drew again; surfacing from her wonder she recognized it as a menstrual cramp. She hugged him and squirmed out of his embrace, feeling the sheets for blood. In the bathroom, blinking in the bright light, she searched for a tampon. There was no blessing for getting your period, either. What would it be? *Who renews our days as of old.* Now, if they were orthodox, she would not return to him: they would keep their own beds, and rejoin again in two weeks. *My soul failed; I sought him and could not find him.* She could not contemplate withholding her body from him. In the darkness—now darker than before she had switched on the light—she returned and found him, moving into his arms and searching for something to kiss.

Her lips on his face encountered skin astonishingly soft; she let them rest there without quite knowing where she was. A little while later something moved under them, and she identified it as an eye: her lips were resting on his eyelid as he slept. That was more strange than all the rest, that he should not wake: that his body should trust her body even with this. The eyeball flickered beneath the lid in a dream, and he breathed slowly, entirely unaware of her.

CHAPTER 19

> She hath left me here alone,
> All alone, as unknown,
> Who sometime did me lead with herself,
> And me loved as her own.
>
> —"The Holy Land of Walsinghame"

> For there is something miraculous in a man finding in one woman a pleasingness which he can never find in another, as say the experienced.
>
> —Thomas Aquinas

Alan had found it agonizing, but in another sense not difficult, to be chaste until he was married. Even in the late sixties and early seventies, when it seemed that all his contemporaries were leading each other into temptation, he had refused to be led. The silence in his house on sexual matters had been so profound that he did not know how his parents would phrase an explanation of where babies came from; his sisters thought that kissing would make them pregnant. The visible rituals of sex in their neighborhood were conducted in a brash night-club atmosphere whose underlying mood he sensed as raw fear. When at twelve he had watched with new eyes the Italian girls in the school (the Irish girls were too much like his sisters, too pale and too practical) he had been disturbed by their power to draw him into that atmosphere from the calm masculine competence of the Church. He wanted to be a priest; he did not want to be stirred by the swinging of dark hair, or by a smooth leg crossing under a uniform skirt (how it lifted the pleats!), or by the straps and hooks of a bra through a sheer white shirt. He was repelled by the boys' avid muttering about how *it* was done and which girls were likely to do it; he was mortified to find his alarmingly mansized tool stiffen, on any pretext or on no pretext, and to have to skulk to the bathroom and make it shoot its sticky load into a furtive kleenex. He was never so grateful as when he discovered Augustine, and found that the great saint had endured the torment of lust; he read the *Confessions* and all *The City of God*, then picked his way through them in Latin, and his teachers thought he was studious but he was merely clinging to a mind that understood his condition. In *The City of God* it said that if man had not fallen, the organs of generation would have been moved by the will—the same way Tony Buscemi could wiggle his ears, the same way Tim McIlwaine could fart on command; yes, yes, he said to himself, by the will, and much later, when I'm twenty-five or so and want children, and then only as many times as it takes to beget them. This is too much, too young, I can't stand it, I will shoot the soul right out of me one of these times. But what am I saying, I'm going to be a priest, I'll never have children. O God, take this terrible lust away from me. Only not yet. O Saint Augustine, human and troubled saint, you suffered this all as I suffer it: *ora pro nobis*.

He had wanted to be a priest from a very young age; it did not matter what the little girls said about his not being able to get married, it did not matter what his bad Uncle Joe said about priests not being real men, for the priests of his parish were obviously the best and most powerful of men, as the nuns were the most formidable of women. He loved the sweet smoky air of the parish church, the bank of flickering and guttering votive candles and the statues with their eyes rolled to heaven: it was the one place in his world where holy emotion was present full-strength, the very wood and plaster so saturated with it that the priests' voices did not have to be. As soon as he became an altar boy he studied their manner, hoping that when his voice changed it would develop a rasp like Father O'Rourke's. He said Mass in his room at night with his dresser as an altar, the whispered Latin transporting him from the routines of his dingy old house to the divine housekeeping of the consecration. He imagined hearing confession, practiced a mood of authoritative kindness. When his voice changed it did not develop a rasp, and no one had told him about the plague of impure thoughts that accompanied the change. (Did Father O'Rourke—? Oh, no, it was not to be thought.) But he did not understand, then or later, the notion that trouble with impurity should keep one out of the priesthood. He had a vocation; his body would have to be mastered.

At fourteen he entered the minor seminary; in those days one began it in high school, and at least he was taken out of the presence of girls for those hours. When he was sixteen the beloved Pope John convened the Second Vatican Council, and for the first time Alan got a sense of the wider world: for the first time he saw what the service of God might mean beyond the mystery of the Mass and the ordinary work of the parish. On fire with the vision of converting the modern world to the timeless doctrine, he followed all the reports; when the Pope died in the second year of the Council, he grieved as if he had lost a near relative. The assassination at the end of the same year of the first Catholic president (the only Catholic president, as it now appeared) was a deeper shock, and a call to a new kind of seriousness. And in the years that followed the Council a more insidious distress began to unfold: the terrible irony of the Council reforms in practice. It seemed that instead of the Church converting the modern world, the world had converted the Church. The plainclothes religious appeared—the priest as buddy in shirtsleeves, the nun no longer mysterious and terrifying in a long habit but dowdy in knee-length skirt and cardigan sweater. Droves of priests and nuns shed their vocations and married each other. The tenor of services changed, the Latin replaced by wretched English and the priest no longer facing away from the people, bearing their solitude and awe to God, but beaming at them fatuously from behind the altar. Alan was ashamed to serve at the new Mass. The Blessed Sacrament, his sole and compelling reason for continuing in this disintegrating Church, was surrounded by profanations: the relentless shallow optimism, the sacerdotal buck-and-wing of passing the peace, the banging of out-of-tune guitars. By the time he was twenty-one he had known: his life work was gone before he could begin it.

He mourned, in a prolonged cold anger; he wrote. His first published piece was an impassioned protest against the new order in the Catholic press. Seminarians were forbidden to publish—he was by now in the major seminary—so it was an act of open defiance: he was ready to leave. He preferred to do it this way, with a clear statement, rather than go quietly and let everyone assume he was unable to handle chastity. It was the seminary itself that was becoming unchaste. Only that month he had sat through a lecture on the hypostatic union that had suddenly turned grotesque: against the Docetist heresy, which maintained that Christ was not flesh but a spirit and a semblance, Father Taylor had suddenly calmly asserted, "Why, Jesus had a penis." He spoke as if it were the most natural thing in the world to say it aloud, as if he were talking to three-year-olds. "He urinated . . . defecated . . ." he went on in a voice of sweet reason, while each long pause shrieked with silence; "there's no reason to think he didn't have nocturnal . . . seminal emissions." He strolled up and down the aisles, while the seminarians, even the guitar-banging ones, sat rigid and drenched with sweat. "Fully God *and* fully man," he concluded benignly. "A man's not a ghost . . . not a eunuch." Alan had fled the room when the lecture was over.

He looked for another life work, as if one could pull such a thing out of the air; he did not know where he would find it. Teaching? Clearly one became too full of oneself; in any case teaching was going the way of the priesthood, egalitarian and slack, and one was likely to end up with lackadaisical students who came to class stoned—it happened sometimes even at the Catholic university to which he transferred. Journalism—no; he intended to keep writing, but he was too angry to write rapidly and wittily and to order; he wanted to set his own pace. By default he settled on law, because it was a kind of secular priesthood and upheld order; his father did not trust lawyers, but that could not be helped. He hoped he would be able to bear spending his life at his second choice.

When he entered a secular graduate program he lost his draft deferment. "You wanted the world," his father said, "well, this is the world, my friend." He did not understand the war—it was against Communism, it was against the vicious Viet Cong, but it was also against defenseless villages of rice farmers and from the air—but he did not entirely understand the antiwar movement either: it seemed somehow jubilant, as if the accumulated resentments of childhood and school (air raid drills, homework, the Pledge of Allegiance, Eisenhower, Khrushchev, Disney, school uniforms) were splattering forth in a gleeful spray of anarchy. Love? Marijuana? What did that have to do with the terrible possibility of having to kill? He disliked the frivolous bombast of the antiwar students—their guitars were no better tuned—and despised the Berrigans with their violent brand of nonviolence. Death, the only thing that seemed certain in the equation, spread its net further all that year: the assassination of Martin Luther King, of Bobby Kennedy, the invasion of Czechoslovakia, the Chicago convention. The papal defense of the birth control doctrine, which appeared the same year, seemed to him not the disaster that everyone said but the simplest reaffirmation of human life. He did not want to serve death; he did not want to suffer it, though he was not sure what he could live for. In his first month of law school he asked a professor, Jim Molloy, to help him sort out the case for conscientious objection. In leaving the priesthood he had not abandoned his faith; his faith told him not to kill; if his faith—his conscience—told him not to kill, should he not apply for C.O. status? "Don't confuse your faith and your conscience," said Jim Molloy. "Your conscience can justify any damn thing it wants; your faith is a stricter matter. Remember what Chesterton said: the corollary of being too proud to fight is that you leave all the fighting to the humble. Don't get into heaven on other men's backs."

He was stunned: he had never thought conscience could be dishonest. Jim was outspoken about the war's senselessness, but he thought it could be a man's duty to walk open-eyed into senselessness: to let a chance moment in history disrupt your plans or even destroy your life, for the love of Christ and your fellows. In the end Alan's bad eyesight kept him out of the war; after a few anxious months he was declared unfit for service. But the lesson stuck. He attached himself to Jim's mind. Here was the teacher he had hoped to find in the seminary and had not.

From his first visit to Jim's house he dated his rebirth as a layman.

He was not used to the luxuries of professorial living: the big stereo console with records of Lassus and Palestrina and the monks of Solesmes, art reproductions on the walls instead of his mother's cheap crucifixes and portraits of popes and Kennedys—and books, books, books: Teilhard, Simone Weil, Maritain, Hopkins, von Hügel; Augustine, Aquinas, Teresa, John of the Cross; an eclectic range of volumes on history and politics, from Machiavelli to Gibbon to some impenetrable man named Strauss. And a wife who concocted a meal in record time, and who had been—was still—a beauty. Of their seven children only two adolescents were still at home; they were bold and articulate, and Alan felt shy around them. These were the kind of people Vatican II was meant to produce; why hadn't it? What had happened? He wanted to remake himself in their image. When he left that evening he felt a new exultation; *Non moriar sed vivam,* he sang to the stars as he drove home in his fifty-dollar Ford. Perhaps there were other vocations.

And then—it was like an earthquake, a further shift in the tectonic plates of his soul—he thought, *Shall I marry?* It had never struck him before. He had divided the world into good girls and bad girls, like everyone else he knew, but never into women he would marry and women he wouldn't. *The girl that I marry will have to be . . .* his mother and sisters had sung him to sleep with that song. How did you figure out what the girl that you married would have to be? He looked around the next day in the grill at the student union. A girl in tight jeans and a thin peasant blouse—braless—with limp yellow hair that was brown at the roots and a crooked-toothed smile; a lithe, energetic girl in black jeans and green turtleneck—braless too—with a sleek brown ponytail and a volume of Sartre; a large girl in artsy clothes and big jewelry—this one wore a bra—with a volume of Merton. Where did one begin? He'd want to enjoy looking at her, but that wasn't everything; it was best to find someone whose beauty was subtle, surprising, so as not to come to the end of it right away. The artless immodesty of not-quite-beautiful women, those who hadn't studied the rules closely enough or couldn't quite follow them, had suddenly strangely touched him: it was human, preoccupied, not a snare of the devil or a deliberate tease. He had always preferred the "befores" in the beauty makeover sections of his sisters' contraband magazines; the "afters" exuded fear, like the nightclub people. To a "before" girl he might be able to talk.

But he was unlucky with women; he could not find the right things to say. The few women in law school were too tightly wound up: they refused to be deflected from their studies for very long, and they found him emotionally backward. Women from outside the law school he found difficult to approach; he felt pedantic and awkward, and too conscious of his desire. The woman he was most at ease with was his professor's wife, Mona; he had become more or less a fixture at their house as he tried to remake himself, and saw her nearly as much as Jim. Since Mona was beyond him in every sense he could talk to her freely, and he quickly concluded that the girl that he married would have to be just like her: quietly intelligent, at ease in her body, able to make sense of an emotional stalemate kindly and helpfully. The trouble was that now he was not really looking for anyone but Mona; she and Jim occasionally caused him to meet a young woman, and he dutifully went out with each one, but they suffered by the comparison. He could take no one seriously but her. It was safe, but for that very reason it had no future; and in the long run it set him back, because when he left town he was still single, and had an idealized memory of an inaccessible woman to whom every woman he met must be compared.

He was thirty when he met Mira, and he knew as soon as she spoke that she was the one. He had been practicing in Easy Landing for two years—he still smirked at the town's rakish name, and was amazed at some of the characters the ocean cast up on his doorstep—and he had gone one night to a poetry reading at the university nearby. The poet was remarkable for being a relatively young man who wrote serious devotional verse; the critics compared him to T. S. Eliot and Geoffrey Hill. As Alan waited to talk to him after the reading, a small bright-eyed young woman was taking her turn: "Dad says hello. He's so proud of you: you're the first of his students to attain such a height, and he hopes it has something to do with him. He says you almost got him to suspend his unbelief. Stan, it's fine work: the ironies in that elegy for Pope John—"

"Yes," said Alan, not knowing he was going to speak, "that image of the altar dragging its anchor—I wish I'd had that poem when I was in seminary."

"You're a priest?" said the poet—after all, one could no longer tell by the clothes—and Alan said, "No. Under these conditions . . . I found it impossible. So much was lost."

The poet and the young woman gave sympathetic nods, and the young woman said, "I can only imagine. I've come to it just in the last few years, and I keep thinking *Sero te amavi*—late I loved thee—and hoping it isn't *too* late."

Their eyes met for an instant. Someone else moved in to talk to the poet, and they stepped gently aside. "You read Augustine in Latin?" he said, keeping his tone conversational.

She blushed. "Not well. My Latin is very bad. All from choral music; there are big gaps in my vocabulary. But he's so compelling: it's lovely, lovely prose." She pushed her hair back from her face: it was a gesture like Mona's, unselfconscious and easy, and his heart melted toward her. He smiled.

They were still talking half an hour later, when the gathering broke up; they went out for coffee and were still talking at midnight. He walked her back to her dormitory, absurdly pleased that she did not live in an apartment off campus, that he could have a sense of reliving a lost youth he had never quite had. At the big pseudo-Gothic front door he remembered the difference in their ages, and did not move to kiss her lest she find it alarming; she turned away with a delicate shrug of regret, resignation, impatience, and so far did the gesture exemplify the accidental display he still found so moving in women that he imagined he saw, beneath her fall jacket and two layers of turtleneck shirts, the bare shoulder move in the socket. He promised to call her; he called her the next day.

She was a senior in the humanities residential college, planning to go on in philosophy; she was new to the Church since college, though her family on both sides had been Catholic until recent generations. On the Irish side—her mother's—a great-grandmother had eloped with a Protestant; on the Italian side her father had simply abandoned the faith. She had lived as completely in the secular world as Alan had in the

Catholic one; she had some hair-raising ideas, which with her graceful good will she took at their best, but she was young and would surely question them as soon as she saw the alternatives. She had never thought she would marry; her friends ignored the possibility of marriage for looser attachments, and so far she had judged no candidate suitable even for one of those. Thank God he had found her in time. She went by the unlovely nickname Mim; within a month he had renamed her Mira, in oblique homage to Mona and in thanks for the wonder of her appearance.

    She admired his writing; she wanted to write, but was not sure she was good enough. She dreaded the business of earning a living: there were no jobs in philosophy, or in philosophy of religion which she did not like the feel of anyway, and she expected to labor in some tiresome job on the sidelines in order to do what she loved. She was not sure about children—she disliked the idea of marrying just any congenial man in order to have them, and so had refused to think much about it—but though she said her first response to the idea of motherhood was sheer terror, she supposed in a few years. . . . But she radiated a springlike sensuality, a profound readiness to be loved, that set all his nerves humming. *O God*, he prayed, *let me have her.* It was not simple lust: with one of Jim and Mona's young women he had indulged in some fevered gropings and two vertiginous episodes of heavy petting, and he knew the difference between that and his present desire. That had disgusted and shamed him—he had not even liked the girl; this was a love for the whole life they would live together, for the lives they would make, for the truths they would teach their children—all the lost beauty of the Church, so far as they could supply it, as well as the moral valor and the promise of salvation that remained. Once they were married, once she was secure in his love, it was not to be imagined that her natural fears of motherhood would not pass quickly away.

    By the day of their marriage they were still virgins, but only just: it was too easy to be alone together in the modern world. At first he was scrupulously careful not to see her alone in private; when he drove her somewhere he would not even kiss her till they were out of the car. But in public they drew closer and closer, holding hands and then holding each other as they walked, sitting close together on the harbor cruise or huddling under a blanket at the open-air concert, and at last in the campus woodlot they had begun the long descent: on a crackling sheet of clear plastic, their bodies replete with wine and sandwiches and new strawberries and smelling of citronella, they had lain back and kissed, and he had pulled her up to lie on him fully clothed, and as he lay beneath her carefully unmoving she had begun to move, softly and experimentally she had pushed against the swelling in his chinos, and after the fourth or fifth push had jumped back in surprise and confusion, throbbing with (it turned out) the first orgasm of her life. She had been too abashed to continue that day, but she had wanted the sensation again; now whenever they met they enacted the same halfway measure, in her room and at his apartment and even once in the car, troubled and trying to resist but finally unresisting. It began to take longer: once she began seeking the sensation it began to evade her, and she begged him to enter her—"Alan, we're not adolescents"—but he would not take her virginity till they were married, though the substitute made him sore. By the time they had bought a house and were moving in just before the wedding, things had become very difficult: they had left the mattress propped against the wall in its corrugated box lest they be tempted to use it. But on the new couch in the living room they had handled each other, she had permitted his hands to go everywhere, she had even held the hastily proffered kleenex as with the other hand she held—the second person besides himself to do so—the organ of generation, and clumsily brought him off. The other girl had known how to do it, but Mira's delicate inexperience was thrilling: there was such love in her touch. At the altar they gave each other complicated smiles of forgiveness and hope; they already knew each other a little better than they were supposed to. His mother and married sisters sniffled behind them in the front pews, and his father beamed; her father smirked at the decor of the old parish church, and her mother, looking distressed but brave, tried not to let her eyes wander to the bad statuary. Her mother had seen to the music—the long middle chorale from *Wachet auf* and a piercingly erotic duet by Schütz on the Song of Songs; Father O'Rourke, the rasp in his voice augmented by smoker's cough, said the mass. Jim and Mona had sent an expensive gift. Alan had brought the luggage down from Easy Landing the night before, to store at his parents' house; he caught Mira's eye and they stole away from the reception, not escaping even the cliché of tin cans tied to the car, and drove there. Up in his old room, before setting out for the airport, they accomplished their purpose: they lay down on his bed, the site of a thousand pollutions, and exchanged what was left of their purity.

For all the power of the sexual urge, he found the act itself peculiar: the indignity of it, having to climb right onto and into the woman's body, being compelled to it by the now irresistible motions of one's own body and the blissful warmth of hers—being perfectly happy to do it, too, as long as the fit was on you. It was licit, but it was altogether strange. Why did it involve every part of one's frame? Why wasn't it easier? Why was it fraught with such confusion of mind? Mira had learned to enjoy it quite quickly—to coordinate the processes of arousal, movement, physical climax and emotional transport—and her joy had unlocked his joy; in the first months of their marriage he had finally felt kind toward his body, poor Brother Ass St. Francis had called it, which was now led to its right pasture and set at liberty. Sex was *happy:* the Church had never said that simple thing. It was a form of friendship. But friendship was unnerving when it came direct through the skin.

He had thought the periods of continence would be no worse than his many years of chastity; they were torture. Having once experienced immersion, he wanted immersion; he wanted to feel her rocking beneath him, or (O God) above him, wanted to swim in her permeating heat. His clumsy body could become the forceful, graceful instrument of her pleasure; why should it not become so? She loved him; why should she not have him? He was touched to see her struggle obediently with calendars and temperatures, doing the Church's will, but why did she bother? It was perfectly clear that she wanted him all the time. She was still trying to separate, as the world required, the act and its consequences. He, whose desire had finally attained its object, knew better: all the lusts of his youth had been for this purpose, for the planting of a child in his wife. He would not force himself on her, and he did not want to make her pregnant before she was ready, but why wasn't she ready? What sense did it make to get married and not be ready? Surely if she could just let go of her fear she would see it, she would trust herself to God's will as he trusted his tool to her body (she called it, outrageously, "Gus," as short for Augustine). What was the problem?

But she insisted; weeping with thwarted desire she denied him entry on several nights of the month, and then could not sleep. To comfort her, and to relieve his own urgent desire, he found himself giving and receiving satisfactions that were called licit only by slack modern Catholics, the kind of people he despised. But he did not despise himself: the sweetness of her relief cleansed his pleasure of filth, and his body could not understand, though his mind did, why the early penitentials had prescribed seven-year fasts for these lovely acts. He was moved beyond speech by the intricacy of her tender parts (he never could name them), by their instant response to the faintest slip of his tongue, by the scent of her curly hair as he bent to discover them—and by the searching intelligence of her mouth on him, such a steep and terrible pleasure that he cried at the end like one stricken. And once, on a night of profound mystery that left him silent and sobered, the mineral taste of her blood. That month she made no distinction between fertile and infertile times, and never did again; as he slowly took in that she would no longer speak of it he relaxed deeply within. *Tota pulchra es, amica mea, et macula non est in te.* Soon he would be a father in the only sense he now could be, the literal sense; his remaking would be complete.

But by the end of a year he had developed a quiet doubt of his own fertility; he did not want to trouble her with it, but he could not suppress it. He began to wonder—it was foolish, but he could not help it—if his failure to impregnate her were a punishment for forbidden acts, which they still did for pleasure sometimes. Biologically that was nonsense, but God's will overrode biology, and he wondered whether a faithful man turned faithless might rate such correction. For two months he refrained from the proscribed acts; then his doubt overcame him, and without telling her he decided at least to make sure of biology. Standing in the little bathroom of the doctor's office, holding the ridiculous plastic cup in which he was to deposit his seed, the recollection of her heavy sighs had roused him in an instant to perform: no other woman had a claim on his imagination. But when he learned the results, and knew that her failure to conceive must be a fault in her own body, or else a judgment from God; when he told her, sympathetically and haltingly, of having had the test, and she looked suddenly caught out, cornered; when she confessed, full of shame, that her sterility had been her own doing, he wished her claim had not run so deep: his imagination was wounded at the root. That she, who had yielded him all the secrets of her body, had withheld the uttermost place—that she had abandoned him to these schoolboy fears of God's retribution—that she had lied to him while crying out in his arms—was not to be borne. *Vulnerasti cor meum, soror mea sponsa, vulnerasti cor meum.* He wept in secret, and before her he was cold and angry lest he weep again. He woke and slept beside her and could not touch her.

He would remember all his life the night of their reconciliation: the tears of her capitulation mingling with the tears of his pardon, the agitation of their grief fueling desire till they wept again as they moved into bliss together. *A foretaste of heaven*, he thought. He had won her for heaven: he and not she had preserved her virginity till they were married, he and not she would insist on this deeper obedience. And as the weeks went on, though she tried again to establish a sense of the safe period, she showed more and more a beautiful resignation, a new passivity, in which she could be enflamed by his lightest touch but would make no move toward him, not till by silent wooing he overcame what was never quite resistance and obtained her unutterable surrender.

> *So shee a mothers rich stile doth preferre,*
> *And at the Bridegroomes wish'd approach doth lye,*
> *Like an appointed lambe, when tenderly*
> *The priest comes on his knees t'embowell her—*

a Donne epithalamion she had shown him once, which he remembered as he smiled down at her, moved in her, her eyes shut and her hair spread across the pillow. Her earlier eagerness had not been so captivating as this new modesty. It was true, she spoke less, but there was less need to speak; what was not said during the day was spoken wordlessly at night, in the moment when her unmoving body erupted into motion under his. How could he ever have thought the act of love difficult? If men were made for it he could have kept on all night and every night.

Now, in his mid-forties, when he lay with Claire—less often and less passionately, but still with a sense of friendship—he was troubled to find himself remembering those days sometimes. In the first few years after Mira the memory of their love, so brutally arrested, had reduced him to such misery that he had had to find a way around it in his mind; when he remarried he had had to reconstruct, with painstaking artifice and only half convinced that it was possible, an experience of sex that did not include her. He had chosen Claire because of her unlikeness to Mira: she was practical, safe, not a thinker but a doer—a psychologist specializing in short-term crisis therapy—from a family of cops and contractors like his own. It was unsettling that memories of Mira should return at all, much less return as jolts of excitement at moments of erotic tedium. He was taking longer to make love these days, and Claire reached her compact, self-contained climax reliably and early; he was left to labor on without much sense that she was really interested, though she was kind and tried to be helpful. He did not want to want more; he did not want to remember Mira's extravagant passion, or imagine what she would have done with the extra time. He did not carry the problem into daylight hours, or take it too seriously when it occurred—a flash of memory, a convulsion of ecstasy, a stab of self-contempt, and it was done. But he felt an obscure sense of lack, an esurient sadness, that he thought was perhaps his age.

He was writing a book; he had six months' leave to work on it, and was doing computer searches at the library and putting folders of notes in order. His shift to teaching had been another consequence of Mira's desertion—he had found his law practice unbearable as his life fell apart, and had hoped that by reaching students he might somehow keep them from doing what Mira had done—and the book would be built around themes that had worked their way into his lectures and articles. He had always been interested in the insidious ways that thought played itself out in action, the powerful role of ideas in disrupting the social order; the treason of the clerks had, since his seminary days, seemed an altogether credible danger. Chesterton had a phrase, *intellectual crime,* that suggested the duty of thinkers to keep their doctrines in order. In the book he would be tracing what happened when they did not. When doctrine was abandoned, when man became the measure of all things, morality was eroded: people thought they had only themselves to depend on and only themselves to be responsible to, and as a result they became undependable and irresponsible. Nietzsche said *God is dead,* Sartre said *Man is alone,* and the next stop was Jack Kerouac hitchhiking somewhere on the road, and from there it was no wonder if the road led straight to an abortion clinic. The existentialists had actually retained a quasi-religious heroism—derived, had they known it, from *credo quia absurdum*—but their admirers did not have even initiative. What they thought heroic was really a drifting uncertainty, sensitive to all forms of ecstatic stimulus but never to the needs of others. Mira, who had tried no drugs beyond the occasional polite toke of marijuana at a party, who had an almost Protestant aversion to drinking more than she could hold, was no exception: she had drugged herself on his body, on her own pleasure, and believed herself incapable of raising her own child.

He was discontent with the style of the book so far: it seemed earnest and humorless, angry and pleading by turns. In an age that thumbed its nose at homiletics he would have to do better than that. Claire was always nonplussed by the difference between him and his style: "But Alan, you're such a softie and you sound so rigid on paper." She was probably right, but the self on paper was the true self: the printed word was its refuge. There he could express without compromise all that he had been forced to temper and mitigate in real life. But he sounded desperately, not confidently, uncompromising; he always protested too much. He wished he could be robust like Chesterton, assured of his victory—at least in the realm of ideas, if not in the social order—if only his point were trenchantly enough stated. But he knew what the social order would make of his point; he knew how its incomprehension would hurt it; wars would be fought, people would be tortured and killed, marriages would collapse or never be made, babies would be unconceived or would die unborn because the social order was braced against points like this.

Standing in his study, stuck on a difficult passage, he opened a volume of Chesterton at random for the help of the fine supple prose: "There are people who say that they wish Christianity to remain as a spirit. They mean, very literally, that they wish it to remain as a ghost. But it is not going to remain as a ghost. What follows this process of apparent death is not the lingering of the shade; it is the resurrection of the body. These people are quite prepared to shed pious and reverential tears over the Sepulchre of the Son of Man; what they are not prepared for is the Son of God walking once more upon the hills of morning." No, they were not prepared; they could not be prepared; they would ask for the medieval wing of the city museum and get the living Body of Christ, and it would destroy them. *Not a ghost, not a eunuch,* he thought. Christ omnipotent, God in man's flesh, incontestable. That was what silly Father Taylor had meant, but he had only babbled obscenity.

The mail had arrived. There was a packet of letters from the editor of *The Christian Challenge*, responses to the forum he had taken part in. There were quite a few of them: good! he had hit a nerve. He put the editor's scrawl aside—really, why couldn't the man use a word processor?—and paged through the letters. The predictable incredulity at his defense of the teaching on contraception; the shrill feminist outrage at his "authoritarian" views; a few voices defending the New Age nonsense; and an oddity, not immediately classifiable, whose style drew him in. "Why Lonigan should see as a 'utopian fixit mentality' what could easily be seen as a prophetic urge toward *tikkun olam*—repair of the world—is not clear. The answer may lie in what Leo Baeck (rabbi, philosopher and survivor of Theresienstadt) called romantic religion— religion that centers itself on feeling rather than deed, religion whose response to the world is in some sense profoundly passive. Why is 'fixing' not itself numinous, as it was for the prophets?" Who is this, Lerner? he thought, and glanced at the signature—and glanced again, and stared, while his heart pounded erratically and his peripheral vision greyed. He sat down. Automatically, to calm himself, he tried to follow the argument, but he was unstrung: he heard it in her voice, and joy and distress chased each other around the circuit of his mind. "Lonigan mistakes:"—she would say it not pompously but with a playful erudite mischief—"the numinous is not mocked. It continues, impervious both to the assaults of New Age eclecticism and to the worse depredations of religion, to be present as *it* will be present. After all, the numinous mocks us; perhaps it and we are bound in a mutual mockery, whose disappointment and hostility may be tempered by the work of repair—'may God establish the work of our hands as the work of our hands establishes God,' in the old rabbinic pun—to the religious and the irreligious alike, a durable fire." Good God, he thought, she still loves me. She loves me not. How am I to read this? She is speaking against me and speaking directly to me; she must know she's speaking directly to me. Where does she get all this Jewish stuff? She throws it around with great ease.

His children were shrieking outside, helping Claire in the garden. He shuffled papers distractedly; he went back to the editor's note. "By the way, you've hooked a big fish," he slowly deciphered: "this Peter Perrin is one of the big cigars in the men's movement, and if *he's* worried about you, you must be on the right track. And Mim Como seems to be the rising star of the religious prochoice crowd: our intern showed me some remarks of hers in a newsletter, and she's an interesting mind if a little out in left field. (Must be a *nom de plume*—or *de guerre*—cf. Ezek. 3:10.) Deadline for your reply 9-1 if you can. Keep on keeping on." Religious prochoice—that was which one? of course, pro-abortion—God help her, not that. But God will help her, he must: look, she still speaks of God.

Adrenalin and the morning's coffee made him feel hollow; his concentration was gone. He wondered what he should do. Should one play intellectual footsie in print with one's former wife? Suppose he answered in print and the editor—or the readers—found out that they had been married? Suppose they found out how it had ended? He imagined Mira on a talk show, explaining how he and the Church had oppressed her, making political hay of their private pain. Would she do such a thing? Should he write her?

He applied himself with some effort to his work. It was worse than usual. His sentences seemed to hiccup, to want to break into direct address, to say *Mira, how did you*—? *where did you*—? *do you still*—? *have you ever*——? *how* are *you*? When he came out of his study at last he said nothing to Claire; she saw his preoccupation, but he only said his work was going badly. How could he mention Mira, to her of all people? Claire had patiently healed him of her—he knew, though she never said so, that he was her most difficult case—and he did not want to recall those unhappy days. He was surprised at how easy it was to say nothing, to keep a small secret from someone he loved.

He tried, in the next two days, to put it all from his mind; he began composing his reply to the other letters, avoiding Mira's, since the only answer he could yet think of was the *ad hominem* query of how killing unborn children was 'fixing' anything, and he would not descend to that tactic. After the first shock he could work on the book again, and even got a new charge of energy from the strangeness of her reappearance. But beneath the energy he felt instability, as if he were running too fast, overbalanced, and must keep throwing his legs before him faster than he could control in order simply not to fall.

At last, with a sense of compulsion, he sought out the phone books in the library. Phone *fiche,* they were now, for everything but the large cities: he fumbled with the small rectangle of film, smudging it with his thumb, as he tried to insert it right side up—it took him three tries—into the machine with his hands shaking. She was there. *Como M,* no address: a fanatical feminist self-protectiveness there, as if all men were obscene phone callers, stalkers. He could not write her. But the same number—it made the hair rise on his arms—that he had called in the old days, over and over, begging her to come back: it swam its way up from memory, and a host of miseries with it. He put the fiche back in its box and moved off feeling stalled, weightless, as though his forearms might float up to the ceiling: he hoped he was not catching flu.

That night he told Claire about Mira's letter. "Oh honey, oh no," she said, distressed that Mira should resurface at all in his life after leaving it in such ruin. She read the letter and pulled down the corner of her mouth. "She sure likes to hear herself talk," she said. "She missed your whole point, didn't she?" Did she? He hadn't noticed. "She's smart, but she's so self-absorbed. Such a *cold* person. Come tuck the girls in." Cold? The words seemed to him intimate, ardent, like laughing whispers in the dark.

His daughters' good-nights and Claire's old pink pajamas secured him once more in the present, but tenuously: he felt like a kite, or an astronaut tethered to the ship as he walked in space. The phone number reverberated unbidden in his head. Somewhere one is always alone, he thought: as a devotional matter he reminded himself continually that one is always alone before God, but this time he meant something like *single*, alone without limits. Autonomous? alienated? he said to himself caustically, oh, Lonigan, *you*? No, orphaned: divorced: disemparadised. And a few nights later, when Claire had taken the girls to the mall for back-to-school shopping, he quickly got up and called. So little time it took to punch in eleven numbers; if he had had to wait for a dial's whirring each spin would have ticked its judgment, he would have stopped and hung up. Did the ease of sin actually rise with the advance of technology? There were some clicks on the line, and four rings. Thank God, a machine. He felt simultaneously a knee-weakening relief that he had not reached her and an agitated desire to hear her voice. He would listen and hang up and not leave a message: she need never know.

But it was not her voice: it was a male voice, amused and a little arrogant, nasal with the shade of a New York accent. He conceived an instant dislike for it. *If you've reached this number, I assume you know what you're doing. Please leave a message.* Alan felt his throat emit a soft syllable of protest; then the beep came, and he hung up and stood shivering by the phone.

"Another anonymous well-wisher? Those people have found out my number."

"I think it's for me. You know, that call forwarding thing. I shouldn't have done it; I gave in to the hard sell. I don't want to get phone calls here. At least we should change the message; they must have thought they had the wrong number."

"You have reached the Palindrome pad. If you wish to leave a message for Mr. or Ms. Palindrome . . ."

She had a man. Well, of course she would have a man. She had probably had several by now; at least it wasn't a woman. But maybe even a woman—at least, a nice woman—would be preferable to this supercilious voice, with who knew what body attached: with who knew what body attached to hers. He was jealous: it was monstrous to be jealous, and he a married man with a family, but he was. This was why marriage was eternal, why there should be no divorce. He had once read somewhere that divorce was bad metaphysics; he felt he had lived his whole life with women under bad metaphysics. If he could have been a priest and avoided it all— He had a sense of disintegration, or a sense that perhaps he had disintegrated years ago and not known it. He gripped the table; he prayed the Anima Christi. *Passio Christi conforta me; O bone Jesu exaudi me; intra tua vulnera absconde me; ne permittas me separari a te.*

Ari, on the way to the kitchen to scrounge for a snack, stopped next to Mim as she wrote at the dining room table. She would not use his computer, which reminded her too much of work; she wrote longhand in a green notebook. She turned, smiling: the luxury of idle affection had never seemed, so far, to interrupt. She pressed her face to his belly, and he stroked her hair and put a hand down the back of her shirt; she ran her hands over his body, in the black turtleneck and jeans he affected sometimes. She could feel his nipples through the cloth. With one hand she reached down and kneaded his left buttock, and he gave a contented low rumble of arousal; she smiled again and nuzzled his belly, and moved the other hand down to follow (as well as it could through denim) the miracle of expansion. She eased the pull of the zipper over the lump. Astonishing, always: the tender skin and the seemingly impervious standing flesh, as if it could never be limp; the poignant alternation of power and restraint in his movements as he abandoned himself to her mouth and she brought him, standing, to ecstasy. She laughed softly as he recovered, swaying against her. "Not what you were expecting?"

"I have learned," he said breathlessly, "always, from you, to expect the unexpected." He put a hand inquiringly on a breast. "Do you—"

"Later," she said. "Whenever. Love, it's a present."

CHAPTER 20

The accomplished cannot be annulled, but only confused. It is for this purpose that our rationalizations were created.

—Kafka

Is the Evil Impulse indeed good? Incredible! But for the Evil Impulse, however, a man would not build a house or marry a woman or beget children.

—Genesis Rabbah 9:7

Lisa, Ari's sister-in-law, sent Mim an orthodox manual for young wives, as a curiosity: "Romance isn't dead," she said. The book was gorgeously produced, with photographs of babies and sunsets and fields, and it flatly (and not altogether talmudically) prohibited birth control. Abortion it mentioned once, with profound contempt, as if convinced that women went seeking it for enjoyment. Mim read it and sighed. She had seen at the clinic last weekend a woman raped by a friend of her husband's, a girl of sixteen and a woman of twenty-seven who thought it was a sign of bad character to have contraception, and a woman her own age whose husband was already working two jobs to support her and their three other children. The women were all convinced that abortion was murder; none of them saw their way to another choice. She was feeling thin-skinned.

Still, it struck her how benevolent some fundamentalisms were, at least up to a point: extremely orthodox Jews might insist on a great many pregnancies, but not for anyone outside their own circles, and they knew what else sex was for. She was peculiarly moved by the description of the menstrual laws—the laws of family purity, as they were called—which did not read like an exhortation to the unwilling but like a good dancer's explanation of the steps of a dance. Of course she knew them in outline: abstinence during one's period and for a week after, with immersion in the ritual bath (the same bath she would enter for her conversion in six months or so) as the boundary between the times of separation and union. It was roughly the opposite schedule of abstinence from the rhythm method, the separation ending in time for the fertile period. Among the rationales the book offered for the practice—besides the essential one, that it was commanded—was the assurance that the children conceived by it would absorb their parents' strength of character, their power to subordinate a compelling bodily urge for the sake of heaven. ("How to curdle a good cheese," she murmured to Ari.) But what moved and surprised her was the frank statement that sexual love was renewed by the separation: that each month there was just that degree of desperation that new lovers have, that the method was proof against boredom, that it was a means of both containing and intensifying sexual passion. "Damn it, I love this religion," she said. "It's so kind; it's so sane; it works *with* the body's needs, not against them. Where I come from, purity in marriage means never doing it at all. Ari, did your parents do this?"

"I didn't inquire," he said. "They may have; they had separate beds. I hope you're not planning to try it."

"So do I. It sounds horribly difficult: in this version, you have no physical contact whatever for half the month. I couldn't bear not being touched."

"Well, you have all those children to touch you."

"Of course." She read on. "They say it's a way of teaching young couples to talk. Forcing them to develop their resources. We can already talk," she said hopefully, searching for loopholes.

"Ilene and I could have used it," he said sourly. "Nobody was making a rationalist pitch for it in those days. Nobody was saying a thing about it, actually; it was just one of those primitive blood taboos. It's a good thing they weren't; God, we'd have murdered each other in a week without sex. It takes more than a strenuous discipline to make people compatible. Don't go in for feats of piety, sweetie: fanatics are so ungenerous."

"I'm not saying I want to," she said slowly. "Only that the seriousness of it is appealing: you have so much respect for the power of sex that you can refrain from it all those days, and return to each other like magnets. Not because you're afraid of it but because you understand it. Like observing the Sabbath: you surround your rest with so much work that it's a real change, a complete suspension of ordinary time. Of course we don't do that either."

"Ohh, I knew it," he said, sinking down in the shoulders. "You're going to want to be *frum*. I've got to warn Lisa not to send you any more of this stuff; you're too susceptible."

"I'm scaring you," she said. "You're trying to censor my reading matter. Love, not to worry. One can't make decisions about sex unilaterally. I promise we'll never make this one unless we both want to."

"I'll never want to," he said. "Who needs to intensify—my God, every time I get into bed with you I could cry. What good would it do not to touch you for half the month? Forty-seven years of not touching you isn't enough? I feel, every time, like the king in the *Winter's Tale*, when the statue of the queen comes to life, after sixteen years thinking he's killed her. Ever see the PBS version, with Claire Bloom? I forget who it was played the king, but he knew, he knew—sixteen years of desperation in his voice when he clings to her and gasps out, 'Oh, she's warm!' Is he going to get bored with her, is he going to take her for granted, without some carefully controlled regimen of when he gets her and when he doesn't? Not on your life: he's going to pray he has enough years of potency left to please her whenever she wants it. You can have your calendars and your rationales and your laws straight out of the Torah: a woman's body gives me my mitzvahs direct, and your body—" He shook his head, wordless.

"My love," said Mim, shaken, "what would Reb Sigmund say?" She pulled him down and took his head in her lap. He moaned and searched under her blouse.

"'Say he knew it all along," he said indistinctly. "Oedipal; can't tell my lover from my mother; trying to get back to the womb. What would Moses say, too. Or the Pope. Mim, oh God, let me love you."

She moaned in her turn as his mouth warmed her nipple; her vulva was struck with wetness as with lightning. Newspapers crunched under her elbow as she slid down to meet him; she rubbed the fly of his jeans. "Damn birth control." The diaphragm was in a decorative box in a drawer in his bedroom. The cervical cap was at home on her bathroom sink; it developed a purulent smell after two or three days of wear, and she was annoyed with it.

"No, sweetie," he said, struggling up, "never say that. I can blaspheme the Torah of Moses, but you can't blaspheme the diaphragm. They're tricky little characters; they get even. No, you just stay there. I'll get it." He staggered into the bedroom and returned bearing it, a drooping rubber disc in a dismal off-white shade, which he had already filled with clear gel.

Mim looked at it and rebelled: it was an insult that the force of his passion, the curious pathos of his willingness to serve her, should come down to the insertion of this unpleasing little object. It made him ridiculous. "Oh, please," she said, "I can't bear for the first thing inside me to be this cold mess; I want *you*. Couldn't we—just for a minute—"

"Mim," he said hoarsely, "you know perfectly well—"

"Ari, please," she whispered, holding his eyes. Some profound chain of reflexes, old as the world, had been started; the risk itself intensified her desire. Her lower parts streamed with it; she did not know what she felt; was it heat or cold, stillness or motion? She undid the buttons of her blouse, not removing her gaze; she bared her breasts to his sight.

His face was so intent it was almost blank: no irony, no self-consciousness, no smile, his lips seeming tumescent from having been on her. He reached his free hand to her, and they went without speaking into the bedroom. Outside it was raining: beyond the high window the drops pattered into the bay, and the room was filled with grey light.

He lay behind her, the front of his body furry against her back, his penis slowly stroking her swollen folds. "Like stupid kids," he whispered. "Ilene and I used to do this for hours on end." The consonants were distinct and quiet against the huge sound of the rain. She laughed a soft unfocused laugh; then flexed her spine so that on the next stroke he went part way in. "Ah," she said, "that's so lovely. Just a little ways; just *open me*. Oh, let me turn around."

She faced him; guided him into her, just a little ways; felt her muscles close on him spontaneously as he entered. His hand spread, sure and familiar, on her buttock; if it gripped her she would rock forward and fill herself with him. He kept it still. "Crazy lady," he said. "We've got to stop this real soon." "Very soon," she said, but she held him; sensed, motionless, that he trembled on the edge of motion; melted in every cell toward his desire. *Open me,* she thought again, and though she did not say it aloud his control gave way: he thrust twice into her, slick, setting her haphazardly and helplessly pulsing, and withdrew gasping, "Oh, God. Sorry. Please." He clumsily slid the diaphragm into her, her outraged nerves responding with pleasure in spite of themselves to the clammy rubber and gel, and when he had hooked it in place re-entered, now from above and insistently. Three strokes more and he shot: he gave a broken cry and collapsed on her, pumping slowly, his erection relaxing as she tried to complete her own half-finished climax. She cursed D. H. Lawrence in her heart: those women in *Lady Chatterley* who preferred men flaccid, the gamekeeper's first wife who tore with her beaklike pubis to get her pleasure. Let him, like Tiresias, live in a woman's body, let him suffer this moment before he spoke of such things. "Ari," she said gently, stroking his leg with her foot, "it's all right, love. It's all right."

"It's wonderful," he said tiredly, rolling out of her. "In a confused sort of way. Are you all right? You're not, are you?"

"Don't worry. I'll figure it out." He gave her both hands, and she hissed and shrieked as he touched her: at once satisfied and thwarted she plunged against them as he took her back to the height. It was not what she wanted, but on its own terms it was bliss; it was some time before she could stop moving. The cat, arriving from somewhere too late for the show, purred right against her head. The rain went on, and Ari's breath deepened beside her; he had fallen asleep, leaving her to contemplate the nature of erotic selfishness and generosity, and the difference between theory and practice.

She had never seen him so silent as when he woke; he brooded the rest of the evening, and their good-byes the next morning were quiet and strained. She wondered from time to time during the day how wrong things had gone: was he angry, or ashamed, or merely embarrassed, and what would it take to put it right? She had no patience with the details of protocol at work, Cedric's irritations and the importunate ringing of phones, the interminable trivial talk outside her door—the Acquisitions clerks reading printouts aloud from start to finish merely to fill the silence, their supervisor giving her braying laugh. She hoped one of the phone calls might be Ari, but it never was; occasionally he did call her at work, to ask for a book or tell her what he was thinking or simply to make her blush, but apparently this had confounded him. *I'll do anything that doesn't stop us talking,* she had said at the start. Apparently, unerringly, she had found what would stop them talking.

    She called him when she got home. "Do you want to come over here, or shall I go there?"

    "Oh, God, I don't know," he said wearily. "I'll come to your place." She was dismayed at his tone, and could not think about supper; she paced around her bedroom trying on clothes. What did one wear for a caesura in a relationship? Clothes that he liked? Clothes he had taken off her? Clothes that had no history between them yet? Not yesterday's blouse. Was there time to run down the block and buy something new? Damn the whole business, she thought: more pettiness, more protocol. Was he worrying about what to put on for her? At last she wore a T-shirt and shapeless pants lest she seem to be too seductive, but she knew that her father had considered her mother most seductive in ratty old clothes. When Ari arrived they drank seltzer and sat at the kitchen table; they both avoided the couch.

    "I've been trying to think how to say this," he said. "That was some of the most incredible sex we've ever had—not some of the most competent, but some of the most intense—but please let's not do that again.

If you want a baby, let's talk about it like people; don't play games with your unconscious to get it."

"Ari," she said, unnerved, "is that what you thought? I think I know my unconscious well enough—it's not in any rush to decide that. It wanted just what it said it wanted: a physical sensation."

"But—"

"I know. Elementary cause and effect. But everybody knows that, and sometimes it makes no difference. We're not any smarter than the patients. It doesn't mean subconsciously wanting a baby; it doesn't with them."

"Well, if you don't want a baby, for God's sake don't play games with that either," he said. "You're a grownup; you know what's at stake."

He might have been saying the opposite. "Ari," she said again, "don't talk to me like this. We took a risk and we shouldn't have; you took it along with me, though of course I agree that I started it. Don't psychoanalyze me and order me around. Can't you believe I—"

He was barely listening. "I won't do another procedure on you," he said. "There are limits. I mean, one should be willing to do anything, but I don't think I can do that; if you're by any chance pregnant, I—no doubt it's a weakness, but I can't. I don't mean to say you shouldn't go to somebody else."

It silenced her. "I don't think I'm—" she stammered. "And if I were, I wouldn't ask you to—"

"All right, but you might ask someone. It's totally up to you. Only—if you do, please don't tell me; just go take care of it somewhere and don't let me know. You know who else there is to go to."

She stared at him, unbelieving. "Take care of it somewhere," she said. "Is that what you'd want me to do? By myself, in secret, as if it were none of your business? As if it were shameful? You don't treat the patients that way."

"I don't mean that," he said. "No, that's not what I'd want you to do. I meant—"

"You meant it's my problem, if that's what I happen to want," she said. "Ari, good God. Do you think I could worry about being pregnant, and find out I was, and say nothing to you about it? And just disappear for a day without telling you why, and go to Sue Packard or someone, someone who knows you, and—? To begin with, I'm not that secretive."

"You used to be."

"Oh, my God." She shrank down. "There's no forgiveness for sins, is there? Never make love to your priest or your doctor: they're up to the elbows in your mistakes."

"Oh, God, I'm sorry, Mim." He reached a hand to her instantly. "That was a hell of a thing to say."

"Yes, it was." She squeezed the hand briefly, without warmth. "It was true—those things always are—but it's pointless to say it. You know why I did that to Alan. I won't do it to you." She could not look at him; she sat sideways in her chair and stared at the floor. "Anyway, it's not at all likely I'm pregnant. It's the wrong time, and one's not that fertile at my age. And we weren't that careless."

"Sometimes it doesn't take any more carelessness than that. Funny things happen."

Neither spoke for a while; they leaned dejectedly, he over the table and she over her knees with her feet propped up on the chair rung. She wondered what had possessed them to be even that careless. She did not like what it brought out in him. Did people have an urge to test their relationships at the weakest link? Did love have a death wish? Did she go directly, with any man, to exactly the position on birth control that he could not tolerate? "You know what my unconscious wants?" she said finally. "Roulette. There's no excitement so high as taking the risk. Isn't that sickening? You go through something early in life, half frightened and half willing, and all the rest of your life that's what sex is to you; even when you get something more trustworthy, you keep trying to get back to that."

"Well, everybody's first experiences—" He was gentler, trying to make amends. "They're so muddled, and so riveting, and somehow nothing you do later when you get good at it is quite so branded on the mind. I've been wondering all day, what was I thinking? I could have put on a condom, I could have pulled out and stayed out, I could have done lots of things. But one reverts to confusion."

Good, he was willing to accuse himself too. Surely the worst was over. "It's the loss of control," she said, responding as much to his tone as to what he said. "It's like all those good feminists a while back who found they couldn't do without rape fantasies. Only that's understandable, somehow: one knows the difference between fantasy and reality, they weren't saying they wanted to be bruised and called Bitch and made afraid for their lives. They were saying they wanted to be wanted—like you wanted me yesterday, with that energy, that abandon, that one-pointed concentration." Even now she blushed as she spoke of it. "But what I'm doing is worse. I'm treating the whole process of conception as if its only purpose were to turn me on, as if it were pornographic. I'm reenacting the old days. I have to play Alan now, and put myself to the risk: it's the only way to lose that degree of control, and it's artificial, it's decadent. I know I don't want the risk. The worst thing in the world is to take the risk without knowing you want the result. It's moral aphasia."

"Which is why it's such potent stuff," said Ari. "The one thing you never allow yourself is moral aphasia."

She looked at him. The theater of all my actions. "My God, you're right," she said. "Only what's genuinely forbidden is genuinely erotic; only what's really wrong is that desperately tempting. There's no such thing as psychosexual health, is there? You're better off feeling guilty for the little things; then you don't have to push it so far."

The complicated muscles around his eyes registered relief and love and amusement. "Sweetie, you're so Catholic," he said. "I've never heard anyone use the word *decadent* seriously, without a certain sly relish. Come to Papa."

His sheer outrageousness made her laugh. "Ari, you have no scruples." She leaned toward him across the table, and what was forbidden became eclipsed by what was available.

But only for a minute; when they reached the next stage, when he said "Mm?" against her lips to ask what she wanted, she leaned back in her chair and collapsed again into dejection. "And it all starts over again," she said. "What's the use? We'll do it, and we'll like it, and we'll risk whatever we risk with the cap—six percent for perfect use, right, and eighteen percent for typical—we're getting awfully typical, aren't we?—and I don't want to take the Pill again, and I don't trust myself any more. Why on earth does one do this? Why does it matter so much, to wrap ourselves up in each other and—"

"I don't know, sweetie," he said. "I forget from one time to the next."

He sighed and sat back; he looked out the window across to the campus trees, as if resting his eyes with distance. His raptor's face. Ari king of the crows, she thought: his feathers a little scruffy, the lines of his body weary with approaching age. Once upon a time the king of the crows fell in love with a beautiful maiden—well, not quite a maiden—whose dearest wish was not to have a child. O wise king, learned in lore and physic, what can I do to rid me of this babe? One didn't hear stories like that. Though there were a few songs: the cruel mother's punishment, seven years a fish in the flood, seven years a bird in the wood. "Look," he said abruptly, not looking at her. "Do you want me to have a vasectomy?"

"No," she protested softly, without even thinking. "That's if I'm pregnant right now, or if I'm not? No, I don't want you to do that."

"Out of some atavistic reverence for the vas deferens? Because Alan's perched on your right shoulder telling you not to?"

"Because—" Her heart began pounding; her throat went suddenly dry. "Ari, look. Let's just face the question of what happens if I am pregnant right now. It's not only up to me. Will you answer me seriously and tell me if you want a child?"

Still he did not look at her. His face became blotched with red; tears stood in his eyes, and she could sense the tightening in his sinuses and beneath his jaw. "Ilene used to tell me," he said, "during the painful transition from the old order to the new, that it would never matter a damn if I adopted feminist attitudes: I oppress women by the way I move and speak and the pitch of my voice. It's probably my Myers-Briggs, some inescapable confluence of nature and nurture that I can't do a thing about. If I say what I want, you'll do it; that's coercive without even meaning to be. Mim, I can't answer. If I did, there'd come a time when you'd be out of here as fast as you were with Alan, and for the same reason. Do I want to speed that day? All I can do is hold back and say please, this must be your choice, I will do whatever you wish. Please don't ask me for more."

She did not know whether to be grateful or furious. "You're a purist," she said. "It's more than prochoice; you think even your own wishes are a kind of undue influence."

"I'm an uncomplicated old-world papa at heart," he said. "I've already had one family disappear on me. I don't even want to think about kids if you're not sure, I don't want to push you, I don't even want to remember . . . just the *delight,* that and sex are the only times I can trust the world, though why should one trust the world. Oh, God, I shouldn't even think of it, with the antis on this endless rampage, how could I put a kid through the kind of life—Listen, do you want to do the morning-after thing, the two birth control pills now and two in the morning, you never have to know if you were pregnant or not. My God, even Alan didn't have to watch you decide—at least he only knew afterwards—"

She got up and embraced him closely; she put his face between her breasts. "Ssh. Ssh. Ari. Love. Don't. I'm not going to decide that."

CHAPTER 21

Out of the mouths of babes and sucklings hast thou ordained strength because of thine enemies.

—Psalm 8:2

Art and Politics may certainly sleep together, but they should use protection.

—Michael Kuch

Sarita managed well enough, usually: she did not howl at the moon for Mim, or have dreams about her, or do any more than kick savagely at pebbles in the street when she thought of her. It was galling to be asked advice about having children, but at least that was real conversation; she had Mim, fully and thoroughly, for as long as such a conversation went on (and thus also had a powerful incentive not to press her own case and risk the loss of the conversations). Her emotions were more or less controllable nearly all of the time. But once in a while things caught up with her; they had done so this evening.

Mim had come by after work, looking rather withdrawn. "I wanted to ask," she said. "Bob and I are going to get married, and I want to give him a present."

Sarita was willing to smile, but the moment seemed wrong. "Are congratulations in order? I can't tell if you're happy."

"One falls in love out of happiness; one gets married out of pity and terror," said Mim. "I don't expect to survive it. I hope he survives his work." She did not sit down. "What I want is a sort of amulet," she said indistinctly, toying with a scrap of blue cotton. "Since the shooting he wears a bulletproof vest at work; I want—another sort of protection."

"Oh, Mim," Sarita protested, "why come to me?" She had never said anything to Mim about her experiments, or only once and obliquely; it unnerved her to be solicited point-blank. "My influence with the celestials isn't reliable."

"Whose is?" said Mim. "I'm not asking for something that works. It's only—a way of containing anxiety. Telling him I accept the conditions he lives under. I don't need a warranty."

Sarita was not reassured. "What *is* an amulet really? Is it a spell? Aren't they little medallions or scrolls, or bits of stones and bones tied up with a string? What does that have to do with what I do? He won't wear it, you know."

"No, he won't. Oh, God. I don't know what I want." She paced to the window. "To be spared. Passed over. What we need is our own private golem. *Golem* really means embryo, did you know that? We've got enough of those around, do you s'pose we could find one willing—" Her voice went shrill.

"*Mim,*" said Sarita. "Sit down. Good God, what's the matter?"

She sat down. "They showed up at his house."

It had happened two days ago—Saturday: Mim, on her way to find breakfast, had been arrested by the familiar noise of prayer from outside the kitchen window. Not the buzz of davvening, of synagogue prayer, but the rise and fall of Calvin Hardy's hortatory tenor, punctuated by Amens from his Protestant followers. (The Catholics meanwhile would be praying the rosary and trying to pay no attention.) He was quoting the Gospels: "But Jesus turned back unto them, and said: Daughters of Jerusalem, weep not for me: but weep for yourselves, and for your children." It made the hair rise on Mim's neck: she knew what was coming. "For behold, the days are coming, when men shall say: happy are the barren and the wombs that never bare, and the paps which never gave suck. Then shall they begin to say to the mountains, fall on us: and to the hills, cover us. For if they do this to a green tree, what shall be done to the dry?" She stood at the cupboards, riveted; she could not move. "That's the Gospel of Luke," Hardy went on, "and we can see clear enough that Jesus was talking about today. Planned Barrenhood, isn't that what they call it? These abortionists and fair-weather mothers, they're proud of themselves." The pun released her—she could almost laugh at it, even now—and she went back to the bedroom quickly. "Ari, they're out there."

"Shit," he said violently. He was half-dressed; he flung on a shirt, buttoning it on the way to the door. "They usually warn you. They make some obnoxious call or leaflet the neighbors. What the hell are they up to now?" He was at the door in a few strides, snapping the locks.

"Ari," she said urgently, "you know what they want. You don't have to talk to them. Ari, put on your *vest*."

"What's it matter? People know to aim for the head, if they're going to." He waved her back, opening the door. "Good morning," he said loudly. "To what do I owe this unexpected pleasure?"

Calvin Hardy stopped preaching. "Good morning, doctor," he said. "I think you know why we're here."

"I know in the broad outline, of course," said Ari, "but in the short run what are you after? Murder? Mayhem? Trying to stop me from getting out?"

"We're here to witness to the power of Jesus Christ in the world," the minister said evenly. "And yes, Jesus might use us to block the exit."

Ari nodded appreciatively; Mim knew his expression by the drop of his head. "Should it happen to cross his mind," he said. "Interesting instrumental view of yourselves there. Just God's little roadblocks." And then, as the thought occurred to him, "God wouldn't ever use me, of course, to end an unfortunate pregnancy."

"God doesn't do that," said Hardy. "If you knew *anything* about God, doctor, you'd know that."

Ari made a self-deprecating gesture. "Of course. Just spontaneous abortions. Never steps over that line. Silly me."

"Very funny, doctor. Just funny enough to deny your own sin."

Mim squeezed into the doorway. "What about *your* sin? How dare you come threaten him after all he's been through?"

A few of the protestors tittered; a few appeared shocked. Benoit LaGrange was there, and averted his eyes. "Oh, Mira, not you."

"Benoit, that's her *car*," whispered one of the women. "The little blue one. I thought you knew."

"Yes, of course me," Mim said, exasperated. "And stop calling me Mira. What's the matter with you—all of you—turning up in this way? Get out of our privacy." It was too early in the morning; she could not think. How could Ari talk about instrumentality before coffee?

Calvin Hardy, tireless and quick with an answer, had already had his coffee; or maybe God was his coffee. "What is privacy next to the saving of a single baby? What is privacy next to the saving of a single soul? That's why we're here, you know. You may have given up your souls to fornication and murder, but we haven't. Jesus loves you. And *we* love you."

"Yes, we do," said a woman. Others picked it up. "We love you. We love you, doctor. We love you." They did not look at him; they stared into middle distance, enraptured.

Ari was impervious. "No, you don't," he said. "This is Spain, this is Poland, this is Russia. It was love every time. The whole thing is bankrupt; you've been running on empty for generations and don't even know it. Don't tell me about your love."

One of the men, an intense little grey-haired one, boiled up into speech. "Spain?" he said. "Russia? What are you talking about? No, doctor, this is the U.S.A., and *you* may prefer Russia, and *you* may prefer atheism, but we prefer Jesus Christ and a Christian nation, and you'll just have to deal with our love."

Ari's face twitched—damn it, Mim thought, he would go to his grave laughing—but she cut him off before he could speak. "What about our children?" she said. "Does a Christian nation want only Christian children? Do you care if our children get born? Will you love them the way you love us, which we can't tell from hate? Will you leave them a living father?"

"Young lady, you watch your tone," said the little man. "Don't try to tar us with the same brush as that Del Marlin. He belongs with you—you and him are the killers; we have nothing to do with that. Your children, if you really have them, if you really have the guts to have them, they'll have to deal with having killers for parents; what could we do to them worse than that?"

But one of the women—thin-faced, in her middle forties, with dyed red hair pulled away from her face in a high girlish ponytail—was looking at Mim in bewilderment. "You want to have *children?*" she faltered. "You and him?"

"Yes," said Mim, a bit plaintively. "Is that so peculiar?"

"But I thought people like you—" She shook her head, and did not finish the sentence. The others looked on: white faces, mongrel European faces, *goyish* faces, which Mim recognized with a sudden pang of kinship. "Are you going to get married?" said the woman, not insinuatingly but simply, wanting to know.

They had not discussed it; Mim was not sure what to say. Either a yes or a no would be inaccurate; to say she supposed so would sound merely offhand and frivolous. And what explanations did she owe to these people? She waited a little too long, and then took refuge in what was worst of all, a quotation: "Ask Reverend Hardy to explain *a bridegroom of blood,*" she said—and fled back inside, where Ari found her a minute later ("Look, buzz off," he said as he slammed the door) crying with shame because she had met a genuine, humble question with arrogance and mystification. She should have been able to take hold of the situation; she should have been able to talk these people into oblivion; but she was with her lover, perhaps she was pregnant, and she was afraid. They were all shouting outside. Ari called the police. He comforted her, and they ate breakfast, and Mim lost her breakfast soon after from sheer distress, and that afternoon driving home from the clinic he put his hand apologetically on her knee and said, "So *are* we going to get married?"

"A bridegroom of what?" said Sarita.

Mim explained. It was toward the beginning of Exodus: after Moses talked to God at the burning bush, he set out with his family for Egypt to fulfill his commission, and God tried to kill him on the way. It was a strange thing to do to one's newly designated mouthpiece, but God had a habit that way: look at Abraham and Isaac. "But Moses' wife was no fool: she sliced off her son's foreskin, touched it to Moses' privates, and saved him from harm."

"I do remember that story," said Sarita. "Terrifying stuff in the Bible."

"And elsewhere," said Mim. "Here's how it looks in Hebrew. *Ki chatan damim atah li:* For you are a bridegroom of blood to me."

She had written it in a small notebook. Sarita studied the incomprehensible letters. "Well, there's your amulet," she said. "It's an extraordinary one. Have it engraved in his ring: he'll have to wear that."

"Oh," said Mim, disappointed, "oh, of course. Though I'd have to think of that poor woman each time—but you're right, of course that's the thing."

"Unless you want to hold out for the foreskin of your firstborn."

"I don't think Bob could handle that," said Mim drily. "And one can't be sure of having a boy. And what I meant anyway, when I said it, surely you know, was that—was that my first-*un*born—"

"I understand that," said Sarita. "Don't try to say it rationally."

"You understand everything," said Mim, getting up. Clearly she was not used to being held by anyone but a lover: her body molded itself to Sarita's, familiarly and with trust. Sarita was no longer used to being held by anyone at all. Mim's breasts and belly were soft through her thin summer clothes; she smelled slightly of sweat. "Make us *something*," she said. "I know you'll know what to do. Your blessings are hard currency; one can't have too many."

When Sarita looked back on it, she knew all about amulets: she had devised some of her own in third or fourth grade. Oppressed by the lovelessness of school and wanting to bring some love with her, she had cut out pictures from the newspaper and carried one with her each day. They were drawings of pretty ladies from the comics or the fashion ads, usually just the faces—it wasn't their clothes she was after in those days, but their pensive looks—and now and then during the day she would glance into the palm of her hand and be reassured. What holy pictures must do: provide a reminder of some other realer world. During gym class she could not keep holding the picture, and would leave it in one of her street shoes; eventually the gym teacher found out and had Sarita up to her office, where she probed for some deep-seated maladjustment and sent a note home to her parents. Why she had made so much of it, Sarita had always wondered: surely other little kids had odd habits. We're idolaters, that's all, she thought: from teddy bears and security blankets we make other accommodations. We sublimate it all finally into our books and our jewelry and the colors we wear and how much hair we prefer, all of which can look more or less normal and deceive people into thinking we're healthy. But we're not: we cling to inanimate things for comfort and safety, because the animate thing that once gave it, the mother's warm body, recedes from us farther and farther.

She borrowed a Hebrew dictionary from the calligrapher. She stretched a two-yard length of silk like a canvas, and mixed her dyes. She sat watching the silk. Preposterous, tasteless ideas presented themselves: slogans, floating fetuses, copulating couples in cave-painting style. One had to be serious: even now Rushdie languished in hiding for the crime of not being serious. But the situation had passed the point where seriousness could be helpful; one could only laugh or despair.

She had an odd sense of movement in some fold of her mind: as if something were stirring, trying to get her attention. Always before she had solicited the invisible realm through something she made; this time the invisible realm was soliciting her, before she knew what to make, and the sensation unbalanced her. She shut her eyes. It was darker than she expected, as if an eclipse came over her eyelids, and she opened them again in surprise. But after all, eclipse was her present condition: she might as well see what it was like in the dark.

"Baby Wittmer!"
"Sir!"
"Muster the infantry."

There was a shrill whistle, and as Sarita's eyes grew accustomed to the dim light she saw a vast flat plain crawling with movement. The ground was alive, seething and thick as an animal's carcass with maggots; disoriented, she could not tell size or scale, and could not see what the creatures were. Gradually she made out that they were babies, crawling along the ground, squirming in constant motion. They all seemed to be the same age, just come to full term, and they were all dressed alike in grey diapers, though they came of all races and showed some difference in size. They seemed to be moving, with the aimless method of babies, toward their places in some military order, and as she watched little banners appeared among them: fluttering pink and blue pennons, streamers with writing that she strained to read. UNBORN NATION. LIFE, LIBERTY AND THE PURSUIT OF SUSTENANCE. WHATEVER YOU LOOSE ON EARTH SHALL BE LOST IN HEAVEN. And behind a small group to the right, a big flag painted in red: KILLER BABIES FROM LIMBO.

The babies reached their places on the field, but they had no parade-ground decorum: they kept discovering each other, and giving each other long fascinated stares and slow toothless smiles. A few broke rank to explore from another angle; some hugged, and she noticed one thoughtfully sucking another's fingers. From the group on the right came another loud whistle, and suddenly there was silence. And all the babies, with their topheavy heads and weak legs, strained and stood up on their feet, an exceeding great army.

The baby who had given the commands stood under the flag, flanked by six or seven large babies who seemed to serve as his officers. "Interrupted infants of the world!" he declaimed in ringing tones. "We are gathered here to strike back at a confirmed and mortal enemy, a man who has sent too many of us here. For twenty years he has dislodged us from our mothers' wombs without compunction or contrition, remorse or regret. We are as deeply opposed to his future life as he was to ours, and though we cannot harm him directly we will work by any means for his unhappiness." He looked down at the front ranks. "Baby Lonigan, you are particularly concerned in this matter. What do you have to say?"

A dark-haired baby in a rumpled diaper uniform answered lethargically. "Oh, nothing much. Sir."

"Nothing much! When this monstrous event, this charade, this mockery, is taking place! Where is your sense of duty?"

The baby looked around vaguely, making delicate gestures with its hands. "I don't know," it said. "Is that something we're equipped with yet? I thought we didn't even get the rudiments until potty training."

The leading baby went red in the face and let out a bawl of outrage. "You are a discredit," he said, "to your parents and to the faith in which you were not baptized. Let me remind you of the grotesque and ludicrous circumstances surrounding this inquiry. Your mommy, through a comedy of error that doesn't even bear thinking about, is marrying the man who murdered you. She's *happy* with him; she's thinking of having another baby with him, one that will be born this time. Does this mean nothing to you? Do you feel nothing at all?"

"What should I feel?" said the other. "And more to the point, what do you expect me to do about it?"

"Punish her! Stop up her cervix. Wrap yourself around the egg so that his sperm can't get in."

"I keep forgetting. Do we or don't we believe in birth control?"

"Don't be insubordinate! We believe in God's vengeance. Do whatever it takes. Sit in her womb and don't let the baby settle. Or pry it loose once it *has* settled, and give her a miscarriage. Wait till she knows it's there, and then pry it loose."

The other baby rubbed its eyes with its fists. "Wait, I'm really confused. If what they did to us is so wrong, how can it be right for us to do the same to that baby?"

"Oh, you stupid . . . zygote. People who do wrong deserve to be punished. That baby is just the means."

"You know, I've been wondering if that's fair. If grownups want so badly to do that thing that they get us even when they don't want us, could there be something going on besides right and wrong?"

The chief baby rolled his eyes upwards. "Baby Lonigan, it's just as well you *weren't* born. You wouldn't have been on our side. You'd have been one of those clever hairsplitters who can find an excuse for anything. What *is* there besides right and wrong? Situation ethics?" He sneered, and his cadre of officers sneered too; they gave little bleats of disdain like infant gangsters.

Baby Lonigan's dark eyelashes fluttered. "You know, I have no quarrel with my mommy. She was scared and trying to do her best, and she told my daddy so, and the only reason I'm here at all is because he wouldn't listen. I was a little worried about my daddy from the start; he seemed . . . nervous. I'm not sure he would have liked me as I was."

The chief baby's eyes narrowed. "Mommy's little defender, is that it? Defender to the death. What were you, scared to be born, like she was to have you? Why can't we fight for our lives? Why do we go helplessly into these doctors' hands?"

There was a disturbance in the ranks: another small group was cheering wildly and hoisting a banner that read SUPPORT YOUR RIGHT TO ARM BABIES. The chief baby waved at them indulgently. "Later, boys." He turned back to Baby Lonigan. "Well?"

"Well, the doctor, I thought he was nice. *He* wasn't nervous at all, and he had the most thrilling voice. I can see why she likes him."

"You are disgusting. That's such an inappropriate thing to say. You don't even have a sense of your own interests."

"That's just what my mommy says about *her*self! Oh, to resemble her in just this little way!"

"To say nice things about the man who killed you—!"

"Ah, but if one has to die . . ." said Baby Lonigan languidly. "There are worse ways."

The chief baby screamed, and his officers picked it up; that set off the whole multitude, and the parade ground rang for a while with earsplitting cries. When at last the noise died down, the chief baby said accusingly, "I submit that we shouldn't have to listen to this filth. All that lies before us is our duty, and I submit we should do it."

"Baby Feerer, what duty are you talking about?" said Mim's baby with dignity. "Who would we obey if not our mommies?"

"The higher law," the chief baby said. "The law of life, the law of God. How often do we obey our mommies anyway?"

Baby Lonigan's eyes, Sarita thought, were really most expressive. Right now they were tragic, big and blue with a film of tears that made them gleam. "Baby Feerer, I loved my mommy. Oh, how I loved her. I could have stayed in her body with such joy till it was time to be born; she was exquisitely warm and protecting, and had everything I needed to be in perfect bliss. All but one thing. She didn't want me. She tried to want me, and she regretted that she didn't want me, but she didn't; and I think she did a hard thing and a noble thing by sending me back. I'll always remember her with love, and if she and the doctor love each other and can get a baby together that they love, why I don't see that I can do anything but wish them happiness. You're just not a realist, Baby Feerer."

"You're not a real baby," snarled Baby Feerer. "You're an impostor; you sound like you're thirty years old and in therapy. Let me tell you about hardship and nobility; let me tell you about realism. *My* mommy was a ranking member of Iowa Aid to the Embryo. When she discovered she was pregnant with me, she knew she loved me. She wasn't like your mommy, Baby Lonigan, a scaredy little snip of a feminist with more brains than placenta; she wasn't a teenage slut, like *your* mommy, Baby Wittmer, or yours, Baby Gonsalves, or most of you babies' mommies. She was a good mommy to my brothers and sisters, and she treated my daddy with love, like a man should be treated." He drew himself up and looked sternly and slowly about him. "All the rest of you babies who got here after me? She did it for your sake; she did it in mourning for you, you babies who came here before me. She didn't have time to work for you and me both. She didn't think twice: she knew her duty and she did it, and there wasn't a soul she could tell except for the enemy. Now *she* was a hero. And it's my duty to carry on her work. What's the matter with the rest of you?"

He looked around again, more quickly this time, and the rhetorical question took on a note of alarm. "What's the matter with you? Where are you going?" For the rank-and-file babies were falling out: some were quietly crying, others were curling up in the fetal position and sucking their thumbs, still others were crawling toward the periphery. "What are you doing? Where's your revolutionary discipline?"

"We don't like politics," they whimpered. "We want our mommies; all this talk of our mommies is making us lonesome. We want our mommies, and we know we're not going to get them, and you can't give them back to us, either. Baby Feerer, even you think your mommy just did what she had to. Why was it right for her and wrong for our mommies? Why aren't they heroes too?"

Baby Feerer raged; he seized a rattle from one of his officers and hammered it on the ground. "Baby Lonigan," he said, "you started all this backtalk and you'd better stop it. What are you going to do?"

Baby Lonigan was roused to frank insolence. "Listen, fetus: we're all real tired of your bombast. And you know what? We're already dead; there's not a thing you can do to us. I think I'm going to go to sleep now, and maybe later on I'll play with my toes. Would you care to join me?"

"I hate you!" shrieked Baby Feerer. "You're not worthy to call yourself unborn! You're an irresponsible, nasty, effete little—Hey, are you pink or blue anyway?" He beckoned to his officers, and they rushed Baby Lonigan and tried to unpin the diaper. Baby Lonigan screamed, really terrified, and Sarita found herself swooping into the scene, picking—him? her?—up, and swooping back to reality. "Mim would have loved you," she murmured, "what a pity she couldn't have known you. From what I know of your father, you'd have scared him silly, but not her. Are you all right now?"

"Not really," the baby said. "I mean, I am dead. I don't like having been so hypothetical." It sighed. "I know all the reasons it had to happen this way, but I think it's too bad. Of course you can't say that to *them*." It nodded backward, meaning the other babies. "But I did want to keep on being. It's all you know how to want at that age," it added sagely.

"You weren't hypothetical," said Sarita, not knowing whether that would comfort or grieve it. "Whatever it amounts to, to have existed for a few weeks, you were plenty real."

"But what *does* it amount to? Everybody keeps fighting over it. I'm too young for an identity crisis. It's all so sad; grownups don't know what they're doing." It wrapped a pale hand around Sarita's first finger.

"No, we don't," said Sarita seriously. "That's not part of the human condition. It's what you had to look forward to, you know: being as confused as the rest of us. You may be well out of it."

"I've thought so sometimes." It yawned and looked up at her, and relaxed. A change came over its face: a limpid blue gaze, a trust so extreme or a guile so disingenuous it could not be fathomed. "Poor mommy. Poor daddy. Poor doctor."

"You can bless her?" she said, hesitating. "Even though—"

"Yes," the baby said tiredly. "She was all I knew; of course I bless her." It was becoming very small; it was reverting from a full-term baby with a precocious vocabulary to a seven-week fetus with dark smudges for eyes. It curled in the palm of her hand. She wondered vaguely what sex it really was, and the words came into her mind from it, *Wouldn't you like to know?* Then it winked out: it just disappeared, leaving a little light in the hollow of her hand, which she pressed at once to the center of the cloth. Around it she traced two interpenetrating triangles, her finger leaving no impress on the silk. She marked the place with a paintbrush. She studied the Hebrew dictionary for perhaps twenty minutes, and then laboriously wrote the letters for *tikkun olam,* the mending of the world, across the surface of the star. Nothing was visible on the cloth.

When Todd came to work the next day he found her collapsed in the armchair, half-coherent and sick, and the finished piece still framed on the cutting table. Dyes, brushes, Q-tips were spread out in chaos. Some books were open on the table; there was an unplaceable smell in the air.

One of Todd's former lovers had once tried to kill himself; he had looked just like Sarita looked now, queasy and poisoned, nearly inert. Todd panicked. "Oh my God," he said. "Sarita, what did you take? How long ago was it? I'm going to call 911."

"What did I . . . what?" she said. "You mean take, like pills? Nothing. Todd, no, don't be helpful."

"Don't lie to me, Sarita," he said. "I'm not going to let you do this. You have to live." He reached for the phone.

"Todd," she said, weakly but steadily. "I didn't take any pills. Don't bother the EMTs."

He wavered. "What was it, the dyes? What's that smell? You're not careful enough with toxics." He put down the phone, doubtfully, and opened the window. "You're not trying to fake me out?"

"No," she said. "You whiteboy shamans, you don't know what you're looking at. There's not a pill in the world that could cause this."

He was a small man, perhaps thirty pounds lighter than she was; he pulled her up in the chair. "Something is very wrong," he said. "Sarita, have you been here all night?"

"No," she said, beginning to laugh oddly, "I flew off with Peter Pan and Wendy to the island of lost—" The laughter took over and she could not finish the sentence. "Yes," she said finally. "I've been having an aesthetic miscarriage."

"This thing in the frame? Can I look?"

"No," she said. But it was only two steps away; he was already looking. She watched his eye travel critically over the silk. A ground of dark red, with shadings into purple and scarlet and brown. She had sprinkled crystals of rock salt on the wet fabric, which made the colors creep; there was a polypoid, corpuscular effect to the surface. In the center was a huge dark yellow sun, on whose expanse the salt left only a faint undulation. Around the sun flared out a corona of grey; on closer inspection it turned out to be a swarm of tiny white comets (squiggles of gutta resist from a paper cone) with elegant snapping tails. "What is it, the Big Bang?"

She gave a faint laugh. "You could call it that."

He studied it. "Oh," he said at last with an air of dim recollection, "this is one of those straight-people things. That's Big Mama Egg, with all the little spermlets crowding around. Jeez, it's a wonder anybody's born queer. It's so elemental."

"It's kitsch."

"Is it? It might be a little campy, but the technique is to die for. It's like nothing you've ever done."

"It's kitsch," she said. "The technique is all right, it's the . . . the method, the part you don't see. Supernatural voyages. Bunge among the celestials."

"What are you talking about?"

She sighed. She was not going to tell the whole story; he would think she was crazy, and there was no reason ever to say what she did after hours. She had already said too much. "When you were a kid, did you ever want to go on a quest to save the world?"

"God, no," he said. "I wanted to go to Hollywood. You mean like in *A Wrinkle in Time*, where they travel to other planets and meet that awful pulsating brain?"

"More or less." How could one convey the urge, if he had not shared it?—the sense of absolute possibility, at least between the covers of a book if never within one's own family, the sense that one's powers were real? "There's a lot of writing for kids—not all of it for kids, either—that makes you imagine it possible. A brave little band of spiritual warriors resisting some modernist menace. Sometimes they dredge up someone from the past to help them—King Arthur or Merlin, nearly always somebody Celtic. Some *magus ex machina*. Sometimes they do it all by the power of love, just stand and think the right thoughts, and there are signs and wonders and good wins out over evil in some fabulous cataclysm."

"Nice work if you can get it," said Todd.

"Well, it sounds like *possible* work to someone like me, who doesn't trust politics and lives a good deal in her mind. There's this sense of making an end run around the real world, in which money has to be raised and people have to be convinced: you just go straight to the source. You flip the right switch and God does it for you." What was that quote from St. Paul in *A Wrinkle in Time*? *The foolishness of God is wiser than men, and the weakness of God is stronger than men. . . . For God hath chosen the foolish things of the world to confound the wise; and God hath chosen the weak things of the world to confound the things which are mighty; and base things of the world, and things which are despised, hath God chosen, yea, and things which are not, to bring to nought things that are.* She got up, hobbling a little, and stood next to Todd at the table; she stared at the yellow sun. "But it's *moral* kitsch. The world isn't saved that way; the world isn't saved at all, because every answer we try becomes a new problem. The foolishness of God is still foolish, and the weakness of God is still weak, and he's parceled it out pretty evenly among us. How do you know who's who? Who's weaker and more despised—a fetus, a pregnant woman, an abortion doctor, a fundamentalist? A Jew or a redneck? Who's supposed to confound whom?"

"Oh," said Todd, comprehending, "This is something to do with Mim?"

"Oh, of course," said Sarita apologetically. "How would you know that? I'm sorry."

Todd took it in. "But Mim *is* the modernist menace, isn't she? I mean, in her own small way. So are you; so am I. The emancipated woman and the godless artist and the shameless cocksucker. All destroying the family twenty-four hours a day for all we're worth. Why should any of us be able to flip the switch? God's probably pulled the wires."

"No he hasn't," said Sarita, with such offhand certainty that Todd raised his eyebrows. "That's the trouble; he doesn't pull anyone's wires." She unpinned the silk from the stretcher, gathered it carefully to contain all the grains of salt, and shook it out the window. The next step was to set the dyes: she would roll the piece in brown paper and steam it in a tube of aluminum stovepipe (wrapped in a fiberglass batt to hold the heat) on the stove in a canning pot.

"What does Mim want with an image like that?" said Todd. "It's the poster child for prolife."

"It's a wedding present," said Sarita. "She's marrying Bob." With movements a little too deliberately casual, she took up the brown and gold satin she had dyed a few weeks ago. She would drape and cut it today, make a new design that had nothing to do with Mim. First she would go down to the restaurant next to the bus station for an omelette. Bacon and mushroom.

"She would," said Todd. "Hets are so unimaginative. All they ever want is one thing."

CHAPTER 22

And mariage is then most brok'n to him, when he utterly wants the fruition of that which he most sought therin, whether it were religious, civill, or corporall society.

—Milton

This world can be made beautiful again by beholding it as a battlefield. When we have defined and isolated the evil thing, the colours come back into everything else. When evil things have become evil, good things, in a blazing apocalypse, become good. There are some men who are dreary because they do not believe in God; but there are many others who are dreary because they do not believe in the devil. The grass grows green again when we believe in the devil, the roses grow red again when we believe in the devil.

—G. K. Chesterton

Somewhere beneath all thoughts admissible to consciousness, Alan was deeply exhilarated by his upheaval. Mira's speaking against him had roused his spirit: it was as if, instead of the vague succubus of his night memories, he had had restored to him her whole mind, lucid and bantering and serious and piquantly wrong. His work on the book was going wonderfully, because with every page he refuted her; surely if he just turned a phrase this way, made that point a little sharper, she could not fail to concede. Even his daily life with Claire and the children became part of the refutation: his family was not just the imperfect peace he had managed to find in a life full of disappointments, but the proof that his principles held. Whereas hers. . . ? They gave her only a life with a scornful man, a fixation on defending her crime, a pathetic sophistication. *Paiens ont tort, et chrétiens ont droit,* he quoted to himself from *The Song of Roland,* for the first time in many years; he had never studied Old French, but it had been a rallying-cry of Jim Molloy's. Pagans are wrong, Christians right, it still comes down to that finally.

He had resisted, so far, writing to the editor of the *Challenge* to ask what this newsletter was, the one where their intern had seen some writing of Mira's; it would have made better sense than trying to call her, but it would have been a public admission. Of course it was utterly natural for a commentator from one camp to show interest in a commentator from the other—perhaps that was even why the editor had mentioned the piece, to give him the opportunity—but that was why he could not do it; it was too impersonal, like a denial of their former relations. In another sense it was too eager, as if he had seen her ("Uh-cross uh *crowd*-ed room," he heard in his sister Maureen's voice, exaggeratedly rapturous) and whispered to someone, *"Who is she?"* He could not do that.

A few days after his attempt on the telephone, he was working again in his study. He had found himself on a circular train of logic, and had switched on the radio, a habit he had developed to give his mind a quick shake. The news: more about this awful business in the Gulf, the president and one of his petty dictators squaring off like schoolyard bullies. All about oil, really. More factional fighting among South African blacks. Somewhere there had been a bad storm. Idly Alan remarked how the announcer leaned on the names, like the italicized names in old books: "Jury selection begins Monday in the trial of *Del Marlin,* accused in the shooting of abortion doctor Robert *Morgenzahl* in September of last year." He remembered the case: he had wondered at the time if that had been Mira's doctor, and been vindictively glad and then been ashamed of gloating at another's misfortune. Now he thought, *But she'll be there.* If she were taking some activist role she would be marching outside the courthouse, talking to the media, upholding the party line. He could go there and see her outright. It would not be a question of secretly calling her, writing her terrible bleeding letters as he had once done, putting his marriage to Claire in some obscure jeopardy: it would be a clean political quarrel, on which their mutual past need never obtrude. He could be there observing the scene; he could interview the doctor and the assailant; he wouldn't interview Mira (though if she said anything good of course he could quote her), but he might find a way to have one real conversation. He imagined her face when she saw him among the reporters. *That'll settle her hash,* he heard in his mother's voice, but it wouldn't be vengeance; it would be a kind of pursuit for the sake of mercy, a rescue, a harrowing. Jim Molloy had once lent him a book, an extraordinary series of interviews some woman from Europe had done with the jailed commandant of one of the Nazi camps: she had not been content to transcribe what the prisoner said of himself, but had forced her way into his heart, and broken it—literally: he had died soon after admitting the extent of his crimes. But he had died confessed, she had harrowed him out of hell, and that was what Alan would do for Mira. She would face what she'd done, and call it by its right name. Who knew what reconciliations might begin to occur, within the limits of what they were now permitted, if he could have that one conversation? The rekindling of God's mercy. A durable fire.

He called *Saecula,* the Catholic journal for which he most often wrote. So convinced was he by the germ of the article that had just sprung to life in his mind—and so fired by all that he was not saying—that he persuaded the editor at once and found himself with the assignment. He began drawing up lists of questions. He would need to make a run to the library for background reading. He would need to make plane and hotel reservations. He would need to tell Claire.

But Claire was dismayed: "Oh, honey, I don't believe it. To take off and do this, at the beginning of your sabbatical, without even thinking it through—to get sidetracked by this issue, of all things—why? You don't need the grief."

"But it's time I took up the issue. I've always avoided it. It's not a sidetrack; it's—"

"You've avoided it because it almost destroyed you. I don't believe what I'm hearing. Don't you remember when those kids from the parish asked you to picket with them, and you snapped at them and then came home and had nightmares? You shouldn't go near this issue. You haven't made your peace with it yet—and you're not going to do that in public, with all sorts of preachers and pundits screaming about it, including the woman who did this to you in the first place."

"Claire, I'm not sure it's peace that's asking to be made," he said. "I don't know if these things can be resolved. I'd like to be able to forgive her, if that's possible." Forgive: the word glowed at the pit of his stomach.

"Well, it's not possible if she's not repentant, and she's not, from the sound of things."

Sometimes Claire reverted to basic catechism; it was not an attractive habit. "You don't know that," he said. "This special pleading, this apparently rock-hard certainty, is often the thinnest veneer. You know that as a psychologist. It's like ice on running water, very fragile. Claire, she still talks about God."

"In that ironic, profane, dig-you-in-the-ribs kind of way. That means nothing."

"I think she could be reached."

"And you're going to try and reach her, and you're going to come home in pieces because you can't, and I'm the one who's going to have to put you back together. I don't ever want to see you so hurt as you were when—"

"Claire, please! Let's not dredge up old troubles. You did a good job; I'm not going to end up like that again. This is a piece I have to write; I think I'm well suited to write it. I can draw on my own experience without having to whine about it. I can use my personal knowledge without making a spectacle of myself."

"Alan, you're the last person in the world who's suited to write about this. To interview your ex-wife—to confront the doctor who probably aborted your baby—that *is* making a spectacle of yourself."

"I won't *interview* her. I'll just talk to her. And the doctor won't know. He must see thousands of women, and it was all years ago. He'll have no way to make the connection."

"Well, then, it's dishonest, and you shouldn't do it. You should—what's the word—recuse yourself, not go seeking it out."

"Claire, I'm writing this as a Catholic and a citizen, someone who cares about this country's public life. My personal connection to the subject is irrelevant, except as it enables me to write a better piece."

"Your personal connection to the subject is enough to make you a basket case. Alan, I won't *allow* it."

He looked at her, feeling weirdly distant. "Claire, do you realize that what's hurt me most as a married man has been what women won't allow?"

She looked stunned; her round, freckled face went blank for an instant, and then her eyes filled. "Alan, that's terribly unfair! If you mean to compare me with Mira, I don't know what I've done that's the equivalent of what she did. I have never told you a lie; I've never—"

"No," he said. "Claire, I didn't say that. Please, I shouldn't have said what I said. But can't you see, I have a responsibility. Mira's caught up in this movement. I have to help her."

"Your ties with her were dissolved. You knew her for a couple of years. Is this some mid-life crusade, where you have to track down every loose end of your life—"

"Dad?" A little voice, sleepy and diffident, came from above their heads. Chrissy, aged five, had come halfway downstairs in her nightgown, trailing a blanket. "Are you and Mom fighting?"

Claire gave an anxious sigh. "No, honey," she called, "everything's fine. We're just having a disagreement."

Alan got up and went to put her back to bed, gathering the warm little body close to his chest; the fine reddish-blonde hair was fragrant under his nose. "Everything's fine, cricket," he said. "Sometimes moms and dads disagree, but it's because they care about each other. Everything will be fine."

"You're not going to get a vorce?"

"Sweetheart, no, never! What would give you such an idea?" What a time to grow up in, that a five-year-old should have such a worry. "No, we're both going to stay right here."

She sat, alert, on the bed. "Daddy, who's Mira?"

O Lord, what else had she heard? "A lady I used to know."

"Did she do something bad to you?"

"A long time ago. But it's all right now." Whether it was or was not, his children must never know what Mira had done. It had not crossed his mind that they might hear of her and be curious.

"Is she someone to pray for?"

Alan almost dissolved. It was a family formula, devised by his firstborn, Grace, which had been applied to everyone from sick relatives to the President. He felt a twinge of incongruity, but also a sense of longed-for completion, at having it applied here. "I think so," he said softly. "She's not a happy person; she needs God's help."

"I'll put her on the list," said Chrissy importantly. "And I'll say a Hail Mary right now. English or Latin?"

Alan smiled in the glow of the nightlight. "Which do you want, sweetheart?"

"Latin. 'Cause Latin is your favorite."

It was her favorite too. No, better not say that. "Okay."

Grace, in the next bed, stirred and muttered as her sister recited the prayer. Alan listened, half present, assailed by the concurrent reality of this scene and Mira's own life. Somewhere, unknown to them all, was a ghostly sibling; if that child had been born he would never have had this family. Chrissy finished and flung herself down expectantly, waiting to be tucked in. Alan complied and kissed her. "Sleep tight, now." He closed the door to a crack. Outside, on the landing, he stood collecting himself. He stared unseeing at the print of the Botticelli Christ: resurrected, eyes weary as if just waking, the blood of his wounds beginning to run again. Would the ghost-child be resurrected? Augustine had devoted some thought to that question; Alan was too tired to remember what he had said. All his protestations to Claire now rang false, like a little boy's wheedlings, one try after another to see which one would succeed.

When he came downstairs again Claire was sitting immobile; she had been crying. "All right," she said. "You're going to do this, and I know I can't stop you. But I want you to know I've been *deeply* shaken tonight. Always before I've had the satisfaction of knowing that I gave you what she couldn't give you: peace, and a good home, and sweet children that love you. Tonight I've seen that you would walk away from all that in an instant if you could have her. I'm just second-best. Her lies are better than my truth; her immature flightiness is better than the best work of my adult life."

"Claire, don't demean yourself by comparing—"

"She's the target of all the romanticism you have; I never have been. You may think that because I'm practical and steady I don't need romance, but I do; and to see you direct it all to this glorified memory of someone who hurt you unbearably—" She shook her head and blotted her eyes. "All I can hope is that seeing her again will break the spell. She's not twenty-one any more; she's probably settled and stable in her own fashion. She may even have kids of her own." She watched his face as she said it; he tried to keep the shock from his eyes. "I have to believe that you love me enough—I think you love the children enough—to come back and be yourself after seeing her. But I have to tell you, I'm very disturbed. Men can just become strangers to women. This is the kind of thing that happens to my clients; I never thought it would happen to me."

"But what are you worried about?" said Alan, feeling outclassed. "I just want to talk to her. Of course it will be an emotional conversation, and I may never know if I've changed her mind, but—but I'm faithful to you, Claire, you don't ever have to fear for our future. Surely you don't imagine—"

"Physical faithfulness can be very *pro forma*," she said. "If you're physically faithful to me but always have one eye out for what she's been writing—if you're going to go into some emotional spin every time— Oh, God, it even occurs to me to wonder if she wrote that letter as some sort of sick flirtation. It's the kind of thing a woman like her might do. Alan, this really feels dangerous."

Since it had occurred to Alan to wonder the same thing—without the epithet *sick*—he scoffed at the notion. "Oh, sweetheart, don't diagnose long-distance. I think she was just showing off. It was a chance to stand on her political soapbox, and to get in some personal digs at me without anyone knowing it, and I don't think we have to probe any further into her motives." *Besides, whoever this man is, I bet he's probing pretty far into*—but he couldn't say that. He would have to pay that phone bill as soon as it came. He hoped it wouldn't come while he was away. *Pro forma* indeed.

"I think there's a lot you're not seeing," said Claire. "You know a lot about morals, but I'm not sure you know yourself."

Later, in their room, the dispute had unbalanced their physical affection: they were both cautious, ingratiating, warily kind to each other. "Would you like to, you know—" she said, gesturing with her head.

"Oh, no, that's all right, Claire. I know you don't like it that much."

"Well, it just has bad memories. But if you want to, you can." And then, as he hesitated, "Or would you like *me* to—"

"Oh, sweetheart, please, I love you just as you are. You don't have to make yourself over." She had no great love for what they had taken to calling "the extras," which her two former lovers, in her days of half-hearted rebellion against the Church, had insisted on loutishly; he might still have liked to do those things, but felt (the few times they tried) that he was imposing on her body the cravings of Mira's, and it seemed a crude violation. He could not, in any case, recover the sense of wild risk he had had when he engaged in those acts with Mira—partly because the risk had been real: he had suffered such heavy losses. "We're going to make love like grownups," he said, rearranging their nightclothes and sliding to the preliminary position, elated at the onset of lust. "We're out of the oral stage. There, isn't this what you like?" They moved side by side.

"Oh, yes. But I need you to *be there*," she whispered. "It feels so mechanical lately, you seem so distant and sad. Please, Alan, I need you."

"I'm here. I'm with you," he said. He slipped easily into her; she moaned softly and pushed. They moved slowly together: her counterthrust a little delayed, not simultaneous but syncopated with his thrust, a requital and an invitation. He found it delicious and soothing. Two boats rocking together as the same wave passed under them, not at once but in a close rhythm. She tugged at his shoulder; he rolled onto her, burying himself. "Why do I need you so much?" she said helplessly. "It makes me so angry to need you." Then, quickly, a violent climax: her pelvis churning, her breath hissing raggedly (cries would have woken the children), her nails gripping his back. He was startled into release: he did not think of Mira or of anything, unless the obliteration of thought that overtook him were somehow the thought of God.

CHAPTER 23

> The belief is not the content of a testimony, but rather the power of reproduction. The Jew, engendered a Jew, attests his belief by continuing to propagate the Jewish people. His belief is not in something; he is himself the belief.
>
> —Franz Rosenzweig

Mim went away for the weekend before the trial. She did not quite want to, but there was a retreat in the mountains led by a rabbi whose books she had liked, and Ari said, "You should go. I keep stealing your Shabbes." Of course he would not go with her. She wished he would close up the clinic for the day and go anywhere but to work: a vigil was planned Friday night at Our Lady of Sorrows (Mim and Alan's old parish church) to pray for "an end to abortion," and what might happen next morning was anyone's guess. She drove up through the little hill towns, past general stores and gun shops and yards full of old junk cars, wondering uneasily if some of these people were antis, and "anti" enough to come down to Easy Landing and prove it. She knew some of the women were patients from time to time.

In the Hebrew calendar it was the month of Elul; in the common calendar it was September, and the nights were cold in the mountains. The group sat in the lodge on pillows, studying text. Elul, the rabbi explained, was the month of preparation for the High Holy Days, the month of *teshuvah* or turning; *repentance* was a wrong translation, suggesting shame and renunciation rather than purpose and hope. (Latin again, Mim thought—though *conversion* might have had the right flavor: *Hierusalem convertere ad dominum deum tuum.*) In fact, the rabbi went on, the four letters of Elul—aleph, lamed, vav, lamed—were the initial letters of *Ani l'dodi v'dodi li*, "I am my beloved's and my beloved is mine"; the word was an acronym, an encoded message of the profound trust between God and his people. Mim gave herself up to allegory. The group was small, only thirty people or so, along with six children; they hummed and muttered fervently through the long services, enveloped in prayer shawls. Some of the prayer shawls were tie-dyed: the group was hippie rather than Orthodox, people who had been through drugs and Gestalt therapy and Buddhist meditation and were bringing it all back home. Now and then everyone spontaneously burst into song. Mim felt at once profoundly at rest and ready to jump out of her skin: she wanted to stay here forever, but she wanted to run for her car and drive off, away from these people who before the Friday night meal had taped on the bathroom light switches in all the cabins, lest anyone, forgetting the Sabbath, should switch them off and force their cabinmates to brush their teeth in the dark. She felt a sense of incongruity amounting almost to pain: was this the only way to get close to those texts, with their mighty irony and their liberating reach, to knuckle under without a syllable of dissent to shtetl piety? Of course amulets were shtetl piety too, and she had been ready enough to ask Sarita for one of those; she had no right to complain. But she had planned to call Ari some time on Saturday, to check on the state of the clinic, and the telephones were off limits. To call she would have to petition one of the organizers of the retreat and explain that no, Ari's life was probably not in danger, and that she could do nothing from here to save him if it were, but that she did not want to wait till the evening to find out how the morning had treated him.

She lay awake after the Friday night study session, her eye drawn to the pool of light from the bathroom, her mind running in circles. In the bunks behind and beneath her, women breathed in the dark. The couples and families were housed in the other cabins. The peace was extraordinary: the moist silence of the chilly forest outside, the quiet approval of the women for Ari's work, the complete absence of danger. It made her soul ring as one's ears ring when a loud noise shuts off. Taking advantage of the light she climbed down from her bunk and went into the bathroom, hoping to see a streak of blood on the retreat center's scratchy paper, but there was nothing. Silly to think the near-accident had actually made her pregnant, but she would not know till she knew. Ari's anxiety and her own impulse to comfort him had made that narrow chance seem the only possible one. She had said she would have the child, so now there would be one: the universe would pounce and make sure it came true. What had she let herself in for? At supper she had sat next to a shy boy of twelve who sang sweetly, who was preparing for his bar mitzvah, who was mourning his grandmother. He was pudgy, hesitant, beautiful. She had never found children beautiful before attending to Jewish children. People loved their children—loved them blindly, shatteringly, no matter what they were like. Now that she had Ari, she wondered if she could love at that pitch and live. She would not have thought she could love any man as she loved Ari. But with a man one could have beforehand some sense of the price, and refuse to pay it if it threatened to be too high. With a child one learned the price only gradually, and never before it was too late.

She went outside and stood on the concrete porch of the cabin, breathing the comforting pong of forest rot. It was raining a little; drips fell from the roof to the leafmold. Last night—it seemed weeks away—she had run into Edith Tyrell, Sarita's formidable assistant, in the supermarket, and they had gone out for a beer and finally had their long talk. Nobody would talk to her these days about anything except pregnancy. Edith had had one, years ago now, that had ended badly; she and Fred, unmarried then and intellectual rivals at their little midwestern Bible college, had one night stopped arguing doctrine and started kissing, and a few weeks later one rapid and unintended coupling had left her not with a normal pregnancy but with an ectopic one. She had been rushed to the hospital in pain and with full public fanfare, and the embryo and the tube had been removed while her parents bewailed her virginity in the next room. They had tried to spread a rumor of appendicitis, but somehow everyone knew; when Edith and Fred married at the end of the school year they received an anonymous gift of a plastic fetus, with a note that read "Jesus remembers." Fred had lost his faith in the aftermath—"I told him he would, he was trying to prove God by science, and that's just begging for atheism"—and still said he would rather believe in blind chance than in the caprice of a God who would hurt a young woman that way. "But he's wrong," said Edith, "I don't want that chivalrous pity. Whom the Lord loveth he chasteneth. That's not caprice."

"You think he keeps track that closely?" said Mim. "Sits up there judging which sparrows deserve to fly and which to fall?"

"He can tell us apart," said Edith. She had never been pregnant again: the inflammation that had prevented the egg from descending had affected both tubes, and after two years on the Pill—during which she and Fred had kept reinfecting each other—she had found she could not conceive. A hard punishment for a rather venial sin, Mim thought—supposing it to be a sin at all—and far worse than anything she had suffered. She told Edith some of her story. "What year was that?" Edith said. "Oh, too early. If only we could line up the years the way we want them. I'd have taken the baby."

Mim jumped; occasionally she had referred a patient to the local adoption agency, but she could never get used to the way women coveted the fruit of their neighbors' wombs. "Edith, I was married. What was I going to do? *Surprise, dear, I'm carrying your child and I'm going to give it away.* That's just incoherent. Abortion at least makes sense."

"I don't think so," said Edith. Her face was severe in the ersatz Tiffany light of the little bar. All the same, she hated the protestors; they gave no quarter, they sent plastic fetuses to anguished young women, they let other people's sins dissolve their restraints. "It's your job to keep their temper," she said. "They can be as immoral as they like in defense of morality. Goons for God."

"They're trying to save souls," said Mim. "It transcends etiquette."

Edith grinned painfully and downed the rest of her beer. The beer itself must be a sign of defiance; where Edith came from there probably wasn't any. In the parking lot of the mall, as they said goodbye, Edith gave her a long look. "Do you think of it now—having children?"

Crickets shrilled in the field alongside the mall. "Is that anyone's business? Yes, I think of it now." She searched for her own intrusive question. "And do you still prove God by faith?"

·

"Well, God proves me by it," Edith said dryly. "And how about you? Do you prove God by any method at all?"

"Oh, by his caprices," Mim said. "Because he still wounds without reason."

But standing in the damp Sabbath darkness at the retreat she did not feel wounded; she felt held, expectantly, by the women in the cabin and by all the trees of the wood, as if the whole creation waited to hear the little SO AM I that might speak from her body. A hundred miles south, on the coast, the antis kept vigil; Mim waited to see if anything stirred in her womb.

Alan, arriving in town late Sunday afternoon, decided not to eat in the hotel; he would walk the short distance downtown and find someplace cheap. He was curious to see what had changed in the years of his absence. The gentrifying trend that had hit every other town had not spared Easy Landing: the hotel was new—postmodern brick with complicated green pointed roofs—and the ratty bayside road had been prettied up, even the derelict textile mill given new windows and turned into condominiums. But the big pile of salt was still there, disreputable as ever, and between the patisseries and fine craft shops on Water Street some signs of the old life endured. Harbor Books was still there—he went in and bought some vintage Dr. Seuss for the girls, and a book on the famous local gardens for Claire—though part of the window was occupied by a mannequin in a fantastical sea-green gown advertising a shop upstairs. The public library, of course, was still there, with an ugly new addition (not postmodern) and homeless people parked on the benches outside. The little Greek restaurant was still there, worse for wear—He las Café, the sign said—and the Crow's Nest was still there!, and he jubilantly went in and bought a lobster roll and a beer. Afterward he kept walking, past his old office—it was still a law office, though two of the names had changed—and past the big Buckingham Hotel with the stone lions, and past the old Bennett House where someone had erected an unfortunate chain-link fence. Idly he read the sign: Women's Health Center; Cara Lizotte, D.C.; Mitchell Tannenbaum, D.D.S. He had gone on half a block before it registered. Good God, that was the place. Smack in the middle of town. It hadn't been there before: did that mean that Morgenzahl *hadn't* been Mira's doctor?—and Alan's happy exploratory mood was ruined as his mind was caught up again in the treadmill of speculation. He refused to walk back and examine the place more closely. He would get a good enough look in a few days, when he went to interview Morgenzahl. Had that been a security guard at the door? Had that been barbed wire at the top of the fence? Morgenzahl had not seemed suspicious on the phone Friday afternoon; he had sounded uncommonly gentle, deferential almost. ("Yes, certainly I know your work," he had said.) Something faintly familiar about his voice.

The walk was spoiled; he turned back to the hotel. For old times' sake he bought an ice cream cone at Frenier's, but of course it did nothing to help. He was glad for the habits of family life, through which he could call Claire at the girls' bedtime and get his mind off the past. Grace was reading the first Narnia book, and told him that the lion's name was almost like his, except his was missing a letter. He said that was nice, and only later remembered that the lion was Narnia's God; what a useful paradigm that was of creator and creature, the creature in the same image but lacking something. Chrissy giggled on the phone and sang him a song about bugs. Claire was patient and watchful. He sighed as he hung up the phone. Now for the worst call. He had put it off until now; he did not, when it came to the point, want to talk to the real Mira, only to refute the political Mira and have the perilous liveliness of the erotic Mira somehow available without sin. Certainly he did not want that man to answer the phone. What should he say if that happened? *This is Alan Lonigan. May I speak to my wife, please?* He laughed ruefully at his own melodrama and punched in the number; he braced himself as it rang.

Her voice: "Hello?" His heart raced.

"Mira?"

"Alan." She sounded flustered but not surprised.

He was flustered himself. "I'm in town for a few days," he said, reciting his prepared words, "and wondered if I could see you."

"You're here for the trial," she said.

"You knew that? Yes, I'm writing about it for *Saecula*."

"Bob Morgenzahl said you had called him."

Good God, did she know him socially? Well enough to find out within two days? "Will you be there too?"

"Yes. Not as a witness, just—watching."

Marching around with a sign for the cameras, no doubt. Well, don't be bitter. "When do you have some free time?"

There was a brief silence. "Is—is this personal or political?" she said. "I mean, is it for the article, or—"

"No, no, just to see you," he said. "I—you—your letter to the *Christian Challenge*, which was so generous—I thought it wasn't impossible you might like to see me. The editor sent it on," he added; "it was quite a surprise."

"Oh," she said. Her blush was almost audible over the phone. "My God, that never occurred to me. Of course, they give the authors a chance to respond. I should have just written you—but, but I wouldn't have. And you'd said it in print, and it seemed worth refuting in print. Not that you'll think I refuted it."

"It was very persuasive," he said, glowing with the thought that she wanted to refute him too. "Personable. A great sense of confidence to it."

"Thank you!" she said, sounding startled. "Of course that's easy in print; it's just my persona talking to your persona. A very different thing—now that I hear your voice—from me talking to you."

How like her: so shy and diffident, and then absolutely direct. Absolutely disarming. How angry she would be if she knew what was going on below his belt right now. Indeliberate desire. Stop. Stop. "You've been well?"

"I've been fine. And you?"

"Just fine. And Claire and the girls are well." He had better make it clear that he had a family. "Still working at the library?"

"Oh, Alan, what a grim question. Still revolving around the sun? Still made of six carbon atoms? Still sitting at the right hand of God? Yes, I'm still there."

"And discouraged about it."

"Fed up with it. Are you still teaching?"

"On sabbatical, at the moment. Writing a book. But I can tell you about that when—"

"Of course. And about your family. At least—at least, *is* this a friendly visit? Or does your persona want to talk to my persona? Because I'm not sure I can do that."

His mind swam. "Mira, I know it's awkward—"

"It's very awkward."

"—considering that we've both made public statements about these things. But a private conversation has nothing to do with that. Of course, I don't know what you may be doing about the trial. Will you be making any public statement about that?"

"I don't think so," she said warily. "Does it matter?"

"Well, then it's fine," said Alan in great relief. "If you were planning to say anything, I suppose I might want to quote it; I'm sure it would be worth quoting. But if you're not planning to, there's no conflict; we can just talk." In one stroke he was cleared of dishonesty, at least as far as she was concerned: exonerated, at least a bit, before Claire. Of course there was still the problem of Morgenzahl, to whom he had presented himself simply as a journalist. "Could you just tell me, though—since it turns out you know Dr. Morgenzahl. I'd just like to know how well. I mean, is he likely to know you and I were married at one point."

A long, dismayed silence. "Alan, what are you doing here? Yes, he knows."

"Does he—I'm sorry, we *don't* have to talk about this, but I just need to know where I stand—does he know that you . . . that I . . . about the baby, does he know it was mine."

"Where you stand," she echoed miserably. "Oh, my God, Alan. Yes, he knows that."

"I see," he said. "Thank you. I'm sorry to mention it." Cleared of dishonesty there too, though not quite intentionally: that interview would be dreadful. Why had Morgenzahl even consented to see him? Had he not known the whole story till afterward? Had he said Alan's name to Mira, perhaps at some pretrial activists' powwow, and she had said Oh my God, we used to be married, that was *his* baby you. . . ? Or had he known it beforehand? He had spoken so gently: surely because he knew. Mira was speaking again, almost stammering something, clearly something terribly private; he cut in hastily, "No, Mira, please, you don't have to say more." He supposed she was trying to tell him that Morgenzahl had done the abortion, and that was clear enough now; let her hang on to whatever dignity she had left. "It's all right. Let's just let it pass. When can I see you?"

She made a small distraught noise. "I don't know, I don't know. When are you talking to Bob?"

"After the verdict," he said. "I suppose you know, they don't expect the trial to take long. It's a pretty clear case."

"Let's wait till after you talk to him. I don't want to—I don't want anything to—"

Her voice shook; she was nearly in tears. "Mira, what's wrong?"

Another long pause. "For God's sake, Alan, don't hurt him."

"Mira!" he said, almost laughing. "People who write for *Saecula* don't attack people physically. What an idea." The paranoia these people must live with. "I'll call you in a few days. And you know, you can always call me," he added, swept by emotion, the erotic itch swamped by real charity; "if you need anything I'll always be glad to help. I'm at the new Merrimac, down on Bridge Street; if there's anything I can do—"

She did laugh: a hysterical giggle. "Right across the street—" she said, and broke off. "No, Alan," she went on sadly, "I won't need anything. It's nice of you, but I won't."

He was exhausted. The conversation had contained every possible draining emotion: politeness, embarrassment, shock, attraction, concern. Thank God he had already called Claire. There would have been no way to dissemble, she would have had the whole conversation out of him in five minutes flat. He spent an hour reading in preparation for the trial, but his attention was very bad; finally he switched to his recreational reading, a new Arthurian novel by the daughter of one of his colleagues. It was extravagantly Celtic and pagan, and quite anti-Catholic. He gave up and went to bed. He slept uneasily; he dreamed of the impotent

Fisher King and woke in a sweat; he dreamed Mira was next to him, naked and murmuring, asking if his persona's name was Gus.

At the courthouse the press was put in a room with a closed-circuit television. Outside it was raining; protest and counter-protest had been rather small, though a man with a sign saying WHO SPEAKS FOR THE BABIES? had hailed him and remembered his name and said something pitying about Mira. Good God, did the whole world know, and how much did it know? There were more activists in the courtroom: the judge was just now warning them to keep quiet. Jury selection was taking a long time. Alan chatted with a local reporter named Jerry something, who had been covering the Marlin story from the beginning and who seemed to know everybody. He had spent a lot of time with the defendant (hadn't Alan seen his piece in the *New Yorker* last week?), knew a lot of the activists on both sides, had cordial relations with Morgenzahl. When he finally took in that *Saecula* was a religious journal, he lit up with helpful interest. "Talk to Morgenzahl's girlfriend if you get a chance," he said. "She's good at the religious angle. Talks about God at rallies and gets the prolife demonstrators all confused. See if you can't track her down."

"I'll do that," said Alan collegially. "What's her name?" A theological girlfriend was more than he would have predicted for Morgenzahl; he would have guessed either a trashy blonde or a lawyer in a grey suit. How did a woman interested in theology get interested in a man who—

He named her; and it was only because in the split second before he did so Alan had guessed that he could say almost smoothly, "Oh, I've—actually got her number, I didn't know they were . . ." and trail off diplomatically without giving their conduct a name. Why hadn't he known? Why hadn't he suspected? Why hadn't he recognized Morgenzahl's voice when he talked to him? Why hadn't he understood from Mira's silences? Why hadn't he simply known that the world was like this, one loss after another, one betrayal after another, no single thing in it worth wanting, only in heaven? *Passio Christi conforta me.* Oh, Mira. Oh, no. No.

At last the jury was seated. Numbly Alan attended to the proceedings. The judge began his preliminary address to the jury: the morality of abortion is not on trial here, you are only considering the innocence or guilt of Delbert Marlin. You must not take the indictment to be part of the evidence; it's only the charge. Marlin, a slight red-haired man, stood as the charge was read. Morgenzahl took the stand, first witness for the prosecution: forties, dark, balding, distant, businesslike. Unmistakably, now, the voice on the answering machine. Absolute confidence: never self-pitying, never playing too much on the trauma, just the right touch of dignified martyrdom and a breath of acidulous wit. How long had he been Mira's lover? What kind of woman would lie down with a man she had paid to destroy her child? Was she in the courtroom, looking on as he spoke?

The arresting officer; the emergency medical technician in charge and the emergency room doctor; two protestors who had seized Marlin just as he shot. The mastermind of the protests, Reverend Hardy, who assured the court ringingly that his group would cast out anyone who planned to do violence. *Phony*, Alan thought sourly. He had no reason to disbelieve the man, who was surely sincere. But he was submerged in grief, drowning in grief, and it was all he could do to take notes as the trial went on. When the first day ended he downed a stunning Scotch and water at the hotel bar, and went for another long walk.

Mim, in the courtroom, listened in a similar distraction. The phone call from Alan was only one more anxiety; it vied with several others for her attention. All around her were protestors from both camps, none of whom reassured her; Calvin Hardy was there, and the hot-tempered patriot from the protest at Ari's house, and (on her own side, more or less) Ceridwen from Laura's party last fall. Ceridwen was wearing a respectable corduroy blazer, but it fell open to reveal a T-shirt that read KEEP YOUR ROSARIES OFF OUR OVARIES. Del Marlin wore his dark courtroom suit as if it had been a T-shirt, with easy insouciance; he looked around curiously, nudging his lawyer with whispered comments and laughter. Mim watched the lawyers and the judge with an obscure envy: she could have done this, she could have gone to law school and learned to speak articulately of justice, if she had had the right kind of self-trust. Alan had made it through law school; he had met that man Jim Molloy who had had such an influence on him, and who was to say there might not have been someone—maybe even a woman—waiting to influence her? What *was* Alan doing here? What did he want from Ari? What would happen if Del were acquitted (surely, surely he wouldn't be)? If he weren't acquitted, what would happen after he served his sentence? Or if someone else tried to get to Ari before him? What would happen if she were pregnant? (A quick check of her body's frontiers: no nausea, no prickle in the breasts, no odd taste in the mouth, no sensation of any kind in the uterus; no tickle of descending blood. Thirty-one days.) How could it be fair to bring a child into this perpetual tension? How could it be decent to Ari not to? She was abashed at having asked for time off from work to attend the whole trial; she could just as well have worried about pregnancy at her desk. Shots of fear, little squirts of adrenalin, flashed out from her midsection to her limbs at the thought of every uncertainty. She kept turning to Ari to make sure he was there.

The Friday night vigil at the church had become a large protest: at dawn the fifty people who had prayed through the night had gone in procession to the clinic, their faces sleepless and bright, and been met in the next few hours by three times their number. Father Rafferty, the senior priest, was in charge, and had insisted they all keep silence, so that rather than Calvin Hardy's hoarse shouting and the usual jaunty hymns there was merely a sound of filled space: two hundred jacketed bodies crowding the sidewalk. By Ari's account the regular protestors looked ready to burst with frustration: Father Rafferty, though a respected man and an asset to the cause, had taken little part in the movement up to this point, and they did not like his pre-empting the tactician's role. This blanket of silence, punctuated by the occasional cough or whisper, was no substitute for their own more volatile evangel. After all, there were counter-protestors; they taunted and could not be answered; no doubt the silence was meant to make their taunts ring as brassy and profane as they could, but it was bitter to let the name of Jesus be mocked. But when the police began to make arrests—the crowd (however slow) was after all blocking the entrance—Father Rafferty showed what he was made of: he let the teenagers sing. They had some simple chants, with very few words; the music spread through the crowd in waves, everyone taking it up (except for those few who abjured Latin), some weeping from sheer relief, till the whole street resounded as the people in front of the gate went limp and were carried singing away. The clinic staff, watching from the windows, on the whole liked the music—"At least it's pretty this time"—but Anne Shattuck said it gave her the creeps, and she'd seen too much to appreciate anything these jackasses did, and wouldn't this look pretty on the news, where no one would have to think about suffering women? By ten the protest was done: the last arrests made, those who had not risked arrest walking off deep in thought, the remnant of the sleepless drifting away last and blissful. Then some of the patients got in.

The arrested protestors were now out on bail; they included the two men who had wrestled Del down as he shot, who were witnesses for the prosecution. They had been at the overnight vigil, and still kept something of its euphoria, as if the trial were merely the third phase of a prolonged session of prayer. Their voices lilted a little as they testified. Mim knew all the signs; she had spent days in that state herself, and not only when she was younger. No doubt she had sounded just like that at her first dinner with Ari, spilling her soul to him over the scallops and shrimp. *Ani l'dodi.* Oh, God save us from religion, one of her father's colleagues had always said, his voice going plummy with glee at his own paradox. But that was the last thing God would save his lovers from. God knew all about paradox. Certainly he would never spare them the shame of being seen to love him, in the most paradoxical ways—like these men, unaccountably on the wrong side of their own quarrel for valuing human life enough to defend a man they despised for destroying it.

Del, the next day, dismissed them as mere ingenues. "Poor simps. They have to understand, he's not going to stop. Why should he? He's making too much off it. It gets into some people's blood. You see it all the time in the Bible—like in the land of Canaan, where they sacrificed their sons and daughters unto devils? Those knives they use for circumcising, you know—"

Mim focused all at once, with a perilous rushing sensation: it was like the moment in a plane's landing when, descending from the higher velocities of the sky, one suddenly feels it rushing with intolerable speed over the ground, surely toward no manageable end, surely toward collision. The defense attorney was interrupting, but Del sailed happily on. "No, you listen to me," he said. "God told them to make sacrifices. It's a commandment. They don't sacrifice the he-goats and bullocks no more, 'cause the Temple is gone—remember, the veil of the Temple was rent in twain when Jesus died—but the commandment isn't repealed. You don't so easily get away from what the Lord requires you to do. So what do they sacrifice?" He looked over the room—the judge, the jury, the antis, the allies; he caught Mim's eye for a beat on the way to Ari's.

The judge—a steely-eyed Yankee—was speaking sternly. "Just answer the question," he said. "You are not being asked for your theological stance; you're just being asked to explain what you were doing on the morning of the twenty-eighth." Del rounded on him. "I swore to tell the truth, the whole truth, and nothing but the truth, so help me God," he said; "You're not going to keep the whole truth out of this courtroom. Remember what the prophet Hosea called his children? The ones he had with the wife of whoredoms? Lo Ruhama and Lo Ammi, no mercy and no people. *That's* what happens when God's chosen go astray."

There was a moment of blank shock, then cacophony—spectators shouting, the judge pounding the gavel, Del's harangue going on—but Mim could not take it all in, she was rising and weaving toward the door, she was staggering down the hallway to where she had seen a restroom. She fainted on the floor of the stall for a moment; she heard rather than felt her cheekbone smack on the tile. Then as her breakfast came up she struggled into a crouch to let it fall in the water, still not knowing if this was pregnancy or simply the terror of history, the body winning out over theory at last.

CHAPTER 24

> Terrorism . . . is political activity without manners, without form; therefore it is incapable of yielding much meaning and is inevitably without hope. In some crucial way, it is not serious; it has no stake in the future.
>
> —Mary Gordon

> Every controversy that is for the sake of heaven shall in the end have a resolution, but every controversy that is not for the sake of heaven shall not have a resolution.
>
> —Pirke Avot 5:20

Alan looked at Del Marlin through the glass. It had an odd similarity to the closed-circuit television in the courthouse: one could not get near enough to sense a full human presence. Del looked remarkably self-possessed for a man who had thrown a courtroom into disorder, who had had to be taken out, who had in the end been sentenced to ten years in prison. But then his self-possession was his whole problem; he had no doubts and no inhibitions. His eyes were too bright; he had all the answers. Alan was glad he had gone to early Mass before driving to the prison, for a fortification subtler than answers. He braced himself and began. "Are you disappointed?"

"Well, sure," said Del easily. "If this wasn't a godless nation they'd have hauled *him* up on the stand and said Guilty guilty guilty, and the death penalty for you, doctor, because you really *did* kill those babies. I mean, *I* just wounded him. But if you mean am I surprised, no I'm not surprised. A Christian has to expect to be persecuted. I knew I would serve some time." He leaned back in his chair.

The answer led almost too easily to Alan's next question. "When Christians are persecuted," he said, "it's not for attempted murder, as a rule. How do you justify violence?"

Del eyed him, amused. "You mean why don't it bother me to kill for the sake of life? People keep asking me that. You intellectuals, you're so hung up on words. Obviously the only way to save the babies is to get rid of the people killing them."

"But you're a Christian."

"You bet your sweet ass I am, mister. Did I not make it clear?"

"Well, you're talking strategy, not morality. What if morality forbids the most practical strategy? What about *Thou shalt not kill?*"

"Aw, come on," said Del. "When a man runs a murder mill, he's the one breaking a commandment. What am I s'posed to do, sit back and watch?"

"What about reaching the women, like the other protestors do? Morality is a matter of changing the heart."

Del smirked. "Some of those women have their hearts set on it," he said. "I wouldn't say they were real reachable. That sidewalk counseling shit, it's more for show. You don't see it work too often. It takes how long, maybe ten minutes, to destroy your average unborn baby? Versus how long to convince her to keep it? A bullet wins hands-down for sheer speed. Save the babies first, and let the women figure out how to cope; they've been doing it for a million years. They made their choice when they played around."

Alan felt a flash of rage at Del's brutal finality, and tried to get hold of himself; losing his temper would accomplish nothing. "But you didn't save any babies," he said. "You know yourself that they brought in another doctor and business went on as usual. And even if you could kill or scare off every doctor, women would still find ways. They've been doing that for a million years too. That's why you have to reach them. Yes, they have their hearts set on it, but that's partly because they need help: moral help, financial help, spiritual—"

"Hey," said Del, "they can always go on welfare." He laughed, and the laugh turned into a cough, and it took him a little time to regain his composure. "Oh, my," he said. "They can be welfare queens, sitting up there having one baby after another at the taxpayer's expense. What do they want to kill their babies for? They got it made."

Alan found himself speechless at this twist of logic. He had increased respect for the European woman who had interviewed the Nazi commandant: how could one keep confronting the criminal's moral evasions day after day? He looked down at his notes, to get his bearings. When he looked up again, Del was fumbling with a piece of paper.

"Here," he was saying. "I found this down in the library the other day. You'll never get anywhere talking to dumb women who don't know any better than to kill their own babies. But this makes it all clear." He unfolded the paper, held it in both hands, and paused. *"To grope down into the bottom of the sea after them,"* he read with emphasis; *"to have one's hands among the unspeakable foundations, ribs, and very pelvis of the world; this is a fearful thing."* He sat back and nodded as if making a conclusive point.

"What *is* that?" said Alan, disoriented. "It sounds like—"

"*Moby Dick*, by Herman Melville," said Del. "Bet you didn't think I read classics. Well, I don't really, but I opened it up and this jumped out at me, just like when you ask the Bible a question. I had to write it all down. 'Course," he added, "the guys in high school used to say Moby Dick was one of them social diseases, what today you would call an STD."

"I guess I don't get it," said Alan. "No, of course I get the joke, but what does this quote have to do with—"

"It's the *doctor*," said Del. "He has his hands among the unspeakable foundations. That Herman Melville, don't he have a way with words?"

"But Melville's not talking about an abortionist," said Alan. "He's—"

"*I* know that," said Del impatiently. "Man, you intellectuals, you always think working people are dumb. *I* know he's talking about these guys on a whale hunt. But it's like reading scripture, you know? You'll be reading along, like in the Psalms or something, and you'll come across this thought that if you didn't know any better you'd think it was just what it said it was, but you know it's really a prophecy of Jesus. So who's to say Herman Melville wasn't prophesizing, seeing through a glass darkly what would come to pass in our time?"

"If you want to give secular humanists credit for having prophets," said Alan, "I suppose you can read it that way. But I think it's stretching the point. He was probably thinking of an anatomist dissecting a body, or maybe a surgeon operating." What an odd thing to be talking about.

"But *I'm* thinking about an abortionist," said Del firmly. "After all, there's one way it's not like scripture: you can't go to hell for reading it your way. Right?"

"Okay," said Alan, defeated. He did not see the use of explaining either scriptural exegesis or literary theory to this man. "What's your point about the doctor?"

Del began to speak, and stopped short. "Let me look at it again," he said. "You've just about ruined it, picking it apart."

He immersed himself in the words and looked up again, rapt with effort. "That to have your hands in there, it's a fearful thing," he said. "That he's groping down to the bottom of the sea after them. He's a hunter: he hunts babies in their natural habitat. But it was Esau that was the hunter, not Jacob. He's lost his birthright. It's not him whose name will be called Israel."

Alan shifted uneasily. He did not want to get Del started on the Jews. "I agree it's a fearful thing," he said, "but to get back to my original point, to substitute force for due process—"

"I'd call this an overdue process," said Del. "I tell you, mister, I begin to question whether people like you aren't just content to let most of the babies die, as long as you can save a few others in a leisurely way and feel good about yourselves. Man, I know one thing from reading the Bible: when the Lord tells you to move, you move! You don't sit there and say Uh, buh, buh, I can't do it. He'll burn like a fire in your bones." He held Alan's eye with a blue stare. "You're no prolifer. You're prolife like this bunch here in town. Chickenshits! When I first got to this area I went to one of their meetings. They were teaching each other these cute little chants and gearing up for a letter campaign, this petty sniping kind of stuff, and I just thought Oh you guys, get real, you're never going to save any babies that way. You're scared to get your hands a little dirty, and meanwhile *his* hands are groping all around the unspeakable foundations, dismembering babies. You know what that means? That means little old me has to get his hands real dirty. But I was ready. God had been preparing me all my life to kill in a righteous cause, and I knew this was it."

Alan broke their mutual gaze. There was the faintest echo in Del's reasoning of what Jim Molloy had said about Vietnam: if you're too proud to fight, you leave all the fighting to the humble. But this wasn't a war of that kind; it was a war for souls, a war for the understanding, which couldn't be won by fighting. When Alan was ten he had met and argued with a fundamentalist boy at a playground: at that age he had met very few Protestants and for a while had thought all of them were like that, fierce and intrusive and stark raving mad. "What do you mean, preparing you?"

"He told me when I was real young," Del said. "It was like Jeremiah, you know, who God came to when he was just a scared little boy, and he didn't want to be a prophet but God wouldn't let him alone. I used to lay awake nights worrying about it, saying God, you got the wrong guy. But he never let up. Finally I thought if that was how things were going to be I better get some practice, so I practiced on some squirrels and possums and this old tomcat that used to hang around my Aunt Bobbie Ann's barn. But it never really made sense. I mean, it wasn't like they did anything wrong, so why kill them. Or it wasn't like hunting, where you're going to use what you kill." Again the rapt stare. "Finally when I was old enough I went in the military, figuring that was what it was for, and God was getting me ready to kill a commie or an Arab or something. But I never saw any action. Actually God was quieter then than he was any other time; too many other guys around, maybe, not enough privacy. Anyways, when I got back here and everybody was into saving the babies, it started to make some sense. I spent some time down in Florida, and they're serious about this stuff there; none of these half-assed little singalongs. They think the pro-deathers need a taste of their own medicine. So then I figured it out. That was what God was trying to tell me in those dark nights. To kill a killer, to stand in the way between death and the victim, that's not an evil thing."

Alan shivered. He thought of Claire's clients, who seemed remarkably often (in the generic, anonymous hints he had had of them) to have histories of torturing or being tortured. *Is he someone to pray for?* He resolved to add Del to his list. "Are you sure it was God?" he said. "You can't always trust those night voices. He doesn't seem to talk that way to the men that stopped you, and they were prolifers too. They stood between you and *your* victim; they valued even his life."

"Bunch of simps," muttered Del, discontent. "Jesus might be able to love a man like that, but no human being should have to."

"There's at least one who does," said Alan.

Del met his eyes at once, as if sensing some vulnerability. "Unh," he said speculatively. "That pretty woman sitting next to him in the courtroom. Yeah, they're an item; I saw her give him a look that woulda burned wax. Damn, I bet they had to hose off the seat when she left."

Alan looked at him blankly; then, as the meaning dawned, had an impulse to strike him. Thank God the glass was between them; he would have laid him out flat. "She may save his soul," he said, barely knowing what he was saying, "she may be his only chance. Is that all you think love is?"

Del burst out laughing, as if he had hit the bull's-eye. "Is that how they save souls in your religion?" he said. "Oh, my. That's better than cake and ice cream. What's he doing with a girl like that anyways? A killer like him? Lucky stiff." He arched back in his chair; his whole skinny torso looked phallic. "Why do the wicked flourish. Man oh man." He yawned and came out of the stretch as if deeply refreshed. "Listen, how much longer is this gonna take? You're doing an awful lot of preaching for a reporter. You got any more questions?"

"I'm not sure I do," said Alan, shaken by his own outburst. "You've told me a great deal."

"I've told you things I never said to a soul," said Del. "That clown Jerry Kaplansky, I'd never tell him. That boy has no sense of right and wrong. But you're a Christian—at least, Catholics are pretty close to Christians, I met a few good ones in Florida—so I can expect a lot out of you."

Do you think I'm writing to vindicate you? thought Alan. "I do have one other question," he said without warmth. "What happens when you get out?"

"Well, that depends, don't it? If they make abortion illegal, there won't be a problem. If they don't . . ." He shrugged and grinned. "Of course, there's other folks out there who might beat me to it."

"So you anticipate no change of heart."

"Listen," said Del, "a minute ago it was the women who had to change their hearts. Make up your mind. I still think you're soft on pro-death."

Alan began to pack up his tape recorder. "You've been very helpful, Mr. Marlin. Thanks for your time."

"Oh, I got nothing but time."

"And—" He hesitated, wanted simply to get out of the room, decided to say it anyway. "Pray, will you? And make sure you're talking to God before you start listening to him. Pray for other ways to oppose sin than by violence. I can tell you, there are some."

"Not that work half as good," said Del cheerfully. "Thanks a lot for your time, uh . . . Alan? Send me a copy when it comes out. You take care."

He sat outside the jail in his rented car. He felt soiled: by Del, by Mira's attachment to Morgenzahl, by his own compulsion to talk of Mira on any inadequate pretext. What nonsense had he been babbling? Did he really think Mira's love could save Morgenzahl's soul? Of course not; it was much more likely that she would take on his hard supercilious gloss and lose her own soul, though he did not think it had happened yet. He understood now her fear that anyone—a bereaved father, a writer for *Saecula*—might threaten or hurt Morgenzahl: Del's existence, the existence of such profound craziness, was enough to shake one's faith in the sane.

He drove back to town. He was seeing Morgenzahl at two-thirty; there was plenty of time. He ate in one of the patisseries, wishing it had a view of the water instead of a poster of the Mediterranean; he needed a respite from people. He made a few changes to the questions he planned to ask. He knew he would not adhere to them strictly once the interview was in progress, but if he went over them carefully now perhaps he would not find himself suddenly alluding to Mira. Reassured, he put the questions away and went on with the Arthurian book. He wished it were shorter—why were all Arthurian stories so deadly long?—so he could be done with it. Morgan le Fay was seducing Arthur, with some fancy justification about redemption through sin. Only an act against nature, the conceiving of a child by her brother, could restore the land to fertility. What kind of sense did that make? That was how love saved souls nowadays: it wasn't love and it wasn't salvation. He had met his colleague's daughter; she was a nice girl. How could she write this filth?

Morgenzahl's very look seemed to recruit him into some confraternity of civilized male experience where disagreements were handled by dispute and détente and not by wild accusation and violence. Alan shook his hand with reserve. He did not like men with charisma: he felt swept into their orbit against his will, compelled to agree with them by the force of their own conviction. Even if this man had had no connection with Mira he would have resented him; even if he had been doing blameless, admirable work he would have felt faint dislike.

 They were meeting in one of the counseling rooms, a genteelly appointed parlor like somebody's Florida room: rattan furniture with floral upholstery, a coffee table, a Georgia O'Keeffe poster. There was even a potted palm. Very feminine: probably meant to put the patients at ease, to lull them into an acceptance of what they were doing. Why weren't they meeting in Morgenzahl's office, he wondered; he pictured an alchemist's study with retorts and alembics and jars of pickled fetuses. Surely it wasn't like that. Unbelievably, they were chatting: he was himself being lulled, or perhaps they were both just avoiding mention of the one experience they did have in common. How much did the man really know? Alan switched on his tape recorder. "Let's begin. How do you feel about the outcome of the trial?"

 "Reassured for the moment that a jury of Del Marlin's peers has no trouble convicting him." Unmistakably, now, the voice of the answering machine. "Ten years doesn't seem long enough to keep him out of the way, but they can't lock him up for life for not killing me. It's as much reassurance as we get in this world, I guess. Of course," he added, "no doubt there are more where he came from."

"You're going to keep doing abortions?"

"Of course."

"Is it different now?—knowing that these people mean just what they say? You must be prepared to make an immense sacrifice for your cause."

Morgenzahl looked at him a moment before speaking. "You'll understand if I'm a little tired of the word *sacrifice*," he said. "This is a medical service that women need. If somebody wants to martyr me for it, that's his affair."

It was the indifferent, world-weary tone that set Alan on edge; no wonder the man had no compunction about killing a child in the womb. He didn't care about anything. "From your perspective it's simply a medical service," he said, "but—you'll forgive my speaking frankly—from another point of view it's a moral outrage. Del Marlin's animosity didn't come out of nowhere. A great many people find the killing of unborn children deeply repugnant. When you put this medical gloss on it, you make it look acceptable. You legitimize abortions of convenience to women who would never have considered them before. One doesn't have to be a zealot to be worried about the future."

"I think you mean convenient abortions," said Morgenzahl, unperturbed, "as opposed to the kind you have to search for in the underworld. I don't think the motives have changed. All sorts of women had abortions in the old days; they weren't just waiting, you know, to be told it was okay when *Roe* was decided. They make the decision the way they've always made it: because they're alone, or because they're ashamed, or because they can't afford a child, or because they're overwhelmed with other demands. Perhaps the shame has gotten a little less—partly owing to your side saying that abortion is the worst possible sin, worse even than illegitimacy, so that illegitimacy has itself become, as it were, legitimized." He smiled thinly.

Alan gave an incredulous laugh. "You're blaming *the Church* for illegitimacy? That's a new one."

"Yeah, well, the Church is a past master—*magistra?*—at double binds."

Oh, the man knew his stuff: someone (Alan bet he knew who) had been telling him the nasty jibe that went around among malcontent Catholics after the encyclical *Mater et magistra*. ¡Mater, sí—magistra, no! Keep your temper, Lonigan. "Let's not lose sight of the point. I'm suggesting that as abortion loses its stigma, good women will seek it for pathetically inadequate reasons. In the Church's eyes no reason is adequate, but of course one is sorry for poor women or very young girls, or single women who've made a mistake and then find that their boyfriends won't marry them. But as the laws get more and more lenient, the threshold of what's intolerable gets lower and lower. Women who would have braced themselves and taken the pregnancy in stride fall apart and think they can't cope; affluent, thoughtful, morally serious young married women opt for abortion because they think a baby is a disaster. It's tragic—stupid and tragic."

"How much do you think that happens?" said Morgenzahl curiously.

"I have no idea what the percentages are. I know it happens." He was slipping already.

"It's rather rare. Money and shame are by far the most common reasons—especially when there's some sort of instability, abuse or what not. That and the inability of young kids to believe in the link between sex and parenthood, which surreally enough is the quickest way to become a parent. Affluent, thoughtful women are generally very good at birth control." He held Alan's eye for an instant.

Alan, stung, saw a number of things at once: what Morgenzahl thought of Mira, what Morgenzahl thought of him, how much Morgenzahl knew about the most intimate details of their unhappy past. *How long have you been seeing her?* he wanted to say. *Do they still fuck women on the table before the abortion?* "I don't think that will cut any ice with the readers of *Saecula*," he said. "That isn't their view of marriage. They think it's barbarous for married couples to spend all this time avoiding pregnancy."

"Birth control is barbarous, I'll agree," said Morgenzahl glumly. "Should God ever inquire of humanity, he'll find we have major design complaints. He should have consulted a doctor. But the readers of *Saecula* won't care for that either, will they? What would they like to know?"

"For one thing, they're concerned about the effects of abortion on the marital bond," said Alan with a steady look of his own. "Obviously if a woman can go through the whole process without ever involving the father, that bond is incalculably weakened. With an unmarried couple, it doesn't even get a chance to form; the father who doesn't know can't do the right thing. With a married couple, the deceit destroys an already established bond."

"In my experience—which amounts to twenty years by now—when the woman finds secrecy necessary, the bond is already destroyed." Morgenzahl looked away delicately, his averted eyes as authoritative as his glance had been. "It's very complicated, Mr. Lonigan. Some fathers don't do the right thing: they just disappear, or say they want the baby and *then* disappear—or stay and feel trapped and start beating the woman for being pregnant. Some men are great: the pregnancy stuns them into adulthood, and they get jobs and stop doing drugs and turn overnight into good solid citizens. A lot of men don't. Often couples sit down together and make the decision to abort, sometimes with a great deal of anguish; and sometimes the man tries to bully the woman into the abortion, as you must surely know. Some of these situations are very sad—my God, they're all sad—and sometimes I see a potentially solid relationship crumbling away when a small shift of feeling might save it. But the baby won't save it—not all by itself: that's a myth."

"So marriage means nothing," said Alan. "It's not a sacrament, it's not even a contract, 'one flesh' means nothing at all."

"Well, we're not certain altogether what it means, are we?" said Morgenzahl rather gently. "We know what we'd like it to mean, but it often doesn't."

Was it sympathy or mockery? Mockery, Alan supposed. "At one very obvious level, it means the child," he said. "I know it's not easy to accept the Church's teaching on birth control; it demands a great deal of faith. These days even most Catholics sneer at it—even the readers of *Saecula,* some of them. But it's not a cruel doctrine. Birth control is what's cruel. When there's no interference, no break in the continuum from sex to conception to birth, you take a position of absolute welcome: you have this extraordinary tenderness toward the world."

Morgenzahl shook his head, unbelieving. "As I understand it, the Church upheld its stand on birth control mainly for political reasons," he said. "Not to say that it's not a nice feeling. I have kids; I know that sense of creating the world. But after you've created enough of it . . . my God, after the eighth or tenth kid she might start to wear out; then what do you do?"

"We're made to wear out," said Alan urgently, "we're not meant to hold ourselves back. Modern life is so cautious; people are so afraid to throw themselves into living. Conception is the biological purpose of marriage, that's what it's for. To interfere with it, to hedge your bets, is to withhold yourself from full union."

"Oh, so is fighting over how to handle the toothpaste tube," said Morgenzahl irritably. "You want ways to withhold yourself from full union, they're not hard to find. Look, Mr. Lonigan: the Catholic Church is marvelous at symbolism, and everybody *wishes* sex and pregnancy didn't have to be consciously disconnected, but they do: conception's too easy, we're way more fertile than we need to be, there are lots of practical problems. Sure, it sounds big-hearted and lavish to throw yourself into living, but what happens when your wife is thirty-five and walking around with a prolapsed uterus and you've got eight kids to support and somehow you can never quite manage to withhold yourself from full union? Maybe we're made to wear out, but what does she think? What do *you* think when she dies of the next pregnancy and you miss her? Is that just another case of God's will? We're not animals; we can take control of these things."

"Control: I knew we would get to it. A woman's right to *control* her own body, that whole pack of lies. Control means restraint, Dr. Morgenzahl: it means if you don't want to conceive you don't do what leads to conception. It's not liberating to women to be able to indulge without consequences. It's unthinkable that that should be liberty—the power to destroy their own children."

"Unthinkable?" Morgenzahl said. *"That's* unthinkable? Where have you been? That's a benign biological fact. It's a messy fact, but it's very easily thinkable; compare it to Eichmann on the phone to the Reich Transport Ministry asking for group rates." He shook his head, flatly dismissive. "That's the other side of all that marvelous symbolism: it's completely detached from real life. It exists in this airtight little realm where the thinkable is unthinkable and the really unthinkable never makes an impression. It's a fairy tale: God incarnate, and Christ resurrected, and Jesus the King of the Jews, and all the rest of it. But up there in the endometrium, that isn't the way it works."

Alan, for the moment, had forgotten what the endometrium was; he vaguely connected it with the empyrean. It was not a word he used every day. But he was deeply and quietly offended by the insult to his faith, and determined to shake Morgenzahl's confidence. "You're the one with the fairy tale," he said. "A baby can be wished out of existence, and people can be adolescents forever, and sex is nothing but pleasure." (He saw for an instant, before he could stop himself, the man buried up to the hilt in Mira's body; Mira astride him, naked and disheveled; Mira with a mouthful of cock.) "Let's just move along."

Morgenzahl was immovable. "Oh, Mr. Lonigan," he said pityingly, as if teaching a child the alphabet, "is sex ever *nothing but pleasure?* Only celibate priests, who aren't getting any, could think that. Look at it from experience. Sex is all kinds of things: you could probably reconstruct the whole of religion and ethics, if you weren't getting those, just from it. What wouldn't you have, just in the nature of the act? There's that same overpowering longing; the same need to decipher necessary cues from fragmentary communications; the same struggle with inattention as people who pray get with prayer; the same need for forgiveness sometimes; the same sense of enormous possible consequences, which have to be handled with absolute rectitude. And the same need to time yourself by somebody else's calendar, whether that means the lunar calendar or just the flow of response on a given occasion. And this terrible sense of the contingency of everything lovely: for a few seconds you have this extraordinary bliss—with luck, *she* may have it for several minutes—and then flop, there you are, and you're not sure where you've been and you can't get back there, and you're shut out again from the one place that really matters. It's not so profane."

Alan listened to this caprice half repelled and half fascinated; had it been anyone else he might have been willing, for the first time in his life, to talk man to man about sex. Here was someone who might understand the misfirings of married affection between him and Claire, and who did understand—better than anyone else in the world—the cues Mira gave to a lover. (Several minutes? Good God, what did the man do to her?) But it was impossible: he was gloating, it was intolerable. "I'm not here to talk sexual technique with you, Dr. Morgenzahl," he said coldly. "I'm trying to understand your view of your own work. You used the word *rectitude* just now; how does abortion fit into any concept of rectitude? Who judges the rectitude of the women who come to you? A doctor isn't a gas station attendant; it's a very recent thing for highly trained people to abdicate moral influence over the people they serve. Do you see yourself as having any responsibility at all in their choice?"

"Certainly. They're making an extremely serious decision. I have to let them make it. If they have the baby they've got to be able to care for it—physically at the very minimum, and in the best case with some understanding of a child's emotional and mental development. Or they've got to be able to bear giving it up to somebody else who can, and for most women that's a lot harder than an abortion. If they abort, they've got to be able to handle *that*. They have a very short time to decide, and they're under tremendous pressure. Of course I have moral influence."

"Which you use to say they should do whatever they want."

"Not at all. They should do what they can bear to. That's a much narrower range. Look, rectitude is a practical matter: they have to be able to assent to the child with their whole body, with their whole future. If they're pregnant without being able to do that—and the fetus just *takes* their assent, you know, whether they give it or not—it's a complete violation, a rift in their integrity. How can I tell them which way their integrity lies? I can tell them it's that kind of question, but I can't answer it. The best I can do—well, look, we have a little proof-text about it up here." He gestured above Alan's head.

Alan got up, curious and a little annoyed. Some calligraphed words in a frame: black italics appearing pressed, as it were, between two lines of grey rocks, which on closer examination turned out to be thick Hebrew letters. Alan could read the Hebrew letters when they had vowels, but this was beyond him; he looked at the English italics. The words slowly registered, with muted King Jamesian eloquence: *Behold, thou desirest truth in the inward parts, and in the hidden part thou shalt make me to know wisdom.* And in tiny Rapidograph lines: Ps. 51:6.

The words seemed obscenely twisted to Alan. "What's that supposed to be? Some sort of free-lance absolution?"

"A confirmation of what most of them already know: that this is serious, it's mortal, and it's between them and God."

Alan turned and looked at him, sizing him up. "And what qualifies you to talk about God?"

A shrug. "Oh, well, Mim put it up. She's better at that kind of thing."

He went rigid. He sublimated every response that occurred to him into quietly switching off the tape recorder. "Can't we end this charade?"

"Certainly," said Morgenzahl calmly. "It's not my charade. What do you want to say?"

Alan gestured over his shoulder at the calligraphy. "This cynical, self-serving—" The open use of accusing adjectives ignited his anger, and he was suddenly so enraged he could barely form words. "To use her as a front for your sins—"

"Mr. Lonigan, I assure you—"

"Oh, for Christ's sake, call me Alan." He sliced the air with his hand in a thwarted gesture. "You've scraped my child out of my wife's uterus, you might as well call me by my first name."

There was a silence. Morgenzahl gave a long sigh. He looked tired and distressed. "Please sit down," he said. "This is going to be very difficult. We'll have to go carefully."

Alan was trembling. "We," he said. "I'll give you no cooperation. I'm not going to meet you halfway."

Morgenzahl shook his head. "There is no halfway. But we can try—yes?—not to use the whole arsenal." He gestured toward Alan's chair. "Please."

Alan sat. Automatically he said, "I'm sorry, I—"

"Don't apologize. I'm sorry too, but how far does that get us? We're not going to change the past."

"What are *you* sorry for? You don't have a thing to regret."

"Sorry you got hurt. Everybody gets hurt in these situations. I do think you walked right into it, but no doubt that just makes it more painful."

"What do you mean, I walked into it? She walked into marriage. If she didn't know what it meant—"

"She walked into marriage, she didn't walk into bondage. She expected to negotiate with a good man who loved her, not to be browbeaten with dogma."

He was surprised to hear the word *good* from Morgenzahl's lips, apparently unironically. It must be an oversight. "Browbeaten," he repeated. "Is that what she says. She thinks I was a tyrant. I don't know what all she's told you. But she was dishonest." Of course there were aspects of the problem this man would not understand. "Catholic teaching isn't negotiable in that sense. I'd have loved to rewrite it all just to please her—believe me, I would have—but it's not in my power. I had to be faithful to it. God knows I paid the whole price."

Morgenzahl shook his head. "You were fleeced," he said sadly. "Nobody else pays a price like that. Why should Catholics have to? Why, at a point when we finally have reliable birth control—"

"Oh, come off it," said Alan. Was this what the man called not using the whole arsenal? "Do you think the Church condemned birth control because it wasn't reliable? This is an old, old battle. It goes all the way back to the decline of the Roman Empire. Roman fathers used to decide whether each newborn child would be kept or exposed, you must know that. And the Manicheans were great on birth control. All those Gnostic sects, then and later, thought children were a grind and a burden, not a proper occupation for the *perfecti*. Sounds a lot like modern feminism, doesn't it, that thinks children aren't a worthy occupation for women with minds?" He was so angry he felt slightly dizzy; he spoke louder as if to keep his balance by sonar. "You know, everywhere you look modern feminism is rehabilitating the witches—just these harmless old ladies who worshipped Mother Earth and made herbal medicines. But you know why the witches were hated? They destroyed unborn children. As a boy I thought that meant they caused miscarriage by cursing the pregnant woman, but with all this new scholarship it's clear enough what went on. The witches did exactly what you're doing here, Dr. Morgenzahl—"

"Bob," said Morgenzahl belatedly, raising an eyebrow.

"—and it was a heresy then, and it's a heresy now. It's psychologized now, or politicized, but it's just a new version of something very old and very evil and very basic: hatred of children. That side of feminism is just the Gnostic heresy in new dress."

"Mim told me you thought that," said Morgenzahl, suddenly interested. "I didn't believe her at first. Now I see how you do it. Very ingenious. *My* favorite witch accusation is the one in Kramer and Sprenger about the stashes of stolen penises—these little hoards of them, twenty or so to a box, that squirm around and eat oats, remember that one? One doesn't *admire* the mind that can think of that, but one appreciates God's sense of humor in letting it happen."

"You're mocking because you're desperate," said Alan. "You can't prove me wrong."

"Desperate? Not me," said Morgenzahl. He held up his hand peaceably, but an edge came into his voice. "I'm just trying to steer you away from the perfidious Jews and little Sir Hugh of Lincoln, before you say something you may regret."

"Oh, please," said Alan. "That's the cheapest shot in the book."

It was impossible; he was not going to change the man's mind. He was not even going to shame him, which he supposed was what he had come to do. Beyond shame, both he and Mira: lovers, practically smelling of it, for every boy reporter to sniff. The battle was lost; it had been lost before it began, and he was sitting here with a cheapened verse of the Psalter behind him, and across the room a poster of a blowsy red poppy with a big hairy mound.

He heard Claire's voice suddenly: "Use an *I* statement." She said that to the children sometimes; it was a tried and true mediation technique. "Grace, don't call Chrissy a pest, use an *I* statement. *I* feel crowded when you play with my toys without asking." I feel unmanned when you play with my wife. "When I first met Mira," he said rapidly, not stopping to think, "she was instinctively spiritual. I've never seen anyone so transparent at worship, so ready to rise up to heaven with adoration, if mortal flesh could. She didn't know what to do with it: all she had was this passion, and a lot of chaotic thinking from secular culture that couldn't help her sustain it. And one of the wounds of my life has been that I couldn't help her: that I failed her right at the point where I meant to lift and ennoble her. She had a weak moment, and you were right there, and I lost her. I'm just sickened: that she's defending your work; that you and she are—'involved,' I suppose you must call it; that she's using the rags of her faith in this grotesque way. My God, what did she want?" he burst out. "We had enough money, we had a nice house on Grant Drive, she had a husband who loved her and would have been faithful for life. What more does it take to come up with the willingness?"

Morgenzahl did not answer. Alan imagined him knowing and refusing to say. At last he spoke, rather softly. "I wouldn't worry," he said, "about her not being spiritual. What that comes down to, you'd better take up with her; not what you'd wish for, of course, but she scares *me* sometimes. As for what she wanted, it seems pretty obvious to me, but it wouldn't perhaps . . . common sense is not too common. Well, you probably don't want to take advice from Voltaire. Shall we wrap this up, do you think?" he said, not unkindly. "You've said what you came to say, and we're not going to get anywhere. Anything more I can do for you in your official capacity? Anything for the readers of *Saecula*, who languish on hold?"

Alan glanced involuntarily at the tape recorder. "Oh, God," he said. "I can't use any of that."

"Sure you can. Just delete all the subtext. They don't have to know *why* you're asking those questions. That's the way it always is with this issue: the real stuff all goes unsaid."

Alan gave him a long look. "What are you not saying?"

"You'd rather not know."

•

"Relative humility 55%," said Ari. "He's willing to see his own failure, but not why he failed. Poor schmendrick, one feels this urge to protect him."

"My God, not you too."

"It's too bad. If he couldn't handle his own life, why does he insist that other people handle theirs on the first try?"

"Because he believes in moral absolutes," said Mim tiredly. "You know how it works. It's the doctrine: what does it matter if he couldn't attain it, or if nobody could attain it? It's perfect. We're not. Q.E.D."

"*Torat Adonai t'mimah*," Ari hummed. "Damn it, now you've got *me* singing the stuff. Well, he's right in a sense: doubtless a male sense, but a lot of men's moral law is aimed at controlling the unruly member, which is a fairly absolute presence on the human scene. The *Dong an sich*, as John Hollander so charmingly suggests. We've talked about that before: it's the shepherd and the shepherdess and their covenant."

"Yes, and I said I didn't like their covenant. The shepherdess loses whether she holds out or gives in."

"Well, that's the problem: what's women's place in men's law? Are they exempt from it, are they supposed to help the men keep it, what's their relation to it? If you look at Genesis up close, it can appear that men's job is obedience and women's is transgression."

"Of course. Men wouldn't know how to handle transgression."

"Zissele, I will transgress with you right here on the carpet if you wish it. Just let me move some of these newspapers."

"Exactly: if I wish it. At my invitation. That's obedience, and where would we be without it? But if *I'm* obedient—oops, be careful, you'll hit your head on that thing—either I'm obedient to you, which contravenes the whole purpose of the law, or we're both obedient to the law and can't get any closer. And what is life worth—wait, there's another button on this side—if we can't get any closer?"

CHAPTER 25

Nobody can remain content with the mere knowledge of good and evil in itself, but must endeavor as well to act in accordance with it. The strength to do so, however, is not likewise given him.

—Kafka

We do not ask that the Christian shall not violate the Christian law; we only ask him to know that he is breaking it when he does break it. This seems to me admirably brought out by the remark of Cardinal Lavigerie who was asked: "What would you do, Eminence, if some one slapped your right cheek?" and who replied, "I know what I ought to do, but I do not know what I should do." *I know what I ought to do,* and therefore what I ought to teach.

—Julien Benda, *The Treason of the Clerks*

Alan waited in the restaurant Mira had chosen. It was a dockside place called the Lobster Quadrille that had been new during their courtship; it had weathered and the crockery had been updated, and a new generation of effeminate waiters had taken the place of the old, but the view of the bay was still fine and the spectacular seafood paella remained on the menu. He was very tired. He could not believe he had scheduled all three of these conversations in the same day; how could he not have known that each one would require a night's sleep? And he had just talked to Claire on the phone. "They've been praying for Mira every night since you left. What did you tell them? I don't wish her ill, but I don't want to hear about her every night of my life." He had not told them anything much: Chrissy had asked another question or two, sensing reluctance, and her imagination seemed to be doing the rest. How had Claire handled it? "I said she needed help for bad thoughts. Alan, what could I say? Let's hope it wears off soon." How were his interviews going? "I've talked to the doctor," he said. "He's a bitter man. And he's sleeping with Mira." She gave a long, martyred sigh.

He had taken a booth in the back where they could talk quietly; he had his notes for the article with him, to work while he waited. He stared at his handwriting blankly. A beer would have helped, but there was something seedy about waiting for one's ex-wife with a beer in one's hand. Ex-wife: contemptible term, oxymoronic. People who flirted in nightclubs had ex-wives. How had this happened to him, what had he done to deserve an ex-wife in his past? Eternal damnation, yes, but *divorce*—the anathema of his old neighborhood, the thing no good person did, the thing you would never need if you took marriage seriously . . . the thing his children thought practically normal, normally frightening, a contingency they might at any time have to confront. You wanted the world, well, this is the world, my friend: the horror and humiliation of Mira's deceptions, the crying of all his flesh toward no answer when she was gone.

His eyes were looking inward, at the shape of his life; they took in the outward scene without intelligence. The restaurant was filling up. A line had formed at the door, and a woman in an elegant hat had squeezed past the line and was saying something to the host, scanning the tables intently. Automatically he watched her, admiring her energy and her stance. It was not till she started toward him that he saw it was Mira.

There were lines around her eyes: they crinkled up as she smiled at him, coming close. The subtle beauty of a woman out of her youth, the ripeness, the pang of mortality. The sense of peace in her body firmly established. (Was there a hint of sexual scent as he took her coat? How like the man to put his mark on her before sending her here. Like a dog at a fire hydrant. Damn him.) She was wearing a dress of an unusual color, an unevenly dyed reddish-brown, that looked like something out of a 'thirties movie. But she was not suave and amoral like the women in movies: there was still that slight hesitation, that hint of self-doubt, the lively mind being brought up short by its conscience. The first sight of her was worth everything that Morgenzahl had said to him, and everything that Claire would.

Mim looked back at him from across the table. He seemed to be just the same: the same thick light hair, the same nondescript clothes, and the same quiet vigilance which he channeled into courteous attentions, rising at her approach and taking her coat. But his eyelids were fragile, the flesh of his face was beginning to sag, and there was a sense of restriction about his joints as if he never stretched them very far. Poor man, she thought, there aren't any grownups, are there? Our bodies just age. He was wearing a heavy gold ring, which struck her suddenly and dangerously funny: men's jewelry is so functional, she thought, what time it is and whether or not they're married. Better say something fast. "How did the interviews go?"

"Well enough. There's a lot to absorb. I talked to Del Marlin this morning, and he's a very odd fish: crazier even than he looked in the courtroom. *Culturally* crazy, if that makes sense, as much as personally. Though if he'd told the truth to his lawyers, they'd have had enough for an insanity defense. Funny what people will tell a writer they trust." He took a sip of his water, his eyes not leaving her face. "And this afternoon, of course, I talked to your friend."

Your friend. It was not a good sign. "I should apologize," she said. "I should have told you about us. I tried, sort of, but I was confounded and let you stop me. I think I hoped you would just interview him and go away, and it wouldn't have to be mentioned."

"Oh, he'd have mentioned it," said Alan, his courtesy fraying at once. "He was obviously dying to mention it. He would have found a way."

"He gave you a hard time."

He shrugged irritably. "I made a fool of myself," he said. "I suppose I set myself up. Claire was right: I got in over my head. I didn't think he would remember you at all, much less be—"

"Whatever you want to call it," Mim supplied.

"Yes," he said vaguely. "Have you—how long have you—"

"May I get you folks something to drink?" A waiter had appeared at their elbows. His voice seemed familiar, but Mim was looking at Alan and at first could not place it. "Mim! Is that you?"

"Todd," she said, looking up. "What are you doing here?"

"I work here," he said. "You don't think Sarita pays enough to keep a poor boy in gloves. Oh, that's the new dress! The Weimar knockoff. Beautiful; very retro. I saw it being made up. Oh, and congratulations, Sarita said you and your sweetie—" He took in that Alan was not Ari and broke off with a quizzical look.

Mim blushed violently. "This is my old friend Alan Lonigan," she said. "He's here for—he's writing an article on the trial. Alan, this is Todd..."

"Erway."

"Erway; he works for one of my friends."

"Pleased to meet you," they both muttered more or less amiably.

"So can I get you something to drink," said Todd, reasserting his function.

"Sure, of course," said Mim hastily. "A half-liter of white? Is that okay with you, Alan?"

"We have a nice white Bordeaux," offered Todd, with a hint of self-parody.

"That's fine," said Alan, and Todd disappeared efficiently. They looked at each other, nonplussed.

"I'm sorry," said Mim, hardly knowing what for. "I had no idea he worked here. What were we saying?"

"I don't remember," said Alan. "Oh, I was asking—well, really it isn't my business. How long you and—and Dr. Morgenzahl have been in this relationship."

"Just since this winter," she said. "I wrote to him after the shooting.

We went out a couple of times, and I started volunteering at the clinic, and—well, and one thing led to another. It was an odd thing to happen, but we're very attached."

"I can't say I'm happy for you," he said. "I think he's taking advantage of you. But I guess I'm happy you're happy."

"Taking advantage?" she said, smiling wider than she decently ought to. "Oh, no, I'm taking advantage of him." He looked away, either because he did not take her meaning or because he did; there was an uncomfortable silence.

Todd arrived with the wine. He took a long time over it: put the glasses down painstakingly, filled them, placed the carafe with infinite care and near-silence. "Are you ready to order?"

Mim had not looked at the menu. She remembered it more or less from other occasions. "Do you still have the fish curry? All right, I'll have that."

"The paella," Alan said blandly. Curious how easily one could make the shift from raw self to dispassionate customer; was that how people with servants dealt with their servants?

"And what kind of dressing on your salads?" said Todd, as if settling in for a long siege. "We have a sweet poppyseed dressing, a creamy dill, balsamic vinaigrette, gorgonzola—"

"Vinaigrette." "Gorgonzola." Her voice, then his, taking no time for thought.

"Toasted almonds okay on your salads?" Todd went on sunnily.

"Sure."

"Thank *you*," he said, and was gone.

They touched glasses and drank. "*L'chaim*," said Mim, with a sense of multiple ironies. Alan looked inquiring, but nodded and drank.

"Anyway," he said after a moment, "your friend casts me very much as the villain. The heavy husband in clodhoppers. Accused me of browbeating you."

"I hope he was civilized."

"Eminently. He gets all his barbarism out in another way; he can afford to be. But the whole thing is opaque to him. He just doesn't get it."

She had wondered how soon they would settle down to the subject; it was going to be right away. "What would you want him to get?"

"Well, that you don't interfere in a delicate religious matter between man and wife," he said, as if he had been rehearsing it all these years. "That when a naïve young woman comes running to you for protection from her own nature, you don't play the role. That it wasn't his business."

She drew a long unhappy breath. Was there any use in having this conversation? "As a matter of fact," she said, "he asked if I intended to tell you. Insisted I should, unless I was really afraid of you. He did have you in mind."

"Good for him," said Alan, unimpressed. "It didn't cost him a cent. Why should you be afraid of me?"

"Well, the whole altercation over the Pill—"

"Altercation," he said. "But we talked about it rationally; Mira, we never raised our voices. I thought we'd agreed."

"What would have been the use of raising my voice?" she said. "You had a whole catechism on your side, and I only had a little tentative self-knowledge. You could destroy it with a well-placed criticism or two; you could have done it in a whisper if you'd wanted."

"That speaks for the power of the catechism, I guess," he said, with the ghost of a smile. "I was just hurt, and shocked. I never felt I gave the Church's view well enough; if I had, you couldn't have doubted."

"You gave it all right," she said. "Surely I doubted because I wasn't good enough to believe. Isn't that how it works? Of course you would feel you had failed me, but that was just another mark of your superior character. Of course a saint would have a tortured conscience."

"Oh, Mira," he said with his little helpless half-laugh, "I'm an unlikely candidate for sainthood."

"Well, we all are. But I didn't think so then. With the Church behind you, and only my whining, duplicitous little scrap of self behind me—"

"But all secular culture was behind you," he said. "You had all the support in the world for doing what you did."

"Oh, the world," she said. "But the world was disqualified. It didn't get a vote. I was just that little scrap of self, begging not to be annihilated. I know, you'll say that's what the self is for; you'll say if you have to choose between annihilating the self and annihilating a fetus, you go for the self every time. But I couldn't do it. I know feelings don't have moral standing, but they get in the way." She ought not to do this; she should be polite and neutral, ask after his job and his family, eat her food and go home.

He looked miserable. "If I hurt your feelings, I'm sorry," he said at last, lamely. "I'm sure I said all the wrong things. I don't know that my character was so much better formed than yours. I know you always worried about your character, and thought you had a long way to go, but I didn't see it. I saw a lovely young woman who would have been happy with a child."

"Lovely!" she said. "Does that matter? It may have been true," she added, remembering some pictures she had dug out to show Ari: she and Alan in her parents' garden, giving each other affectionate looks and squinting into the sun. ("A luscious young woman," said Ari. "Wasted on him.") "But it takes more than loveliness to be good at raising a child. You can't get by on just being nice to look at."

Alan sighed. "I don't mean that kind of loveliness. Young women take their physical grace for granted, I'm sure, but it's more than that: there's loveliness of soul, thoughtfulness and humility and a kind of moral sweetness. And you had that; I know you thought you didn't, but you did. And how you could feel that the growth of your character stood in the way of—of the growth of your character . . . I'm sorry, I'm not making sense. What I mean is, you thought you had more moral growth to accomplish before becoming a mother. But it was motherhood that would have made you accomplish it."

"That's a chicken-or-egg question, isn't it?" she said, deliberately sour. "And I could reply: of course I didn't have enough character yet, because I aborted the child and a woman of character doesn't do that. Q.E.D." Damn it, he was making her think in syllogisms: this was the second time in two hours she had said *Q.E.D.*

She had hurt him; he was losing his temper. "All right. I did say it to myself, in moments of rage: *She was right, she was morally infantile, how did I miss it?* But I don't think you were. I think you were trying hard—maybe too hard; you doubted yourself, and there was a quick fix available in the secular world, and you fell for it. That intense devotion, that hunger for spiritual things—I suppose hunger is really a sign of malnutrition; underneath the outward devotion was this cold pragmatism, which you'd grown up with and which you had no idea how to do without. I thought I could help you; it was more than I knew how to handle."

She was startled. "Alan!" she said. "Pragmatism isn't cold; it's a good deal warmer than dogma. At least it's willing to deal with the given conditions. Don't you know that ninety percent of motherhood—"

"Fresh ground pepper on your salads?" Todd again, putting down flat bowls of leaves and little gravy boats full of dressing; he flourished a foot-long pepper mill. Alan winced.

"Oh, *no* thanks, Todd, we're all right," said Mim swiftly. Good God, how frivolous: how could you sit here and talk about character when in the next breath someone was going to offer you pepper?

Todd had barely retreated before Alan attacked. "Pragmatism is spiritual vulgarity," he said. "You can get anything you want by saying the conditions demand it."

"How is it noble to ignore what the conditions demand?" she said. "Maybe we're all just vulgar, Alan."

A leaf of his salad was not cooperating; he took a minute to rearrange and impale it. "Does it have to be argued at this level?" he said. "Sometimes I wonder if original sin isn't just the compulsion to argue—to think twice, to worry a thing to death, always to insist on reasoning against a doctrine that never claimed to be reasonable. We're not supposed to have children when the conditions are perfect, we're supposed to have them when it's God's will. It's not an intellectual question."

It's not rational, sweetie. No, it wasn't: or she wouldn't be sitting here on the thirty-fourth day still wondering what she wanted. "An intellectual hatred is the worst," she said automatically, "so let her think opinions are accursed." In spite of everything there was a melancholy pleasure in speaking the lines; Ari didn't know his way around Yeats. "But then what do we do? Just go back to instinct? Stop using our minds?"

"You could do worse," he said. "You can indulge or misapply instinct, but it's not so corruptible; you can't cut it loose from natural law. It was the intellect that fell: *knowledge* of good and evil."

"*Daat tov v'ra,*" she murmured. The whole multiply inflected bliss of her attraction to Judaism came over her; she rested in it a moment. "Jews, you know, don't call it original sin. It's just history—the given conditions, which we have to deal with but don't ever have to settle for. The intellect on the whole is friendly: you don't distinguish between good and evil without making the intellect work very hard."

"Is that so," he said. "In that case your friend needs to make his work a little harder."

"Oh?" Her mother's voice sounded through her voice: pleasant, encouraging, dangerous.

"Well, he defends what he does by saying it's not as bad as what Hitler did. It's a pretty poor argument."

"He can't have said that." She attended again to her plate. "His mind doesn't work that way. Besides, most of his family died under Hitler."

"Getting even, is he?"

It took her a moment to understand him, and when she did it was as if the world rocked under her briefly. "Christ, Alan, what are you thinking? People don't do abortions because—you sound like Del Marlin."

"It's a legitimate question," he said. "People do abortions because they have no respect for life; it has to come from somewhere. I have a hard time with Jews who expect you to countenance anything they do because they suffered during the war. It's just like Israeli politics, there's only so much you can justify—"

Her belly knotted. She put down her fork with a snap. "Oh, hell! Don't talk to me about Israeli politics; don't talk to me about Jews you have a hard time with. I never knew you went in for that." She groped without looking for her purse and hat on the bench. "You can say anything you want about *me*, but I'm not going to sit still for this—this half-baked—"

He looked stricken. "Oh, damn it. Mira." He put down his fork and braced himself to get up. "We can stay off the subject; it's not important to *me*. Don't overreact. Please don't go."

She stared at him. "Overreact."

"I've come a long way to talk to you. I want to be reconciled. We both made mistakes; we both need forgiveness. I want us to forgive each other."

She felt her face form a look it had never needed before: exasperated, bemused, patient because impatience could make no difference. Alan's face did not change. He looked unhappy and tired. Maybe he had begun to wear down; maybe, like her, he was driven to say what he said by forces beyond him that he did not know how to resist. Were ideas a kind of daemonic possession that took hold of frail people, giving them voices too big for their stature and a task too great for their energies? "You didn't come here just to talk to me," she said. "It was a by-product of writing the article."

"No, the article was a by-product of it." He smiled guiltily. "It's an alibi; a transparent one. Claire is furious. But when I saw your letter to the *Challenge* I couldn't help thinking . . ." He looked away, phrasing it carefully. "That I saw kindness in it, and that I still felt kindness for you."

Before she could imagine an answer, Todd appeared with their plates. Hers first, the curry, redolent and yellow; then the paella, preposterous in its hugeness, a big mound of rice mixed with shrimp and sausage and crab and peas and tomato and onion and pine nuts, two little cups (one held drawn butter, one wine sauce) embedded in the rice, and an armor-plating of mussels still in the shell in a ring around the perimeter. Alan stared at it: apparently memory had not preserved its full grandeur. "Cushlamochree," he said.

She gave a burst of surprised, involuntary laughter; then they were both laughing, shrill with relief. It was cartoon Irish, from a book they had both known as children about a little boy named Barnaby and his cigar-smoking fairy godfather who had pink wings and the style of a ward politician. The word came in handy for all kinds of astonishment, for a skid on an icy road or a crack of thunder; Mim remembered it at least once in bed. She could not stop laughing. It would turn to sobs in a moment if she did not stop. Alan was glowing with happiness and relief. "See, Mira?" he said. "The bad times weren't the whole story. We liked each other. I was never your enemy. Never."

She squeezed the laughter to silence. She ran her hand into her hair in a gesture of speechlessness. She drew a long breath. Turmeric, fenugreek, cinnamon, coriander, cumin, asafoetida, cayenne. "Alan," she said, "do you know how little it takes to browbeat a young woman who loves you?"

Her words and her gesture undid him: already relaxed from the laughter, and warmed by the wine, he let himself slip from intellect into instinct. "Gus", as if at the sound of his mistress' voice, half-flooded, tingling and warm. Beautiful Mira: the maturity in the bones of her face, her self-assured bearing, the fall of the rough silk dress from the curves of her shoulders. To hear her speak a quick articulate sentence was pure pleasure—even if it was a wrongheaded sentence, even if it was shortsighted or full of error. He lowered his eyes, to hide their delight; he ate. The dense and savorous rice, the buried explosions of taste as he popped a green pea or a pine nut; the embarrassing mussels, slippery and tasting of sea, with their folds and flaps and the little nubbin between them. It was a while before he trusted himself to speak. "I never meant it as browbeating," he said. "I really am sorry. There's just so much explaining to do. The way you were raised—you know, modernists all think they're blank slates, encountering the world absolutely uninfluenced, but they can be slaves to a historical pattern and not even know it. Even your fear of having a child—you thought it was a spontaneous feeling, but it was a conditioned reflex. There was a long line of—well, I have to say it, apostates—urging you to feel that way. And behind them an enemy so old that he predates the world. You were so unprotected."

She groaned; in his heightened state he heard it almost as pleasure. "Oh, Alan, can't you go for five minutes without sniping at modernists? I was helplessly drawn to the Church: I thought I was going to the crucible of all Western art. How modern is that? I know, I know," she said as he made to speak, "facile aestheticism, and tapes of Gregorian chant. All the Church really wanted was to empty my mind and fill my womb. But I wanted to *give* it my mind; why wasn't that possible?"

She was quoting him; she must know that article nearly as well as he did. Claire didn't quote him. "So you went to the one who emptied your womb and filled your mind, was that it?"

She rolled her eyes, out of patience. "Oh, Alan, damn it, can't we just eat? Bob doesn't like you either. Leave it at that."

He did, disappointed; he had hoped for some other response. How could he reach her? He puzzled and waited. At last a phrase from the afternoon presented itself. "He said"—it was curiously troubling to say, once he had begun to—"that poverty and shame are the main reasons women do this. You weren't ashamed, were you? Of, of having a mind *and* a womb? There was no other reason for shame; after all, we were married . . ."

She looked up at once. "Alan, of course it was shame. *Because* we were married. What business did I have being married to you? I couldn't tell you the truth; you couldn't hear it; I was trying to do what would please you, but the risk was too serious. I was playing with somebody's life. You don't let someone start growing in your body if you don't want them there."

His face fell. "You admit it's a life," he said bleakly.

"What else would it be?"

She was not weeping; she spoke with gentle reproach; the thought was not new to her. "But how could you mistake—?" he said. "We went through the pre-Cana thing, you did *know,* though they did a perfunctory job of it. How could you want me and not want the child? What did you think marriage *was?*"

"I don't know," she said wearily. "I thought it was friendship; I thought it was prayer and study; I don't know what I thought. To pray with the person one loves, what an extraordinary thing. I wasn't sure how children fit into it. I'm still not sure." Her eyes flickered. "A relationship is a sort of shared mind, isn't it?" she went on. "You understand things together; you're part of a history and a climate of thought. You have a spiritual framework and moral imperatives and a sense of your task together. And the task can include having children, if you think your shared mind has room. But it might not."

His and Claire's shared mind had no room except for the children. Jealousy gnawed at him. "And do you pray with Bob too?"

She looked startled, and looked away, beginning to formulate some complex answer he was sure he did not want to hear. "Because I can't see what spiritual framework you and he share," he went on, preventing her, "except this extremely dubious feminist notion of liberation from motherhood. Is that enough to get by on? After all, what's his task? One little murder after another, the mass production of—"

"Oh, please, I hear this all the time—"

"—of freedom for women," he said, noting with satisfaction that she had expected to hear something else, "and that isn't how you get it. It has to be carefully wrought, soul by soul; it's never the same twice."

"But that's—my God, Alan, surely you see it. Do you think women who have abortions aren't trying to make their souls? Sometimes they know it better than the ones having babies. There's this extraordinary line from the psalms—"

"He showed me," said Alan shortly. "That quote on the wall. Mira, that doesn't cut it. Prayer is a plea for guidance, not a varnish we slap on over our own desires."

"It's a gravitational pull," she said. "This terrible, visceral cleaving to what we trust. Thou desirest truth *in the inward parts*—"

"—and you'll let me do whatever I want with my inward parts as long as I'm open and honest. That's not prayer, that's a monologue. Choice for its own sake, choice just because you can choose. I killed my baby, I walked out on a husband who loved me with all his heart, but I did it *my* way." Oh, now he had really done it. Why couldn't he stop turning these nasty phrases? But he knew why: it was the quickest way to her feelings. If hostility were the strongest passion he could arouse in her now, he would go for hostility.

But it was not hostility, only a mild, remote scorn. "Oh, Alan, you have no ear. I don't think you want to fix anything even slowly. God knows I'm sorry I hurt you, but what could I do?" She turned back to her food.

He tried to return to his; there was a lot of it left. He saw that he was not going to make her angry. He had said his worst and she had not broken down, and she was not going to break down, and his mission had failed. He had come to reconcile her to God, and here she thought she was already reconciled, by some extra-ecclesial means; she thought she had a direct line. He ate without pleasure. Mim was eating fast, almost done with her curry. At last he saw a faint penumbra of promise in what she had said: one way still to reach her, perhaps. "If prayer is a gravitational pull," he said, "is it still that for you? Do you pray?"

She softened; looked rueful. "Without ceasing," she said, "or damn near. I can't seem to do without it."

"What do you pray for?"

"It's not *for*. It's not like that. It's a current; I think it prays me."

His heart was wrung; if she ever repented, she would be far greater than he. But she might not repent: there had been heretics who prayed, and prayed in the wrong way, and sent the whole force of their devotion down some hellbound sluice. "Be careful," he said. "It's a gift. You've always had it, and God must mean you to keep it. But it can be dangerous."

She shook her head. "Of course it's dangerous. You think religion is a prescription drug, this careful maintenance dose of cure for the human condition. It's not: it's a street drug, the real unregulated opium of the people, that we can't let alone because of what it does to our brains."

He did not smile back. "You don't go to Mass," he said, sure of it.

She blushed. "I'm converting to Judaism. I've been studying all this year."

It fell into place: the references to Leo Baeck and rabbinic puns in her letter, the tripwire reaction to what he had said about Jews. "Mira, are you going to *marry* him?"

She was laughing at him: through a mouthful of curry she was laughing and trying to swallow, and coughing as something went down wrong. "Is that the only reason you can imagine?" she wheezed. "Yes, we're getting married, but we decided that a couple of weeks ago. I decided to convert before we were lovers. Certainly not for *his* sake. He worries I'll make him keep kosher." She drank water and coughed again.

He sat back, feeling winded. It was a removal he could not imagine. Not simply to walk away from the Church, but to go somewhere else; not simply to reject Christ and the Blessed Virgin, but to erase them from your devotions. "Mira," he said, "have you really thought this through? It may be a more comfortable place, given—your history with me—but can it really be satisfying? Is it true? To give up so much—to pretend Christ never came, to deny yourself consolation—"

"Consolation is easy," she said, still a little hoarse. "A religion that won't console is the best of all. You can apply your ardor to anything, can't you? It's the ardor that's permanent, not the object you fix it on. But where ardor isn't the one note you're permitted to sing—" She was radiant, animated, in spite of the scratch in her voice. "You can say *Shema Yisrael* one minute and *Choose another people* the next, and the blasphemy binds you as closely as the assertion. That's a place I can live in. It's even a place I can people; if you can believe it—" She broke off; her eyes widened briefly, and in a different tone, breathless, dispassionate, she said, "Alan, excuse me, please. I'll be right back."

The knot of tension in her belly, which had held steady since it arrived, had resolved itself into a cramp; a warm gush announced that the waiting was over. In the bathroom stall she stood still. She felt the air around her like a force-field of isolation: at the moment of discovery, she thought, one is always alone. From nowhere she remembered the moments after her abortion, her bitter weeping in the procedure room of Ari's old office, the brief unexpected touch of his hand on her shoulder. This was a simpler reprieve.

There was a synthetic marble wallboard in the bathroom, white and dull peach: clouds of motion, random and bland. She stood there so long unmoving that her eye began to see figures in the clouds, obviously not put there on purpose and full of an anguish no American designer would dare try to sell to a restaurant. A little goblin reaching up through a swirl of cloud with its left hand, while its right articulated itself from a loop of vapor that poofed out from its clothes and rested downward along the face, the wrist and fingers delicately turned. Its mouth and right eye were cavernous, the other eye small; the expression of the face was at once distressed and abstracted, like a mask of tragedy. Near it was a woman with a snub face, drifting horizontally, her long hair streaming out behind; a zigzag of cloud suggested an arm and an elbow reaching backward, a thigh and a knee reaching up. Again an abstracted expression, but intent, pugnacious. Below her, as if cradled in her clothes, a huge head, squarish and balding, that resembled Gerald Ford or Frankenstein.

A cow's head, or a dog's, with shut eyes and gently cocked ears. A wallaby, one ear disappearing into a curl of wind. A great tree that scooped up the winds beneath it and tossed them out overhead; over its branches floated the goblin with the anguished face, like Doré's Satan falling or Giotto's angels mourning the death of Christ. She did not weep; she did not sigh with relief; she did not think of what she would say to Ari. *Elohenu shebashamayim,* she said over and over to herself: a phrase from the retreat, not a week ago, a name of God by which one entreated God.

Alan, at the table, made some headway with the paella. His tongue probed a mussel—he had not let himself do that while Mira was there—and his mind tried to take in what she had said. He had not made any sense of her last few words. That she was marrying the man was bad enough—of course in one sense that ought to be heartening, but it wasn't—but that she was taking on his religion, which he himself didn't take seriously, was incomprehensible. What did she want with it? She seemed deeply at home in it, affectionate towards it, both in her letter to the *Challenge* and just now; there was something lovely about that, about the judicious and even maternal look it gave her. But she was placing herself with full knowledge outside the Church, even along one arc of what Chesterton had called the halo of hatred surrounding it; it was a reaction against Catholicism as much as an attraction toward its elder sister. Not that all Jews hated the Church, and Alan certainly didn't hate Jews, whatever Mira assumed; all human souls, through their sins, had earned a share in Christ's death, and it was mere ignorance to hold the Jews specially culpable. All the same, there was something: the sheer abstention from Christ made all explanations of Judaism he had encountered seem strangely vacant. But what do they *do?* he wondered. He had been to a bar mitzvah once—the son of one of Claire's colleagues—and there was no consecration, no sacrament: just a knot of people clustered around a Torah scroll, and the boy giving a speech and chanting a text. At the end, while everyone chatted and folded their prayer shawls, the boy had sung a couple of lines over a chalice of Manischewitz (the bottle was right on the table) and a loaf of that braided bread, and everyone had absently answered *Amen;* it wasn't part of the service, it was the preliminary to lunch. That carnal people, Augustine had always called them. Expecting an earthly Messiah, a heaven on earth. And in modern times seemingly unruffled by birth control and abortion. Perhaps—Alan's hand paused on the way to the plate—perhaps, after all, that was what made the difference, the belief that God had been born as a human child: perhaps if you fully accepted that you could never look at an unborn child as dispensable. He reached for his notes. *That* was the vindication of Catholic teaching, that was what he could say in the article: that those who could see most clearly the enormity of abortion were those who believed God took flesh in a woman's womb. *The planting of God in the womb changed childhood forever,* he wrote at high speed. *The fetus's right to life was established in history: before only an intuition, after the Blessed Virgin's* fiat mihi *it became unalterable law, protective, eternal. The God who was born among us was first unborn . . . Jesus was a fetus . . .* Damn. He needed quiet and time to write this, and here was this simpering waiter coming back for Mira's cleared plate, and here was Mira herself coming back from the restroom, looking subdued. There was a short consultation about dessert (Oh, you're kidding) and coffee (Yes, please), and Mira sat down and looked at him searchingly and said, "Tell me about your children."

Slowly—was it reluctance?—he reached into his hip pocket and drew out his wallet. A picture of a small friendly-looking woman with a reddish-blonde pageboy haircut, flanked by two diminutive copies of herself. They were all over her: the older one giggled against her face, the little one played with her hair. A woman surrounded by love. For Claire, having only a man would be emotional famine. "They're lovely," she said.

"They are. This one is Grace—she's seven—and Chrissy is five. We think Grace is going to be musical: Claire's brother gave her a pennywhistle, the tiny shrill kind that's small enough for her fingers, and she can actually get sweet tones out of it and not blast our eardrums. We know right away when Chrissy gets hold of it." He grimaced. "Chrissy's a live wire. We don't know what she's going to be: maybe a civil engineer. She likes earthworks in the back yard."

And he had met Claire at the parish church when they both volunteered for a food drive, and she was part of a group practice in psychotherapy, working (part-time now) with the newly bereaved or betrayed; and it was wonderful to have children, it met some deep need in him, he hoped she didn't mind if he said so; and it was terrifying to have daughters, one worried years in advance. By the time the coffee was gone they were talking like old friends, without rancor or sorrow. But as they got up—he insisted on paying the check—he gave her that look of reluctance again, and said, "It's good of you not to laugh."

"Laugh?" she said, puzzled. "At what?"

He was helping her into her coat; that might have made her smile, in another mood. "Can we go for a walk?" he said.

There was a little park at the end of the street, where they had sometimes gone in the old days after eating at the Quadrille. They walked there now without touching, which made the progress both familiar and strangely untuned. Alan sniffed at the chilly salt air. "It's almost as if nothing had happened," he said. "As if we were still together, and it was back then. Isn't the mind strange? I can just revert to a former time and make my wife and children wink out of existence."

Mim chuckled sadly. "That's not a choice we get."

The park was a few picnic tables, a few trees and a fishing pier. No one was fishing. They leaned on the fence and looked over the dark water, now at low tide. At Ari's place one could look out the bedroom window straight down into the brine and see starfish sprawled on the sand; she wondered if there were starfish here. "What were you afraid I would laugh at?"

"Oh, the classic two children," he said. "I thought it would strike you funny."

"It didn't occur to me." She and Ari had joked about it; they had counted the years of his marriage to see how many children one could produce at full speed in that time, but when the moment came she had forgotten to think of it. She had wanted simply to be taken out of her own complex grief, to hear about *someone's* children, to see Alan happy with his own and imagine herself and Ari happy with theirs. If happiness was quite what one got.

"Well, now you know," he said. "Aren't you curious about how it happened?"

"Alan! There are all kinds of ways it can happen. It isn't my business."

"I think it is." He did not look at her; he spoke into the dark. "Claire wanted children," he said. "She'd just about given up on finding a man who did. They all want to pretend to be twenty-one forever and have no ties. Of course doctors like your friend play right into that. So she was happy to find me, and I was—well, you know, I was in very bad shape. To have any woman be glad I could give her children—" Mim was near enough to sense his tight shrug. "She didn't want *lots* of children—it's still possible, if you look around, to find Catholic women who do, but I'm not very good at looking around—and at that point I couldn't argue. I can't be the enemy of my wife. I suppose that was what you showed me: women have an absolute veto. It used to be enforced through virginity, now it's abortion. If you don't get the conditions you want, you withhold the gift."

His voice was soft, but the words were corrosive. "If that's how you think of it," Mim said, "it's extraordinarily good of you to live the way she wants to live."

He gave a snort of dismissal. "No, it's not good."

"But—" she said, her persona suddenly compelled to talk to his persona, "then you write these long impassioned indictments of birth control while you're practicing it? Why? What does Claire think of that?"

"One indictment," he said. "I've only written at length on the subject once. She lets it roll off. She says I'm writing about the ideal but we're living the real." Actually she had said, "Honey, I love you, but you're a classic Four on the Kohlberg scale. When are you going to see that the rules aren't the end of the story?"

"But why?" said Mim again. "Isn't it awkward, exhorting people to do something you don't do? Isn't it embarrassing?"

He shifted his weight. "Of course it's embarrassing, Mira, but it's the doctrine. What am I going to do about it? Try to tear it down just because I'm a coward? It's not a false doctrine. I know all those pitfalls and consequences because I live them. Even a bad priest can administer valid sacraments; I hope even a sinful interpreter can give a valid interpretation."

She stared across the bay to the lights of the navy yard. Somewhere over there, there were nuclear submarines: a whole submerged clockwork of mayhem poised to go off. It had not occurred to her to read his article as self-accusation; she had not imagined him defending the moral high ground in theory while abandoning it in practice. It seemed too much like herself. Yes, the numinous mocks us. "Alan, good God, you poor man," she said. "I knew argument couldn't change you, but even experience can't change you."

"I've never believed in getting my principles from my experience," he said wearily. "You relativize them that way, you end up implying *I have to believe this because of what I've been through.* I may have to *live* like this because of what I've been through, but I won't say it isn't a sin; I won't try to bend the truth to spare myself pain."

She reached out and stroked his shoulders through his light canvas coat; she made a small noise of distress. When she settled her arm once more on the railing, his arm went around her; then he pulled her in close, he bent his cheek to her cheek. A shudder ran through him.

"Mira, look," he said in a whisper, "when Claire and I—"

He could not speak for a bit. She waited, unmoving. "We were eager for children. But when I finally had a woman who wanted my children, we couldn't—I—couldn't perform. The thought of, you know, entering her body with intent to create a child—the risk—when my first child had been—" He held her more tightly. "I used to think of it all the time when I was with you, would this be the time, it—used to excite me—but that feeling had been so crushed. And it was so incongruous to try to feel it with someone else. There are parts of a man's body that can't, you know, transfer allegiance—"

She put her arm round his waist. "Oh, Alan. Oh, my dear. You of all people."

"It took several months to get over it. Claire's a therapist, she knows all the psychological tricks. She got me working again. But it was miserable for us both. Even the second time, when we were trying for Chrissy, I had a few failures. I've never once had a problem when Claire *was* on the Pill; my reflexes are all backwards now."

She leaned into him, swaying. "My God, what we do to each other."

He rubbed his hair slowly against her hair. "No, Mira. I don't blame you. Neither of us knew very much. After all, what I did to you . . . in a way I drove you to all of it. It's the pattern of my own sins. I mean . . . let me say it this way. Claire and I could have stopped making love when we had our two children—but I chose lust; I didn't seriously contemplate anything else. And with you I had the same choice. I think what you really wanted was a chaste marriage—friendship and prayer and study. I could have let you have that. If you had wanted children later I could have waited. But I chose lust. One—gets used to it, you know; when I didn't have it I felt half-alive without it."

"Of *course* you did. Alan, that's crazy. I didn't want a chaste marriage. How much do you remember about me?" She stood upright again; if she were going to say things like that it was better not to be touching him. "Claire doesn't stop wanting you just because she has her two children," she said. "What's the point of chaste marriage? To put ourselves through spiritual contortions in honor of the God who made us this way? He made us with brains too. Don't you think he laughs at us, watching us too scared to use them?"

He withdrew his arm. "I think he weeps, watching us too selfish to use our will." There was no piety in his tone; it was disappointment. "There's nothing intelligent about sex for pleasure," he mumbled, almost inaudibly. "It's not even that pleasurable. This monotonous lust, and this constipated fertility."

What could she say to that? She was silent, breathing.

"You really want to know what I think?" he said. "I think we can only reconcile the filth of the body and the purity of the soul through our children. I know you won't like that; they got you a long time ago, the hedonists and the gnostics, who don't care if the two can be reconciled. But look at a child: the way filth and purity coexist there so simply, so plainly. That grubby preoccupation with bodily functions and that dazzlingly innocent mind. We have nothing like that. Adult bodily functions just make us ashamed." His hands held still on the railing. "What's wonderful, what's redemptive, is that our shame can produce more innocence. Our children redeem us from our carnality. If our carnality goes toward producing them, it stops being wrong. Never otherwise."

No words occurred to her. The spirit that filled her with words in a public place was not equal to this private challenge. Our carnality stops being wrong whenever it's kind. It was never wrong in the first place. Carnality *is* incarnation. "Alan, let's go."

They stood outside his hotel. He too could find no last words: forgiveness, as he had imagined it, did not seem to be in the picture. At last he simply opened his arms, and she came into them, simply; her hat brim got in the way, and she pulled the hat off and dangled it at his back as she leaned her head on his chest. He stroked her hair, his heart breaking: he might never see her again. "Mira—"

She looked up then and kissed him: warmly, twice, with closed lips. "*Intimior intimo meo,*" she whispered: one of Augustine's names for God, which she had hijacked when they were lovers. He felt slightly faint. He was painfully, fiercely aroused—that was where all the blood had rushed from his head—and refrained with great effort from giving a sign of it. It would be so easy to bend his knees, to fit himself against the arched bone, to do what he had done before they were married—but not here, in a public place; and he would never get her to his hotel room, they would both think better of it before he did, and Morgenzahl no doubt was waiting. Too civilized to move, he stood still.

"Mira," he said, "if you marry him—try to make him get out of this business."

"No, I won't do that. For heaven's sake, Alan, he's a doctor, it's not a 'business.'"

She let him go; they stood awkwardly. This time it was she who spoke first. "You really thought my having a child would redeem you? From—from having desired me? You think so still?"

"I'll never have a chance to know, will I?"

CHAPTER 26

> As cloth in the hands of the draper,
> Who drapes or twists it at will,
> So are we in your hands, O jealous God.
>
> —The Yom Kippur liturgy

Fall light had its own quality. It rose out of the ocean later and farther south; even at ten in the morning—the hour when Sarita habitually opened the shop—it fell on the bay at a new and more temperate slant. Approaching the equinox: the even season, when briefly light and dark balanced before they changed places. When earthly things made even atone together. Fall always restored her: summer was feverous, one might as well not wear clothes, but fall called forth her energies.

The man who came into the shop was no one she recognized: a trim, sandy-haired professional type in his forties, reserved in his movements, mild in his speech, clearly heterosexual in his simultaneously interested and slightly phobic handling of the dresses on the rack. "I'm looking for something for my wife," he said with a gesture of helplessness. "I saw your display in the window, and—"

"Look around," she said comfortably. "If you don't see something you like, there are other designs in these notebooks; not everything is made up. Or I can invent what you need if you can describe it."

He fiddled with a hanger. "You see, I'm from out of town," he said. "I was hoping to bring something back."

"Oh," said Sarita, "that's tricky. You know her size?"

"Ah, twelve," the man said. "She's not very tall, about this height, and—is it hopeless to go about it this way?"

"Not necessarily. These designs are fairly loose-fitting. Take a look, and we'll manage something. Remember it's most important to match her coloring."

He took some time looking; Sarita made notes for an order of silks from a catalog. After a time she looked up to see him standing before the scarf display, blinking back tears. "Your work," he said, "it's remarkable. I don't know what it reminds me of. Who would have thought to match pale pink and pale grey and white? What is that shade of dark blue called? And those crackles of color, I don't understand how you do it." His face was serious, rejoicing. "Of course. I remember. I must have been four or five. My sister was in a wedding. She took me along when she bought her dress material. It was before Christmas, and there were these rows and rows of deep shiny colors—cloth with sequins and glitter, I'd never seen anything like it. I suppose it was pretty tasteless, compared to this, but I didn't know that then. I thought heaven must be like that." He shook his head. "Well, I can't buy the whole store. What did you mean, match her coloring?"

"What colors does she look best in?" Sarita refrained from condescension or irony; a lot of perfectly intelligent husbands couldn't manage the language.

"She—actually, she doesn't wear them too often," he said. "She wears a lot of those pale washed-out colors. Pastels. And those forbidding suits when she has to go to a meeting. There's one—navy blue with these big red buttons—a lot of red on it actually, the pocket flaps and the cuffs and I guess the collar. Like a suit of armor." He shuddered. "But she looks best in those colors that don't have names. The ones that fall somewhere between green and blue, or green and brown . . . she says they're depressing, but I think they're interesting. I'd thought about this one." He turned to the rack.

It was a long shift in gold and brown: the piece she had made a few weeks ago to distract herself from thinking about Mim. "You don't have a picture? That might help me to tell."

"Oh, of course I do; here." He slipped it out of his wallet. A woman and two little girls in an affectionate pose, with identical short straight red-blonde hair. The girls were in cotton print dresses, the woman in a pintucked pink blouse. Appalling. And the colors clashed with the photographer's blank blue wall. Sarita covered everything but the woman's face with a fold of the dress; she became instantly handsome. "Oh, yes," said the man, "that's much better."

"Well, try it," she said. "If she doesn't like it, of course you can send it back. And she may like it. Women sometimes don't know . . . or rather, they *do* know, always, but they may be afraid. You can dress to say what you are, or dress—not to say it; it's an effort to cross the line."

"I think she'll like it," he said uncertainly, putting the picture away. He looked at the price tag. "I hope so." He gave her his credit card.

She gave him one of her business cards in trade. "Here's my address, in case you do need to send it back."

He watched her ring up the sale. "It's really a sort of peace offering," he went on, "but it may be the wrong idea. It's so hard to tell . . ."

"Whether it's the right offering? Or the right time?"

"Whether it's worth it," he said, as if making the admission at last. "It wasn't a match made in heaven. Well, we knew that. But—I'd *had* a match made in heaven, once before, that turned suddenly into a nightmare. I was glad for just ordinary unhappiness. But it's so unhappy."

The door slammed downstairs, and a clamor broke out: two sets of feet climbing the creaking stairs, two exuberant male voices singing. Sarita swore to herself; it was not a moment for the Todd-and-Andrew revue.

"We'll stay together," the man added hastily as she bagged the dress. "We're not the kind of people who wreck our kids' lives just because we're a little unhappy. But it's so hard . . . being able to tell the difference."

The song came raucously closer, in harmony:

> *Sad King Arthur once looked out*
> *In the glow of even;*
> *There the bold Sir Lancelot*
> *Guinevere was swyvin'.*

The man scrawled his name at the foot of the credit slip. Sarita took it from him just as Todd and Andrew burst in. "Good luck," she said urgently, hoping she would be heard. He nodded thanks, and exchanged a startled look with Todd as they passed in the doorway.

"Lovey," said Andrew, unpacking coffee and croissants on the glass display case, "what was *that* all about? Do you know this man?"

"Sarita," Todd said, ignoring him, "what was *that* all about? Do you know who that was?"

She glanced uncomprehendingly at the signature.

"That's *Mim's ex*," he said in a stage whisper. "They were having this wrenching conversation in the Quadrille last night, one didn't know where to look. What was *he* doing here?"

The writing became legible. Alan Lonigan. "Buying a dress for his wife."

Todd hooted. "And so he might well." But Sarita could not enter into the spirit of it; the man's anguish had been so palpable, and his love for her work so surprising, that she did not care who he was. She saw how Mim had been drawn into marrying him, and into lying to him: one wanted to see him at rest. And when, a few hours later, she grew imperiously sleepy, she did not refuse: she left Todd and Edith in charge and lay down in the laundry room, with piles of cloth beneath her and a length of wool for a spread, and gave herself up to whatever might need to happen.

•

Alan had planned to write on the plane, but did not have the stamina; the fatigue of the previous day had not yet worn off. He felt a thin perilous jubilation at the core of his tiredness: Mira had tempted him and he had resisted, she had held him, had whispered to him, the excursion had not been altogether a failure. Between one and the other triumph he had not slept well, and toward morning had gotten up and polluted himself and a bar of the hotel soap, on his knees in the shower in an ecstasy of desire. Now the raw airline coffee could not keep him awake.   •

He had come into Sarita's shop in an excoriated, highly sensitive state: he would never have talked that way about Claire, even to a stranger, had he not been wondering how to return to her after Mira. He had wanted some last extravagant gift as a form of insurance: he knew Claire couldn't be bought, but during their last quarrel she had sounded as if she might like to be flattered. And this woman's work was so moving: those swirls and blotches of color had judged him, had pardoned him. They had taken him entirely out of himself, where for a moment he had wanted nothing to change. He had seen Mira and was going home to Claire; he had no needs or regrets. How could a color pardon? Colors weren't God.

He had the dress with him; he had not wanted it to get crushed in his luggage, and having paid so much for it he was not sure he wanted to let it out of his sight. He peeked at it in the bag. The colors were tawny, leonine: lighter around the shoulders and gaining in intensity to a dark bronze around the feet. It's *chaste*, he thought, and was not sure what he meant. The neck wasn't chaste; it seemed to be rather low. He could not imagine Claire wearing the dress in public. He imagined her wearing it in private, and shut his eyes. Better not to fall asleep in that mood. A hundred and fifty dollars for a nightgown.

He tried listening to his interview tapes through the headphones, but work could not revive him; his head would drift back, and Del Marlin's voice would dissolve into nonsense. "Converting to Judaism? Honey, that's going backwards. It's like, it's like trying to unconceive the Christ Child." He never said that, Alan thought, but could not fight the undertow of sleep. "He's there, you know," Del's voice went on, "floating in you, sunk in your womb, and all you might feel now is a little unease, a little sickness and dread in the mornings, because you know how your life is going to change when He comes to term. And you think you can escape Him by going to the doctor, you're going in desperation to that murderous man, saying *Doctor, scrape Him out of me, I'll pay you anything.*" Alan woke and pushed the fast forward button, or dreamed that he woke and pushed the fast forward button, but the voice went naggingly on.

"Now you can abort the Christ Child," it said, "you have that free will. But the difference between Him and your ordinary unborn baby is that you can't kill Him. He'll be there, watching you and loving you, and when you turn back—" Hell! thought Alan, and woke. He put in the Morgenzahl tape—surely *his* voice was not lulling—and tried to take notes, but the pen felt blunt in his hand. "The least of these my brethren, that's the phrase, isn't it?" the voice was soon saying. "Inasmuch as you've done it to the least of these my brethren, you've done it to me. And a fetus is the littlest brother of all. But women aren't brethren, are they? You can do things to them that don't get passed on to him. You can't get Jesus pregnant against his will. No, seriously, if you think he's God—God is the ultimate multipara, you know, absolutely untiring, never refuses to bear, never gets overwhelmed. Easier when you're pure spirit, of course. But up there in the endometrium—" He woke again, woozily; he was just conscious enough to turn off the tape and pull off the headphones.

He leaned his head between the seat and the window. The plane's vibration buzzed against his skull. He brought the dress in its bag up to use as a pillow, but the paper crackled annoyingly; half asleep, he pulled the folded garment out and laid it against his face. The astonishing softness of satin. Warm, like Claire's skin. Mira's skin was so long ago that he could not remember it. He must not go to sleep in that mood. He should get out his colleague's daughter's Arthurian book; maybe irritation would keep him awake. Sad King Arthur once looked out in the glow of even. Two or three times he dreamed he reached for the book; once he got as far as thinking he had fumbled and lost the page. A vague sense of its quasi-archaic language passed through him; then he gave up and slid into a long dream.

King Arthur went hunting on a day; alone without his companions he stalked a hart deep into the wood, and shot it, and the hart fell down and bit the grass. And as he stood by the hart's body an old man came near, clad in a broad-brimmed hat and a many-colored coat, and watched him and said, "The king of the pagans has sacrificed his horned god."

The king was uneasy at these words, for he was a Christian man. "By thy long grey beard and glittering eye," he said, "why mockest thou at me?"

"I do not mock," said the old man, "but I am a student of souls, and

I know that for every sacrifice a scapegoat is required. See, you have made this hart's body pass from warm life to cold and ungainly death: look how his eye is dulled, and his muscles slacken, and his blood sinks slowly to the ground. Will you bear the guilt for his death? Will you punish your arrow? Or will you, because I stand here, give me the blame?"

"Old man," said the king, "if your accents were not those of a wise man I would think you a fool. Why should I charge you with what I myself have done?"

"In a long life I have seen such things happen," said the old man. "I was by at an execution long ago; when I read the accusation above the man's head, and said, 'Not *my* king,' one said, 'Let him live until he acknowledge it.' And I have lived since then a thousand years with the blame for another's deed."

The king looked long at him, and fear dawned in his eyes. At last he said, "I have heard tell of you, I think. Are you not he they call—"

"*Der ewige Jude*," said the old man. "In the tongue of those who will someday find me most burdensome. And you are Arthur of Britain."

The king acknowledged it, but his mind was distracted. "You saw Our Lord," he said.

The old man nodded. "But he was not my lord. And I cannot tell you of him. I am on my own business, sir, not yours."

The king frowned at his temerity. "And what, pray, is that business?"

"Talk," said the old man mildly. "Through talk we unbend the rigor of the Law. Through talk we relax the paralysis of limbs. Through talk we attain the secrets of the heart. God made the world through words, and through words we maintain it."

The king had never heard such dark sayings, and he thought on them deeply. "The secrets of the heart," he said. A haunted look came on him; he listened for his companions, but there was no sound in the wood but the small birds piping. He spoke in a low voice. "Sir, is my wife chaste?"

The old man gave him a pitying look. "I am no seer. Ask her, if you would know."

The king spoke still lower. "When I was young I lay with my sister. She bore our son. None knows of it. I was under enchantment and knew not what I did."

"Ah," said the old man with a little smile, "the uses of enchantment."

"I knew it not!" said the king angrily. "And now my wife is barren, and my kingdom will fail, and my one heir must not be acknowledged because he was born of sin. Old Jew, what have you done to me to make me tell such things? Are you also an enchanter?" And he drew his knife, with which he would have gutted the hart, and held it at the ready.

"Slay me not!" said the old man. "I bear no weapon, and have neither touched nor harmed you. I will not tell your secrets. Does your Lord mean so little to you, that you would kill me in this wise?"

Arthur stood, and his breath came heavily. "Your talk is a maze," he said, "and you stand at every corner of it, bewildering the mind." He sheathed his knife. "Howbeit," he went on, "I am a Christian knight, and I will not slay a man unarmed. Yet if I do not slay you, I must buy your silence, for you know what would overthrow me. What is your price, old man?"

Now for the first time the old man looked at him with contempt. "My price," he said. "You could not pay my price. You could not comprehend it. Let us go our ways; you have spared my life, and I will keep silence. Let us have no talk of prices."

The king did not understand. He thought on the words, and at last discovered a meaning that he could grasp. "I see," he said, "I have offended you. You are a holy man, and Our Lord sustains you in life till he come again; you have no need of gold or favours." Then, suddenly moved, he knelt and said, "Old father, I have sinned. Absolve me."

"How changeable you are," said the old man. "One moment you would kill me out of fear, the next you kneel to me in trust. Get up, sir. I will not absolve you; that is not our way. Your sins are your own burden. Yet if you would earn my respect—and that is the only gift of mine worth having—come back in a year and a day, and answer me one question, which all my years and all my knowledge have not answered."

Arthur, who had not gone on a quest for many years, rose with a sense of hope and returning youth. "What is that question?" he said.

The old man leaned close, and looked searchingly into the king's eyes. "*Was will das Weib?*"

So Arthur blew his horn, and his lords found him, and together they bore away the deer. And as they rode homeward all saw that he was troubled, but none dared question him. But that evening he and his knight Gawain sat alone, and he opened his heart to Gawain and told him of the strange quest. "And if I fail of my answer," he said, "what shall become of me? He knows the secrets of my heart, that only Christ knows else. His scorn is fearful. He made no threat, but I doubt not I shall be dishonoured."

"Sir," said Gawain, "you shall not be dishonoured through me. Let me ride out with you, and we will go two different ways, and ask whom we find for the answer, and put all the answers we find into a book. We shall not fail."

So they rode out, and when they met again each had a thick pamphlet of answers. "Sche lovyth to be wele arayd." "To have the love of men, and the prayse of wemen." "Securitee against ravissement." "A man wyth a bygg dycke." "She longyth for goodly babes." "For beaute that wyl not fade." "Salvacioun." "The lineamentes of gratifyed desyre." "A yerde lyk a horscok." And Gawain, who was interested in names, had noted in the margins some of the curious ones he had encountered on his way: *Touchepryk. Fillecunte. Cruskunt. Clevekunt. Scrattayl. Twychecunt.* "We shall not fail," said Gawain, well satisfied.

"I am adread," said the king.

Next day he went again to Inglewood, where he had killed the hart, and there he met a lady. She was the foulest woman that ever he had seen: her face red, her nose snotted, her hair clotted, her teeth like yellow fangs; her great eyes bleared; shoulders a yard wide with a hump between them, a body like a barrel and paps that would have burdened a horse. Indeed she was mounted on a horse, a fair steed gaily appointed, and she rode right up to the king and spoke her mind. "Sir, I know your quest, and I know that not one of your answers will avail you. Grant me a boon, and I will give you the answer, to spare you dishonour."

"What boon, lady?"

"Give me Sir Gawain to wed."

"Alas," said the king, "I cannot give him; I will put your case before him, but he must choose. Yet he will be loath to deny me, for the saving of my honour; yet so foul a lady I never saw go upon ground, and what shall I do?"

At these words she sat still. "Sir king," she said, "an owl has choice of a mate, and I am a lady."

So the king went back, and opened his heart to Gawain; and the knight said, "Is that all, sir? For your honour I will do that and more."

"You are the flower of knighthood," said King Arthur. And he rode forth again.

On the day when he must give his answer to the old man, he met again with the lady. "Gawain will wed you," he said; "you shall have your desire both in bower and in bed. Now tell me the answer quickly; I am in haste."

"Ah, sir," she said, "tarry a little; women like not haste. Some say we like finery and flattery, and to be much courted; some say we like many strange men, and to be often married. All this is foolery; it will not avail; but I will speak the truth. On one thing we meditate day and night, one thing we desire of man, and that is sovereignty. List! Alone we enter the world, and alone we leave it; alone we carry our burdens and choose our ways. Whether a man wish us to lean on him, or whether we wish to lean, we must know and do our will, for the joy of the bed is fleeting and life is lent. Tell that to your student of souls, and he will be wroth with you; he will curse me that taught it to you, for he fears the undoing of his work. But that is the truth: women desire to have the sovereignty."

So the king rode on in great haste, and at last he met again with the old man. The bearded face was mild, but the eyes were subtle; King Arthur quaked to meet them.

"Come down," said the old man, quietly enough; "tell me your findings."

The king took out the two books.

"Ah," said the old man. "Of the making of many books there is no end. I will see whether these hold anything new." He turned the pages slowly. "No; no. Ah, that is cleverly said, but it is an old answer; it has been proven wrong. No, these are charming collections, but I have seen everything in them. They may perhaps do in the realm of folklore."

"Wait," said the king; "I have one answer that will make all sure."

"Yes?"

"*Women desire to have the sovereignty.*"

The old man lost his melancholy demeanor; he became distraught, and paced to and fro in the grass. "I know who told you," he said; "that was my sister, *das ewig Weibliche,* and little she knows what is good for her. If she would consent to protection—! But she denies her need to depend. *Sovereignty,* she says, but in truth all she desires is a man's member to be grafted to her body; the envy of it has turned her foul. Look how her railing against destiny distorts her anatomy. Good day, sir king; you have my respect, as I promised, but your answer is all my despair."

King Arthur rode away, much bewildered. When he had gone a little way he met with the lady again. "I will ride with you to the court," she said, "and see your promise done. I will not part from you till I meet my husband, and I will not be ashamed."

But the king had great shame of her as she followed after. When they reached the court she would ride in in the full sight of all, and they had never seen so foul a thing; when they entered the hall she would not retire, but said, "Let fetch me Sir Gawain, that I may be made secure and our troth plighted; bring me my love at once."

Sir Gawain came forth, and when he saw her he did not blench, but said, "Sir, I am ready to do that I promised."

"God have mercy," said the lady; "for your sake I would I were a fair woman, you are of such good will."

She would not be married but with a great cry through all the shire, and all the ladies of the land invited; but Guinevere advised her to be married privily and early in the morning.

"Nay," she said, "I will not to church till high mass time, and I will eat in the open hall among all the rout."

"As you will," said the queen, "but I am minded of your dignity."

"As for that," said the other, "this day will I have my dignity, I tell you without boast."

She was wedded in a dress worth three thousand marks, as fair as she was foul. At meat she ate as much as any six, breaking her meat with her long nails; she ate three capons and three curlews, and she ate up great baked meats. None would sit with her, but men looked on and bade the devil gnaw her bones. But when the feast was over she and Gawain went to bed, and there he lay with his back to her and did not stir.

"Ah, Sir Gawain," she said, "since I have wed you, show me your courtesy in bed. It is my right. If I were fair, well I know you would do another dance; but for Arthur's sake kiss me, and let see how you can speed."

He said, "Before God, I will do more than kiss!" And he turned to her.

But when he turned, he saw the fairest creature that ever he had seen, naked between the sheets. "What is your will?" she said.

"Ah, Jesu!" he cried. "What are you?"

"Sir, I am your wife, surely; why so unkind?"

"I cry you mercy," he said, "but now you are a lady fair in my sight, and before you were the foulest I had seen." Only a moment he looked, and then embraced her. "Well is me, lady, that I have you so!"

"Sir," she said, "so you shall have me, but be ware: my beauty will not hold. Choose whether to have me fair by day or by night; one or the other you must have."

Then Gawain was greatly dismayed. For if he would have her fair only by night, it would do him no honour in the hall, and she would suffer the scorn of knights and ladies. And if he desired to have her fair by day, then at night he would have a simple repair. His courage rose at the sight of her fair body, but his heart trembled. "Do as you will, my lady," he said at last. "I put the choice in your hand. Loose me when you list, for I am bound. To you I have vowed before God both body and goods; to you also I give the choice."

"God's kindness on you, courteous knight," said the lady, "for now I have my dignity. You shall have me fair both day and night, and ever while I live as fair and bright. For I was shaped by magic by my stepmother, God's mercy on her, to be foul and misshapen till the best of England should wed me and give me sovereignty. And this you have done, for me that will not grieve you early nor late. Kiss me and be glad, for well is me begone."

"Ah, lady," he said, "I am glad as grass in the rain to take joy of you."

There they made joy out of mind, in talk and in the act of kind, until the dawn broke. Then the lady would have risen, but Gawain said, "We will sleep until prime, and then let the king send to wake us." And she agreed.

At midday the king said to his knights, "I am afraid for Sir Gawain, lest the fiend have slain him; let us go see if he lives." And they went together to his chamber door, and the queen with them, and behind them unseen an old man in a cloak.

They knocked and called, and Gawain called out, "Will you not let me be? I am full well at ease. But stay: you shall see the door undone."

Hand in hand with his bride he went to the door. There was a fire lit in the chamber; she stood by it in her smock; her hair hung to her knees red as gold wire. "Sir," he said, "this is my wife, Dame Ragnell, who is healed of her misery and who saved you from dishonour."

Then they all marveled, and she told the tale of her enchantment by her stepmother. "Yet let me not blame her," she said, "for so she got me a man that will not rule over me, except it be for our joy."

Then the old man came forward, and King Arthur saw that it was the old man of the wood, and fell back in fear. But he passed by the king and said, "Sister, I am glad at your restoration and pleased at your pleasure. But—" And he dropped his voice so that only the lady heard what he said.

When she heard it she laughed; and then she answered softly, so that besides the old man only Gawain and Guinevere heard her. "Ah, brother," she said, "the sweetness of that length of flesh is such, that if a man wield it kindly we desire to serve him with all our soul. Yes, we desire to possess it, but not as you think. But in the daylight and in his clothes, what living man deserves such service? Kind he may be, yet he does not know all. So in all that touches the rule of our bodies let him yield us the sovereignty; and from that freehold we will yield him service and friendship, that he may always know it is given and not compelled."

Sir Gawain lived with his lady in great bliss; she bore him a son who in after years became a good knight of the Round Table. But she lived only five years after; she died in childbed with their second son, and the babe died also. And of all the ladies that Gawain loved, he loved her ever the best.

But King Arthur mused on old wrongs, and on the secrets of his heart; and he consulted with the abbot of King's Cull, who mused on old texts, and the abbot told him of Eusebius and Ambrose and Chrysostom. And late that same year Arthur drove all the Jews from England by fire and sword, for the killing of that Christ whom some call the horned god of the pagans and some the king of the Jews.

The signal to fasten seat belts sounded; Alan woke. Disoriented, he stuffed the dress back in its bag. Elements of the dream replayed themselves in his head as it gradually cleared. He searched for his tapes and his notes. The vividness of the dream disturbed and enchanted him; it made him laugh, it left him deeply refreshed, as if every distress of the past few days had found its expression and need not distract his mind as he went to meet Claire. He had never been good at stories: when he put his children to bed he would read them books, or tell them the classic fairy tales or saints' legends, but he could never make anything up. As if the one story that must never be told sat blocking the well of Story, inhibiting his imagination or threatening to poison anything that came out of it. And now, for some reason, his imagination felt purified, drenched—baptized?—not because there was any purity in the story, God knew, but because it had come to him strangely, a gift and an oddity, surely not from *his* mind. He saw the Arthurian book as he repacked his briefcase; perhaps he wouldn't finish it now.

Claire was waiting at the gate, a daughter in each hand. Her face was carefully disposed in a look of greeting. Grace's eyes held a quiet scrutiny, missing nothing, as if she were studying marriage for her own future. Chrissy, oblivious, was jumping and shrieking "Daddy!" He got down and let them kiss him and climb on him; he tousled the small heads and got up and hugged Claire. Her head lay on his chest at the same place as Mira's. They were the same height. *Intimior intimo meo.* He was instantly full of contrition for thinking the words. He kissed the top of her head: a new gesture.

Much later, when the girls were asleep, he gave her the dress. "Oh my goodness, Alan," she said, and stared at it silently; at last she left the room to go put it on. He hoped that was a good sign. He sat on the bed, nervously wondering if she expected him to come after her. At last she reappeared, golden, with naked arms. The dress *was* low in the front. She stood uncertainly, her hand still on the doorknob, her brows gently knit in a look of appeal. Decidedly a *before:* no made-over woman would let that look cross her face. He smiled. "Gee, lady," he said, in the accents of his old neighborhood and on an impulse entirely new to him, "are you sure you got the right room?"

Her look softened; her mouth smiled, but her eyes were still anxious. "Alan," she said seriously, "is this how you see me?"

It never had been; he hoped it was going to be. "I'm not sure I've ever seen you before," he said. He did not say that even at the births of their children, and in their infancy, it was the children he had seen and been glad for; that Claire had been a substitute, an expedient. He must not blame Claire for not being Mira. He opened his arms; he rested his cheek on her belly. The extraordinary warm softness of the silk, this time with her warmth behind it, with her familiar curves at his face and hands.

She stopped his hands as they traveled. "Alan," she said again, on a note of warning. "What happened with Mira?"

"Nothing," he said, answering the question she was really asking. "We talked; we couldn't change each other's minds; that was it. She asked me about the girls."

"You seem different," she said. He was: strangely, he was present to her presence as he had never been because he had been with Mira. His desire was for both of them, as innocently and clearly as if it had been commanded. He wanted, purely and lightly, to be in a woman's body: his wife's would do fine, his wife in this wonderful dress and all soft in his hands, and Mira's body inaccessible but not hostile, she did not hate him, his desire was heavy and thick in his lap because she had whispered to him. "She knows everything," he said. "I told her everything, about—about us. I mean, about—"

"Of course," she said, rather distantly, "you would need to." He did not ask what that meant; psychotherapy would uncover all kinds of uncouth motivations. To punish Mira for hurting him, to restore his intimacy with her at Claire's expense, to prove that after all he had learned his lesson. All true, no doubt. But he could not care. Those colors were on Claire's body, they pardoned him; surely so would Claire in a minute or two. "She asked about you," he said. "How you put up with me writing the things I do."

"What did you tell her?"

He did not want to answer; he did not want to lose momentum. "I said you let it roll off. You probably don't, do you?" Why wouldn't she just lie down? "Please, Claire, you're so beautiful—"

She dropped his hands and moved a few steps away. "I've been doing a lot of thinking while you were gone," she said. "You know why I let it roll off? Because you've been good for me; you've been good for me in a way no other man was. Even though I wasn't your first choice. Or *because* I wasn't." She spoke very softly, so the girls if they woke would hear nothing. He tried to listen without ceasing to look. "It's not just that you wanted a family. It's—why is this so hard to say? I can pry these things out of my clients in the first couple sessions. It's that I knew I wanted you. Not just to get pregnant." She bowed her head: not quite shy, but not quite meeting his eyes. "When I was with Mike and with Darrell—they always wanted sex first, and wanted it all kinds of ways, and I never had a chance to want anything first, or even to know what I wanted. And you gave me that chance. Is that terrible? Is that emasculating? I mean, it was your, your potency that I *wanted*. But because you were so unhappy . . . you know, if you hadn't been I could never have decided Yes, I want this badly enough to try. I used to hate Mira for what she had done to you. But if she hadn't, I'd never have known."

He reached his hand to her. They gripped tight across the space: he from pain and sympathy and impatience, she from the effort to speak.

"I understand why you write these mournful things about disobedience and lust," she said. "I grew up the same way you did. I think it's sad; I think you're lining up with the wrong people; but no one else can stop you from thinking that way. All the time I was with Mike and with Darrell I believed what the nuns said, that girls were just a temptation whether we wanted to be or not. But they were wrong, weren't they?—about you and me at that time? I couldn't tempt you even when I wanted to. So the nuns didn't know everything. And the priests don't know everything either. It's not their fault: it's their vows: they have to resist, forever. But we have to unite. And it's not just for having children. It's for the pure joy."

He could feel it in his body, but he could not receive it in words. *They have to believe that because of what they've been through*, that's what she was saying. "Men aren't pure," he burst out. "Women don't understand about lust. Of course the nuns didn't, but even Mira, who knows all about it, thinks it's just a nice thing. It's not nice: it's relentless: it's like being raped by your own body. I'm no different from Mike or Darrell. It's that or incompetence. There's no middle ground. We're all led around by the whatsit." He was vaguely conscious of sounding ridiculous. "It's completely impersonal: it's not for you, it's not even for Mira, I might as well be by myself."

She came close. "You're not by yourself."

She caressed his head, pressed it between her hands; he made for the space between her breasts and attached himself. His arms went around her, and he felt the little shiver at the base of her spine. When she lay down he took her hand and clutched it within his, over the aching flesh. Underwear, shirttail, pants, oh Claire get me out of here. She did: not with her bare hand but with a fold of the dress, ineffably soft. He cried out, too loudly: oh God, let the children not wake.

She laughed: quiet, tickled. "I think it's for me, Alan, isn't it?"

"But, Ari, I have the best excuse in the world. I'm going to stop being a vulnerable, neurotic shiksa who needs you and become a demanding Jewish woman compelling you into fatherhood. I'm going to give you what you want for reasons you don't even like. Now do you believe me? I cry at bar mitzvahs, and a tear is an intellectual thing; I've been working up to this for a long time."

"Religion is not a reason. Do you need me to tell you?"

"It's not a religion, it's a people with an attitude. You said so yourself. Besides, you'd like having a child; you'd like it for its own sake, and you'd get a tremendous charge out of being the man whose child I would have. Ari, you're blushing, look at you. That's reason enough."

"Mim," he said, "you don't need any reason except that you want to. But you're in love with the attitude; what happens when that wears off? What happens when shul is no longer exciting, and I don't remind you of it against my own will, and one more eight-year-old anti has just told your sensitive child that his or her daddy kills babies?"

"Our sensitive child," she said, unruffled, "will write a rude verse, and maybe I'll set it to music. Sensitivity always has enormous reserves of derision. We'll manage."

He gave her an admiring, though still dubious, look. "You'd make an interesting mother."

She blushed in her turn, and shook her head. "Not to the child. No child ever thinks its mother is interesting."

"Oh, I did," he said helpfully. "I was the original Oedipus. Oediyahu. What did the very ordinary Max Morgenzahl do to deserve the beautiful Sarah Eichel? I was just as good as he was."

She whooped and collapsed on his shoulder. "My God," she said when she could speak again, "what will you do if we have a boy." But family life wasn't wholesome; if Alan thought it was, he was shutting his eyes to a lot. When she was little her father had encouraged her, any time she happened to be watching her mother dress, to say in a piercing singsong, "Maaa? *Why* d'you wear a gir-dul?" It was at the end of the fifties, when women wore armor under their clothes; God forbid they should appear to have anything soft and palpable under there. It suddenly struck her what he had really been doing. If she and Ari tried anything like that, the child would turn them in to the social workers.

"If we knew what was going to happen we couldn't do this at all," she said. "It's absolutely unreasoning. It's just like the patients, but in reverse: she gives you one excuse after another for why she's going to have that baby, and that's all they are, excuses."

Sarita laid out a soft cotton twill on the cutting table. She could cut it almost without marking: a shapeless plain gown, the neck slashed in a V to below the breastbone, long sleeves that could be rolled up. The skirt was long too, but in the original painting it was hoisted to the joints of the thighs: Hendrickje Stoffels, Rembrandt's beloved mistress, wading into a stream. It would be her last gift to Mim. It was voluminous and would accommodate pregnancy without alteration. Armisael was the angel that governed the womb. The angel Laila governed conception. She would write their names on the hidden seam of the facing.

She had seen the picture in London on an art-history trip in her last year of college. It was greyer than she had expected—some of the reproductions had a gold cast—and it seemed dwarfed by the larger canvases in the room. Oils were always humbler in person than in their own glossy photos, but this one was almost humiliated by being hung between larger pieces and near a doorway. At the focal point of the room a class of seven-year-olds in red uniforms sat crosslegged staring up at Belshazzar's Feast. "Do you know what that writing says?" prompted their guide. "Noeüüü," they chorused obediently, young enough to be tractable. Sarita struggled to shut out the voices. The warmth and musk of the woman's body almost sensible from her pose; her head tilted downward in quiet absorption or modesty, her legs mirrored in the still water, her right thumb firm on the bunched cloth. The love of the human eye for the female body. Yesterday it had been the Elgin Marbles in the British Museum, ripples of stone like water on breasts and thighs. Sculptural driftwood, bleached of paint, a skeletal frailty as affecting as if hammer and gunpowder had damaged warm flesh—the defaced votaries, the headless reclining goddesses, the castrated wrestlers. That night in the pub her professor's face, which she had learned to read in the dim light of his slide lectures, showed the same frailty; when they got back to the little hotel on Gower Street she took him into her bed. The ban against touching the works of art had become too severe.

"Jack shall have Jill, nought shall go ill," chanted Todd, looking on as she worked. "Et cetera. But never for you, Sarita. You never go anywhere. You never do anything but work. When are you going to find someone?"

Sarita cut steadily from one chalk dot to another. "I am the cat that walks by himself," she said. "No man cometh to the Father but through—oops! that's another story. What does it matter, Todd?"

He did not answer directly. "Do you know Kay Geoffrey's work?" he said with unusual diffidence. "She does oils—abstracts—very austere, very fine. You'd like her colors. She has a show opening tonight. You really don't know her? She's been around for a while. And she's a dyke. And she's single."

Sarita rolled her eyes. "Todd, I appreciate—"

"You do not. Take that pained look off your face. Edith, tell her I'm only trying to help."

"Todd, she's perfectly happy. She likes to work."

"She fell *asleep* in the laundry room yesterday. People who are perfectly happy don't do that. I think it's a warning sign. Sarita, really, I'm not just trying to fix you up. I do think you'd like Kay's work."

"But you're trying to fix me up too," she said, with resolute, distant good humor, and went on cutting. But after Todd and Edith had gone and the gown was finished, she locked the shop and rested from all she had made; she took a scrap of the cotton twill and went down to the water. She found a big rock on the breakwater, an egg-shaped granite one the size of her fist. She tied the rock in the cloth. She walked a block to the park with the fishing pier. She leaned on the rail, holding the wrapped stone to her forehead, whispering verses. She dropped it and it fell with a muffled plop.

She came back to the lit street. She walked the three blocks to the gallery and took a plastic cup of wine and a crabcake from an attendant and stood sorrowing over the paintings, which seemed, had her heart not already been broken, to be trying to break it: the colors of the stillness in a damp greenhouse, the stifle of night, the soft shine of light on a smooth treetrunk. These things were not kindly and healing; they were not benignant; they were the weary implacable patience of living matter, the ground-bass of all human relations. They were the grave. This woman understood that. Sarita looked over and found her; she stood near the desk with a wineglass, enduring chat. She did not look weary: clear-eyed, very quiet, waiting, as if she had cleared everything from her personality but the primordial longing for contact. Sarita fought an impulse to go up to her and say *Look, I made this dress, it says the same thing you were saying.* She turned instead to the price list. She knew she could never afford these—was it on Bob Morgenzahl's wall she had seen one, or even two?—but she hoped the cold douche of commerce might stop her from doing anything rash. The prices were high. Good: the woman deserved them. The titles lined up at the left margin. *The fowl of heaven. Too long a sacrifice. Stones might rejoice in levity.*

All Sarita's chromosomes stood on end. She turned; she looked at the artist; she crossed the room.

EPILOGUE

There are only chosen peoples: all who still exist.

—Elias Canetti

Mim was fifty and Ari was sixty-three; she might have been their grandchild. She stood holding the handles of the scroll with nonchalant self-possession. If her age had not been announced by the very fact of her being called to the Torah for the first time—*Ruchama bat Aryeh v'Tzipporah, maftir chazak!*—she might have been any age between twelve and twenty; the dress Sarita had made her conferred ripeness. The slightly duckfaced look of her childhood had given way to a wary grace. Mim and Ari, as recipients of the last honor, stood to one side of the table, next to the new rabbi, a woman in her forties who was wearing one of Sarita's dresses too—as of course was Mim: Sarita had done nearly as well as the caterer from the event.

The name on the birth certificate was Anna, for Ari's lost sister, but no one ever called her by it; while still in the womb she had become and remained Roo (whereupon Mim became, irresistibly, Kanga, and Ari eventually Eeyore—"Because that's Ari spelled inside-out and because he's a cynic," the girl had declared at six). In her honor Ari had privately renamed their street the rue Morgenzahl; it was one of a maze of winding streets in a subdivision, chosen for its obscurity, and he felt safe enough there to walk her up and down it devotedly. He was besotted by her, starry and foolish.

She finished chanting her three sentences of the Torah; the scroll was lifted and displayed to the congregation and dressed in its velvet robe. Mim and Ari sat down, and Roo was left alone on the platform. In the rows behind Mim and Ari sat Ari's family: Jay and Lisa, Marcie with her husband and two sons, David and his second wife and their new baby daughter, Jay and Lisa's son Evan with his wife and their one-year-old son, and Dina, twenty and unattached; Mim's parents, in their seventies and curiously deferential as they would not have been in a church, sat next to Mim in the front pew. The room was full; Sarita and Kay had seats near the back.

Roo took the podium and looked down at her printout. "The book of Genesis," she began, her voice now shaking a little, "ends with Jacob and the seventy people of his household going to live in Egypt because of famine. The book of *Sh'mot* or Exodus begins four hundred years later with the children of Israel still in Egypt. Now they are slaves, and have become so numerous that they 'swarm.' Pharaoh is alarmed at their birth rate and takes steps to reduce it: he tells the Hebrew midwives to kill the male babies as they come out of the womb. The midwives don't openly refuse, but they don't do it; they tell Pharaoh that the women give birth too fast, before they can get there. They take for granted that no one would harm the boys once they're born. But Pharaoh's next order is to the Egyptians, to throw the Hebrew boys into the Nile."

She looked up: a second to brace herself. Her duty as a bat mitzvah was both to summarize and to interpret the week's Torah portion; in this crowd and with this subject matter, the interpretation would be heard with great curiosity. Mim, who knew what was coming next, was as tense as if she did not: Roo had just assumed a persona, as if she had put on the mantle of public life along with her prayer shawl. The uncanniness of seeing her own and her mother's mannerisms reproduced gave Mim, for once, an unambivalent pride.

"Even then," Roo went on, her thin voice now steady, "there were disagreements over who had the right to forbid or permit birth. Moses, Israel's first and unequaled prophet, the friend of God, was sentenced to die at birth by a state policy. He was floated down the river in a basket so he could live. In our time, state policy allows women to choose whether or not to give birth, and no one is supposed to interfere with their choice. But if they choose not to, the people who help them are always at risk. The two situations, ancient Egypt and modern America, are totally different. Perhaps the one thing they have in common is this: to be born is to be chosen to live." A soft, percussive breath, like a bracketed exclamation point, went up from the congregation: she had negotiated a difficult corner adroitly and even surprisingly.

It had taken two years to conceive Roo: two years of treading water, with Mim still uncertain whether pregnancy were drowning or rescue. Once it occurred she was pretty sure it was both. From the morning of Roo's birth she had been shattered by the intensity of the bond—how involuntarily her body loved the child's body, how her milk sustained life and her comforting really did comfort and her whole soul exploded with joy toward the small face. And how Ari came rushing home every day to be with them both, to lie flat on the floor and bounce Roo on his chest, to sing her jingles and babble at her in Yiddish. In another sense she felt trapped in a false position from which there was no escape. She was not sure—then or now—that she was a mother in more than the physical sense. She believed in pragmatism, but she was not good at it; she believed in it *because* she was not good at it, as a sinner will believe in a sinless God or a lofty and self-isolated thinker in mutuality. The unrelenting need to think of the future—the next meal, the next morning, the next school year, the college fund—oppressed her; the blank irrelevance of her earlier life to Roo made her feel effaced. Even in Roo's first year she never stopped giving speeches, but they seemed less and less real; she would write them between interruptions, and it was the interruptions that were the commanding moments. Roo's life was the real one, her own the dream: the hunger or the wet diaper or the ominous cough the reality, intellect and religion and public policy the idle abstractions of people with time on their hands. She understood the antis then as well as she ever would: if you gave your allegiance early enough to the realm of wet diapers and coughs and irrepressible joy, or if you could not imagine your way outside it, nothing on earth would seem solid enough to replace it. She would recognize this, and wonder whether the reality of Alan's child would have compensated for the ambivalence of its conception, and then she would finish writing her speech and strap Roo into a car seat and drive to the college or conference or rally where she was speaking, chattering compulsively all the way about pretty trees and cattails and doggies. Her self, split between two works, felt near dissolution; how did Ari's self remain so unassailable?

"The trouble is," Roo said now, "some people are chosen to live instead of others. The firstborn of the Israelites were spared and the firstborn of the Egyptians were stricken; and it wasn't because the Israelites were any better, because once they got out of Egypt they were a disobedient rabble, a burden to Moses and a disappointment to God. But they survived and the Egyptians didn't. In the twentieth century"— now over, and how peculiar it was to hear it spoken of as the past— "Hitler tried to reverse the process, and chose the Jews not to live; again, survival had nothing to do with being good or bad, only with good or bad luck. And what it's taken ever since to maintain the state of Israel shows that the need to survive can make you think of goodness as a luxury you can't afford.

"And when any child in the womb," she went on, studiously not looking at her parents and reading a little too fast, "is chosen to live and another is chosen not to, it never has anything to do with what they deserve; they haven't deserved anything yet. What does it mean to be alive when someone else might have been? What's the price of being chosen to live?"

Two months after Roo's birth the first abortion doctor had been killed. Ari had come home at the first possible moment, found the spot in the house farthest from any window, and sat shivering for an hour with Roo in his arms. Over the next two years, as there were several more deaths and a slow exodus of doctors willing to do abortions, he and Mim had several times considered closing the clinic. The local antis were actually somewhat quieter, as if chastened by the lethal power of their own slogans, but there was no telling when some other friend of the militant wing like Del Marlin might appear on the scene. After the Brookline shootings Ari decided, not to close the clinic altogether but to close it on Saturdays; that would not prevent a determined person from doing harm, but it would make it harder for the less determined to set the scene for harm. He began—to Mim's considerable surprise— going to shul occasionally, not because he felt any different about religion but because it was restful: she and the baby were going, there would be two and a half hours during which every move was predictable, and chanting the words calmed his mind. It was his downfall: someone found out he knew how to read Torah, and recruited him for the task once a month or so.

In the first grade Roo had gone through a time of shouting sharply to drown out the radio news; she was retaliating against the power of the outside world to disrupt their meals. Mim sympathized; she too would rather have ignored it. But she was registered with a speaker's bureau by now and had to keep up with the news, and Ari wanted no delays in finding out if there were ever another shooting. (Only the most spectacular bombings were ever reported.) "Couldn't I just not listen?" Roo had said, and Mim would have allowed it, but Ari answered first. "Annaruchamele, look," he said, taking her on his lap, "this is not something you can escape from. Think of it as part of your education as a brilliant neurotic Jewish woman. We come from a profoundly crazy religion that insists knowledge is better than ignorance; not everybody insists on that, and for the most part ignorant people run the world, but that's just one of the things we have to know. It's not bad to understand this at a young age." Roo was silent, bedazzled—Mim knew all the symptoms—by the heady mix of tenderness and severity; thereafter when she listened to the news, whether she understood it or not, she pronounced on the ignorance of senators, movie stars and foreign heads of state.

When Roo was in second grade the Christian millennium rolled over and Del Marlin got out of jail. As if the change in the calendar from so many nines to so many zeroes caused a similar blank in the mind, a rash of prophetic movements broke out; not all of them owed anything more than their timing to Christianity. A new voice arose on the Internet calling the enemies of abortion to desperate acts. Late in the year a sixteen-year-old boy put his new driver's license in his pocket, loaded his father's truck with ten gas cans, and totaled it against the clinic wall. He lived—with whiplash and a cracked sternum from the grip of the seatbelt—and the fire department arrived and the gas cans did not ignite; when questioned the boy identified the man on the Net as his inspiration and the source of the cash. (Marcie e-mailed Ari at once: "You were right, I was wrong. Sorry.") The man used the name Ahab; Alan might have guessed who he was, had anyone asked him.

Parent-teacher conferences had played no great part in Mim's conception of motherhood up to that point. When she received a summons to talk to Roo's third-grade teacher about some disturbing drawings, she was not so much worried about Roo, who seemed to be holding up reasonably well, as unhappily surprised at the eruption of public life in another sphere. The confiscated drawings showed a large yellow house on fire, a burning bush, and a burning crib. "That's my daddy's clinic; that's God; that's my daddy's sister who died in a fire and I'm named for her." Mim felt a crawling chill, not at the drawings but at the teacher's insistence that Roo was on the edge of breakdown, that she might begin setting fires, that she ought to see the school counselor right away. *No*, Mim thought, *Roo's older than you are, that's all*. Even explanations only roused the young woman to the assertion of a lamblike authority: "I find that the kids who come in with these violent Bible stories are some of the most troubled kids in the class. Isn't she saying that God set those other two fires? She doesn't need a God she has to be scared of." "But the clinic didn't catch fire," Mim reminded her, wondering if Roo wished it had. She concurred with misgivings to the school counselor; she disliked the ploy of telling children to draw what they felt and then keeping their feelings under surveillance, but she wondered if her own suspicion of therapy (inherited from her father) were a form of lingering antisemitism and so gave in. But Roo was outraged at the counselor in the first session: "You think it's *inappropriate* for a little girl to draw fires. That's so ignorant. For heaven's sake, I'm not going to *stay* little." Sarita crowed when she heard of it; she offered to take Roo one night a week for art lessons.

She was an apt and obedient pupil, and was delighted to be given the run of the shop; it was a world familiar from her earliest days yet unlike anything at home. Edith lost her heart utterly to the child, and would sometimes keep her for weekends while Mim was away and Ari was on call. (Todd and Andrew had moved to New York, where Andrew was assistant choirmaster at St. John the Divine and Todd had opened a restaurant.) Roo did not, perhaps, have the makings of a real artist—she never anticipated what Sarita had not yet told her or took risks with materials—but she drew what she wanted and stayed out of the teacher's way. (From a classmate she learned a standard method of drawing horses, and did that in class.) The week after she entered the fourth grade—it was then 2001—everyone, suddenly and without warning, grew up to her age.

"We don't know," she continued, "what Moses thinks about being chosen to live. We know what he thinks about being chosen to be God's messenger; he doesn't want to. God's messengers are almost always reluctant, and they pay a high price for their missions. In the haftarah I'm about to read, Jeremiah is reluctant too; he doesn't want to be a prophet, he wants to be a child, but God won't let him. Later on in the book he accuses God of raping him, as if God chose him by invading his mind. But he does go ahead and prophesy, and Moses does lead the people, and maybe that's what happens to anyone who's chosen to live: they have to keep on choosing it for themselves.

"Is that what it means when God tries to kill Moses on the way down to Egypt? Is he testing whether Moses is firmly attached to life? The traditional commentaries say God was angry with Moses for not circumcising his son, but why wouldn't God just have told him to? One modern commentary points out that it's hard to tell who God was trying to kill, and that maybe it's really the son: he's putting Moses' firstborn at risk like the firstborn of the Egyptians, and he has to see blood drawn to spare him like the firstborn of the Israelites. That sounds more likely, but I think really God wants to know if Moses can choose his own life. And I think Moses isn't sure. It's almost as if his wife has to choose it for him at that point—so swiftly and decisively doing the circumcision, protecting Moses from God. But by the end of the Torah, Moses is so strong in his own life that God has to tell him, *die*, as if he could do it on purpose. It says that he died *al-pi Adonai*, from the mouth of God: the rabbis say that doesn't just mean 'at the command of God,' it means 'by God's kiss.' Even Moses couldn't endure it and live. But he could deserve it."

Sarita shivered at Kay's side, wanting to whisper to her: what a subject for a painting, and if only Roo's eye were as good as her remarkable associative power. The minute she heard of the three fires, the clinic, the crib and the bush, she had known Roo was trying to understand the power and nature of fire; had she added a fourth image, the Sabbath candles, the contained and domesticated version of fire, the teacher might have understood and been mollified. But Roo went in for immensities; she could have remade Renaissance painting with these neglected biblical scenes. Imagine Moses' death from God's kiss as common a set subject as the Annunciation; imagine the circumcision of Moses' son as a chaotic night scene, the wife's gesture precipitous and forceful as Judith's beheading of Holofernes in the Gentileschi painting. Imagine God's rape of Jeremiah a representable subject, like Leda and the swan or Zeus and Ganymede; remember Rembrandt's Ganymede, no gorgeous seductive youth but an ugly toddler, pissing into the air with the fright of flying. (And remember Henry Ossawa Tanner's Annunciation, the stunned girl cringing from the light.) Sarita had not worked in oils in twenty-five years; Kay was not about to start doing history paintings. Would it be worth pressing Roo to develop as a painter, even when she did not seem to have a genius in that direction, so that if genius did strike she would have the competence? Should Kay take over the art lessons?

Sarita had not, since meeting Kay, made any ventures into the spiritual realm; it would have seemed adulterous. The spiritual realm had come to her, in full force and in the flesh: its intimacy, its mordant hilarity, its inexhaustible drive. Nothing she could do with cloth and imagination could match what she and Kay could do in an evening together, in a mergence so profound, so painful and so healing that nothing said of its physical expression could serve to explain it. They regretted the necessity to say they were lovers; it was a pigeonhole, a category, which said nothing of the meeting of mind and mind or the terror and moral rigor of consent. ("Christ, Edith, you were right," Sarita had said, coming to work bleached and sleepless one day in their second year, "ethics does take precedence over aesthetics.") Mim had talked of couples growing a joint system of mycelia, but it was worse than that: it was a joint nervous system that could not bear too much parting and reuniting. It became painful to live and work separately; they had both established with effort the conditions they needed for living and working alone, but those conditions no longer held. At last, in great trepidation, they bought a building together; Sarita's shop was downstairs and Kay's studio and their apartment were upstairs. Then the uprooting process that took them away from each other's voices and back to work became bearable; the filaments between them, which had seemed to tear at each separation when Kay lived in the country and Sarita in town, could stretch and hold at that distance. Their work changed: Kay's dark canvases were slowly suffused with color in a series she called *Purgatorio*, Sarita developed a sideline in erotic toys. Occasionally they collaborated on a project, a piece of public art or a theater set.

Roo's speech was ending. "And what is the message that Moses and Jeremiah and all God's chosen messengers are so reluctant to deliver—the message that all of us, chosen to live by somebody else, have to speak from our unchosen condition? That we're free: that we can change our condition. That justice and mercy are in our own hands. It's the most terrifying message there is. All we want, having been chosen to live, is to get through it, not to have to say yes to it every minute as if it was our idea. The Israelites didn't thank Moses or Jeremiah or God for telling them they were free, and maybe neither do we. But if we ever learn how to thank God, it will be the first thing worth thanking him for." She put down the printout and reached for her book.

She began to sing: the yearning trope to which all the prophetic readings were set. It was Mim's favorite music in the service: she found it melancholy soothing, and once in Roo's infancy Ari had come home from a late-night birth to find Mim humming it as she stirred a pot of the Indian rice pudding on the stove, Roo asleep in a basket beside her. The Jeremiah reading was an unconventional one: it belonged to the Sephardic liturgy, not the Ashkenazic, but Roo had gone for it instantly when she saw the two texts together in the book. The rabbi had made no objection. "Any kid who's paying that much attention deserves to do what she wants," she had said with faint weariness. Mim followed the reading, finally at ease between Hebrew and English:

> Before I formed thee in the belly I knew thee, and before thou camest forth from the womb I sanctified thee; I have appointed thee a prophet unto the nations. Then said I: "Ah, Lord God! behold, I cannot speak; for I am a child."

She felt an astringent and overpowering love for her daughter, who was capable of such strength. The skill and labor required of an ordinary bar or bat mitzvah were substantial enough; that Roo should also be capable of this protest—a protest against the whole condition of her life, yet so rooted in the pattern of synagogue practice that she could deliver it without breaking, even without speaking in personal terms—was more than she could take in. She had been staring at that face ever since it was squinched and red and scarcely more than a cry; she had held that body when it weighed no more than a cat's, had carried it in her body when it weighed nothing; she had known Roo's smells, sweet and foul, had watched her learn to play, intent and autonomous, had heard her language assemble itself day by day; and she did not know her at all.

Mim had been reading Roo verse from the very beginning: to lull her with rhythm, to maintain a foothold in adult life and sanity, to hold out against television. She had not always troubled to keep it simple. "Fern Hill" and (of all things) Geoffrey Hill's "Mercian Hymns" had been great successes; a milestone had been reached when Roo, not yet four, had found one line emerge from the eloquent noise: "'I liked that,' said Offa, 'sing it again.'" ("Oh, Ari, she's quoting!" Mim had cried; he had raised an eyebrow and said the *Shehecheyanu*, the blessing for first occasions.) In the spring of fourth grade she had come home with a poetry game. She had a prodigious word-hoard already, and could write things like "Never the elephant fails to remember" and "Still stars hide behind the day." They started playing the game at home on quiet evenings, having agreed to turn the radio off: Roo messily adventurous, Ari effortlessly brilliant, and Mim choking with forty years' unwritten lines. One night after putting Roo to bed she found herself crying; she dug in a box for a folder of unfinished poems, some of them dating back to her college years, and saw that of *course* she had a feel for the shape of a poem, of *course* she understood off-rhymes, if she had not she would never have known enough to worry about it; she was not, not at heart, and never had been, a demagogue. The poems began to be finished; when they were finished she went on and made new ones; they came from the place that her speeches came from when they took fire, the place that was not quite her mind. It was a mania, a congestion of desire, as obsessive as her first months in the synagogue; it was the first thing to rival the synagogue in her imagination. She wrote poems to Roo, and in spite of Roo, and in competition with Roo; she read poems along with her speeches; she turned down speaking dates in order to work on poems, and then when poems did not arrive on demand she agonized about the money she had refused that might have gone for Roo's education. She knew it was perilous, she knew she had arrived at the really impermissible pain she was going to inflict on her child, but she could not stop without stopping her own language at its source. It was a third pregnancy, unintended but wholly desired, which she must carry to term or despise herself all her life. Roo, who already had so much to allow for in her parents' lives, allowed this too, without comment; when Mim tried to discover how she felt about it she squirmed and said, "Aw, Mom. Everybody's mother does *some*thing. Is it important?" Mim, rebuffed, went back to her notebook. Poems at least were something she had been born to; she had only converted to motherhood.

Roo finished her chant; on the congregation's *Amen* the young children pelted her with candies and came scrambling up to retrieve them as the congregation sang *Mazel tov*. Then she carried the Torah in the procession, down one aisle and up the other, everyone reaching to touch it with prayerbooks or fringes; her own dark red prayer shawl was slipping down on one shoulder. The scroll was put away, and in a final anticlimax Roo was presented with a kiddush cup by the head of the ritual committee. Mim and Ari had declined to "say a few words," having seen too many parents make fools of themselves by that method; they held her tightly between them as the closing prayers were sung. Ari said softly, "You've arrived: you're a scary lady, just like your mom." He and Mim made a private face at each other over her head. And then everyone pressed into the social hall for a great spread of bagels and lox and whitefish and hummus and babaganoush and spanakopita and fresh fruit and vegetables, and brownies and cookies and cheesecake and rugelach and poppyseed cake and meringues.

Sarita and Kay, trying to eat without being jostled, were gradually edged toward the windows. David, Ari's son, stood nearby, surrounded by a crowd of Roo's friends; he was newly famous on television for his spoof cartoon series (*Zeitguy, a Superhero for Our Time*) and a magnet for smart little girls. Ari circulated, at some distance; Mim was too short to locate. Sarita talked in Kay's ear about the paintings. "Of course," said Kay, lighting up. "The dormition of Elijah. Scenes from the life of Moses. The stations of the forty years in the desert."

The crowd thinned somewhat, and it was possible to cross the room to the coffee urn. Kay went and brought back two cups. David was teaching Roo's friends a fast wordless tune. The grownups heard it and began singing and clapping, backing away to clear some space in the room; there was Mim, hastily seeing to the moving back of the food tables. The girls began to dance, the cluster unraveling away from David into a long snake as they joined hands; Roo, at the end of the line, pulled Mim into the dance as they passed her. Sarita and Kay put their cups on the windowsill so as to clap along. A small heap of prayer shawls in bright velvet bags had been piled there. Roo's prayer shawl did not have a bag; it lay among them, sliding out of its folds. The upper corner that showed was a rich maroon; a couple of silver squiggles meandered across it.

Sarita stared. She had been able to manage with only minor discomfort while Roo was actually wearing the shawl—just as she had managed when Mim and Ari used it for their wedding canopy—but the unexpected proximity was a shock. Kay put a hand on her shoulder. "So there it is," she said. "Bunge's revenge. What do you think of it now?"

Sarita shook her head, recalled by the touch. "*You're* Bunge's revenge," she said. "But that never was. Just misplaced effort. My God, we do bad art when we mean well."

"Even when we don't," said Kay. "Of course I can paint over mine. Did you ever think of destroying it?"

"All night," she said. "But I couldn't. I couldn't bring myself to. The same thing that made it a failure made it impossible to destroy. The—" She stopped. She had never told Kay all that had gone into the piece.

"The kid," Kay finished for her as if it were nothing unusual.

Sarita turned pale. "You know too much," she said. "How do you know so much?"

"Apple-knowledge," said Kay very softly. "It's just the sort of thing you'd let yourself in for. Besides, he had a history of opportunism."

"Oh, so he was a he, was he?" said Sarita, trying to recover. "I thought he probably was."

The clapping intensified. Roo's friends lifted her up on a chair and danced her around the room, Roo holding nervously to the seat with a fixed smile. "He'd—he'd already been destroyed once," Sarita said haltingly. "It didn't seem fair to put him through it again. And the hope that he if anyone could protect Mim—" She looked over to where Mim stood, weary and glowing, on the other side of the room. Ari, beside her, bounced the newest Morgenzahl grandchild in time to the song. "Of course," she added morosely, "he's Roo's problem now. He stands between her and God every time she prays."

"Well, that's protective."

Sarita shot her a look. "Maybe," she said. "But it puts me right in with the antis, doesn't it? Easy for me to save him; I don't have to raise him. She does."

NOTES

Chapter 6 In a time when clinics that provide abortion services were understandably reluctant to allow visitors, Dr. Warren M. Hern's textbook *Abortion Practice* (Philadelphia: Lippincott, 1984) was invaluable for its clear presentation of the organization and procedures of abortion clinics. I am also grateful to the nurses, counselors and activists who answered my questions in telephone interviews, at conferences and in private conversations.

Chapter 12 The snake cheats: it takes advantage of Sarita's ignorance of Hebrew. *Daat* is a trochee, not an iamb.

Chapter 15 For Japanese rituals honoring the aborted fetus see William LaFleur, *Liquid Life: Abortion and Buddhism in Japan* (Princeton University Press, 1992).

Chapter 17 For Hildegard and the cheese theory, see Barbara Duden, *Disembodying Women: Perspectives on Pregnancy and the Unborn* (Cambridge, MA: Harvard University Press, 1993), 56-57.

Chapter 26 The epigraph is adapted from Morris Silverman's translation in *The New Machzor* (Bridgeport, CT: Media Judaica, 1977). The translation is rather free; in the Hebrew, an embroiderer makes the work straight or crooked, and for "jealous and vengeful" Silverman uses "righteous." The image of the cloth and the draper was irresistible for my purposes, but "righteous" is mere bowdlerism; I have restored the original meaning.

Alan's Arthurian dream is taken—with many liberties—from the Middle English poem *The Wedding of Sir Gawain and Dame Ragnell*. I used the text in *Middle English Verse Romances*, ed. Donald B. Sands (New York: Holt, Rinehart and Winston, 1966). For the word "dignity" as a translation of "worship" I am indebted to George Brandon Saul's translation (New York: Prentice-Hall, 1934). The line "I am as glad as grass in the rain" is adapted from the ballad version, no. 19 in *The Oxford Book of Ballads* (Oxford: Clarendon Press, 1910). For further elaboration of Ragnell's ideas on sovereignty, see Elizabeth Cady Stanton's 1892 speech "The Solitude of Self."

The curious names that Gawain collects for his book appear in Jan Jönsjö's *Studies on Middle English Nicknames* (Lund: CWK Gleerup, 1979).

Printed in the United States
789300001B